THE
Great Lakes
Lighthouse
BRIDES
COLLECTION

7 Historical Romances Are a Beacon of Hope to Weary Hearts

THE
Great Lakes
Lighthouse
BRIDES
COLLECTION

Lena Nelson Dooley, Rebecca Jepson,
Carrie Fancett Pagels, Candice Sue Patterson,
Kathleen Rouser, Pegg Thomas, Marilyn Turk

BARBOUR BOOKS
An Imprint of Barbour Publishing, Inc.

Member of the
Evangelical Christian
Publishers Association

Printed in Canada.

Contents

Anna's Tower

by Pegg Thomas

Dedication

This story is dedicated to the brave men and women who kept the lights burning in towers around the Great Lakes. Often isolated in inhospitable areas, they guided ships across the five lakes and various rivers to bring the pioneers who settled the nation's northern heartland. Then sailors on these ships carried out iron, copper, and other metals from this resource-rich land to build a growing nation. We owe them all a debt of gratitude.

Chapter 1

The wail of a ship's whistle jerked Anna Wilson from sleep despite the cotton wadding she'd shoved in her ears before bed. Another blast sounded, and then a third, while she untangled her nightgown and legs from the quilt. Heart pounding, she pushed Barnacle out of her way and ignored the sleepy meow of protest.

The whistle was too loud and too close to the island. Thunder Bay Island's fog signal moaned its response as she pulled the cotton from her ears. The ship's whistle blasted three more times while Anna charged down the stairs, her bare feet smacking the wooden steps.

Auntie Laurie poked her head from the downstairs bedroom. Gray hair fanned in all directions around her nightcap. "What's going on, child?"

"It's a distress signal."

"Of course it is. I'll awaken Gretchen." The old lady shut the door.

Anna raced through the arched brick passageway to the foot of the metal circular stairs leading up to the lighthouse tower. She stopped on the bottom step, cold metal against her feet, her hand clenching the handrail.

"Uncle Jim?"

The stairs vibrated as Uncle Jim descended. Anna let go of the rail and stepped back.

"What could you see?" she called.

"Not a thing. Fog's too thick." He stopped at the bottom, wrinkles deep around his eyes beneath the rolled hat brim. "Doug's gone to the mainland. I can't leave the tower, not on a night like this."

She straightened her shoulders and smoothed her hair away from her face. "Tell me what to do." After all, this was what she'd come for.

Uncle Jim stroked his beard. "Could be a bad one. That whistle's close."

"Too close?"

"Aye. She's likely on the rocks." He clamped his hand on her shoulder and squeezed. "Go to the lifesaving station. Remember the way?"

Could she find it in the dark through the fog? What choice did she have? She nodded.

"Run and change." He sighed. "Suppose the aunties will go with you, even if you try to stop them."

"I imagine they will."

"Go. I'll join you at daybreak if you've not returned by then."

Anna ran back to her bedroom, faster with each wail of the ship's whistle. Garbed in her work dress with woolen stockings and a heavy shawl, she hurried to the back door for her boots.

Auntie Laurie, hair neatly tucked under a wool scarf, stomped into her boots while Auntie Gretchen, looking for all the world like a scrawny bear rousted from hibernation, grabbed quart jars of canned chicken from the pantry. She shoved a basket of potatoes into Anna's arms then thrust a sack of onions at Auntie Laurie.

"What are these for?" Anna clutched the basket to her middle.

"Soup." Auntie Gretchen wrapped her shawl around her shoulders. "If they fish any live ones out of the water, they'll need warming up from the inside out."

If.

The word hung like a specter in the room.

"Now sister," Auntie Laurie said. "Of course some are alive. Someone is sounding the distress whistle, after all." She settled her shawl, tucked two jars of chicken under her arm, picked up the onions, and stepped outside, holding the door. "Let's not delay when men need rescuing."

Auntie Gretchen mumbled under her breath as she grabbed the remaining jars and the lantern.

Anna followed the two old women into the damp darkness, thankful that they'd taken the lead. This was her first time to respond to an emergency at the lifesaving station. There'd been a few minor accidents with fishing boats this summer, but those had happened in the daylight, and Uncle Jim had been there, leaving Anna back at the lighthouse with the aunties, shielded from everything.

Tonight she'd be in the thick of things, but what if someone died?

She swallowed even though her throat had gone dry. When she'd cajoled Uncle Jim into letting her come to the island after Father's death this past spring, she'd overlooked this aspect of what it meant to live in a lighthouse. It wasn't all keeping the lamp burning to guide sailors on their journey. She made a fist of her hand that had grasped the handrail to the tower steps. That wasn't the only thing she'd overlooked. But she could do it. She had to do it. Anything was better than being the dependent little sister living with one of her overbearing brothers. She hoped.

"Hold the light higher. I stumbled on something." Auntie Laurie limped in front of Anna.

Auntie Gretchen lifted the lantern higher. "My arm isn't a ship's mast, you know."

Anna hustled up beside the old women. "Here. Let me." She reached for the lantern and held it aloft. "Can you see better?"

"Thank you, my dear," Auntie Laurie said. "So thoughtful."

The ten-minute walk took almost twice that long through the darkness and fog. Droplets clung to Anna, weighing down her shawl and making it sparkle in the torches outside the lifesaving station.

Auntie Gretchen opened the door and they filed in. Finding the main hall empty, they headed for the kitchen in the back, the source of warmth and the aroma of strong coffee.

Mrs. Persons stood near the huge black stove. Her air of quiet authority settled the nervous tumult brewing in Anna's middle. Only Captain Persons inspired more confidence to those on Thunder Bay Island than Celia Persons.

"Got a sinker out in the bay, eh?" Auntie Gretchen's voice dominated the room. It was said that if the fog signals ever failed, they could use her vocal cords for a replacement.

Auntie Laurie shrugged out of her shawl and hung it next to the stove, wisps of steam rising from the damp wool. "How can we help?"

"Let's assume the best and plan for the worst," Mrs. Persons said. "You brought the makings for soup. Good. You start that while Anna and I light a fire in the hall stove and then roll out the cots and blankets. God willing, we'll only have a bunch of cold men to feed."

"Amen," the aunties murmured in unison.

"Oh child." Auntie Laurie came forward and cupped Anna's cheek. "This is your first shipwreck, isn't it?"

"Yes, ma'am."

"We've had a long run of good luck. It was bound to give out sooner or later." Auntie Gretchen hung her shawl next to her sister's. "I hope they fish a few out alive, at least."

"Now sister." Auntie Laurie's hands settled on her hips. "Let's do like Celia said and hope for the best."

Auntie Gretchen snorted and thumped her quart jars on the table. "All right, but you know as well as I that the lake wreaks havoc on a night like this." She rolled her *r*'s, a reminder of her Russian heritage that grew more pronounced when she was agitated.

"Don't mind her, child," Auntie Laurie said. "She'll soon have soup made fit to snatch a man back from death's door. Oh." She pressed her hand to her chin. "Not that we'll need to, of course."

"Hurry. They'll be back within the hour," Mrs. Persons said over her shoulder.

Anna swallowed against the dryness again before scurrying after her.

An eerie flash from the lighthouse broke the gloom surrounding the dock as Maksim Ivanov stepped from the rescue boat. The fog swallowed the beam before it could reach the dangerous waters beyond. If only the captain of the SS *James Davidson* had seen that beacon in time.

The men around him spoke too fast, and he didn't understand much past the words *ship*, *rocks*, and *fog*. Pavel Orlov had been herded onto the other rescue boat, leaving Maksim with three sailors from the *Davidson* along with the burly rescue crew speaking their hurried English.

He followed the men along a pebbled path until a building formed out of the fog, torches lit on each side of its door. The scent of something savory mingled with the cold mist. His stomach growled. One of the nearby rescue workers laughed and smacked a meaty hand against Maksim's shoulder. Maksim managed to grin while keeping on his feet. The man spewed a tangle of English words that meant nothing, but Maksim nodded and followed him into the building.

Warmth radiated from a flat-topped stove in the center of the room. Maksim, along with the sailors, pulled off his gloves and stretched his fingers toward the heat. How much worse it would have been had they been thrown from the ship when it ran aground on the reef. The fog had dampened everything, but at least they weren't drenched.

A diminutive woman clapped her hands and commanded their attention. She made an announcement. He understood *coffee* and *soup* and smiled along with the rest of the men, two of whom broke from the group and returned from the back room with a steaming kettle and the largest coffeepot Maksim had ever seen. Behind them came a young woman with hair some shade between red and brown. She carried bowls and smiled as the men lined up to receive a helping of the fragrant concoction.

Maksim got in line. He nodded his thanks when the tiny woman—who appeared to be in charge—handed him a cup of dark coffee. He stepped closer to the younger woman ladling the soup. A smattering of pale freckles splashed across her nose. She tilted her head and asked him a question. His English was improving, but tonight he couldn't concentrate on the words. He shrugged and shook his head.

The sailor behind him answered her. The word *Ruskie* pooled in a ball of resentment in his hollow belly. He didn't need to know much English to know that most of the sailors looked down on him. In fact, most of the people he'd met since coming to America had looked down on him.

The young woman in front of him smiled. A beautiful smile. She pressed a bowl into his hand then gave the remaining bowls to one of the rescue crew and filled his ears with hasty English words. She turned and hurried to the back room.

Maksim balanced his bowl, stepped out of the line, and took a cautious sip of the scalding coffee. The chairs around the tables were full. He looked for a place to sit.

The young woman emerged a moment later with two old women in tow.

"Welcome, boy, welcome," one of the old women said. The words were stilted and heavily accented, but they were Russian.

Homesickness tugged at Maksim's heart. "You speak Russian?"

"*Da*, we do." She pointed at the other woman. "This is Auntie Gretchen, and I am Auntie Laurie."

He set his bowl and cup on the end of a nearby table then pulled the knit cap from his head. "I am Maksim Ivanov."

"You're bleeding." Auntie Gretchen pulled a cloth from her pocket. "Bend down." She held his chin and scrubbed his forehead with more force than gentleness. The pretty girl with the freckles hovered close by. He did his best not to wince with her watching. Once Auntie Gretchen released his chin, he nodded toward the girl.

"Is she your granddaughter?"

"*Nyet*, but we'd claim her if we could." Auntie Laurie beamed at the girl. "Her name is Anna, and she lives at the lighthouse. As do we."

Auntie Gretchen leaned closer and gave him a bold wink. "She isn't married."

Maksim took a step back, at a complete loss for words. . .in either language.

"Sister, I swear the most untimely things fall from your mouth. Anna would be so embarrassed if she understood you. And this poor boy looks like he just swallowed a frog."

Auntie Gretchen shrugged and winked at Maksim again. "Some opportunities don't come twice. A wise sailor knows when to drop anchor."

But he wasn't a sailor. He was a stowaway.

Chapter 2

Maksim and Pavel shared the edge of a cot and ate their soup. An elbow to his ribs pulled Maksim's eyes from the pretty girl across the room.

Pavel leaned close. "We need to talk."

Maksim scanned the room. The two old women disappeared into the kitchen, and the girl followed them, shadowed by a blond man roughly the size of a haystack. Nobody else near them spoke Russian as far as Maksim knew. "What troubles you?"

"I overheard the head of the rescue crew talking to the captain. This is an island we're on. They've sent someone to the mainland to telegraph the company."

"This is good, da?"

Pavel shrugged. "For me, but maybe not for you."

His friend's troubled scowl made the chicken soup in Maksim's stomach sour. "What do you mean?"

"If they can't free the *Davidson* and sail her out of here, they'll send another boat for the crew. There's no way I can sneak you onto the rescue boat."

"But the captain, he knew I was on the *Davidson*. He let me work off my passage."

"He did, but he won't admit that to his bosses." Pavel rasped his fingernails across three days' growth of whiskers. "He wanted your free labor, so he broke the rules. If the company finds out, he'll get in too much trouble. He won't risk it."

"But—" Maksim stopped when Pavel shook his head.

"A rescue ship will have a list of who they are picking up. Your name won't be on it."

Maksim set his half-eaten bowl of soup on the floor. "What will I do?"

"Pray that we get the *Davidson* afloat." Pavel shrugged. "If we can't, try to find another ship heading to Duluth. There's still time. The St. Mary's River won't close for a couple of months. There should be plenty of ships heading into Lake Superior before the ice sets in."

Duluth. Maksim had no burning desire to go to that western city on the Great Lakes, except that it was far away from Rachel and known to be a growing agricultural area in need of laborers. Maksim knew farming. He could start over in a place like that.

The pretty girl—Anna, the old woman had called her—worked her way around the room picking up used bowls and spoons. Her graceful movements reminded him of Rachel, although her hair was straight and fine, nothing like Rachel's ebony curls. When Anna reached their cot, she spoke to Pavel. He handed her his bowl. She stooped and picked Maksim's off the floor, asking him a question. He glanced at Pavel.

"She asks if you're finished with your soup."

He looked into her eyes, such a dark blue he'd mistaken them for brown when they first met. "Da."

She smiled and moved off, the sway of her skirts commanding his attention.

"There's a girl who could take your mind off the Jewish one." Pavel stressed the word *Jewish* as if it were something distasteful.

Maksim gritted his teeth and shook his head.

Pavel walked away, mumbling to himself. He'd never understood how Maksim could become attached to Rachel. Pavel's family may have come to America before he was born, but they'd brought their old-world prejudice with them. The same prejudice that had taken Maksim's father from him. That had taken Rachel from him.

He grabbed a folded blanket off the end of the cot and wrapped it around his shoulders, grateful for its warmth. Then he made his way to the window near the door. The beam from the lighthouse broke the darkness with a dim glow, muted by the same fog that had befuddled the *Davidson*'s captain.

Maksim had been a fool to think that leaving Russia meant leaving the prejudice behind. He'd been a fool to think he could fall in love with Rachel. He leaned his shoulder against the wall and watched Anna return to the kitchen, the blond haystack in her wake. He'd been a fool who'd stowed away on a boat captained by a man who'd run it aground, leaving him a castaway.

"I'm here because Uncle Jim couldn't leave the lighthouse." Anna pushed down her irritation and forced the words over her shoulder at Ernest Kindt. Why must he seek her out when she'd done nothing but discourage him since she'd arrived?

"You shouldn't have come here on a night like this." Ernest stepped in front of her, blocking the entrance to the kitchen. "What if you'd tripped and twisted your ankle? You could have been lying out there for hours before anyone knew to look for you."

"The aunties came with me," she said through clenched teeth. Ernest was more annoying than her bevy of older brothers back in Detroit. Just because she was the youngest didn't mean she needed someone to watch over her. Not family and not Ernest. She was eighteen, for pity's sake.

"I still don't like it."

Anna pulled the tray of dirty bowls against her waist and took a steadying breath. "It's not your place to like or dislike what I do."

"It could be if—"

"Get out of the way, boy. Let the girl through." Auntie Gretchen smacked a wooden spoon against Ernest's shoulder.

He stepped aside, rubbing the spot.

"I was just—"

"In the way." Auntie Gretchen grabbed hold of Anna's arm above the elbow and hauled her into the kitchen, calling over her shoulder, "We've work to do. You'd do well to mind your own duties."

Ernest reddened but backed away from the door. "Yes, ma'am."

"That boy's a nuisance," Auntie Gretchen muttered.

"Don't I know it." If only he'd take one of her many hints that she wasn't interested.

Anna had dried the last bowl and put it on the shelf when Auntie Laurie poked her head into the kitchen. She joined Anna by the sink.

"They have fifteen cots here, but nineteen sailors. I've told Celia that we'll shelter four of the men. I'm sure your uncle won't mind."

"No, I'm sure he won't."

"We'll bring the Russian boys. Gretchen and I will—"

A low rumbling came from the corner of the kitchen where Auntie Gretchen slouched against the wall precariously seated on a three-legged stool.

Auntie Laurie smiled. "We will walk over with the sailors. You can take the lantern and run ahead to make up the beds. Take your blankets to our room and make a pallet under the window."

"I will. I expect they'll sleep like the dead after tonight."

"They'll be out at first light to try and move the ship and barge off the reef."

"Barge?"

"Seems the *Davidson* was towing the barge *Middlesex* behind her. They will be plenty busy for several days." Auntie Laurie raised her voice. "Won't they, sister?"

Auntie Gretchen snorted and straightened on her stool. "What?"

Anna giggled behind her fingers. The aunties were something special. "I'll hurry."

She braved the dark and foggy path alone—she was more than capable despite what that oaf Ernest thought—and arrived at the lighthouse, where she dashed upstairs. Uncle Jim used one of the four bedrooms for his office. She entered the spare room first and removed some mending she'd left lying on the bed. She fluffed the feather pillows and smoothed the quilt over the top. Then she hurried into her room.

"Barnacle." Anna scooped the long-haired calico off the middle of her bed. "We've company coming for a few days. You'll have to find some other place to sleep." The cat purred and blinked her emerald eyes. Anna set her on the floor. "Go find a mouse."

Barnacle stalked from the room with an offended flick of her tail as she crossed the threshold.

The silly beast would be back, but the sailors should be used to cats. Ships often kept a cat or two on board for help with rodent control. Barnacle did her duty in that regard in the lighthouse, the tower, and the arched brick passageway that connected the two structures.

Anna gathered what she needed from her room and carried it to the only downstairs bedroom, which the aunties shared. She had a pallet made and was stifling a yawn when Uncle Jim came through the passageway. She explained what had happened. He nodded his blessing at housing the extra sailors before returning to the tower. On a night like this, he'd stay up there to be sure the light shone its warning.

Someday, she'd be tending that light by herself. She pressed her hand to her belly and clenched her teeth. She would find a way to make that happen.

Chapter 3

Something plopped onto Maksim's legs, pinning him beneath the quilt to the soft mattress. He raked the hair off his forehead and away from his eyes. Not for the first time, he wished he'd had the money for a haircut before boarding the SS *James Davidson* in Buffalo, New York. He elbowed Pavel and earned a grunt in response.

"Get your legs off me."

"What?" Pavel rolled over and pulled the quilt from Maksim's shoulders.

Maksim squinted into the predawn gloom. If Pavel had rolled over, then what was on his legs? He sat upright, earning a second grunt from the other side of the bed, and came face-to-face with a pair of unblinking green eyes.

"*Privyet*. You probably don't understand Russian either." Maksim scratched the cat's chin. "I say to you, hello."

A rumbling purr returned his greeting.

Maksim rubbed his face and glanced out the window. The fog was gone. Soft gray light filtered into the room. Wind moaned around the eaves.

Pavel snorted and buried his head into his pillow.

The cat bumped against Maksim's arm, and he answered the plea by stroking the animal's long fur, earning a louder rumble.

"We should get up now." He gave Pavel's shoulder a shove. "Didn't the captain say to meet at the ship this morning?"

Pavel lifted his head, opened one eye, and then dropped back onto his pillow. "It's not morning yet."

"It will be by the time we walk there." He shook his friend again then stood and stretched.

The cat jumped onto Pavel's shoulder. "Leave me alo—ugh!" Pavel fell out of bed then sat up and rubbed his cheek. He glared at the cat. "That thing licked me."

Maksim laughed. "She did you a favor. Now you are out of bed."

They dressed and entered the hallway, the scent of frying bacon greeting them at the top of the stairs. That put new life into Pavel's step, and he beat Maksim to the bottom. They entered the dining room as the feeble rays of predawn gleamed through a pair of windows.

Maksim would work hard today with the sailors. He'd do his best to earn the captain's notice. Perhaps then he'd put in a word with the rescue boat's captain and secure a spot for Maksim. Pavel didn't think so, but he had to try.

What else could he do?

Pushing a stray lock of hair under her head scarf, Anna glanced around the kitchen. Uncle Jim had told her to make breakfast early because the men would be leaving at first light to try and salvage the ships. After barely two hours of sleep, she had everything ready. The aromas of coffee and bacon should bring the men down soon. Feet thumping on the stairs confirmed it. She filled cups with coffee and put them on a tray with a pitcher of cream and the sugar bowl. Russian words greeted her as she stepped into the dining room.

"Here you go." She placed the tray on the table the aunties had already set before they had disappeared to tidy themselves. "The others should be down shortly. Please, sit wherever you like."

"Thank you, miss." The first sailor executed a short bow.

"Thank you, miss." Although heavily accented, the Russian's words were understandable, and he mimicked the other's bow.

Heat warmed her cheeks. When had a man—much less two men—ever shown her such courtesy? Not her brothers and certainly not Ernest. Wishing she had something to do with her hands, Anna dipped a quick curtsy. "I'll be right back with the food." She fled the room, bumping into Uncle Jim in the hall.

"Steady, girl." He cut a look into the dining room. "Is something the matter?"

"Not at all." Her cheeks burned. "I was just hurrying to fetch the food." She ducked her head and scurried into the kitchen.

What was the matter with her? What must Uncle Jim think? She waved a towel in front of her face. It was the aunties' fault. All their chatter this morning about "that nice-looking Russian boy with the darkest eyes." And now he was in her dining room, thanking her in that husky Russian accent.

She didn't have time for such foolishness. When she had the tray filled with platters of bacon, eggs, and warm biscuits, she straightened her back and marched down the hallway. All five men were seated, but the two Russians stood when she entered.

"For heaven's sake, sit down." Anna refused to look at Uncle Jim as she set the platters on the table and took her seat.

The aunties joined them.

Uncle Jim cleared his throat. "I'm Jim Wilson, the lighthouse keeper." He gestured toward Anna. "This is my niece, Anna Wilson." He gestured to the aunties. "And these are Auntie Gretchen and Auntie Laurie, our housekeepers."

"I am Pavel Orlov, and this is my friend, Maksim Ivanov. He doesn't speak very much English."

"Don Boston."

"Carl Henderson."

"I wish you the best of luck today," Uncle Jim said. "I'd join you, but with my assistant keeper not due back until tomorrow, I must sleep so I can maintain the light tonight."

The sailors murmured in agreement. Nobody knew better than they how important the lighthouses were on the Great Lakes, especially in the fall with its fierce storms.

After the blessing, the food disappeared at an alarming rate. Anna would need to bake a larger batch of biscuits tomorrow. Good thing Uncle Jim had filled the flour barrel his last trip to the mainland. The men ate without talking. Once finished, the handsome Russian took a final gulp of coffee and stood.

His English-speaking friend stood as well. "Thank you for the fine meal, miss. We'd best hurry. The wind is picking up. If it gets much stronger, the ship will be battered to pieces on the rocks before we can shift her." They bowed before leaving the room. The other two sailors looked at each other, shrugged, and then followed without a word.

Uncle Jim chuckled. "A bit of the Old World come to the shores of Lake Huron."

Anna jumped to her feet and gathered the empty plates and platters.

"There's nothing wrong with good manners," Auntie Laurie said.

"Nothing wrong with a good-looking lad or two at the table either," said Auntie Gretchen.

Auntie Laurie smiled and nodded.

Uncle Jim leaned back in his chair. "Although why Anna'd look elsewhere when young Kindt is ready to declare for her, I'm sure I don't know."

Just what Anna didn't need, first the aunties and now Uncle Jim wanting to marry her off. She shot him a look meant to skewer him to his chair and ignored Auntie Gretchen's cackling laugh. They didn't understand. They'd not been the youngest of a large family—the only girl—always treated like the baby, always told she couldn't do this or couldn't do that. Those days were done, and she had no plans to put herself under another man's thumb. She could do whatever she set her mind to.

In fact, she could take care of herself and run the lighthouse. Without her help, Uncle Jim might step down as lighthouse keeper at the end of the season, what with his rheumatism and all. With him, she wasn't a burden; she was an asset. He was her father's oldest brother. Anna being the youngest of a large brood of siblings, Uncle

Jim was more like the grandfather she'd never known.

When Uncle Jim decided to step down, she planned on stepping into his place. The assistant keeper was almost Uncle Jim's age and had already been talking about retirement. There were other women who kept lighthouses around the Great Lakes. She set down the tray and clenched her fists. One day, she'd be the lighthouse keeper here on Thunder Bay Island. She'd be the one to keep the light burning.

The beacon at the very top of the tower.

Chapter 4

Cold, wet, and disappointed, Maksim trudged behind Pavel to the lighthouse. They'd dumped more than a hundred tons of coal from the *Davidson*'s hold, but it hadn't been enough to lift the ship off the rocks. Sore shoulders and weary arms were his only reward for the hours spent shoveling the black rock.

At least the sailors had been able to gather their belongings. Maksim had retrieved his canvas bag containing all his worldly possessions. That amounted to an extra pair of trousers, two shirts, a pair of mittens his mother had knitted, his father's pocketknife, a pair of socks in need of mending, and his wooden flute. Everything he'd escaped Russia with.

He had less than two dollars in coins left from the money Rachel's father had handed him, saying, "Go west. Your future is there, not here. Not with us." That there had been a hint of sadness in the old man's eyes had helped a bit. Not much, but a bit.

Maksim and Pavel tromped into the back room behind Don and Carl. Miss Anna Wilson met them at the door, her clipped English far too fast for him to understand, but the towels she handed out and the washbasins got her point across. Maksim wasn't the only one covered in coal dust.

She pointed to their bundles and spoke another flurry of words.

"She says we can leave our clothes here and she will wash them." Pavel dropped his bag to the floor. "I told her to call us Pavel and Maksim, since we're close in age." He grinned and wagged his eyebrows. "You never know. Being shipwrecked here could be to your advantage."

If not for the overcast day, he'd think his friend had been out in the sun too long. Maksim was still just a Russian immigrant, and a stowaway at that. He had no prospects beyond his willingness to work, and all that had earned him was a one-way ticket to nowhere.

The other men stripped down to their long underwear and splashed away the day's grime. Maksim followed their lead, dunking his head in the basin as much as he could to rid his hair of the clinging coal dust. Pavel passed him a cake of soap, and he hurried to finish as the others dressed in their clean—or at least cleaner—clothes. Then they filed into the house.

Maksim stepped into the kitchen and breathed in the scents of onions, stewed fish, and fresh bread. His stomach rumbled. They hadn't stopped working to eat at the ship. Breakfast was a distant memory.

Anna brought in the food, Mr. Wilson prayed, and then the sailors plowed through their portions while the aunties chatted to each other. Maksim licked his spoon and was battling a jaw-cracking yawn when Anna stood and left before he could rise. He pushed back his chair, but Pavel shook his head, a grin on his face. Moments later, she reappeared carrying a golden-crusted pie. The scents of cinnamon and cloves teased his tired muscles back to life, and he sprang to his feet.

"Please, sit. You pop up like a rabbit from its hole."

Pavel translated, and warmth crept up Maksim's neck. The other men looked at him. They hadn't moved from their chairs. He hadn't been around many American women yet. This would take some getting used to.

But not everything in this new country would. Being served a meal like this by a pretty girl who had offered to wash his clothing made his life a little more bearable, a little less lonely. He glanced at the plate she slid in front of him with its generous slice of apple-baked goodness.

If only he knew what tomorrow would bring.

The clink of forks against china ended, and the sailors relaxed back in their chairs. Anna did the same. She'd been on her feet all day, and there was no hurry to wash the dishes.

"How did it go out there today?" Uncle Jim pulled his pipe from one shirt pocket and a pouch of tobacco from the other.

Mr. Henderson also produced a pipe. "The tugboat *Swain* nudged the *Middlesex* free."

"The barge? Was she badly damaged?" Uncle Jim asked.

"Not a bit." The sailor spoke around the pipe's stem in his teeth. "Quite a miracle, that. They've taken her to the nearby port at Alpena."

"Same can't be said for the *Davidson*," Pavel said, sending a look toward Maksim. "They've sent to Detroit for a diver and pumps. She's taking on water."

"They'll never raise her." Mr. Boston shook his head. "We shoveled coal off her all day, and she didn't budge an inch. She's cut on the bottom, for sure."

"The diver will inspect her," Mr. Henderson said.

A gust of wind rattled the windows. "If she don't break up on the rocks before he gets here." Mr. Boston's words settled over the room, dampening the relaxed camaraderie.

Pavel leaned close and whispered in Russian to Maksim, who glanced out the window, color receding from his cheeks. Auntie Gretchen leaned so far in their direction that she risked falling off her chair.

Anna rose and collected the dishes. Uncle Jim stood and invited the other men to join him in the parlor. Maksim followed last with Barnacle padding at his heels. The man turned at the doorway and glanced at her. What caused the sadness that lingered in his eyes? She almost asked, but he wouldn't understand. She certainly wasn't going to ask the aunties to interpret. She offered what she hoped was an understanding smile, and he bowed in response before leaving the room.

She turned her back on Auntie Laurie's approving nod and carried the dishes to the kitchen. Why did his obvious distress affect her so?

Once the dishes were cleaned and the aunties had retired to the parlor, Anna stepped out the back door. She'd check one last time for eggs. It was getting cold enough that a late egg might freeze before morning, and they had all those extra mouths to feed at breakfast.

The chicken coop was a lean-to on the side of the barn. Anna entered and hung the lantern from the hook on the ceiling. She spoke to the speckled hens that remained tucked up on their perches. Two brown eggs lay nestled in one of the boxes.

It was a good thing she'd come out to check. She stroked the smooth feathers of the hen closest to her. It ducked its head and gave a low-pitched squawk. Anna slipped the eggs into her apron pocket and lifted the lantern from its hook.

A note pierced the night air, followed by another. Not a ship's whistle. This came from somewhere near the barn. The notes collected into a melody, mournful and slow.

Anna snuffed out the lantern and stepped from the chicken coop. A myriad of stars shone overhead, their crystal light a perfect backdrop for the clear tones coming from the other side of the barn. She made her way along the barn's side and across the back as quietly as possible. The haunting notes drew closer. She pressed against the far corner, inching her head around until she saw who created such music.

Maksim.

He was sitting with his back against the barn, one knee raised, the other leg stretched out before him. The moon cast a dull gleam on the wooden flute in his hands. His eyes were closed as his fingers drifted across the open holes of the instrument as if in a slow waltz. A shiver that had nothing to do with the cold worked up her spine. The poignant tune tugged at her heart.

He might lack words, but the expression in his music told a tale. Alone in a strange land, buffeted by events beyond his control, missing. . .what? His home? His family? A girl he'd left behind?

She pulled back and leaned her head against the rough wood. The sorrowful notes rose and dipped, drawing her into their cadence. When they stopped, she straightened and hurried toward the lighthouse. To be caught listening to such a private moment was to be caught eavesdropping. Maksim had poured his soul into his song.

Her fingers smarted from the cold. Her heart smarted too, in a different way. A disturbingly different way.

Chapter 5

Maksim listened to the captain, his muscles tightening by the minute. If only he could understand more words. Pavel glanced at him and lifted a finger, but waiting was the last thing Maksim wanted to do. At last, the captain ran out of words, and the sailors around them mumbled and muttered among themselves.

"It's bad." Compassion darkened Pavel's eyes. "The diver says there's a large hole in her bow, and the waves have twisted her hull. She won't sail again. I'm sorry, Maksim."

"I have worked hard—"

"You have, but it won't change anything. The captain said we're to load onto the *Winslow*." He nodded to the tugboat that had brought the diver and pumps from Detroit. "We're leaving within the hour."

Maksim sank to the ground and pulled his knees up, wrapping his arms around them. A castaway. His harrowing escape from Russia, the heartbreak of leaving Rachel, his journey to find work farming in a far-off land, and this was where he was, stuck on a lonely island with winter setting in.

"Perhaps one of the lifesaving crew will give you a lift to the mainland." Pavel shrugged. "It's not farming land, but there is work for someone who can cut timber, they say."

"Will there be other Russians there?"

Pavel shook his head. "I asked the old ladies at the lighthouse. They don't know of any other Russians close by."

"How will I—" What was the use? He waved off the end of his question. He was stranded and would soon be alone. He glanced at the tower, just visible over the scrubby trees growing along the edge of layered limestone that served as a beach. At least he could speak with the two old women. Could he learn enough English to speak to others before he made his way to the mainland? Enough to speak to Anna and thank her for washing and mending his clothing yesterday? He'd like to do that. Her freckled nose and ready smile had intruded on his thoughts more than once today.

But it wasn't likely the lighthouse keeper would allow him to stay once he knew that Maksim was a stowaway.

Anna bent her head over the last of the sailors' socks that needed mending. Auntie Laurie hummed as she mended the final shirt from the pile. Auntie Gretchen dozed in her chair, Barnacle snoozing on the footstool beside her feet. The house was quiet, the ticking of the hall clock its only sound until Uncle Jim came down the stairs from his bedroom.

Just in time. Anna snipped off the yarn and tossed the finished sock onto the pile of mended clothing.

"Did you sleep well?" she asked.

He yawned and stretched. "Well enough. I'll be glad when Doug returns. To tell you the truth, I expected him yesterday." A frown marred his brow.

"That wind has been fierce," Anna said.

Auntie Gretchen opened one eye. "Not bad enough to stop a tugboat. I remember back in the fall of '61 when—"

"Yes, sister," Auntie Laurie said. "That was a frightful year."

Auntie Gretchen grunted, leveling a wrinkled glare at her sister.

Auntie Laurie turned to Uncle Jim. "Do you fear something has happened?"

"Could be."

Anna's stomach tightened, and she stood. "I'll fetch you coffee and a sandwich if you like."

"Thank you, my dear."

Anna hurried to the kitchen. What if the assistant keeper didn't return? Uncle Jim couldn't keep vigilance at the light every night. He needed help.

At the top of the tower. Maybe this was her chance.

She pressed her hand to her stomach for a moment before assembling the sandwich and putting it on a tray. She poured a steaming mug of coffee from the pot she'd left on the back of the stove.

As Anna returned with the tray, Uncle Jim said, "Perhaps Mr. Persons could spare young Kindt if Doug hasn't returned by tomorrow evening."

Oh, please, not that. He'd be hanging around her all the time. She didn't dislike him, exactly, but she didn't want to encourage his attention. Not even a little bit. She met Auntie Laurie's gaze from across the room.

"Surely he'll be too busy this time of year," Auntie Laurie said, her voice a balm to Anna's ears. "It's a dangerous time for the boats."

"All the more reason I need help with the light."

Anna set the tray on the side table by Uncle Jim's chair. As she straightened, voices drew her attention. She went to the window.

"The sailors are returning, and it's just midafternoon." What could that mean? They'd not returned before dark the past two days.

Uncle Jim sipped his coffee. "That can't be good."

Maksim, his dark hair covered by a knitted cap, followed the rest into the lighthouse yard, his chin almost on his chest, his shoulders slumped.

No. It couldn't be good news.

Maksim followed the rest of the men into the keeper's house, leaving his boots and coat in the back room like the others. Pavel spoke to the lighthouse keeper in the parlor while the other two sailors headed up the stairs to fetch their belongings.

Maksim stopped and listened, understanding only a few words and then his name. Pavel waved his hand, urging Maksim to join them.

The two old women sat, and Anna stood by the window, but the lighthouse keeper pinned him with a steely stare. What had Pavel told him?

"I told him that you're stranded here. He knows you were a stowaway, that the captain knew about it, and that you'll be looking for work. I told him you're a hard worker."

The keeper stroked his gray beard. Auntie Gretchen said something in English and the old man's eyes narrowed.

"Mr. Wilson had just mentioned needing help with the lighthouse," the old woman said in Russian. "Seems to me you could solve his problem, being as you're marooned here for a while at least." She gave him a long-toothed grin.

Anna's attention alternated between him and her uncle. Was that hope on her face? Why would she want him to stay? An answering hope resonated somewhere deep inside him.

More English words flew between Pavel and the keeper, with both the old women chiming in. Anna stood in silence, her hands clasped at her waist.

Then Auntie Gretchen cackled and slapped her knee. "That's it, boy. You'll stay at least until the assistant lighthouse keeper can be found. And for helping out, Mr. Wilson will see you get a boat for the mainland before winter sets in."

"I don't know what to say." Maksim staggered a bit when Pavel cuffed his shoulder. "I will work hard. Very hard."

More English words and the rigid line of Anna's shoulders relaxed. She smiled at him, and the day seemed brighter than it had when he'd arrived at the lighthouse. A whole lot brighter.

The old woman cackled again.

"I wouldn't know where to begin." Anna pushed a wayward strand of hair behind her ear.

Auntie Gretchen stirred a pot of bean soup at the stove. They wouldn't need all of it tonight. The three sailors had packed and hurried off, leaving just five to feed. "Begin with the simple things, words he'll need to know to help your uncle. Words for the things he'll be handling. The same as you'd teach a child."

"But he's not a child."

"I should say he isn't." Auntie Laurie looked up from cutting biscuits.

"Handsome enough to charm a bee away from a patch of clover," Auntie Gretchen said.

"Mannerly too." Auntie Laurie placed the biscuits onto the baking tin.

"His manners are nice." Anna refused to comment on his looks. It was bad enough that heat crept into her cheeks at the thought. "But how can I teach someone who doesn't understand me?"

"I'll help you, dear." Auntie Laurie placed the tin in the oven and dusted off her hands. "We both will."

"But when?"

Auntie Gretchen grunted. "In the evenings after supper when we're all gathered in the parlor. He'll be grateful, I'm sure."

"And he's got such lovely manners." Auntie Laurie pressed her fingers to her cheeks, leaving a faint dusting of flour behind.

Teaching him more English was the least Anna could do. She nodded and won another cackle from Auntie Gretchen. She owed it to Maksim. With him here, Uncle Jim wouldn't ask Ernest to come.

She supposed she should be flattered by Ernest's attentions, but she wasn't. Not a bit. If he came and stayed, she might lose her one chance to take over the lighthouse. Her one chance to be independent. To take care of herself and help those sailing Lake Huron. Whoever took over would need the approval of the lighthouse board, of course, but if someone was already filling in and serving. . . No, Ernest couldn't come.

Maksim had a roof over his head and a bed to sleep in, although he'd been moved to the bedroom across the hall. He rubbed the back of his neck when he thought about Anna giving up her own bed for him and Pavel those first nights. He also had food, and someone had mended his socks. Things could be much worse. He had the aunties—who had insisted he call them aunties even though they were not related—who could interpret for him until he learned enough English to understand on his own.

If only everyone would slow down and speak without running all their words together.

He unbuttoned his shirt. One button hung by a single thread. Maybe if he asked, someone would sew it back on for him. He sniffed the fabric and wrinkled his nose, relieved that he had a clean shirt to wear. He should ask where the soap was kept and wash this set of clothes tomorrow. Or maybe he'd be too busy up in the tower.

He crossed the bedroom and looked out the window. With no clouds and not a trace of fog, the moonbeams danced on the waters offshore. The beacon from the tower flashed across his view. The sight must be something to behold from the top of the tower.

Tomorrow he'd find out. Tonight he needed to sleep. He stretched out on the bed. The door creaked, and Maksim smiled into the darkness. Silence. No matter how he strained his ears, he could hear nothing until the rotund feline pounced upon the bed.

"If someone oiled the door hinges, you'd be a better sneak." He rubbed between its furry ears. "I hope I'm not stealing you away from whoever you used to sleep with." Contentment rumbled from the cat, and Maksim lowered his voice to a whisper. "But I'm very glad you're here."

The next morning, they assembled in the parlor like they did every Sunday after breakfast. Uncle Jim held his old Bible. "We're done with Romans. Which book should we read next?"

"I believe it's Anna's turn to choose," Auntie Laurie said.

He nodded toward Anna. "What will it be?"

Anna bit the corner of her lip. There was no church on the island. Uncle Jim's Bible readings were more informal than her church in Detroit, if no less heartfelt. She needed to make her choice count. But which book?

Of course. She smiled and relaxed in her seat. "Esther."

Auntie Gretchen cackled. "Fitting."

Heat flooded Anna's cheeks. Was she so transparent?

"God put the stories of strong women in the Bible for a reason." Uncle Jim smiled at her.

She cast a glance at Maksim, his crinkled brow a sign that he was struggling to understand. Had he read the Bible in Russia? Could he read at all? Was he even a believer? There was so much she didn't know about him, but she had a curious pull to learn.

He noticed her and straightened on his chair, a grin parting his lips. The look that did disturbing things to her middle darkened his eyes.

Uncle Jim cleared his throat and Anna jumped, turning her attention back to him. Heat flooded more than just her cheeks. Why did Maksim unsettle her so? And why did she look forward to it?

" 'Now it came to pass in the days of Ahasuerus....' "

Chapter 6

Three days later, dawn's first rays had yet to break the watery horizon when Anna stepped out the back door. The air smelled of frost and woodsmoke as the chimney belched out its ribbon of white above the rooftop. A fog bank was barely visible to the north. She should stoke the furnace in the fog signal building after milking Gertie.

How had she managed to leave the milk pail in the barn? She stomped across the yard, irritation prickling between her shoulders. It must be out there, because it wasn't in the kitchen. Had she taken it out when she'd gathered the eggs after dark? She couldn't remember, which irritated her even more.

When she opened the barn door, a soft light shone from within. The rhythmic *shping-shping* of milk squirting against a metal pail greeted her. What on earth? Anna hurried to the far end of the barn.

Gertie's head was secured in the milking stanchion, her lower jaw swinging in contentment as she chewed her grain. Crouched beside her on the three-legged stool was Maksim, his ebony head pressed against the cow's flank, both hands working in quick rhythm.

"What are you doing?"

He jerked, sat upright, and then rose when he saw her.

It was a good thing his English was so poor. After all, it was perfectly obvious what he was doing. But why was he doing it? Her heart plummeted. Someone else who didn't think she could pull her weight. Well. . .not this time.

"This is my job." She pointed to herself and then the cow. "I milk Gertie."

He shrugged. "I can do. I do in Russia."

She clamped her hands to her hip bones. "This is my job." And he wasn't taking it over. She pointed toward the door.

He looked at the floor then shuffled between her and the barn wall. She stood firm, letting him know that this was her territory. Best he didn't get any ideas about that, no matter how nice his manners or how his dark looks made her insides quiver.

As he walked off, the slouch to his shoulders matched the soulful music he'd played on his flute, and regret poured through her. Maybe he was just trying to be helpful as a way to express his thanks.

Oh. . .what had she done?

Anna ran after Maksim and caught his sleeve. He took a step away from her, and who could blame him after the way she'd just acted? She pointed to the fog signal building then motioned for him to follow.

They stopped outside the door, and she pointed to the north. "Fog." She swirled her hands then cupped them over her eyes as if having trouble seeing.

"*Fog*. I know this word."

Anna dropped her hands. Of course he'd know that word. He probably heard it plenty the night of the wreck. She coughed against the embarrassment filling her throat. "We must stoke the furnace for the fog signal. With coal."

"Coal." He nodded. "Certainly."

She opened the door and pointed to the furnace. He grabbed the coal shovel and went to work.

That was easy. With no more words needed, he took over.

Anna returned to Gertie and finished the milking. If Doug Anderson were here, he'd have started the furnace. Maksim was just filling in while he was gone. He wasn't one of her brothers who didn't think she could do anything useful by herself. He wasn't trying to usurp her position here either, or rather, the position she hoped to inherit.

"Try again." Anna pointed at Auntie Gretchen. "Auntie Gretchen is knitting a wool mitten."

Maksim focused on the woman across the parlor from him. "Auntie Gretchen knittink the wool mitten."

"Excellent." The auntie in question beamed at him.

It wasn't correct. Anna shook her head, but at Auntie Laurie's raised eyebrow, she held her tongue. After all, she could understand what he'd said. Even more important, he understood what he'd said. Quite the improvement in just a few days.

"Very good. What is Auntie Laurie doing?"

Maksim stared at the other sister. He opened his mouth, closed it again, rubbed the blue-black stubble on this chin, and then straightened in his chair. "Auntie Laurie readink the book."

She sighed at his rolled *r* but gave him a nod. "And what will Mr. Wilson be doing soon?"

His eyebrows rose and a smile brightened his face. He glanced at the older man, who was resting in his favorite chair, pipe tucked in the corner of his mouth. "Almost time he light the tower."

"The lamp. He lights the lamp *in* the tower," Anna said.

Maksim's smile evaporated. "The lamp. Certainly. The lamp."

Her heart squeezed at his crestfallen expression. His promise to work hard was as true for learning the language as it was for learning the workings of the lighthouse. Since word had reached them from a visiting tugboat that the assistant keeper was stuck in Alpena nursing a broken leg, one the doctor feared might not heal well, Maksim's willingness to work was a blessing to her uncle. But it still worried her.

She'd made sure to beat him to the barn after supper, even though he hadn't appeared ready to try milking again after the stink she'd caused this morning. She shifted on her chair, embarrassed by the memory of her words and actions.

At least he'd taken over carting coal from the dock to the coal bins in the fog signal building and the lighthouse. That job was getting too difficult for Uncle Jim to manage, and the handcart was too heavy for Anna to fill completely. She'd need to make twice as many trips back and forth as Maksim did. With winter on their doorstep, they needed every chunk of coal the boats would unload for them.

She'd have to ask Maksim to chop wood for the kitchen stove with Mr. Anderson gone and Uncle Jim adamant that Anna not touch the ax. The aunties refused to cook with coal. Auntie Gretchen claimed she could taste it in the food. Auntie Laurie said it dirtied up the whole kitchen.

Of course, first Anna needed to convince Uncle Jim to winter on the island.

A knock on the back door drew her out of her musings.

"I'll answer it." Anna hurried from the parlor. Saturday visitors were uncommon at the lighthouse.

She pulled open the door, and a blast of damp air blew into the back room. On the step, his hand raised as if to knock again, stood Ernest Kindt. He snatched his knit cap off his head, leaving his too-long blond locks in disarray. In his other hand hung a bulky bundle wrapped in paper and bulging against the twine that contained it.

"I've been to the mainland today and brought back a delivery for the aunties."

Anna stifled a sigh. "Please, come in. The aunties are in the parlor with Uncle Jim and Maksim."

Ernest shrugged out of his heavy coat and pulled off his boots in the back room before following her into the house, the bundle bumping against the walls as he carried it down the hallway.

He exchanged greetings with Uncle Jim and the aunties, but his eyes cut to Maksim and narrowed.

"What have you brought with you?" Auntie Laurie asked, setting her book aside.

"I know what it is." Auntie Gretchen rubbed her hands together. "My order came in, didn't it?"

"Yes, ma'am." Ernest dropped the bundle on the floor in front of Auntie Gretchen's chair.

She chuckled. "Fetch me a pair of scissors, girl."

Anna retrieved the pair from the mending basket and handed them over. Auntie Laurie stood and came across the room. When Auntie Gretchen snipped the final piece of rough twine, the package burst open. The odor of sheep flooded the room as fluffy white locks of wool spilled onto the floor.

"You didn't tell me you'd ordered us fleece." Auntie Laurie's eyes shone.

"We'll need something to keep us busy this winter if we're staying on the island."

Staying on the island? Anna shot a glance at Uncle Jim.

Her uncle held up both hands, palms out. "Now wait a minute. I didn't say we would winter on the island—"

"And who's to say we can't stay without you?" Auntie Gretchen sat back in her chair. "With John and Ann Paxton having retired to the mainland, Laurie and I can't stay at the fishing station on Sugar Island anymore. This is as good a place as any to ride out the winter."

"Didn't William take over the fishery?" Uncle Jim asked.

"He doesn't want a pair of old women hanging around," Auntie Laurie said. "Him being young and all."

Ernest stood with mouth open, gaping at each speaker in turn. Maksim stayed in his chair, a puzzled expression on his face. Likely he couldn't follow but half the words. Anna waited for Uncle Jim's response, her toes curling in her shoes.

"Anna's not wintering over, is she?" Ernest blurted out into the room.

Nobody answered him. Uncle Jim moved his pipe from one corner of his mouth to the other, his forehead a mass of wrinkles.

Anna held her breath. If she opened her mouth, she might say something that would tip Uncle Jim's decision the wrong way. He didn't approve of her ambition to be the next keeper, but he'd let her come to the island, so she held firm to that slim thread of hope.

He removed his pipe and tapped the stem against his beard. "We've time yet to decide such things."

The air rushed from Anna's lungs, and she caught Maksim's dark brown gaze. She flashed him a smile and then knelt by the pile of wool while the aunties made their plans to spin it over winter for warm mittens and hats to sell to the fishermen and sailors in the spring.

Maksim paced at the bottom of the tower steps, waiting for Mr. Wilson. It was almost time to light the lamp, which had become his favorite time of day. For a few moments before they lit it, they would go outside on the parapet and lean their elbows against the railing, looking out over the expanse of water. So much of it. Beautiful as the sun lowered, making the passing ships look small beside their shadows. Mr. Wilson would sigh, rub the back of his neck, and then pull a box of matches from his pocket. Even without words, Maksim understood the old man's attachment to the tower.

The words were coming. He knew Anna wished he'd pronounce the words better, but the strange sounds were foreign in his ears, and his lips couldn't make some of them work. He would try harder. Her smile when he got close to the right sounds made it worth the effort.

Rachel used to smile at him, but not in the same way Anna did. Rachel had been a bit of a flirt. More than a bit, as he thought back on it. At least, she had been when her father wasn't around. Had he been nothing more than a game to her? A way to pass the time on a long voyage? That question had robbed him of sleep too many nights. But not in the past week. Being shipwrecked had been a good way to refocus on what was truly important in life.

Having a pretty tutor with reddish-brown hair as sleek as a seal didn't hurt either, her dark blue eyes shimmering with intelligence and something else. Something he couldn't put his finger on. At times he thought she was worried and at other times pleased.

Her uncle's fingers were gnarled and his steps slow. Maksim did his best to anticipate things he could do to make the man's life a bit easier. Mr. Wilson had treated him with such kindness, it came naturally to want to help him. But if it also pleased his niece, lessened her worries, then so much the better.

He was beholden to them. He would make sure they never regretted allowing him to stay.

Mr. Wilson came down the passageway. He pulled the pipe from the corner of his mouth. "Are we ready, boy?"

"We are ready."

"Good. Let's go up and warn some ships."

"Yes, sir." Maksim picked up the can of kerosene he'd filled earlier.

It was slow climbing the spiral staircase behind the old man. The brick walls lent a feeling of solid strength to offset the metal mesh of the steps themselves. The first couple of times he'd climbed to the top, he'd had to force himself not to look down. The height was a bit intimidating. Even now, he kept a tight hold on the pipe handrail set into the bricks. Once they reached the landing under the lantern room, Maksim scrambled up the steel ladder and pushed open the hatch door. Since pushing the heavy door up and open was hard on Mr. Wilson, Maksim had made sure he opened it since that first time. The lighthouse keeper stroked his beard and nodded his thanks. No words needed for the understanding between them.

If only he could understand the niece as well as he did the uncle, because even though his heart had taken a bruising from Rachel and her family's rejection, he now realized that it wasn't broken beyond repair. If it were, those occasional smiles of Anna's wouldn't be distracting him while he leaned against the railing and looked out over Lake Huron.

Then there was the glowering frown from the fair-haired giant who'd brought the wool. If ever a man was staking claim to his territory, it was Ernest Kindt.

Chapter 7

Anna leaned against the doorframe of the barn, the egg basket dangling from her hand, the cool breeze washing over her. Sunlight shone off the vivid yellow and red leaves that clung to their branches while evergreens muted their stark warning of winter's approach. Wet leaves left a tang in the air. Soon, the fishermen's families would move to the mainland for the season. The fishing village would be a ghost town. She shivered and hurried across the yard to the lighthouse.

Uncle Jim still hadn't decided.

She left the basket in the kitchen and was passing a window in the dining room when movement caught her attention. She pushed aside the lace curtain. Maksim attacked the brush and vines that had grown up around the fog signal building, chopping and hacking at the foliage. Even in the chill, he wore no coat, and his shirtsleeves were rolled up, exposing muscular forearms. He stopped to swipe his hair from his face and tuck it under his cap.

Something fluttered beneath her ribs.

"That boy is a worker."

Anna jumped at Auntie Laurie's voice. "I didn't see you."

"I'm not as interesting as that young man outside."

"Of course you are."

Auntie Laurie joined her. "He could use a haircut."

"He could."

"Why don't you offer to trim it for him, mmm?" The wrinkles at the corners of Auntie Laurie's pale blue eyes deepened.

Anna swallowed. "I'm sure he'd rather have a real barber."

"Where is he going to find one? Not here on the island. No. You should offer. He'll accept." And with that, the old woman left the room, humming to herself.

What would his hair feel like? Anna shook her head to clear the thought. And yet. . .her eyes were drawn back to the window. He was such a help to Uncle Jim. Cutting his hair would be nothing more than a kindness. A way to thank him for all he'd done. And he'd look better when he arrived at the mainland. It might even help him find a job over there. When he left.

She pressed her palm against the cold glass.

Maksim stopped to rest for a moment and glanced at the lighthouse. Anna stood there, framed in the window, her hand raised. He waved in return. She whirled and left, leaving the curtain to shimmer across the glass. He leaned against the building's metal siding. His heart pounded from more than just the exercise.

He was falling for Anna.

And he was a fool. He took in the area around the lighthouse. The assistant keeper's house, the barn with the milk cow standing in the fenced paddock, the path leading to the dock with its deep ruts from hauling coal in the handcart. This place was starting to feel like home. He'd only been here a month, but that was longer than he'd stayed anywhere since leaving Russia.

He turned his gaze to the water. It was clean and sweet, nothing like the salty brine he'd crossed to escape his homeland. The homeland that had taken his father. The homeland where he'd left his mother. Alone. Did she live? Or had the pogroms, the anti-Semitic riots that had swept away his father, taken her too? Would he ever know? Probably not. No one back in Russia knew where he was. Even Rachel's family didn't know, except that he'd gone west. Likely they didn't care. Likely no one did.

With a shove of his foot, he pushed away from the building.

He cared. His mother had wished for him to have a better life in this new country. He would have one. A good one. He grabbed the hatchet and set to work on the remaining brush and vines. And if a girl with freckles on her nose who watched him from the window could be a part of that—

The hatchet hit a thick sapling and lodged in it. He tightened his grip on the handle. Ernest Kindt may have laid claim to the girl in question, but it was Maksim Ivanov she was watching from the window.

He grinned and jerked the hatchet free.

Barnacle licked up the last of her dinner scraps and milk. Disloyal cat. Anna missed the warm lump next to her at night. She'd thought the cat was busy mousing this time of year when the rodents left the woods and meadows, hoping to spend the cold months in the warm lighthouse. But no, she'd found out this morning that the traitorous calico had been sleeping with Maksim. Barnacle licked her chops and sauntered away from the clean bowl, which Anna picked up and washed.

With no more reason to linger in the kitchen, she straightened the towel on its hanger. Again. Why was she so nervous? She'd trimmed Uncle Jim's hair twice already, not that there was much left to trim, just a bit of fringe around the edges.

She missed nothing of the hustle and bustle of Detroit, with its clogged streets and smoky skies. She'd known she'd have to make do when she talked Uncle Jim into letting her move here. She relished both the solitude and the spirit of the small community. Part of that spirit was helping others.

Like cutting Maksim's hair. Nothing more than a kindness. Nothing more than anyone else would do. She rubbed her palms down the sides of her skirt. Nothing at all.

Anna carried a dining room chair into the kitchen and hung an old towel over the back, then moved the rugs out of the way. She went upstairs and fetched her comb and embroidery scissors. Those should do the trick. At least she'd be less likely to lop off one of his ears.

With those in her pocket, she went to the parlor and stopped short of the doorway, out of sight of those within. She took a deep breath and blew it out, then straightened her shoulders and pasted on her best—hopefully, neutral—smile before stepping inside.

"Maksim."

He looked up from the lantern he was polishing.

"Auntie Laurie mentioned that you could use a haircut." She slipped the scissors from her pocket and snipped them to demonstrate cutting.

Maksim looked at Auntie Laurie, who nodded but didn't translate.

"Certainly." He stood, setting the lantern aside.

"Come into the kitchen. We'll keep the mess out of the parlor." Anna ignored the knowing glances between the aunties. Really. They made far too much over a simple thing.

Uncle Jim looked up from his newspaper, which had come with the mail that afternoon. "I could use a trim myself," he said around the stem of his pipe.

"Would you like to go first?" Anna asked.

He turned a page in the paper. "No hurry."

Maksim followed her down the short hallway. She motioned to the chair, and he sat on the very edge. She pulled the towel from the back.

"Sit back."

"I am sittink." He looked up at her, his brows drawn together.

She patted the back of the chair.

He scooted back, his gaze never leaving hers until she nodded. She wrapped the towel around his shoulders and pulled the comb from her pocket. The tines of the comb slid through his hair, and his breath hissed between his teeth.

"Did I hurt you?"

"Nyet. No." He squirmed on the chair. "You"—he tapped the scissors in her other hand—"you make hair. . ." He held two fingers a short distance apart.

Why hadn't the aunties translated?

"Yes. I will trim your hair." She spaced her words, emphasizing *trim* by snipping the scissors.

He nodded but didn't relax. Did he think she meant to shear him like a sheep? He could have a little faith in her.

She slid the comb through his hair again. Thick and sleek, still slightly damp around the edges from his wash before dinner. She swallowed then ran her fingers down a lock of his hair and snipped.

Maksim flinched.

Oh, for heaven's sake. Anna pressed her lips into a firm line and attacked the rest of his locks, ignoring him, his flinches, the satiny texture of his hair, the fresh scent of soap. A few times, she tugged him back to the center of the chair when he tried to lean away from her. Not a word was spoken until a circle of black carpeted the wooden floor around them. Anna pulled the towel from his shoulders.

"Finished."

He hopped off the chair as if it had scalded him, and ran his fingers through his hair. Anna pointed at the mirror hung by the back door. He approached it with great caution. She huffed and crossed her arms.

After a long look, he turned and grinned. "Is good. Very good."

What had he expected?

His eyes darkened to almost black. "You make good for me."

"It was nothing." Had that breathy voice been hers?

He stepped close, and she wished she had that breath back. The molasses color of his eyes sparked with something faintly dangerous and delicious at the same time. His fingers grazed the line of her jaw. Her lips parted, seeking the breath that had escaped.

"Did she leave your ears attached?" Auntie Gretchen entered the kitchen, her voice a near bellow. Maksim and Anna sprang apart. At the old woman's cackle, heat scorched Anna's cheeks.

"I'll let Uncle Jim know I'm ready for him." Anna scurried down the hallway, refusing to think about the flurry of Russian words behind her.

Had he intended to kiss her?

Would she have let him?

41

Chapter 8

Ice had thickened around the dock over the past days. Maksim stared across the frigid waters at the approaching tugboat. He pulled off his hat and ran his hand over his hair. If he closed his eyes, he could still feel her fingers on his scalp. At first he'd jumped at her touch. He'd tried to lean away from her, but she'd pulled him back. By the hair. He grinned. Anna had what his mother would have called spunk.

His grin melted away.

What if Auntie Gretchen hadn't walked in when she did? Would he have kissed her? He hadn't planned it, but at that moment...

He jerked his hat back on. It had been two days and still his thoughts came back to her fingers in his hair. He was a fool. Her uncle wouldn't accept him any more than Rachel's father had. The old man perked up whenever that Greek statue model came by the lighthouse. Maksim didn't need anyone to translate that for him.

The tugboat *Aspen* pulled up to the dock. A skinny sailor bundled to his nose waved and tossed a canvas mailbag onto the dock. Maksim flung an empty mailbag back onto the tugboat.

"We've coal," the sailor hollered as a couple of other men prepared to off-load it. "Tell the old man this is the last of it. If he's planning to winter over, he'll need to chop some wood."

"Certainly," Maksim called back, putting together *coal*, *last*, and *wood* to figure out what the sailor meant. The sailor waved again and helped the others unload the black rocks into the coal bin.

Maksim waited until they moved the tug into open water before he pushed the handcart onto the dock. Shoveling coal warmed him. By the time he'd dumped it at the fog signal building, sweat beaded his brow.

Movement near the barn caught his eye. Ernest Kindt walked along the path from the lifesaving station, his blond hair tousled above a knitted ear warmer.

With a sigh, Maksim pushed the handcart back toward the dock. He had at least three more trips to make. Then he spied the mailbag where he'd dropped it to unload. He glanced at the lighthouse. Maybe there was something in that mailbag that Mr. Wilson should see. Now. Not after Maksim finished moving the coal.

He grabbed the bag and strode to the lighthouse.

Ernest stood behind Auntie Laurie, who was washing dishes at the sink when Anna entered the kitchen. She sighed. Sooner or later he had to realize that she wasn't going to accept his attempts to court her.

"Anna." He swiped the ear warmer from his head. "I wanted to talk to you."

Auntie Laurie gave a disdainful sniff.

"I'm up to my elbows in work." And if she hadn't been, she'd have made up something.

He turned the ear warmer over in his hands. "You work too hard. Take a break and walk with me. The fresh air would be good for you."

Auntie Laurie sniffed again, louder this time.

"I've left wax on the parlor's wainscoting. It needs to be rubbed in before it cools and hardens."

"But surely—"

The back door opened, and a swirl of cold air wrapped around her ankles. Maksim entered. He stopped, looking back and forth between them.

Auntie Laurie hummed at the sink.

"Mail come." Maksim half lifted the bag in his hand. "I brink for Mr. Wilson."

"Thank you." Anna smiled and squeezed past Ernest to take the bag. "He's been expecting this. I'll take it to him on my way back to the parlor. Good-bye, Ernest."

She suppressed her grin at Ernest's dumbfounded expression and Maksim's smirk until she was out of the kitchen. She hurried upstairs to Uncle Jim's office and set the mailbag on the edge of his desk.

He leaned back in his chair. "What has you smiling this morning?"

"A narrow escape from spending time with Ernest."

"What do you have against that boy?"

"I haven't time to make you a list, Uncle." But if she did, the way he tried to tell her what she should and shouldn't do would be at the top of it.

He rested his elbows on the desk and his chin on his folded hands. "He's a good lad, and even an old man like me can see that he's handsome enough."

"And he knows it, all too well." She refrained from rolling her eyes. "But he's not my type."

He sighed. "I was never anyone's type either, I suppose."

"Oh Uncle." She came around the desk and hugged his stooped shoulders. "You're the very best type there is." She kissed the smooth skin of his head.

He chuckled. "I am, am I?"

"Yes." She gave another squeeze. "Now, I best return to my polishing." She stepped away from his desk.

"Don't be so hasty to dismiss young Kindt. He's a crack lifesaver at the station, and he leads the island's baseball team. We beat the mainland three out of four games this summer. He knows his way around the lighthouse and the bay. You could do far worse." He opened the mailbag, pulled out a couple of newspapers and a letter. He grunted and turned the letter over in his hands.

"What is it, Uncle?" Anything to distract him from Ernest would be welcome.

"From Doug." He slit the envelope open and unfolded a single sheet.

"What does it say?" She resisted the urge to move back where she could read over his shoulder.

"Hmm." He adjusted his reading glasses on his nose. "Doug won't be returning. The doctor says his leg will heal but climbing the tower steps is out of the question. Seems he'll be retiring earlier than he'd planned."

Would this push Uncle Jim to retire too? Anna pressed her clasped hands to her stomach, her gaze darting about the office, but no ready answer hung on the walls.

He rubbed his hand down his beard. "I must write to the lighthouse board and tell them of Doug's letter. At least we've Maksim to take up the slack for now."

For now. But what about next year? Would he stay on? And why did that idea make her smile?

Maksim walked toward the lighthouse with a stringer of fish tossed over his shoulder. The aunties would be happy. They'd been hinting in their own not very subtle way that they wanted a fish dinner. He'd gotten the coal in with enough time to return to the dock with a pole and a can of grubs. He wasn't sure what kind of fish they were, but they looked edible.

That he grinned most of the way from the dock to the lighthouse had more to do with besting Kindt than it did pleasing the aunties. Anna had taken the mailbag and left both of them standing in the kitchen, but Maksim was pleased and Kindt was not. That put the extra spring in his step.

He entered the kitchen and lifted the stringer.

"Oh my." Auntie Laurie smiled. "Won't we eat well tonight?"

"Do you want for me to. . . ?" He fumbled for the right English word. "To trim it?"

She beamed at him. "Clean it. We clean fish."

Were fish dirty?

Auntie Laurie switched to Russian and explained the meanings.

"English, sister. The boy needs to learn English." Auntie Gretchen's voice boomed from down the hallway.

Auntie Laurie pressed her hand to her lips and winked at Maksim. "I'll clean the fish. You go and fill the lamp."

He handed the stringer over, grabbed the kerosene can from the back room, then headed for the tower. Anna stood on the third step, one hand grasping the handrail, the other clutching her skirts, although she wasn't moving.

"Anna."

She let out a squeal and blanched two shades whiter than her apron. Her foot slipped, and he rushed to steady her before she fell.

"I am sorry." He held her arm and helped her down the two last steps. "I did not mean for—"

She spit out a flurry of English words that tumbled on top of each other.

"Slowly, please." If ever he wished he could understand, it was now. Although, seeing the fire in her eyes, maybe he was better off not knowing what she'd said.

"What's happened here?" Auntie Gretchen hustled along the arched passage that connected the house to the tower. "Did she see a rat? Is that mangy cat not doing her job?"

Maksim shrugged.

"I am fine. Just fine." Anna pulled her arm from his grasp. "And I'd be even better if someone wasn't sneaking up behind me."

She flounced down the passage.

Auntie Gretchen chuckled.

"I not sneakink. Why she angry?"

The old woman patted his arm and switched to Russian. "Some things you'll have to figure out for yourself, boy."

Auntie Laurie poked her head into the passageway. "Who's speaking Russian now?"

Auntie Gretchen cackled and switched back to English. "Go on up and fill the lamp. You won't figure her out standing there gawking."

Whatever gawking was, it certainly wasn't helping him figure out Anna. Nothing else seemed to be either.

Chapter 9

Anna sat with her back to a tree, her knees raised and her elbows resting on them, fuzzy-mittened hands under her chin. What was she going to do if Uncle Jim moved them off the island? The last family from the fishing village had left yesterday. Where would she go? Not back to one of her overbearing brothers, that was for sure. Where would the aunties go? No matter what they said, Uncle Jim would never let them winter here alone.

And what about Maksim?

A gust of wind blew over the island, its icy breath smelling like winter. There were fewer and fewer boats coming by. She'd been gathering the eggs three times a day since the beginning of last week to get them in the house before they froze. She also broke the ice in poor old Gertie's bucket. They'd need to ferry the livestock off the island soon if they were leaving.

And what about Maksim?

Why had he been so. . .so. . . Why was he acting differently toward her? Ever since that almost-kiss, if that's what it was, he'd been popping up every time she turned around. Like last weekend by the staircase.

He couldn't have guessed her secret, could he? She slid her hands along the sides of her neck, their woolen warmth welcome against her skin. Nobody knew. Uncle Jim didn't think it seemly for her to climb the tower. The aunties never went up, of course. But Maksim shinnied up and down like a squirrel in an oak tree.

She stared at the top of the tower. For so long she'd dreamed of running this lighthouse by herself, but what about running it with someone else? Someone with a husky Russian accent. Someone who had been up in the tower many times. Someone who made her feel. . .like she'd never felt before.

First, she needed to convince Uncle Jim to let them stay. If Mr. and Mrs. Persons could winter at the lifesaving station, then they could winter right here. They had plenty of provisions from the garden. She and the aunties had filled the cellar and the pantry and stored—

A sound caught her ear. Maksim's flute. The tune was sprightly, weaving up and down like children skipping along the beach. Nothing at all like the mournful sounds he'd made before. It came from behind the barn. She headed in that direction. Creeping through the trees that pushed up against the lighthouse clearing, she circled around.

Maksim sat with his back against a fence post. Gertie grazed the withered grass from her tether outside the fence. Anna stopped and stroked the cow's thick winter coat. Even with his eyes closed, expressions played across Maksim's face that matched the lighthearted music. The notes skittered to an end.

He opened his eyes and scrambled to his feet.

"That was beautiful," she said.

He cocked his head.

She pointed to the flute. "Your music. It's lovely."

He looked at the instrument. "How you say?"

"Flute."

"Flute." He raised an eyebrow at her. "It make sound?"

"Music."

"Flute. Music."

"Gertie enjoyed it too." She gave the cow one last pat.

"Gertie need eat more." He pointed to the tether.

The small fenced paddock was grazed off. Maksim had tethered the cow where she could reach the dried grass outside it. If they stayed and kept Gertie with them, what would the cow eat?

"I trim for Gertie." Maksim pointed to a swath of cut grass, the old barn scythe resting on top of it. "I trim more, put in barn."

Of course. Why hadn't she thought of that? "It's cut, not trim. Can you cut enough to last her the winter?"

"Certainly. I think enough."

Anna couldn't stop the smile that parted her lips. This was another hurdle cleared for staying on the island. His answering smile sent a delicious warmth through her. If they stayed and worked the lighthouse together, would it always be like this?

He wasn't to milk the cow, but it was good if he cut hay for it. Maksim shook his head. Americans had different customs, but he was learning. And if cutting hay made Anna happy, then Maksim would cut hay. A lot of hay. It was just the wild grasses and weeds that grew in the open meadows of the island that were already cured and dried by the weather, but there was plenty to keep Gertie happy all winter. He forked the last load from the handcart to the empty stall in the barn, now filled with the fragrant hay.

Did he want to stay?

He jabbed the tines of the hayfork into the earthen barn floor and leaned against the handle. Duluth was a long way from Thunder Bay Island, and nobody was waiting for him there. If he stayed here for the winter, his English would continue to improve. Already he understood much of what was said, and the aunties were nearby if he needed help.

He glanced out the open barn door toward the lighthouse as its back door smacked shut. Anna, her red-brown hair escaping her scarf to whip in the wind, walked toward him. The egg basket swung from her hand. She looked out over the water to the south. Her profile mesmerized him. She was lovely. More than lovely, she was spunky and. . .and if they stayed, he risked leaving his heart behind in the spring.

She turned toward him, and a smile lifted her lips and crinkled the corners of her eyes. Maksim's heart lurched. Perhaps it was already too late.

"Hello." She stepped into the barn. "I see you brought in more hay."

"Enough, I think."

She stepped beside him and peered into the box stall filled from floor to rafters. "I'd say so, as long as we get a good shipment of corn from the mainland before the ice seals us in."

"Mr. Wilson, he say we stayink?"

Her shoulders drooped and she shook her head. "Not yet, but I'm hoping he'll agree soon."

"Certainly."

She tilted her head at him. "How did you wind up here?"

He blinked. Had she forgotten? "Shipwrecked."

"No." Merriment colored her voice. "How did you wind up in America? I haven't asked before, but now that you're doing so well with English. . ."

Not that well. How could he explain about the pogroms? His father? Rachel and her family? He jerked the hayfork free and hung it on the wall.

"Come. Need aunties."

He motioned for her to go before him toward the lighthouse. She held up one finger then stepped into the henhouse and came back with her basket of eggs. They walked to the lighthouse together.

The aunties were in the parlor.

"We should scour the wool before spinning," Auntie Laurie said.

"Nonsense. We'll spin it in the grease. That way the mittens and hats will be waterproof for the fishermen." Auntie Gretchen finished her words with a curt nod.

Auntie Laurie laid her book in her lap. "And in damp weather they'll smell like old sheepherders."

"Papa was a sheepherder as a boy in Russia." Auntie Gretchen's voice rose.

"Aunties." Best to cut them off before they got embroiled in a full-fledged argument. "Maksim needs your help translating."

"Of course, dear." Auntie Laurie smiled up at them.

Auntie Gretchen grunted, but she pointed at the sofa.

Maksim waited for Anna to take a seat, and then he joined her there, facing the aunties.

"You translate for me? I tell of how I come here. Anna ask. I not have enough English words."

"Of course we will," Auntie Laurie said.

Maksim switched to Russian. "I left Russia because of the pogroms."

"You're Jewish?" Auntie Gretchen sat up straight.

"If I am, will you think less of me?"

The sisters shared a look. Auntie Laurie lifted one shoulder. "I don't see why."

"Me either." Auntie Gretchen rubbed her chin. "Our parents had strong opinions regarding the Jews, but I don't remember them ever saying why. We've never known any personally, have we, sister?"

"I don't believe we have."

"Well, live and let live." Auntie Gretchen waved her hand. "So, you're Jewish?"

"No. I'm not."

The old women shared a confused look. He wasn't doing a very good job of telling his story.

"My father was a farmer, as was his father and his father before. But with just one son, my father needed help to work the land. He hired Lev Chulak, a Jewish man, for a farmhand. Mr. Chulak brought his family—his wife, two daughters, and three sons—with him. They lived in a cottage on the far side of the farm.

"When the pogroms started, my father was very worried about Mr. Chulak and his family. He helped them dig a room under the cottage. A secret room.

"Then one day, the rioters came to the farm and demanded Mr. Chulak and his family be turned over to them. My father, he led them to the cottage. They searched it but didn't find the secret room. In their anger, they took my father instead."

He stopped and waited while Auntie Laurie, her eyes wide, translated the story for Anna. When she finished, he continued.

"When they were gone, my mother and I went to the cottage and told the Chulaks they needed to run. They were very distraught when they heard that my father had been taken. My mother. . ." He paused and stared at the rug, his mother's face vivid in his mind's eye.

"Go on, boy, just get it out," Auntie Gretchen said, her voice almost soft.

"She begged Mr. Chulak to take me with them. She feared the pogroms would claim me next."

Auntie Laurie translated again. Anna gave a small gasp and laid her hand on his arm. The warmth of her touch helped loosen his tongue.

"Mr. Chulak agreed, but I argued with Mother until she broke down and cried. I could not stay and cause her more grief, and I could not talk her into leaving with us. She said she was born in Russia and would die there, but that I should leave while I was young. That I should find a better place and make a better life. So I left that very day. Mr. Chulak knew some people who helped smuggle us from the country. It took time, but we landed on a ship for America."

After the translation, Anna asked, "But how did you wind up on the way to Duluth?"

Should he tell her everything? He glanced from her to the aunties. Auntie Gretchen nodded as if she had read his thoughts. He swallowed.

"On the ship, we had a lot of time to do nothing. For someone who had always worked, it was difficult. We passed the time talking, mostly me and Rachel."

"Rachel?" Anna's eyebrows rose, and she withdrew her hand. Of course she'd pick out that name from his Russian words.

He nodded. "Mr. Chulak's oldest daughter. She was a year or so younger than me. We. . .grew close on the voyage."

"Was she special to you?" Auntie Laurie asked.

He shrugged and tugged at the collar of his shirt. "I thought so, but now—I think maybe she never thought so."

Auntie Gretchen harrumphed and crossed her arms. "A little flip-skirt, was she?" she asked in English.

"Sister!" Auntie Laurie's voice cut through the room.

Anna's face turned the color of a bowl of borscht.

It took Maksim a moment to untangle their words.

"Nyet. No. Rachel was not a bad girl." His face heated enough to match Anna's. "We did nothink wrong."

Auntie Laurie held out her hands, palms toward him. "No need to explain, my boy." She shot a withering glance at her sister.

"Rachel, she just like to be seen, I think."

"A flirt then." Auntie Gretchen nodded as if justified by his words.

Anna's coloring receded to normal.

Maksim switched back to Russian. "When we landed, Mr. Chulak made it clear that a union between our families would not be welcome. Rachel was Jewish and I. . .I am Christian."

"Why, that bigoted old—"

"Sister." Auntie Laurie shot the woman another warning look, then she translated for Anna.

"You mean, after your father saved their whole family, the man turned against you because of your faith?" What filled Anna's voice wasn't pity, but indignation.

Maksim leaned back against the couch and spoke in English. "He did. He gave handful of money and say 'go west.'" He shrugged. "I go west."

"What happened to your father?" Anna asked.

Maksim studied the rug at his feet.

"The pogroms take people for only one reason." Despite the fire in the grate, Auntie Laurie's voice left a cold chill in the room. "They killed him."

Chapter 10

Two days had passed, and still Anna's heart ached for Maksim. Losing her father had been the hardest thing she could remember, since her mother had died when Anna was born. But her father had died of an illness, something a person could understand and accept even through the pain. To lose one's father to a gang of evil men? She couldn't imagine the pain Maksim carried from that. And then leaving his mother—even though he'd done that to fulfill her wishes.

Her own worries and aspirations seemed shallow in comparison.

Anna backed out of the henhouse and smacked into someone. She gasped and stumbled. Ernest caught her arm to keep her on her feet and grabbed the egg basket before it spilled its contents onto the frosty ground. Her heart hammered against her ribs. She wrenched away from his grasp and whirled to face him.

"What are you doing here?" The sharp edge of her voice wiped the smile off his face. Well, he had it coming, sneaking up on her. Did all men do that?

"I was waiting for you."

She straightened her coat. "More like lying in wait. Why couldn't you go to the door and knock like the rest of the civilized world?"

"Because you're never alone there. If not those two old gargoyles, then it's that Ruskie hanging around."

"That Ruskie?"

"Yeah, what's his name. . .the one who follows you around like a half-brained puppy."

The desire to smack the smirk off his face was almost more than she could resist. But she paused. Why was she so angry about what he called Maksim and not what he'd called the aunties? No, she was angry at both. Equally. She pulled in a long breath and fought for control.

"*Maksim*"—she stressed his name—"is no half-brained puppy, and the aunties aren't gargoyles."

"Well, they're always around when I want to talk with you."

"Did you ever consider that I *want* them around when you're here?"

He took a step back. "No. Why would you?"

The conceited. . . She sucked in another breath, but it didn't work this time. "Because I have no desire to speak to you or spend time with you. And I'll thank you to not bother me in the future." With that, she grabbed her basket from his hand and marched past his gaping jaw. She made a beeline for the lighthouse, fairly certain that smoke was pouring from her ears. The nerve of him, trying to waylay her and calling Maksim and the aunties such awful names.

She pushed open the back door and almost ran over Maksim.

"What is wrong?" he asked.

"Nothing." She stormed past him.

He caught her arm, and Anna's momentum swung her around to face him.

"Somethink is not right."

"Some*thing*, not some*think*."

"Certainly, somethink."

"Some*thing*."

Maksim's ebony brows drew into a fierce scowl as he struggled to make the word sound like hers. "Some-think."

A giggle rose in her throat, but she pressed it down. Her lips twitched before she could stop them.

Maksim's forehead relaxed, and humor twinkled in the depths of his eyes.

Anna covered her mouth, but the giggle escaped between her fingers.

Uncle Jim came from the kitchen into the back room. "What's so funny out here?"

"Nothing." Anna laughed out loud. "Or I should say, no*think*."

Uncle Jim pushed his knitted cap back and rubbed the smooth skin above his crinkled forehead.

"She makes me fun of how I say words." Maksim's grin removed any doubt that he'd taken offense.

Another giggle would not be denied. "You mean 'makes fun of me.'"

"Is what I said, nyet?"

Uncle Jim settled his hat back in place, glanced from one to the other, and then shook his head. "We should move along, Maksim. We've plenty of work to do this afternoon."

Maksim shot her a quick look brimming with humor.

She tucked her chin and squeezed around Uncle Jim and into the kitchen. In the space of five minutes she'd gone from scared spitless to fighting mad to giggling like a half-wit. She was either going mad or. . .

She stopped and pressed her hand to her chest.

The woods around the lighthouse were stark with only a few stubborn leaves clinging to the oaks. Maksim carried a saw and a hatchet and followed Mr. Wilson, who had an ax slung over his shoulder. Maksim didn't need any English words to know what they were about, and he smiled into the breeze that numbed his cheeks. Mr. Wilson wouldn't be worried about cutting firewood if they weren't staying on the island for the winter. There was plenty enough coal to run the fog signal and heat the house for several weeks, and enough wood had been stacked for the kitchen stove.

Anna would be happy, and that made him happy too. More happy than he probably should be. But hearing her giggles and laughter this morning made him feel good. Not to mention catching a glimpse of Kindt's backside heading down the trail to the lifesaving station.

Mr. Wilson stopped next to a tangle of deadfall trees. He thumped on the wood. The sound was hollow, the wood dry and not rotted. Perfect for winter heat. He turned and faced Maksim then put one foot on a log and leaned against his raised knee.

"Anna is a fine girl."

His heart dropped. Here it came. "Certainly."

The older man ran his mittened hand down his beard. "She wants to take over for me when I step down as lighthouse keeper. She's had that dream since she was knee high." He shot a narrow look at Maksim.

"Does she?"

"She does. But it's too much work for a woman. She'd be better off on the mainland, maybe teaching school or married to a man who could take care of her proper like."

The words were spoken slowly and carefully, and Maksim understood them all too well. He braced himself for what would come next. For Mr. Wilson to tell him to pack his things and be on the next tugboat that stopped at the island.

"But she loves it here." The old man's voice dropped, and he looked around at the trees surrounding them. "I guess I filled her head with too many stories about this place. You see, I always wintered with her family. Her father was my youngest brother, you know. I still can't believe he's gone."

"I am sorry." Maksim knew the weight of that type of loss.

"Thank you, son. The aunties told me your story. I'm sorry for your loss as well."

Maksim nodded, his throat tight as he waited to be dismissed from the island.

Mr. Wilson straightened and pointed to another fallen tree. "You start over there. I'll work on this one. Between the two of us, we should be able to put up enough wood to keep the women cooking and the lighthouse warm all winter."

"Then you are stayink?"

"We are staying." The old man stressed the word *we*.

"All of we?" Maksim held his breath.

"I wouldn't consider it if you weren't here. We'll need your strong back and willing hands."

Relief poured over Maksim like a wave breaking over the rocks. "I work hard."

"I know you will." Uncle Jim lifted the ax from his shoulder. "Have a care with Anna. She's the closest thing to a daughter that I have. If you're planning on sailing away come spring, you tell her that up front. Understand?"

Maksim nodded. He wasn't sure he understood all of it, but the important part he did. He wasn't being chased off the island, wasn't being told to stay away from Anna. Maksim Ivanov was part of the *we* Mr. Wilson said was staying.

After the blessing, Anna passed the bowl of mashed potatoes to Maksim. What was he grinning about? He and Uncle Jim had been gone for hours. While Maksim looked ready to burst at the seams, Uncle Jim looked like he might fall asleep on his dinner plate.

"Hard to believe it's dark before we even sit down to supper." Auntie Laurie's glasses reflected the light from the oil lamps on the table.

"What's hard to believe? It does the same every year." Auntie Gretchen shoved a spoonful of potatoes into her mouth.

"The summers seem so short anymore."

The wistfulness in Auntie Laurie's voice tugged at something inside of Anna. This summer had been short. She'd arrived on Thunder Bay Island in April, just as winter's icy grip relented. Now it was November, and winter prowled at their door. Uncle Jim needed to—

"I have an announcement to make."

Everyone stopped, utensils hanging between plates and mouths, and all eyes turned to Uncle Jim. Anna's heart kicked against her ribs. She held her breath. He just had to say they were staying for the winter. He had to. She sneaked a quick glance at Maksim. His grin widened.

"Maksim and I cut wood today. There are plenty of dry, downed trees in the forest. We believe there is enough to keep us warm and heat the cookstove all winter."

Anna dropped her fork. It clattered against her plate.

Maksim's grin widened. He'd known. He'd known what Uncle Jim was going to say, and he hadn't told her? How could he have kept this a secret?

Yet they were staying. They were definitely staying. Disappointment churned where there should have been only joy. If Maksim cared for her as she was beginning to care for him. . .he would have told her.

"Anna?" Uncle Jim's brows drew together. "I thought this would make you happy."

"It does." It should have. "I'm just. . .speechless."

Auntie Gretchen glared a hole through her.

Anna picked up her fork and refused to look at Maksim. "It took me by surprise. I didn't have a clue you'd made up your mind." She plastered a smile on her face. "But I am pleased. I truly am."

She ignored Auntie Gretchen's snort and Auntie Laurie's raised eyebrows. Why wouldn't she be happy? This is what she really wanted. At least, it had been. Why hadn't Maksim told her? She couldn't look at him.

She plowed her fork into the mashed potatoes, filled her mouth, and kept her head bowed while she blinked back unwanted dampness.

The aunties carried on about what they would do over the winter. Plans for spinning yarn and knitting, perhaps even starting a quilt. Uncle Jim answered the few questions they tossed at him, but his gaze flicked to her often, then from her to Maksim and back again.

What if he'd told Maksim first because. . .because he saw in Maksim a young man who could take over the lighthouse? The potatoes weighed like an anchor in her stomach. Hadn't she had the same thoughts only a few days ago? Except, her thoughts had included her by Maksim's side. Not him taking over the tower.

Her tower.

Chapter 11

"Come into my office for a moment."

Anna stopped with her hand on the staircase railing. Uncle Jim stood in the doorway to his office. The office he had moved to an upstairs bedroom when the aunties moved into the lighthouse the year before Anna came. Uncle Jim hadn't needed the help as much as the aunties had needed a place to live when their old shack in the village had deteriorated beyond repair. Uncle Jim was like that. A giving person. Compassionate. The type who would take in a foreigner shipwrecked on the island and teach him to run the lighthouse. Instead of her.

She swallowed her hurt then climbed the last two steps and followed him into the office. He shut the door.

"Sit." He waved her toward one of the chairs across from his desk and then took the other one. He stretched and laced his fingers over his belly. "I thought the news of our staying would make you happy."

"It does." The tiny catch in her voice gave her away.

"But?"

"Why didn't you tell me first?" She gathered the inner edge of her bottom lip between her teeth to keep it still.

"Ah. So that's what's bothering you." He fished his pipe from his pocket and poked it into his mouth without adding tobacco. "I see."

"It's just—"

He held up his hand. "I needed to speak with Maksim first. He's young and strong and willing to work."

"So am I."

"Winters on the island are not like you're used to in Detroit. They are colder, longer, and buried with snow. Why do you think I've never stayed?"

"Because you came to live with us. To spend time with your family."

He moved the pipe from one corner of his mouth to the other. "That's true." He looked toward the dark window. "I still can't believe your father is gone. That he's not waiting to welcome me into his home. That we won't be playing checkers by the fire or arguing over articles in the newspaper."

Anna's chest ached, magnified by her uncle's grief. For the first time since she'd set foot on the island, a wave of homesickness washed over her.

"But life moves on." He patted his pocket and pulled out a pouch of tobacco. As he loaded his pipe, she closed her eyes and willed away the grief. He was right. Life moved on, and she'd thought she could make her life here, at the lighthouse.

When smoke puffed from his pipe, he returned his attention to her. "I'm an old man, and I can't do all the work around here in the winter months. I can barely do it in the summer months anymore. Maksim is willing to stay and shovel snow, cut and split wood, and if the worst happened, make his way across the ice to the mainland for help."

"I could—"

"No. You couldn't. You're young and willing, but you're not strong enough on your own."

She was. . .but she wasn't. Maksim had hauled the coal from the docks because he could haul more in fewer trips. He'd cut the hay for Gertie and stacked it to the barn rafters. He climbed the tower. She'd never made it up there. He could do all that. Without her.

"I see." And she did. It brought a splash of disappointment as jarring as Lake Huron's icy spray.

Uncle Jim leaned forward and placed his hand on her knee, warming her through the wool of her skirt. "I couldn't let you try it alone."

To winter over? Or to run the lighthouse? Either way, he was right. She couldn't do this by herself. An almost physical pain pressed against her as she looked at her uncle.

Pure love shone from his eyes. She knelt by his chair and wrapped her arms around him. "I love you too, Uncle." Her brothers had been right all along. She couldn't do anything by herself.

As he kissed the top of her head, she let go of her dreams.

Maksim understood more English than he had when he'd arrived on the island. Much more. But he didn't understand Anna at all. She'd been avoiding him. Ever since her uncle had announced that they'd stay the winter, she'd changed. She was quiet at meals and in the parlor in the evenings. The aunties had noticed it too, because they shared those looks. Looks that seemed to say more than words but made no sense to him.

And now this. He gave a final squeeze to release the last of Gertie's milk. Anna had handed him the milk pail this morning, then turned and left the kitchen without a word.

He trudged across the yard between the barn and the lighthouse, kicking up the fluffy dusting of snow with each step. He stopped and looked around. The lake's rim was frozen several feet from shore. The trees sparkled with hoarfrost, their bare branches reaching for winter's muted sun.

On a morning like this, he missed his homeland. Not the injustices or the pogroms, but the land. If he squinted, he could almost see his father walking across his fields, his mother shaking a rug by the back door. He sighed. Now that the busyness of summer was over, he'd miss the long evenings with his parents. The time to rest and refresh before the next planting season began.

Could it be that Anna also missed her family with the coming of winter, even though she'd wanted to stay? Did she now regret not spending the winter with one of her brothers?

What could he do to cheer her up?

His eyes were drawn to the tower. That was it. Mr. Wilson didn't think a girl should climb the tower, but Maksim knew that Anna wanted to. How many times had he caught her standing at the bottom of the staircase?

Her uncle would be sleeping now.

Maksim strode to the lighthouse. He'd find Anna and go with her to the top of the tower.

She should be doing something constructive, but Anna couldn't find the energy or enthusiasm for much anymore. Her dream of running the lighthouse had fizzled. Uncle Jim was right. She couldn't handle it on her own. She'd been nothing but a silly girl, running up here with a grand design and no thought to what it would take to make it happen.

Maksim could do it all. Without her. Without even telling her. That still stung.

Envy wasn't a comfortable companion, but it had dogged her steps these last few days. If that weren't bad enough, she had to dodge the aunties. She spent most of her day in her room since their arthritic knees didn't allow them to climb the stairs. Their knowing looks irritated her, as if they knew she wasn't up to the task of running the lighthouse. Doubtless, they only stayed because Maksim did too.

Maksim, who could barely speak English but could do everything else. If only he felt about her like she—

"Anna?"

The object of her thoughts poked his head around her open bedroom door.

"What?" She ignored the warm tide that rose to her cheeks.

"Come with me." His dark eyes glimmered in the morning light streaming through her window.

"Where?"

"You see."

"No—"

"Come." He held out his hand.

She squelched the desire to take his hand, crossing her arms instead.

His grin slipped, and he let his hand drop to his side. "Come. . .please?"

"I'm busy." Busy trying not to lose her heart while losing her dearest dream.

He looked around the room then cocked his head.

"All right. I'll come, but I don't have long."

His grin returned, and he stepped aside to let her precede him down the hall. Which may have been mannerly but was also counterproductive since she didn't know where he was going. Still, she headed for the stairs and tromped down with him at her heels.

At the bottom, he pointed down the passageway to the tower. She shrugged and walked through, letting her fingertips slide along the bricks of the arched walls. When she reached the spiral staircase, she turned and crossed her arms.

"What did you want to talk to me about?"

"Not talk." He pointed up. "Climb."

Anna's breath whooshed from her lungs, the strength drained from her legs, and clammy sweat oozed from her pores. When the room tilted, she clutched the metal handrail to make it stop, leaning against the cold bricks.

"What is wrong?" Alarm filled Maksim's voice, his face swimming before her. "I fetch aunties."

"No." She managed to croak out the word. "Don't."

"But—"

"I'm fine." She took several breaths and stood straight.

"You not look right."

The fellow sure knew how to charm a lady. But he wasn't blind, and if she was half as white as she felt, she probably looked like a sheet of paper.

"It was just a dizzy spell. I'm better now."

He leaned closer as if he could look into her eyes and see her soul. Her heart tripped against her ribs. She took a step back.

He glanced up the spiral stairs and then back at her. "Not climb now."

"No." She hugged her arms over her stomach. "No, that wouldn't be a good idea."

"Tomorrow. Tomorrow when Mr. Wilson sleepink, we go up." His grin returned. Her stomach flopped.

Chapter 12

When Mr. Wilson awoke with a head cold, Maksim's plans changed. He'd have to take Anna to the tower another time. For the next three nights, he was in charge of keeping the light. It was too cold to stay in the unheated tower, so he climbed up to fill and light the lamp then returned to the parlor. Once everyone else went to bed, he sat alone in the quiet room, rocking in Auntie Laurie's favorite chair, and watched the beacon flash across the darkness. It gave him time to think.

Anna had never been to the top of the tower. Spunky Anna who insisted she could do whatever needed to be done. At least, she had until Mr. Wilson's decision to winter over. That's when things changed. Before then. . .she still hadn't climbed the tower.

She went into the tower, like the time he'd startled her and she'd almost fallen from three steps up. He stopped the rocker. Why had she almost fallen from only the third step?

And the time she'd shouted up to him, her hand clutching the handrail even though she was still on the ground. He rubbed his hand across his face.

Then the other day, her face as white as new-fallen snow. Like she might swoon— No. It couldn't be. Could it?

He stood and half ran into the tower, stopping at the bottom to look up. He closed his eyes, remembering his first climb, the way his head had spun when he looked down. Mr. Wilson had told him to keep looking up and the feeling would pass unless he truly didn't have a head for heights. It had passed, and he hadn't thought about it again until now.

Anna's dizziness, faintness, the way she'd gripped the handrail as if her life depended on it.

Anna was afraid of heights.

Anna jumped when Auntie Laurie dropped a pan onto the kitchen workbench behind her.

"You're going to hit the ceiling if you don't settle down."

Anna slapped her hand over her heart and gulped in air. Auntie Laurie was right; she had to get a grip on herself.

"You startled me."

Auntie Gretchen followed her sister into the kitchen, her hair still mussed from sleep, her robe hanging crooked on her wizened frame. A lovable contrast to Auntie Laurie's tidy appearance.

Auntie Gretchen snorted. "You've been as jumpy as a long-tailed cat in a room full of rocking chairs for the past two weeks. What's eating you, girl?"

Anna grabbed a towel and wiped her already dry hands. How could she tell them the truth? Her dreams, her feelings for Maksim. . .all a mistake. A great big blundering mistake. She knew what she needed to do. She needed to catch a boat back to Detroit before the ice sealed the lakes. She didn't belong here. She never had. It had been a little girl's dream. Now it was time for her to grow up and face life as it was, not as she wanted it to be.

Auntie Laurie slipped her arm around Anna's waist. Anna turned to her and wrapped the old woman in a hug.

"There, there. It can't be as bad as all that," Auntie Laurie said.

"It's worse."

"What's this?" Auntie Gretchen's question was nothing short of a bellow. All Anna needed was Maksim hearing that and coming to investigate.

"I can't talk about it right now." Anna straightened. "I have to finish the breakfast and then. . ." She sniffed. "I think I better pack my belongings."

"Pack?" Auntie Gretchen's word filled the kitchen, but Auntie Laurie raised a hand to silence her sister.

"Whyever would you do that, dear?"

"To return to Detroit. . .where I belong." No matter that her heart would always be here on Thunder Bay Island with a certain dark-eyed man who could do everything. "Please don't tell Uncle Jim yet." She'd tell him herself as soon as—

"What balderdash." Auntie Gretchen pushed her sister out of the way, propped her fists on her hips, and leaned in toward Anna. "You fought like a she-bear with cubs to winter here. What makes you want to run out on us now?"

"I'm not running out—"

"What do you call it?"

"I'm not needed here. Maksim can milk the cow. Maksim can shovel the snow. Maksim can cut the wood. Maksim can do everything, even. . .even tend the light."

"Oh child." Auntie Laurie squeezed in between her sister and the sink to get closer to Anna. "You're very much needed here."

"By whom?"

"Me." Maksim stood in the doorway.

Anna's jaw dropped, and she forced it shut with a click of her teeth. He'd heard. And from the pity in his eyes, he understood. He understood far too much.

Auntie Laurie moved away then reached back and took a fistful of Auntie Gretchen's robe. She left the kitchen, towing her sister behind her.

Maksim stepped all the way into the room.

Anna whirled, turning her back on him and clutching the edge of the sink for support. "Didn't anyone ever teach you that eavesdropping is rude?"

"Eavesdroppink? What is this?"

"Listening in on other people's private conversations."

"Nyet. No. In Russia, house is small. Everyone hear everythink."

She turned and faced him, lifting her chin. "Well, you've heard what I said now anyway."

"You cannot leave."

"Of course I can."

He blinked and then rubbed his hand over his eyes. He must be tired. He should be heading up to bed soon, not standing in the kitchen arguing with her. It was almost light enough to extinguish the lantern, which he could do. . .and she couldn't.

"You leave because you afraid to climb tower?"

Anna's fingers dug into the fabric of her skirt. "What?"

"I think about it. How you act. I think how first time I climb make head feel. . . what English word?"

"Dizzy."

"Da. Dizzy. Make feel like wantink to fall."

Shame cemented her feet to the wooden floorboards. She let her chin sink to her chest.

Maksim stepped closer until his breath moved the hairs on the top of her head. "Anna."

The way he pronounced her name, the huskiness of his voice, the hint of kerosene that lingered on his shirt, it all combined to wick the moisture from her throat. And then his fingers grazed the underside of her chin, moving along the edge of her jaw. Her breath disappeared. If only. . . She couldn't look him in the eyes. She couldn't witness the pity that must fill them.

She stepped away, turning her back to him. "I'm going to leave the island."

"But—"

Anna hurried from the room, almost colliding with the aunties in the hallway where they'd obviously stopped to listen. Any other time, their expressions of chagrin and guilt would have made her smile. Not today. Not for many, many days to come. She had to get out of there, get off the island. Go back where she belonged.

Where streets were paved and the houses so close together you could reach out a window to shake hands with a neighbor. Where there were no towers and no ships—no dark-haired Russian who turned her insides to mush.

If she didn't know better, Anna would accuse Uncle Jim or the aunties of keeping the tugboats away. The wind blew another swirling white wall against the side of the lighthouse. The third long day of snow. Maksim had strung a length of rope between the lighthouse and the barn and another between the lighthouse and the fog signal building. Visibility at times was less than six feet. No tugboat would come until the storm passed. No ships were moving out on the lake either. They should all be laid up in safe harbors, riding out the storm, but Maksim kept the fog signal and light operating just in case.

Uncle Jim coughed and rubbed his chest. Anna fetched a knitted throw from the couch and spread it over his lap.

"Thank you, my dear." His voice rasped, and a twinge of guilt pricked at her. She couldn't leave until he was well again. And besides, the aunties had made her promise not to leave until after Christmas.

Another blast of wind rattled the windows.

"We should have Maksim close the shutters," Auntie Gretchen said.

"Oh, but then it's so dark in here." Auntie Laurie rose and walked to the window. "I hate to shut out what little light there is."

"Let the boy sleep," Uncle Jim said.

Auntie Gretchen snorted. "I meant when he awakens of course."

"I can do it." All eyes turned to Anna. "Well, I can."

"No, my dear. You'd need the ladder to reach them. And in this wind. . ." Uncle Jim coughed and shook his head.

The ladder. Of course. She sank onto the sofa. Yet another thing she couldn't do. Yet another reason she didn't belong here. Maksim would take care of it when he awoke. Maksim could do anything.

She wanted to be jealous of him, but instead a hollowness filled her. A loneliness. She would leave the island and never see Maksim again. Which one would she miss more?

Chapter 13

Tomorrow was Christmas Eve. Maksim tucked his flute beneath his coat and trudged out to the barn. For the first time in days, the wind had calmed. The air crystallized with each breath. Snow crunched beneath his boots. The earthy scents of hay and cow greeted him when he opened the door. He hopped onto a grain barrel against the wall of Gertie's stall. The gentle bovine pushed her nose over the gate, and he obliged her with a pat.

He retrieved the flute from his coat and slipped the mittens from his hands, flexing his fingers a few times. Then, with the instrument to his lips, he closed his eyes and let the music flow. The notes of "Silent Night" filled the barn with an eerie longing. A timeless appeal to a stable long ago, a humble place where the Savior of the world appeared among men. Angels had gathered above. A night of hope.

The notes died away and he opened his eyes. Anna stood inside the doorway, her mittened hands clasped beneath her chin, her eyes glittering with unshed tears. Had she felt it too?

"That was beautiful." Her words barely covered the gap between them, so softly had she spoken.

His heart swelled to the point of aching.

She walked toward him. "You play so well. Why do you not play in the parlor? The aunties would enjoy it."

He looked over her shoulder, studied the rakes and pitchfork hanging against the far wall. "My father and I played. Together. Many winter nights."

"Oh." She laid her hand on his sleeve. "You miss him when you play?"

"I miss him all the time."

"Of course." She pulled her hand away. "How silly of me."

He grabbed her hand and drew it back, the wool of her mitten warm against his fingers. "We both miss our fathers, da?"

She nodded.

He slid off the barrel, keeping a firm grip on her hand. She didn't step back, so he stepped closer, close enough that their coats brushed together.

"If you leave, I will be missink you."

She shook her head and turned her face away.

"Please to stay." His heart lodged up against his throat.

"I can't."

"I do not understand—"

"Of course you don't. You can do anything." She pulled from his grasp and waved one arm toward the cow. "You can do all the work I do plus you can man the light. You can climb the ladder to close the shutters. I can. . .I can't. . .my brothers were right. I'm leaving on the first tugboat after Christmas."

Anna whirled and ran out the door.

He stared at the flute in his hands then sighed and tucked it back inside his coat. He had only a couple of days to change her mind.

"We must have a tree," Auntie Gretchen announced at breakfast.

Anna almost dropped her spoon. A Christmas tree? She glanced at Maksim. He shrugged, but one corner of his mouth tugged upward.

Auntie Laurie's eyes sparkled in the light from the lamp. "A tree? When was the last time we trimmed a tree, sister?"

"What does that matter?" Auntie Gretchen pushed away from the table. "Maksim and Anna can find one and bring it in. We'll string popped corn and tie ribbons on it."

Auntie Laurie clapped her hands. "What fun! Maksim, did your family decorate a tree at Christmas?"

"Da. But not on the same day."

"But when would you, if not on Christmas Eve?" Anna asked. "After all, it wouldn't be a Christmas tree if it wasn't up for Christmas. Would it?"

Auntie Laurie answered, "In Russia, Christmas is celebrated on January 6. Since we're here and not there, you two must fetch us a nice tree today." She made a shooing motion toward them. "Go on. Bundle up."

Anna glanced at Maksim. Her heart did some strange contortions in her chest. She shouldn't spend any time alone with him. Not after last night in the barn when she'd been so tempted—so very tempted—to step into his arms.

He grinned and tipped his head toward the door. Her feet moved to join him before she could make them behave. What was she doing? This would only make leaving that much more difficult. They were bundled and out the door before Anna could talk herself out of going.

Maksim fetched the saw from the barn and then pointed toward a stand of trees to the northwest.

"We go there?"

She nodded. "Looks like the place to start."

He stepped back to allow her to pass, and she shook her head.

"Oh no. You can break the trail through the snow. Not me."

His warm chuckle did something to her middle, and while she wasn't sure just what it was, she liked the feeling. Too much. He started across the snowy yard and she followed, knowing she was in dangerous territory. Concentrating on stepping into his boot prints helped keep her mind and eyes off his strong back and broad shoulders.

She bounced off that back and shoulders moments later.

"Hey." She scrambled to keep on her feet.

"Why you run into me?" The laughter in his voice did nothing to even out her middle.

"You stopped."

"Da. I did."

Oh, she was making a fool of herself for sure.

He pointed at a spruce tree that was roughly her height. It came to a nice peak at the top, but it lacked so many branches around its center that it looked malnourished.

She shook her head. "That won't do."

He cocked his head and looked at the tree.

"It needs more branches."

"More branches. Da." He strode off again.

This time, Anna was paying attention when he stopped in front of a smallish white pine. The long needles with their feathery swoop appealed to her, but white pines weren't as common as spruce trees, and she hated to cut one down. She shook her head.

Maksim shrugged and moved on.

They must have traveled halfway across the island before he stopped again. Anna peeked around him to see another spruce. This one was bluish green and lovely. A perfect Christmas tree for her one and only Christmas on the island.

"This one will do."

His eyebrows rose, perhaps hearing the melancholy she'd tried to mask. He was too perceptive, certainly much more so than any of her brothers. But he dropped to his knees and sawed through the tree trunk. In moments, they were retracing their steps through the snow, her leading and him dragging their prize behind.

It might have been a perfect day, if only things were different.

Anna looked up as Uncle Jim entered the room. His expression when he saw the Christmas tree made it all worthwhile.

"You decorated it like your mother used to." Uncle Jim's smile lit the room. "You've turned this old lighthouse into a home."

Her heart warred between loving his approval and regretting that it couldn't last. When he found out she was leaving. . . But she wouldn't think about that today. Today she would let herself believe, for the last time, that she could be the next lighthouse keeper. That she belonged here on Thunder Bay Island.

"Hot cocoa for everyone." Auntie Laurie shuffled into the room with a tray. The scents of cocoa and something cinnamon swirled around her. Anna took the tray and placed it on the table next to the couch while the aunties oohed and aahed over the tree. They all sipped their hot treat and munched the cinnamon cookies the aunties had baked while she and Maksim had trimmed the tree.

Darkness crept toward the now unshuttered windows.

Maksim placed his empty cup on the table. "Time to light the lamp."

Uncle Jim shook his head. "No. You stay and enjoy the tree. I'll do it tonight."

"Are you sure, Uncle?" It worried her that his cough still lingered.

"I'm fine. And Maksim deserves a break after all that work cutting and hauling in the tree." With a wink, Uncle Jim left the room.

Maksim stood. "I go with him."

"No, boy. If he said to stay, then he wants you to stay." Auntie Gretchen plopped down in her chair. "This will be one of the last nights for the tower. The ice is thicker and farther from shore every day. The lake'll be closed within the week. Mark my words."

No doubt she was right, which was why Anna must leave the day after Christmas, or as soon as a tugboat came. If she didn't, she might not get off the island until spring. Anna sat on the couch, slipped off her shoes, and curled her feet up beside her. She would ignore her broken dreams until then and enjoy her one and only Christmas on the island.

"Maksim, will you play your flute for us?" she asked.

"Yes. Please do." Auntie Laurie sat in her rocking chair. "Play us something."

"He knows 'Silent Night,'" Anna said.

"Perfect." The aunties sat with their heads cocked, for all the world like a pair of birds awaiting a handful of crumbs.

Anna wanted to smile and also to weep. She would miss those two almost as much as she'd miss. . . She twisted her hands in her lap and refused to look at Maksim.

"Da. I fetch flute." He left the room.

"Such a thoughtful boy," Auntie Laurie said.

Auntie Gretchen grunted and aimed a pointed stare at Anna.

"He is." That was all she was admitting to. Anything more was too—

Footsteps pounded down the hall until Maksim slid to a halt in the hallway, holding on to the parlor's doorframe. "Come. Mr. Wilson hurt."

Anna scrambled off the couch and ran for the door. "What happened?"

"Come." Maksim ran down the hall and into the passageway.

Anna followed, her stockinged feet silent on the cold bricks. Uncle Jim lay at the bottom of the curved staircase, his head raised, his arms wrapped around one knee and holding his foot off the ground.

"Uncle Jim! What happened?"

The aunties arrived right behind Anna. Auntie Laurie had brought a blanket, which she wadded and tucked under Uncle Jim's head.

"The stairs were frosty and I slipped. I didn't fall far, but I came down wrong on my ankle."

"Let me see." Auntie Gretchen shouldered her way into the tower's crowded base. She held firm to the back of his calf and peeled up his pant leg.

Uncle Jim's breath hissed between his teeth.

"We need to get his shoe off. His ankle is swelling fast." Auntie Gretchen grabbed Maksim's hand and pulled him close. "You hold, here, and hold him tight. This is going to hurt, but it has to be done."

"Oh my." Auntie Laurie's face paled.

"Go turn down our bed, sister. He won't be going up the stairs tonight. Nor for a few nights, I'm sure."

"Of course." The old woman hurried from the room.

"Have you got a tight hold, boy?"

Maksim nodded. Anna held her breath. Auntie Gretchen had her lower lip between her teeth as she untied the shoe and worked it off. Uncle Jim groaned but didn't move. Next she rolled down his stocking and then grunted. Something white and shiny protruded from just above the ankle.

Auntie Gretchen sucked in a loud breath. "It's broken through."

Broken. And no doctor within reach. Tears gathered behind Anna's eyes. This was all her fault. If she hadn't insisted that they winter on the island, then—

"None of that, girl." Uncle Jim reached out his hand.

She slipped her own into it, ignoring its trembling.

"This isn't your fault," he said. "We wouldn't have left the island yet anyway. There are still ships moving on the lake."

"I go to mainland for doctor," Maksim said.

All heads swiveled to him.

"I think that would be best." Auntie Gretchen eased Uncle Jim's foot to the floor and stood. "But first we need to get him to bed."

"I carry."

"No—" Uncle Jim slid onto his hip as if to try and rise, but Maksim was at his side, one arm under the old man's legs and the other behind his back. He lifted Uncle Jim and started down the passageway. Anna walked at his side, supporting the injured foot and making sure it didn't touch the walls.

Auntie Laurie motioned them into the small downstairs bedroom, and Maksim laid Uncle Jim on the turned-down bed.

"I go now." He turned to leave, and an icy-cold spike pierced Anna.

"But. . .the light?"

Time stopped. The only sound was Anna's heartbeat hammering against her eardrums. "*For such a time as this.*" Heaven knew she was no Esther, but Maksim couldn't tend the light and also go to the mainland for help.

She straightened. "I'll do it."

Maksim shook his head. "I can—"

"Go to the lifesaving station and ask Mr. Persons to take you to the mainland. Uncle Jim will tell me what I need to do to light the lamp. Go!" She gave him a shove out of the room and followed him down the hall. She handed him his coat and hat after he'd laced his boots.

"Anna." He pulled his hat over a crinkled brow. "Don't worry about the lamp. We find our way back. I promise."

"There might be other boats out there." She ignored the fear clawing inside her. "I will do it."

He stepped closer, his fingers once again on her chin. His breath stirred her hair. Then he pressed a kiss to her forehead, lingering a moment. His coat smelled of the barn, woodsmoke, and something uniquely Maksim. She shivered.

"You will do it." Then he was gone.

Chapter 14

Maksim ran all the way to the lifesaving station. His breath was coming in frosted blasts by the time he pounded on the door of the living quarters. Mr. Persons answered his knock.

"Come in." He backed up, letting Maksim enter. "Something's wrong."

Mrs. Persons joined her husband.

"Mr. Wilson. He fall. Break leg. Very bad." Maksim bent at the waist and drew several long breaths.

"I'll fetch your things." Mrs. Persons scurried away.

"Most of the crew is gone for Christmas Eve. Ernest and Charlie are in the station. Go roust them. It'll take all four of us to break through the ice. I'll meet you at the boat."

Maksim nodded and hurried back outside. He ran to the station and pounded on the door. Ernest opened it.

"Mr. Persons, he say come. We go to mainland for doctor."

The man's face paled. "Is it Anna?"

Maksim shook his head. "Mr. Wilson. He break leg. Very bad."

Ernest hollered for Charlie, and the two men bundled up, both strapping on cork and canvas vests. Charlie threw one at Maksim. He figured out the buckles and was ready to go when the other men left for the boat.

Mr. Persons was already on board and had smoke belching from the stack. With long metal rods, one end sharpened into a flat spade, they broke the ice around the boat. Maksim hung over the bow, chopping and smashing for all he was worth. He cast a glance back over his shoulder. No light beamed in the darkness as the boat broke free.

"I have no choice, Uncle. I must do this."

Uncle Jim continued to hold her hand as if he couldn't bear to let her go. "It's dangerous. I fell because—"

"I won't fall. I'm well warned of how slippery it is. Now. You must tell me how to light the lamp."

"Anna—"

"Uncle, I insist. Not only may there be ships out there, but the lifesaving crew will need the light to guide them to our dock. It must be lit." She must be the one to light it. There would be no backing out this time. Lives depended on her. On her alone.

With a sigh and a wince, Uncle Jim explained the procedure. Lighting the lamp was simple. But she had to climb the tower. Now.

She squeezed his hand and left the room. Auntie Laurie waited for her at the base of the tower staircase, Anna's shoes and a wad of something in her hands.

"Sit." The old woman pointed to the stairs.

Anna sat and pulled her shoes on. "What is that?"

"It was an old wool scarf." She picked up one of Anna's feet. "I cut it in half. I'll wrap a half around each of your shoes. The metal is slick from the cold. The wool will grip better than your leather shoes."

Anna waited while Auntie Laurie finished. The old woman drew her to her feet, placed a hand on her forehead, and uttered a heartfelt prayer for safety.

Anna opened her eyes. Auntie Laurie took her hands and squeezed them.

"Don't look down. Stop and rest if you must, but don't look down."

Anna nodded, the lump in her throat threatening to choke her.

"You can do it, my dear. I know your fears, but there is something much stronger than fear that drives you now."

"What?"

"Love." Auntie Laurie patted her cheek. "Your uncle Jim and Maksim both need you to light that lamp. Your love for them will bring you through. Remember 'greater love hath no man than this.' You will do what needs to be done."

She wanted to. Oh, how she wanted to! But doubts battered her from all sides. What if she froze? What if she couldn't make it up? What if the boat missed the dock or, worse, wrecked on the rocks because she couldn't light the lamp?

Auntie Laurie pulled her shawl from her shoulders and wrapped it around Anna. "I'll be praying. Go now."

Anna grasped the handrail and turned her face to the stair directly in front of her. She wouldn't look down. *One step at a time, don't look down. . .Lord, give me strength.*

Maksim sat at the front of the boat, eyes scouring the cloudy sky for a gleam of light. Something—anything to show that Anna had made it to the top. He should have lit the lamp before he left. Why had he been so addlebrained? The memory of the bone sticking out of Mr. Wilson's leg made his stomach tighten. He'd needed to hurry, but even so, he should have lit the lamp.

"Where's the light?" Kindt's voice sounded to his right.

"We should be able to see it by now." Charlie scratched a match against the bottom of his boot and lit his pipe.

Mr. Persons stood at the wheel, also peering into the darkness. The doctor huddled in the cabin behind Mr. Persons, keeping warm by the steamboat's furnace.

Kindt rubbed his mittened hands together. "Could be the clouds. They're low."

It could be that Anna hadn't been able to climb the tower. Maksim closed his eyes and silently lifted yet another prayer to the heavens shrouded by clouds. He opened them again. Not a star to be seen, and it must be well past midnight.

Christmas Day.

A faint yellow glow reflected off the clouds. His heart almost stopped. He held his breath and waited for a second glimmer.

"There!" Maksim jumped to his feet and pointed. He looked back into the cabin. Mr. Persons nodded.

She'd done it.

The next half hour was the longest of Maksim's life. Once they got the boat through the ice and tied to the dock, he took off for the lighthouse at a dead run. The beacon shone pure and true from the lighthouse tower. Pride filled him. He burst through the door and charged into the kitchen, not even stopping to remove his boots.

"Merciful heavens!" Auntie Laurie twisted around from the stove, the black teakettle swinging from her hand.

"The doctor come. Where is Anna?"

"What's all the ruckus?" Auntie Gretchen's voice boomed down the hallway.

He started in that direction, leaving Auntie Laurie speechless in the kitchen.

"Where is Anna?"

"Where's the doctor?" Auntie Gretchen stood in front of the downstairs bedroom with her arms crossed.

"He come. Anna?"

Auntie Gretchen pointed toward the passageway. "She stayed up there. Says she's okay. Didn't want the light to go out." The old woman shook her head and returned to the bedroom.

Maksim sprinted through the passageway and pounded up the metal staircase. His foot slipped, and he caught himself, chest heaving. He slowed and made it to the landing. The hatch door was open, but still no Anna.

"Anna?"

"Maksim?" The voice was faint and trembled.

He climbed the ladder and hoisted himself through the hatch. Anna huddled with her back against the lamp, a woolen shawl wrapped around her from head to toe.

"Anna."

With a little cry, she stood and fell into his arms.

"You did it. You climb and light the lamp."

A sob rose from the bundle of girl and shawl in his arms. "I did."

She shook, her whole body shivering against him in a most delightful fashion. He gathered her closer.

"We go down now, warm you."

"No!" The muffled cry tugged at his heart.

"Is all right. Doctor here. Boat safe. We go down now."

"I—I can't."

Maksim looked around the small circular room. Everything was in order. The light was working. "Why?"

"I–I'm. . .afraid."

Ah. So that was it. He chuckled, and the bundle of Anna and shawl turned into a spitting wildcat in his arms.

"Go ahead and laugh. Go ahead. I know I'm crazy. I know I should be able to do this. But I can't. Do you understand? I can't." Fury and passion and fear animated the face now turned up to his. Her blue eyes blazed, and her trembling lips were so inviting he couldn't help himself.

He kissed her.

The fear stopped. The cold dissipated. The anger melted from her bones when his lips met hers. Warmth such as she'd never known blossomed under her ribs. She pressed against his lips. Her fingers burrowed into the hair under the back of his knit cap. Maksim moaned and withdrew a hair's breadth. She couldn't stand it. She rose onto her toes and pulled him close again, their breath meeting and mingling in a warm and frosty combination that heightened her awareness of him. Of them. Of what could be.

If only she were brave enough to stay.

With a gasp, she jerked free and would have tumbled through the hatch if he hadn't caught her. But he did. His molasses-dark eyes shone in the beacon's light. Shone with a dark fire that answered the one burning inside her.

"Anna."

"I—"

He pulled her close again and rested his chin on the top of her head. "I love you.

For long time, I have felt this. I did not think you would. . ."

"I shouldn't." But oh, how she wanted to.

"Why you sayink this?"

"Because you'll do well here as the next lighthouse keeper. You'll need someone who can—"

"Climb the tower?"

"Yes, that's it exactly."

He chuckled again, a deep rumbling in the chest she was pinned against. She bit her lip to squelch the returning tide of anger. Not really at him, but at. . .everything. It was so unfair.

"Look around you."

"What?"

"Anna, you are here. You did it."

Only because she'd had to. Only because there was no choice. And now she was stuck, terrified to climb back down. Hadn't he listened to her?

"I'm afraid to climb down."

"I help."

She pulled away, careful to avoid the open hatch this time.

"I can't."

"Trust me." He held out his hand.

Her insides flurried like a shaken snow globe. Trust. Could she? Did she want to? Oh yes. She most certainly did.

Maksim climbed down three steps of the ladder. "Come, I walk you down. You not fall with me here."

She took a step toward the hatch. And then another. He was still in the room from the shoulders up. She turned her back and stepped onto the ladder, into his arms. Heat flooded as his breath feathered across her neck and cheek.

"Now we go down. Together."

"Together."

His lips grazed the back of her neck. "I should be speakink to Mr. Wilson soon. Very soon."

"Speaking about what?" She forced the words up past her pounding heart.

"Speakink about marryink his niece, if she will have me."

Anna froze. "I don't know if I'll ever be able to climb the tower again."

"You can, if must. But is my wish that you won't have to. Is my wish that I be here to climb for you. For we."

She leaned back another fraction of an inch, just enough to feel the solid wall of his chest against her back. Sturdy. Safe. Like a harbor she could take refuge in. A harbor she could love. A harbor she did love. Anna turned her head until his mouth brushed her cheek.

"You do not have to be doink this alone," he said.

She didn't. Realization shot through her with a rush of warmth and a lingering peace. She wasn't a failure if she needed someone else. Being successful didn't have to mean being alone. And she didn't want to be alone ever again.

"I love you too." She breathed the words more than said them.

His arms tightened around her. Solid. Strong. His lips grazed her neck again, playing havoc with her breathing, making her forget about a silly ladder and staircase. This was far better than doing everything by herself. Why had she wanted that anyway?

"Let's go down and talk to Uncle Jim."

"Certainly."

Historical Notes

Thunder Bay Island sits off the northeastern edge of Michigan's Lower Peninsula near the town of Alpena. While all the main characters of *Anna's Tower* are fictitious, some real-life people are mentioned. Captain John and Celia Persons ran the life-saving station on Thunder Bay Island from 1877 to 1915. John and Ann Paxton ran a fishing station off nearby Sugar Island and retired to Alpena in 1883. The steamer *James Davidson* ran aground off Thunder Bay Island on October 4, 1883, towing the barge *Middlesex*. All hands were rescued. The *Middlesex* received no major damage, but the *Davidson* was a total loss. Her bones still lie off the reef that sank her.

The Thunder Bay Island Lighthouse Preservation Society works to preserve and restore the second-oldest lighthouse still standing along the Great Lakes. Visit their webpage (http://www.thunderbayislandlight.org/) and Facebook page (https://www.facebook.com/lighthousesavers/) for more information and many beautiful photos of this historic place.

Pegg Thomas lives on a hobby farm in Northern Michigan with Michael, her husband of *mumble* years. A lifelong history geek, she writes "History with a Touch of Humor." When not working on her latest novel, Pegg can be found in her garden, in her kitchen, with her sheep, at her spinning wheel, or on her trusty old horse, Trooper. See more at PeggThomas.com.

Beneath a Michigan Moon

by Candice Sue Patterson

Dedication

To my Lord and Savior, Jesus Christ—the lighthouse in a dark, stormy world.

Chapter 1

New Presque Isle Lighthouse, Lake Huron
June 30, 1885

Ava Ryan walked the shoreline of Lake Huron, enjoying the most beautiful day of the year—until she crossed paths with the devil. He was even more dashing than she remembered from their previous encounters.

Wicked dimples sank the inner parts of his cheeks. She looked away from blue eyes as enchanting as the crystalline water, peeved by his presence, more peeved that she was wearing her plainest shirtwaist. But nothing else would do, as she was in mourning. And barefoot to boot. Pretending not to see him, Ava lowered onto a nearby boulder and tucked her feet beneath her skirt.

"Miss Ava Ryan." Hands buried in the pockets of his brown trousers, he sidled up to her as casually as if they'd known each other their whole lives.

She glared at him, though with the angle of the sun peering over his shoulder and into her eyes, he'd think she was squinting. "Mr. Colfax. What brings you this close to the lighthouse? Again."

"It's a perfect day." He sat next to her, making it even more impossible to breathe. Or maybe it was the masculine scent of his shaving soap. "I'm a man drawn to beauty."

Had his hand not been extended toward the gently rolling water, she'd have slapped him. Or at least thought about it. He was too charming not to be dangerous.

Mr. Colfax leaned forward and rested his elbows on his knees. The fabrics of his shirt and vest strained across his broad shoulders. Good heavens, the man could fell a tree bare-handed.

He smiled. "How fortunate we happened to be walking at the same time."

Yes, lucky her. Like Eve, a snake had invaded her paradise.

"I actually came to speak with your father."

Tears pricked her eyes. Ava turned away, blinking to rid the unwanted guests. For her own safety, she couldn't reveal that her father had passed on mere weeks ago. Not with the mass of rowdy loggers who'd recently infested Presque Isle.

His big palms rubbed together, more of a casual gesture than a devious one. "Lightkeepers sleep during the day since their duties keep them up all night, am I right?"

"You're correct."

"Is he awake?"

What business did he have with her father? Surely, it wasn't to ask permission to court her. They'd only met a few times, and their first encounter hadn't been a pleasant experience. Heat rose to her cheeks. Not pleasant for her anyway. "Today isn't a good day, but I'll let him know you came by."

She would too. She just omitted the part about the discussion taking place in the graveyard.

"I believe you spoke that same line to me last week. And the week before that."

She balked at the amusement in his voice.

"I'll take my chances at rousing him from his nap." He started to rise.

"No!" Ava grasped his arm then recoiled. Desperation would only feed his curiosity. And touching him would only feed hers.

She relaxed her shoulders and clasped her hands in her lap. Took a deep breath. "I can't imagine what pressing business the logging company would have with a humble lightkeeper, but you can tell me, and I'll pass the word along."

A breeze rustled the ends of his hair. Brown with hints of blond. Cropped short around the neck and ears. Longer on top. Details she'd fail to notice if he were wearing a customary hat.

He studied her so long her skin prickled. "This is a matter that can only be taken up with your father."

Panic. Dread. And a sensation in her belly comparable to ice cream melting under a summer sun. She licked her lips. "This. . .is a personal call?"

She cringed at the squeak in her voice.

The lines around his eyes crinkled above a slightly crooked nose. "Is that what you're hoping for, Miss Ryan?"

Her mouth fell open. "Of course not. I'm simply trying to deter any unsolicited nonsense. A lightkeeper is far too busy for such things."

Mr. Colfax stood, his lips curved upward. "I assure you, my business with your father is necessary and entirely professional. However, when I see him I'll be sure to compliment him on such a fine watchdog."

Ava rose. "Are you calling me a canine?"

His gaze trailed the length of her body to her bare feet. Blood gorged her cheeks. She dropped again to the rock, praying the earth would open up and swallow her.

His laughter was deep and throaty. "Absolutely not, Ava."

"Miss Ryan." Even if her given name did sound rather nice on his tongue.

Mr. Colfax backed several steps, never taking his eyes off her. "No need to be embarrassed over something as silly as feet, Ava. Or the use of your Christian name. Especially after our rather unorthodox introduction. Besides, I've yet to meet a mutt who wears lace and ribbons."

He winked and headed in the direction of the lighthouse. Whistling.

Her hands curled into fists. How dare he bring up that embarrassing debacle? It wasn't her fault he'd appeared out of nowhere on wash day. Or that her unmentionables had been flapping in the wind like sails on a boat. No one ever visited the lighthouse. Ever. That was one of the pleasures the reclusive spot afforded—fewer underclothes in the heat of summer, grass and dirt beneath bare feet, and the freedom of her father's trousers when climbing the ladder for repairs.

Things a true gentleman would never bring up in conversation.

Mr. Colfax wasn't a gentleman, however. He was a lumberjack. A breed of men who thrived off proving their strength. Banging their chests. Risking their lives.

Let him stand there and knock on her door all day, she didn't care. Except the problem was he'd keep coming back. She couldn't allow him to discover she was the new lightkeeper. It had taken a miracle from God for the US Lighthouse Commission to grant the position to her in her father's stead, even if it was granted on a trial basis. Therefore, the secrets of her personal life must remain hidden from the board members. And from this nosy lumberjack.

Without this position, she'd have nowhere to go. She'd be forced to spend the scant amount of life she had left begging for change on the street.

Mr. Colfax would stay far away from the lighthouse if he knew she was hiding more than her father's death. But it wouldn't solve her problem. If anyone else found out, she'd not only lose her position, her home; she'd also be shunned by the entire town.

Ava and her father had already moved a thousand miles from home so she could have a chance at life. No arrogant, tree-chopping baboon was going to ruin this for her, no matter how handsome he was.

Miss Ava Ryan had a secret. Intrigued, Benjamin strolled toward the lighthouse, recalling the glow of sunlight against her pale skin. Too pale, yet creamy like a china doll. That mass of raven hair. . . The woman was stunning. And entirely too opinionated. All qualities that had kept him from a proper night's sleep since their first introduction.

The warm breeze whipping off the water rustled his shirt, reminding him of clothes drying on a line. They'd both reddened that day when he'd rounded the back of the keeper's quarters. Black waves spilling about her shoulders, her brow damp from exertion, Ava stood at the wash bucket, wet corset in hand. Mouth open, her gaze darted in every direction like a cornered animal. The garment hit the sudsy water with a plop.

The only gentlemanly thing to do was turn his back. He hadn't been embarrassed as much as surprised. After all, he had six sisters, so it wasn't as if such things were foreign to him. He simply hadn't expected to find a woman at the lighthouse, much less one as beautiful as Ava, parading her undergarments. Knowing those undergarments didn't belong to anyone in his family made feelings long suppressed bubble and stew.

Turning his back hadn't helped, because more womanly items hung from the clothesline, now in front of him. Evenly spaced like ducks in a row. Trimmed in ribbons and lace.

He'd better turn the compass of his thoughts north before he burst into flames. He'd come once again to ask permission to climb the lighthouse, to view the forest from the highest vantage point and determine their cutting route. That was all he planned to do here. Even if Ava was the prettiest thing he'd seen in a year of Sundays.

Shame walloped his chest. He never should've mentioned their first meeting. What he'd said earlier was distasteful and completely out of character. He hadn't wanted to embarrass her, only make light of the situation. Instead, he'd come across as crass. Living for years in a logging camp with nothing but men to look at made him forget his manners. His mother would be appalled. Ava deserved an apology.

Benjamin rounded the curved path and started up the hill toward the lighthouse he'd researched since first meeting Ava. Though fifteen years old, New Presque Isle Lighthouse was still considered one of the grandest on the Great Lakes with its Third Order Fresnel lens and double-walled tower built on a limestone foundation. The beacon towered over the treetops. He looked forward to meeting Ava's father, if the man wasn't asleep. Or her mother, to determine where Ava had received those beguiling dark eyes and pert little mouth.

The grounds surrounding the lighthouse were quiet. Chickens pecked in the dirt, sea grass rustled, and waves rippled ashore, yet there was no sign of the lightkeeper. Benjamin climbed the steps to the keeper's quarters and knocked. After several moments, he knocked again, louder.

Still nothing.

Benjamin surveyed the stoop. The space was void, save for a chair and a pair of boots. A very small pair of boots. About the size of Ava's feet.

He strolled around to the lighthouse. When no one answered there either, Benjamin turned the doorknob and peeked inside. "Mr. Ryan?" It was possible the man was in the tower room, but doubtful this time of day.

Oil cans, stacked in neat lines, covered part of the wall to his left, while wicks and an open toolbox sat to his right. Every tool was nestled perfectly in the box, evenly spaced. Even the broom and mop stood at attention like soldiers.

Benjamin tugged the door closed and passed a wheelbarrow on his way to the shed. One of those new safety bicycles, popular in Detroit, was propped against the building's side, a basket hooked on one handlebar. When he called and received no reply yet again, he checked the cellar. All that awaited were shelves of canned fruits and vegetables, perfectly spaced.

Either the lightkeeper was obsessively neat, or his daughter was responsible for most of the work around here. Now that he thought about it, there was no evidence of a man living here at all. And the clothesline—not one article that day had belonged to a man.

Could be that Ava washed her clothes on a different day than she washed her father's. Or that, like the previous lightkeeper, Ava's father was a former military man and craved order. But something around here spoke the absence of a man altogether.

As Benjamin made his way back to camp, he was more convinced than ever that Miss Ava Ryan had a secret.

Chapter 2

Supplies were dangerously low, and so was Ava's spirit. She glanced around the watch room at the scant amount of oil, wiping sweat from her temple with the back of her hand. The thunderheads on the horizon were moving closer to shore, creating a smothering heat in the tower that would make it hard for a person with healthy lungs to breathe, much less her.

Though the worst of Michigan days didn't compare to the humidity back home. A South Carolina low country summer day could suffocate a person in her condition. The cooler temperatures were a welcome reprieve, but how she missed the music of cicadas and bullfrogs on the swampy marsh, the flicker of fireflies for applause.

Something pounded beneath her. She stood on the top step and peered down at the spiral of stairs below. Another pound.

Who would be calling this close to dusk? With speed and precision, she descended to ground level.

"Miss Ryan?"

The deep, muffled voice of Benjamin Colfax seeped through the door.

Her mind must be growing weaker too, as the insufferable—and oh, so handsome—man had been walking around her brain for the last week. Now, it was conjuring his voice to match.

The next knock rattled in the hollow space to the very marrow of her bones. "Miss Ryan?"

She hated snakes.

"Uh, just a moment." Heart racing, her gaze raked over her attire. At least she had shoes on this time. However, her father's trousers simply wouldn't do. There was no means of escape though, and as determined as he was to be a thorn in her side, he'd probably chase after her anyway.

Palm flat against her stomach, which she now remembered was not encased in a corset, she expelled a wheezy cough and opened the door enough to peek her head through. The thumping pulse in his neck met her at eye level. She lifted her gaze, determined to ignore her fascination with the sight.

Fist poised in the air, Mr. Colfax dropped his arm and took a step back.

"I thought I heard a braying mule."

Had she just said that? Her face heated. She'd never insulted a person in her life.

He chuckled. Then reached out and patted the top of her head. "Easy, girl. Don't bite. I'm only looking for your father. I figured he'd be awake ready to tend the light by now, but I've yet to find him."

The urge to slug this man would've been stronger if her scalp wasn't tingling from his touch.

Another cough racked her chest, spreading fire through her lungs. Mr. Colfax frowned, concern radiating from eyes as blue as Lake Huron on a summer day. Every spark of fight drained out of her. "He's not here."

"For a renowned lightkeeper, he sure is gone a lot."

"My mother, he's…with her right now." At least she hadn't lied. However, it was foolish for her to admit she was here alone.

He took two steps forward and looked over her head and into the room. She tried to pull the door closed, but his beefy shoulder got in the way. He dodged to the right. So did she. To the left. She blocked him there too.

A slow, wicked smile curved his lips, offering a glimpse of white teeth. "What are you hiding, Ava?"

"Miss Ryan."

She stepped backward and slammed the door. Leaned against it. Good heavens, it was stifling in here. When the sun set in an hour and she lit the lamp, she'd bask in fresh air on the parapet.

A knock thumped at her back. "I'll come back tomorrow."

She didn't doubt that for a second.

"And the next day…"

If she didn't find out what he wanted with her father, she'd never be rid of him. "What is it you want?" she yelled through the door, fighting another cough.

"To climb the lighthouse. I need the view to determine our best cutting route."

Was that all?

Even though she'd promised her father to never associate with the burly loggers, if granting his request would keep him off her property, she'd gladly comply.

She wiped more sweat, palmed her coif to make sure most of it was still in place, and cracked open the door. The mirth lifting his unshaven cheeks sent a wild round of glorious irritation through her middle. "Tomorrow afternoon. I'll take you up myself."

His eyebrows arched. "I won't turn that down. All the same, I'd like to speak to your father."

So would she. Unfortunately, they'd both be disappointed in the matter. Inhaling a deep breath to ward off another cough, she held her chin high and issued words she'd heard her father say a hundred times when bartering quality cotton to the textile mills when she'd been a small child. "Final offer. Take it or leave it."

A pause.

"Then, I'll see you tomorrow." He squinted up at the sky. "Unless this storm blows us all away."

Which was likely to happen if he didn't leave so she could secure the shed door and close all the shutters the way she'd planned to before dark.

He gave her another once-over and then bowed. "Until then, *Miss Ryan.*"

She watched him go, noting what a fine figure he cut in his pressed slacks and crisp shirt. Something that surprised her from a barbaric logger who lived in an unsavory logging camp. That's how her father had described the lot of them when they'd invaded Presque Isle, anyway. Though nothing about Mr. Colfax seemed barbaric. If anything, his cool demeanor and that boyish light in his eyes promised security and adventure.

He mumbled something that floated on the wind, something akin to "discovering secrets."

She poked her head out farther. "Pardon?"

He continued walking but looked at her over his shoulder. "Hee-haw!"

At least he was speaking his own language now.

She chided herself. Goodness, he was fun to tease. A thing she hadn't had the freedom to do in a very long time. Matthew came to mind, causing her heart to ache. She'd been sixteen when her childhood best friend had spoken pretty words about marriage. Memories that were now scattered into the dust of her past, like so many other dreams after her diagnosis last year.

The wind kicked up, drying tears that hovered on her lashes. After making certain Mr. Colfax had gone, Ava slammed the unruly door behind her, like she'd done months ago when she'd realized all hope of a husband and children was gone.

The angry clouds were closer now, the wind harsher. She rushed to secure the shed door and close the shutters over the fragile glass on the house. A broken window was the last thing she needed.

Rain pelted the earth the moment she stepped under the canopy of the porch. Through the blanket of water pouring off the roof, she spied angry waves rolling to shore. The storm began to howl, much like the one swirling inside her.

Cold and soaked through, Ben walked into camp, each boot sinking farther into the mud on the logging trail. What a shock to his system after Ava's offer to show him the lighthouse, alone, had heated his blood. The exchange was innocent on both sides, yet it spiked his pulse along with a hundred other reactions, making him feel guilty for the direction of his thoughts.

He spent far too much time around riotous men, that's all. Of course he was attracted. But Ava was just a woman like any other. Nothing more.

Wiping rain from his eyes, he set his mind on the long, miserable night ahead. The next few days too, if this torrent didn't let up soon. Cleared land meant mud that could turn into mudslides and snuff out a man's life in seconds. He'd seen it twice before, the most recent incident eight weeks ago. A nightmare that still haunted his sleep. The north side of the hill had crashed into the stream so fast Ben had barely had time to catch his breath. So fast he failed to yell a warning to the man he'd seen rowing downstream minutes earlier, a stringer of fish hanging from the side of the dinghy.

The horror on the man's face would be forever ingrained on Ben's memory. As well as the stronghold of mud pulling on his limbs, making it impossible to reach the man in time. He could still hear the stranger's pleas. Feel the desperation of not being able to save him.

The aroma of beans and corn bread wafting from the cook's tent broke through his thoughts. The same meal they'd eaten the last four days. He missed his mother's cooking, same as he had almost every day for the last six years. And his sister Margaret's cooking too. Alice and Cora's wasn't bad either. Katherine was still watching over Stella and Daisy while the others prepared the meals.

Growing up, he'd never lacked for female company. He'd had his fill of buttons and bows and bonnets to last him a lifetime. Or so he'd thought.

When his father had been injured and could no longer work, Ben had resolved to step into the role of provider. He did his duty without complaint. But as the years passed, he started longing for something else—what, he wasn't sure. Ever since he'd taken a foreman position with the Saginaw Lumber Company, traveling the coast of Michigan, seeing homes and businesses take over the space his team had cleared, the restlessness in his gut became impossible to suppress any longer. He wanted more out of life.

Raucous laughter bellowed through the bunkhouse doors. He trudged to the camp office where his living quarters waited. At least here he could be with his thoughts, away from sixty men with cigars, cards, and tempers. A harmless bunch, really. He'd worked with worse. There was nothing they could do in this rain, so he'd let them have their fun, as long as they were ready to work first thing tomorrow morning.

He left his boots at the door and walked to his trunk for dry clothing. His stomach howled, but Sean was cooking this week. Ben dreaded the taste of overcooked beans and dry corn bread. Stretching out on his bed, he allowed his mind to wander, once again, to the lightkeeper's daughter and her delicious southern accent. The slow, lazy rhythm of her words.

Yep, it was gonna be a long night.

Chapter 3

Ava had never been more relieved to hear silence. For two solid days and nights, smattering rain and gale-force winds had shaken the house, blowing slate roof shingles off as if they were nothing more than weightless pebbles. The fragrant steam rising from her teacup curled around her nose, and she breathed it deeply.

Lemon, ginger, and honey.

She set the teakettle back on the stove to keep it warm. The tightness in her lungs had calmed. Cool, dry air is what her doctor had recommended, but Michigan was as far north as they'd gotten. The lighthouse was supposed to be a temporary detour for her and her father. Now it seemed as if the tower would be their final resting place.

As long as some meddling logger didn't ruin it for her.

She closed her eyes and let the warm tea trail a comforting path to her insides. She had a long day ahead, even if Benjamin Colfax didn't show. She should be sleeping. But the roof wasn't going to repair itself, nor the gate to the chicken coop. Since repairs were in her commission contract, less sleep was on her horizon.

Twenty minutes later, her boots slipped in the mushy yard as she made her way to the shed for tools. Good heavens, this would be a whole lot easier if the hem of her skirt wasn't already weighted with mud. She would've worn trousers, but a certain logging foreman had decided to become a pebble in her shoe. Now climbing a ladder would not only be difficult but dangerous.

The shed door gave an eerie moan. She stepped inside, squinting to adjust to the dimness. The dank space smelled of rusting metal and aged wood. A spider crawled across a shelf of hammer and nails to her left. A chill zipped up her spine. She hated things that crept around in silence.

Mustering her courage, she grabbed the tools she needed—squealing as her fingers grazed a sticky, thready substance—threw them in a bag, and ran for the muddy, and much preferred, outdoors.

"Miss Ryan?"

She yelped and stumbled sideways, her boots failing to grip in the mud.

The bag of tools clattered to the ground.

"Whoa." Ben grabbed her upper arm and propelled her upright then peered into the shed. "What's got you fired up?"

Heat infused her cheeks. Speaking of things that crept around. She pulled from his grip and tugged on her skirt. "Spiders."

"Ah. Would you like for me to rid the pests for you?"

No, she was capable of ridding pests herself. Starting with escorting him up the lighthouse tower so he could be on his way. "No, thank you. I'll manage."

He raised and then dropped one shoulder, causing a lock of hair to curve over his forehead. "Suit yourself."

She peeled her attention away from his hair—once again he wore no hat—and concentrated on retrieving the tools.

Mr. Colfax beat her to it.

She tried not to grimace at the slimy brown glop suctioned to the bottom of the bag as it touched her fingers. "Thank you."

"I'd be happy to carry that wherever you were headed."

She thrust the bag in his hands. "The tower."

The sooner he got what he wanted, the sooner he'd be out of her life forever. She lifted her skirt and tiptoed through the yard to the cylindrical structure, fighting for traction with every step. Mr. Colfax advanced through the muck with the grace of a swan.

"That was quite a storm. Nearly washed our bunks away." He took in their surroundings, craning his tan neck to see the top of the tower. The top button of his collar had come undone. Or had never been fastened in the first place.

He caught her staring and pinned his gaze on her. "I'm glad to see you're safe."

So was she. One hundred and thirteen feet in the air was not a comforting place to be during a storm. The hot lens had turned her normally friendly shadows into menacing creatures of the night. Even her tattered copy of Jane Austen's *Sense and Sensibility* hadn't captured her attention as usual. Not that she didn't already know the story by heart.

However, unattainable love and crushed dreams weren't the subject of the moment, and Mr. Colfax was, once again, prying. "Not even a monsoon can deter you. I'm sure your superior is proud."

"What sunshine you are after a storm."

And what a black cloud he created on a clear day.

He grinned, reached the door of the lighthouse, grasped the knob, and swung it wide for her to enter. Her filthy skirt brushed his pant leg as she passed through the narrow space that now felt suffocating. He followed, then stared at the open door as if unsure whether to close it or leave it open for propriety's sake. He reached a hand out, snatched it back, and nodded at the outdoors.

She bit her lip to keep from giggling at his discomfort.

Planting one hand in his pocket, he squinted up the spiral staircase. "I would normally offer for you to go first, but perhaps I should lead and help you along."

"Thank you for your concern, Mr. Colfax." She hiked her skirt to reveal sturdy, and muddy, boots and began climbing the stairs. "But I do this every evening. You're the one most likely to need assistance."

She bit her tongue at her confession, waiting for his inquiry of why she climbed the stairs if her father was the lightkeeper. The question never came.

The iron steps vibrated with their weight as they climbed. A faint whisper hit her ears. Was Mr. Colfax counting?

She paused, and he nearly plowed into her. His warm hand caught the curve of her waist for support. She gasped.

Breath hissed through his teeth. "I apologize. You stopped and. . .well, it's awkward with this."

He lifted the bag of tools she'd forgotten he was carrying, face aflame. She took the bag and transferred it to the edge of a step, almost feeling sorry for him. "A hundred and forty-four."

She continued climbing.

"Pardon?" The metal vibrated again with his movements.

"Steps. When we reach the top, we'll be in one of the tallest towers built on the Great Lakes."

A wry laugh sounded at her back. "You say that as casually as if telling me what you had for breakfast."

"A four-minute egg, two pieces of toast, and tea."

"Corn fritters, fried eggs, hash, bacon, and beans."

She frowned. "Beans?"

"At almost every meal."

"And you ate all that?"

"I had seconds."

Good heavens. She didn't really care what he ate for breakfast, but at least the conversation had steered them away from the tension following their collision.

At last they reached the lantern room where she'd cleaned the windows just hours before. Mr. Colfax climbed up and stood beside her, making the cramped space feel even smaller. A sheen of sweat glistened on his upper lip and temples. His breaths came at faster intervals.

"You're not afraid of heights, are you?" She moved around the lens to the door that led to the parapet.

He palmed the back of his neck. "I can endure them. If I have to."

A chink in the man's arrogant armor.

She opened the door and passed in front of it to the other side of the still-warm lens. "Endure it as long as you need to determine your best cutting route. I'll be in here, cleaning up."

Mr. Colfax nodded and stepped, a bit too hesitantly, outside. Ava retreated to the watch room to allow him privacy. Here, she spent long hours of the night refueling the lamp, soothed by the hot glowing lantern and the shared angst of Elinor and Marianne Dashwood, fictional characters whose love stories had ended as tragically as her own. At least until the last chapters of the novel, which Ava ignored. For her, the Dashwood sisters' story ended when Marianne was well enough to return home and walk the path at Barton Cottage where she first met Willoughby, to say goodbye. The moment when both women acknowledged the death of their dreams and complied to spinsterhood.

A title Ava might not live long enough to obtain.

The pallet of blankets she sat on every night was still in disarray from the storm. She folded them into neat little squares, hung her shawl on the railing, and propped her book in the corner. She was exhausted but took comfort in knowing her labor might have saved lives.

Despite her lengthening each task to its fullest, Mr. Colfax still hadn't returned from the balcony. As much as she'd like to leave the insufferable man to his own devices, this was her post, and she must guarantee that he got everything he needed in order to avoid future visits.

The air outside was refreshing after the rain. In front of her lay nothing but Lake Huron. To the west, trees filled with deep green leaves covered the landscape as far as her eyes could see. Mr. Colfax stood on that end of the parapet, writing in a small book using a pencil. She leaned her backside against the rail and waited for him to finish.

A few minutes later, he tucked the pencil behind his ear, closed his book, and turned to face her. Color drained from his cheeks. "You shouldn't do that."

He wrapped his hand around her arm and tugged her away.

"Why?"

"You might fall. It's a long way down."

He was twitching like her mantel clock that stuck when the gears wound down.

"This?" Amused, she inched closer to the railing and peeked over. "This is nothing."

She leaned farther still.

"Don't do that." He lunged for her, dropping his book. One corner teetered over the edge.

Using one hand to nudge her against the glass, he bent and retrieved his book. He stood and, for a brief moment, closed his eyes and inhaled a deep breath. Then, blue daggers homed in on her.

"That could've gone badly." She stifled a laugh and covered her lips with her fingers. He was so perturbed, she couldn't help herself and mirth burst through against her will.

His furious gaze melted until he too was smiling. "That isn't funny. You really shouldn't take such risks, Miss Ryan. Especially without anyone here to call upon for help."

Moisture left her mouth, and she swallowed. "My father—"

"Is gone to the Lord." His voice was gentle. "I inquired about the matter in town."

"How I live here is none of your business."

"You're right." He curled his fingers around her elbow.

She stiffened.

He released her. "You are as prickly as a desert cactus."

Tears pushed at the back of her eyes. "I have to be."

"Why?"

The concern in his features and the softness of his tone almost undid her. Like Willoughby with Marianne, Mr. Colfax was a stranger who had the power to break her heart. Only this was real life, not fiction, and broken promises were something she could no longer endure.

"Come down when you're ready. I have things to do." She fled to the lantern room, hurried around the lens, and descended the stairs, picking up the bag of tools on her way down.

She would not cry. She wouldn't.

There were too many repairs waiting to waste time on tears.

She maneuvered through the soppy yard to the house and stepped onto the porch to find a note tacked to her door. A telegram.

With shaky fingers, she opened the flap.

SUPPLY TRAIN DERAILED *Stop* RATION WHEREVER POSSIBLE *Stop* --
US LIGHTHOUSE COMMISSION *Stop*

She placed a palm to her forehead. It was too late to ration. She had enough supplies to last two full nights at most. If the lamps failed and sailors ran aground...

"Can I help you with anything, Miss Ryan?"

She whirled around, tucking the telegram in the hidden pocket of her skirt. "No, thank you. Since you've succeeded in exploring the best cutting route and our paths will never cross again, let me bid you farewell with the best of wishes in all your future endeavors."

Her words were as cold as her heart had grown.

Mr. Colfax frowned, bowed, then stepped backward off the porch. "Even the desert cactus blooms. I look forward to seeing you then, Miss Ryan."

The dashing stranger left her alone to feel as dry and destitute as she truly was.

Chapter 4

The campfire crackled and popped, shooting sparks above Ben's head. McGurdy was supposed to be tending the fire, but when Lenny and his bunkmates had returned from the river spouting about some apparition at the Old Presque Isle Lighthouse—south of Miss Ryan's post—Ben had offered to take over while the men investigated.

McGurdy, being of Scot-Irish descent, wouldn't be able to tamp his superstitious nature to mind his task anyway. One awry spark could be the difference between a full night's sleep and disaster. Problem was, Ben wasn't any more focused than McGurdy. Time and again, he'd yanked his attention away from the beacon flashing above the treetops and back to the flames. Away from the memory of Ava Ryan.

"I have to be." He couldn't erase from his mind the desperation in her words. Her pale skin had glowed in the sunlight like the purest alabaster, but did she truly think she could shatter so easily? What would put such a notion in her head? True, her father and mother were gone, but that did not make her weak.

She pulled at every natural instinct in him, making him want to protect her from whatever she felt she had to fight. Which was madness, since he knew nothing more than her station in life. And how bewitching she was when her ire flared, even while wearing a plain brown shirtwaist.

That line of thinking would never release him from the shackles weighing him down. Presque Isle wasn't his final destination. After he finished this job, it was back to Saginaw to withdraw his money from the bank, then to wherever he chose to go from there. Anywhere away from the woods, the sawdust. Away from beans and corn bread. Most of all, away from injuries and death.

Forward to a life of *his* choosing.

A log snapped, sending another flurry of sparks into the air. Male voices drifted through the trees, growing louder with each noisy footfall. McGurdy was the first to reach camp. He tromped to the fire and dropped onto a stump. Serious lines pulled at the man's eyes as he stared into the flames, his ruddy cheeks ashen.

Ben leaned forward on his knees. "Fire got you spooked?"

" 'Tis spooks, all right." McGurdy rubbed his upper lip. "That there be an apparition. A siren of sorts."

"I don't understand."

"A she-spirit. 'Tis the worst kind." McGurdy fingered his gnarly red beard. "Her beauty, it casts a spell on a man. If he be weak and give in, she'll devour his soul like the devil himself."

Ben would've laughed if the man hadn't been so serious. "This *she-spirit* is at the abandoned lighthouse?"

"Aye. Seen her myself, standin' on the tower all ghostly in the moonlight. Bewitchin' she is with her loose raven hair."

Raven hair? Ben opened his mouth to reply, but the rest of the group returned in a band of raucous voices. Some commented in praise of this "she-spirit." Others, in fear.

"You shoulda seen her, boss." Terrell clamped a hand on Ben's shoulder.

"I stopped believing in ghosts when I was eight." Ben stood and stretched, a mighty yawn swelling his chest.

"I did too, but this one would bring your childish fears to life again." Terrell took the spot Ben had just vacated.

"I doubt that."

Orbin shook his head. "I'm not the superstitious sort, but we heard the noises, and I've never seen a human appear and disappear in a wink. She's an apparition. It's the only explanation."

Ben huffed. "Or it could be because the ugliest group of men she's ever seen scared her away."

McGurdy hung his head. "The only way to ward off a she-spirit is to circle around her nine times."

This time, Ben laughed.

" 'Tisn't funny." McGurdy stood, his bony frame defensive. "We must circle her nine times under a full moon while shouting her name."

Terrell studied the night sky. "Full moon's a'comin'. I'd guess in two nights. How do we find out her name?"

Ben slapped his arm as he moved past. "Ask her."

Let those fools have their spooks and spirits. He headed to his quarters for a restful night's sleep. "Ghosts or not, I expect you ready to work at daybreak."

Two days from now, if his crew hadn't regained their faculties, he'd investigate this *she-spirit*. He had a pretty good idea where to find her.

Ava grunted as she stacked the last crate by the door. Breathing heavily, she leaned against the boxes and wondered how she was ever going to carry them more than a mile to the lighthouse. Her last trip had come by cover of night, to avoid running into any loggers. But the livery where she'd been renting a horse for this job was out of available beasts.

She was fortunate these supplies had been left behind when Mr. Garraty and his family moved out of the old lighthouse fourteen years ago. Though some were no longer usable, what little there was should allow her to keep the lamp burning until another supply shipment arrived.

She swatted at something crawling down her neck and cringed. The building was creepy with its skeletal tower where the lantern had been removed. Every manner of forest creature had inhabited the place since the New Presque Isle Lighthouse had gone into commission. Including the baboons from the logging camp over half a mile west. For some reason they felt the need to poke around at night, and it frightened her to no end. They were infesting the area and would soon discover she was a lone woman without the protection of a man. And when they did, they'd act like a swarm of flies on an apple pie at a picnic, as her father had so brashly described it. The fact that her curiosity often skittered to Mr. Colfax and whether he would be among them was of little significance.

Prickly, indeed. A woman had to be when men exchanged female hearts as fast as they did currency.

She lifted her lantern to examine the oil containers. Whale oil. The stench of it when it burned nearly made her retch. The kerosene gave her headaches at times but was preferable to this ancient method. After setting aside cans that were dented or busted, she placed as many as she could carry in a knapsack and prepared to hoist it over her shoulder.

"You're the she-spirit?"

Yelping, she dropped the knapsack and backed against the wall. Cans clattered and rolled.

Lantern light emerged from the shadows, followed by Mr. Colfax. He glanced around, smiling. "What are you doing in here?"

If her heartbeat would slow down long enough to gain control of her limbs, she'd throttle him.

He fully entered the room. The dancing light drew attention to his sharp, handsome features and bare forearms where his shirt was cuffed to his elbows. Dirt smudged one cheek.

"Ava?"

"I'm gathering supplies, you goon. What are you doing here?" She snatched the knapsack and lifted. It stopped three inches above the ground. If she could just get the end on her shoulder, she'd have plenty of leverage from her backside to sustain the trip home. Or partway, at least.

Mr. Colfax took the burden from her and lifted it onto his back as if it were a dried leaf. "For the last three nights my men have heard all sorts of racket coming from this place. They're convinced a ghost haunts this old lighthouse, along with other spirits. I came to investigate."

She smoothed a hand over her skirt. "As you can see, I'm not a ghost."

"But you certainly have spirit." He laughed and shook his head.

Temper flaming, she reached for the bundle. She wouldn't make another trip tonight in the dark, but this should get her by until morning.

He held her wrist. "I'd be glad to carry this for you."

She jerked away, the heat from his fingertips lingering. "Thank you, Mr. Colfax, but I must insist on carrying my own bundle."

"Ben." He stood taller. "We've spent enough time together, you can call me Ben."

"Ben," she whispered. "I insist on carrying my own bundle."

"Where are you going?"

"Home."

"You can't carry this all that way."

"I can't walk in the dark, unaccompanied, with a man who isn't my husband either. It's scandalous."

One eyebrow rose. "So is walking around barefoot and wearing men's trousers, but that hasn't stopped you."

She gasped like a walleye under the noonday sun.

"Now—" He stopped. Deep, muffled voices sounded through the door.

"Don't let them in here," she hissed, and retreated up the tower stairs far enough to be hidden in the darkness.

Ben frowned up at her. Something thumped against the door. He dropped the knapsack, blew out the lanterns, and jogged to her side. "What's going on?"

His voice was only loud enough for her to hear. He smelled of peppermint and. . .safety.

"They can't know I'm here, please."

The door below them opened, sending a whoosh of air upward.

"Then, *be* the she-spirit," he whispered.

Though her confusion was lost in the dark, he must have sensed it. "Use their fear against them. Make them think you're a ghost, and they'll leave."

"But—"

"Follow my lead."

His warm breath stirred the hair against her ear. Her skin pebbled.

Ben leaned away and made a low, eerie sound while stamping his foot.

"She's here," one of the men said.

Ben pushed at her arm, encouraging her to join in. Well, she did want them gone. As ridiculous as this behavior was, desperate times sometimes called for utter foolishness. She opened her mouth and howled as she imagined a ghost would, if one were real.

"What be yer name, lassie?" The Irish brogue sounded at the base of the stairs.

"Get out!" she shouted. "Get out!"

"It be a full moon, lassie. Tell me your name so we can put ye at rest."

While continuing his banter, Ben reached behind her. Then an object sailed above her head toward the men below.

"Leave her be, McGurdy," someone said. "She ain't hurtin' nothin'."

Shuffling came from the exit.

She started to giggle then covered it with a shriller scream that echoed through the tower like a rabid banshee.

"I'm getting out of here." A door below slammed.

"What be yer name?" the Irishman yelled.

"Keep screaming," Ben whispered. He jumped on the iron stairs and made noises fit for an insane asylum. She kept up her end, feeling both silly and warmed by the fact Ben was helping her scare the wits out of his own men.

In the sliver of moonlight reflecting from the room above, she watched Ben slip off his boot and hurl it down the stairs. A grunt sounded a moment later.

"McGurdy, you all right?" The voice was too close for Ava's comfort.

Ben winced. One Irishman down. How many men to go?

A chant in some language she didn't understand ensued inches from her feet. What would the repercussions be if they discovered her and Ben in the blackened stairwell together, attempting to scare them off? She prayed for mercy.

And received it. The chant, never ceasing, grew fainter and fainter, along with the light that had radiated below. She couldn't say how much time had passed when Ben finally spoke into the pitch.

"I believe it's safe to step out of the underworld."

He grabbed her hand and descended the stairs first, maneuvering with the utmost care. When her feet touched the dirt floor, he released her. With all the talk of ghosts and the darkness surrounding her, she almost wished he'd reclaim her hand.

"Do you happen to have a match?" His deep voice rumbled between them.

"Somewhere."

He moved away to search for one of the lanterns. Moments later, glass crunched beneath his feet. "One of us is now short a lantern."

Which meant one of them was going to have a difficult way home.

The sound of cans clinking together made her jump. Ben mumbled. "I found your bag."

The cans banged together as he, she presumed, hoisted the bag onto his shoulder. She closed her eyes to recall the layout of the room and where she'd placed the lantern before the men had arrived. Then she inched her way that direction, hand extended.

Her fingertips brushed the soft cotton of a shirt and landed on the hard chest beneath. Ben's large hand covered hers, jolting the beat of his heart under her palm. She tried to pull away but it was futile. His grip was determined and, oddly, soothing. "I'll walk you home."

"It's over a mile."

"Which is precisely why I'm not letting you walk it alone."

"Easily two miles from your camp."

"I don't care if it's ten. You're not walking alone, Ava."

Despite the fact that she'd made the trip in the dark alone before, she didn't like doing so. "I appreciate your chivalry, Mr. Colfax—"

"Ben."

"Ben. However, I must decline." She started for what she hoped was the door.

"Stop being stubborn." He caught her arm and took the lead.

"I know you're trying to be a gentleman, but I can't afford to let anything threaten my post. If I'm seen with you, unaccompanied, in the dark, not only will my reputation be lost but I'll lose my position as lightkeeper. It's all I have, Ben. Please, let me go."

She hated the desperation in her voice.

His thumb rubbing along her upper arm stilled her fight. "If a panther, or a predator of the male kind, should happen upon you, keeping your post will be the least of your worries. My team isn't the only one out here greedy for lumber. The others might not run from superstitious notions. I'm walking you home."

She couldn't argue with that.

Chapter 5

Ava gazed up the length of the ladder propped against the house. Each daunting rung shouted a challenge. Somehow, she must manage to climb while balancing her weight, a new shutter, and an old reticule full of nails and a hammer. All while wearing the forest-green skirt she'd carefully brushed, in case a certain lumberjack should appear.

Three days had passed since Ben had walked her home with nothing but the moonlight and the beam from the lighthouse to guide their way. The giddy feeling was still with her, distracting her concentration, lightening her steps. The same giddiness the Dashwood sisters had experienced upon their first encounters with Edward and Willoughby. The same as she'd felt when discovering she was to be Matthew's bride.

How quickly that emotion could be murdered.

Only she must do the murdering this time. Ben was a risk and, furthermore, a logger. Not to mention that his timing was a nuisance. She had a lighthouse to run, a position to fight for, and a solitary life to live, however long or short that may be.

For now, she had repairs unfit for a woman to tackle.

She girded her skirt and tucked it into the front of her waistband. She looked ridiculous, but it might spare her a broken neck. How long would it take someone to find her, should she fall?

At least a week. Every Thursday she went into town long enough to get what she needed and fetch the mail. Since she'd gone into town yesterday, it would be a week before Mr. Easton noticed her absence. And notice he would. The storekeeper always remarked on her punctuality. One of the reasons she made a good lightkeeper.

She stepped on the first rung then the second. When it didn't buckle or sway with her weight, she tucked the shutter under her arm and climbed the rest of the way. Her heart raced. Palms sweated. By the time she reached the top, her breaths came in labored pants. *Don't look down.*

How ridiculous. She climbed the tower every evening without thought. She'd even dangled over the railing to watch Ben squirm. Something about being on a ladder, however, balancing while attempting to hammer, was an entirely different matter. Oh, how she wished her father were here to handle this. Or Matthew. Or—

No. She would not let her mind wander down that swampy road. She was a modern woman—or so she'd like to think—and she could handle this. She wasn't helpless. Yet.

The breeze stirred, and her lungs gave a squeeze. She swallowed the cough, afraid it might send her backward, and caught a glimpse of her reflection in the window. She appeared as young and healthy as any eighteen-year-old woman. But inside. . . How long would it take the tuberculosis to turn her skin paler and her figure to skin and bones? Her youthful vigor to a fleeting memory?

That vigor she'd almost forgotten had reintroduced itself three nights ago. Though scaring Ben's friends had been terribly wicked, she hadn't felt so alive since. . . she couldn't remember when. The truth struck hard. She wasn't living her life. She was existing.

Oh, how she wanted to live.

Tears blurred her vision. Living wasn't meant for the dying. She shook her head, took a deep breath, and braced herself against the ladder, tugging the slab of wood from beneath her arm.

For what seemed like an eternity, she used her shoulder to hold the wood flush with the house and hammered until she thought she'd jar her teeth out. Rivulets of sweat made a path down the sides of her face. Finally, she finished. Arms and legs aching, she eased her way down the ladder, nail-filled reticule dangling from one wrist. Her bottom smacked something solid before a strong grip clamped around her waist, lifted her away from the ladder, and deposited her to the ground.

She blinked then spun. Ben's eyes blazed like blue fire. "Are you trying to get yourself killed?"

Ben scowled, taking deep breaths. He forced his heart to slow to its normal rhythm after the sight of her on a rickety ten-foot ladder had sent it soaring. She lived out here alone, for crying out loud. What if she'd fallen?

He cleared his throat in hopes his words wouldn't sound as harsh as intended. "Stop jeopardizing your life."

One dark brow arched over Ava's piercing gaze. "You're not my father, brother, or husband. I will do with my life what I please."

She started to walk away but stopped and looked down at her skirt tangled through her legs. She yanked and tugged and straightened, her face an angry shade of pink. With one last glare, she took a stride, but he caught her and turned her by the elbow. "You're right, I'm not. But I am your friend, and I'm asking you to stop taking such risks."

Ava glanced at the place where his hand curled around her arm, then back at him. "I was replacing a broken shutter, not practicing trapeze for the circus."

She yanked her arm away and all but ran from him. Her reticule swung like a rope in a hurricane. He jogged after her. "Exactly. You were doing a man's work. You should be safely inside cooking or knitting."

She jerked to a stop and faced him, mouth agape.

His face heated. As soon as he'd said the words, he'd regretted them. With six spirited sisters and a mother tough enough to keep all ten children in line, he knew women were capable of much more than housework. He also knew fear could cause a man to utter some very stupid remarks.

Her dark irises became watery pools. "I have no choice. If this property isn't kept to standard, upon inspection, I'll lose my position. I have no family, nowhere else to go." Her pulse thumped between her collarbones. "I'll end up on the streets."

She needn't elaborate. He knew well what happened to women in such situations, forced to make a choice between morality and starvation. He'd seen a good many men waste their weekly wage to spend time with such a woman.

Her skirts rustled as she continued walking. He followed, calling himself a hundred kinds of fool. He hadn't meant to hurt her. Only to feed his desire to keep her safe. "I'm sorry, Ava. I shouldn't have said that."

She swiped a tear using an angry fist. "Why are you here?"

The subject he should have started with after he'd removed his hands from her curvy waist. "I brought your supplies from the station." He pointed to the horse and wagon parked down the hill. "I know you're perfectly capable of fetching them yourself, but I was already there with the horse and wagon. Figured I'd save you the delivery charge."

She changed directions and marched toward her supplies. Fingers curled around the top of the wagon, she took stock of the contents, counting the crates and eyeing labels. She picked up a small bag nestled between two boxes. "I didn't order this."

He stepped forward and gently took the bag. "I did."

It crinkled as he opened it. He held it out to her.

Glaring at him, she dared to peek inside. "Ribbon candy?"

He held the bag out farther.

She frowned at her hand, wiped it on her skirt, and then reached for a curled strip. "It's not Christmas."

Her youthful innocence was exaggerated by the candy in her grip. He leaned against the wagon. "In New York City, ribbon candy isn't just sold at Christmas. See how the pieces are blue, pink, and yellow? At Switzer's Candy Shoppe you can purchase it year round."

"These came from New York City?" Her fury was quickly replaced by curiosity.

If only he'd thought of the candy sooner.

"A friend of mine works near Switzer's. I sent a telegram asking him to bring these along when we met up in Saginaw yesterday."

She stared at the confection. "I believe I'll save it for later. Thank you. Not just for the candy, but for bringing the supplies. It'll save me time."

He nodded. "Where would you like me to unload these?"

"In the tower, if it's not too much trouble."

Not at all. He'd take any excuse to be near her. She was almost entirely all he'd thought about since their trickery at the old lighthouse. Her laughter, her animated conversation as they'd walked through the woods, the way the moon-light glowed against her hair—it was Ava Ryan in a whole new light. Literally and figuratively. He liked both.

On his way here, he'd envisioned this meeting filled with smiles to indicate his presence was welcome. An afternoon of familiar camaraderie. A little flirting, perhaps.

He'd not imagined witnessing her teetering on a ladder.

From the porch, she watched him as he unloaded the crates. He took his time, enjoying the attention. Goodness knows how long it would be before another woman looked at him.

The horse took some coaxing but finally followed Ben around to the porch. This beast was probably as grateful to get out of the livery as Ben was to get out of the woods. Ava had disappeared from her perch. He looked around and was about to leave when the door opened.

"Thank you for your services, Mr. Colfax." Coins protruded from her fingertips. His pride took a dive.

"It's Ben, and I don't want your money."

She palmed the coins and crossed her arms. Oh, so prickly. His forest sprite was gone.

"I want to help you, Ava. You've not been feeling well. I can hear it in your voice, in the way you cough. You're overworked staying up all night and trying to maintain all this on your own."

Her mouth opened, so he plunged on. "I know you're capable, but you shouldn't have to do this by yourself. Let me help you."

Her features were as flinty as they'd been the night he saw her home when she'd begged him to keep her secret. Fearful of living out here alone in a land infested by ruffians. "It's my own neck."

And what a pretty neck it was. "I don't want you to end up on the streets any more than you want to be there. Let me take care of the repairs, at least until the first frost. Then you'll never have to see me again."

The thought bothered him more than he wanted to admit.

She studied him with narrowed eyes. "What could you possibly gain?"

He threw his palms out. "A break from beans and corn bread."

She blinked. "You want me to cook for you?" Each word came out slow, skeptical.

"I have no ill intentions and no expectations. However, if you agree, the property will be fit for inspection, and you'll have the aid of my protection from all 'invading loggers,' should you need it."

She looked away. "What will people say? It isn't proper—"

"It isn't proper to evict a woman from her home either. I can't imagine you get many visitors here. I promise to be gone long before nightfall."

Closing her eyes, she pinched the bridge of her nose. Her chin leveled, and her shoulders wilted like a flower in the afternoon sun.

Chapter 6

Ava's eyes fluttered open, and she blinked against the afternoon sun pouring through her bedroom window. Her gaze settled on the small brown bag on her dressing table. She smiled. Ben had left it sitting on her windowsill before he left the previous week. The same night she'd admitted to herself she could benefit from his help. Her trial period would expire at the end of summer, and she needed the lighthouse to pass inspection. As long as she wasn't coughing blood, the disease was in remission and not contagious. As long as she kept her distance from Ben, his health would not be compromised.

Neither would her heart.

How many nights since her father's death had she prayed in earnest for a friend? God had answered, even if Ben was of the wrong gender.

She stretched, relishing the breeze that ruffled her lacy curtains. Rest was a blessed thing. Springing out of bed, she quickly dressed, braided her hair and pinned it in a simple coif, then went outside to feed the chickens and collect eggs.

Ben had carted the kerosene and other supplies up to the watch room yesterday, so she needn't tackle that chore. He'd replaced the missing roof shingles and fixed the shed door. In a week he'd managed to do what would have taken her twice as long. She hadn't anticipated having so much time at her disposal.

While she was kneading bread dough at the kitchen table, the weeds in the garden caught her attention. She covered the dough and left it to rise while she tended to the tomatoes, squash, and beans. Every noise brought her head up and her gaze to the path that wound down the hill toward the logging camp.

Ridiculous. Ben and his crew would leave in a couple of months, and she'd go back to being alone. All winter long. She shouldn't enjoy his company so much.

When the sun lowered in the west, she went indoors, chopped vegetables for the stew, and started cooking. She planned to speak with the butcher the next time she went into town to secure enough meat to last the winter. She might even purchase venison to make jerky for Ben. After all, he was working every evening here after a full workday with his crew. The least she could do was feed him well.

Preparing for winter made heaviness settle on her chest. During the months when the lake was frozen over, she wasn't required to light the lamps at night. The Fresnel lens didn't do any good if there were no ships on the water. Most lightkeepers left their stations during winter, but she had nowhere else to go. So, she'd spend her time reading, maybe sewing a few new dresses, marking the long, lonely days in her logbook.

Last year, she'd had Father to keep her company. They'd played chess, discussed philosophy and new methods. Innovative strategies like the one being voted upon in Congress, a World's Fair. How she missed having someone to talk to, share ideas and dream with.

Which explained why her heart was sinking along with the setting sun. Ben had yet to arrive. Shaking her head, she ladled a bowl of stew, cut a slice of crispy bread, and sat at the table, staring at the empty chair across from her. She leaned over her meal and blew a breath across the steam, worry knotting in her belly.

Movement out the window caught her gaze. Inch by inch, the form of a man crested over the hill. Brown hair like chocolate streaked with caramel, broad shoulders, narrow waist, long legs.

The Dashwood sisters would be appalled by her lack of willpower.

She was appalled by her lack of willpower. However, it didn't stop her from standing so quickly she nearly knocked her chair to the floor. Or from reaching the edge of the porch in record time. She had approximately ten seconds to gather her wits before she made an imbecile of herself.

Ben waved. She put a hand to her stomach to calm her nerves. She hadn't been this anxious since she'd waited for Mr. Pickett to finish scrutinizing her through his weaselly eyes and approve her trial basis as lightkeeper.

Ben stopped in front of her, hands in his pockets, trousers filthy, dirt and debris clinging to his stained shirt. He was beautiful.

"I thought you weren't coming." So much for playing coy. She might as well have admitted she'd been waiting for him since he'd left last night.

His mouth quirked to the side. He looked down at his clothing while his palm rubbed the back of his head. Then his gaze flicked away and concentrated on something in the distance. "I came as soon as I could. We started on a new section today, and we had some issues. A man got injured."

"Is he all right?"

A dark cloud of sorrow passed through his blue eyes. "I've seen worse. It's the onset of gangrene we're concerned about."

She hooked her arm around the porch post, wanting desperately to rub away the concern etched between his brows. "What's his name? I'll pray for him."

"Jerome."

She nodded. Were those lines fanning along the skin around his eyes always there? She hadn't noticed them before.

He tipped his head back and rolled his neck. "I'd planned to replace the roof on the chicken coop, but I don't have enough daylight. I'll try again tomorrow."

His voice was somber and full of something she couldn't define. So unlike the Benjamin Colfax she knew.

He took a step backward. Then another. "Sleep well, Ava."

"Wait!" Did she have to yell? She swallowed then lowered her voice. "I made vegetable stew."

As if on cue, his stomach howled. "I promised to be gone before dusk."

That was one of the terms they'd agreed upon, but the man needed to eat. "There's time. I'll be right back."

She went to the kitchen and dished his soup. The outer layer of the bread held a perfect crispiness, while the inside was soft and pliable. The knife scraped along the wood board as she cut an extra-thick slice. She arranged everything on a simple serving tray, including a cup of milk, and pressed the screen door open with her back.

"That smells amazing." He stood from the rocking chair he'd settled in and started to take the tray from her when he noticed his dirty palms. "Um."

"There's a cake of soap by the pump to your right. I'll bring you a towel."

His boots thumped along the porch floor before they silenced in the dirt. She set the tray on the arms of the rocking chair then retrieved a small towel and her own dinner. By the time she returned, Ben waited with wet forearms and dripping fingers.

He took the offered towel and scrubbed. His muscles bulged with the action. She focused her attention on dragging a milking stool in front of the rocking chair then sitting and arranging her skirts. The glance he gave her feet didn't escape her notice. She masked a grin by spooning stew into her mouth. Would he never forget her barefoot walk along the shore?

Ben joined her. He tested the temperature of the stew then ate with gusto.

A comfortable silence fell between them as the summer sun began descending in a ball of fire, painting the sky rich shades of orange and purple. She'd always imagined sitting with a husband on such a night. Rocking babies to the sound of nature's symphony. That dream would one day die along with her. Two to three years, longer if the disease stayed clear of her organs, Lord willing.

No longer hungry, she set her bowl aside. Ben swallowed his bite. "What's wrong?"

His eyes, so earnest. "I wasn't as hungry as I thought."

He lowered his spoon and looked to the horizon. "I should go."

"Would you like more?"

The wrinkle between his brows returned. "It doesn't seem right eating like a king while Jerome is fighting to keep his leg."

A king? She was either a better cook than she thought or he'd been serious about eating beans for every meal. "Jerome's condition isn't going to change whether you fill your stomach or let it go empty. Keeping up strength for the morale of your men might make a world of difference, however."

"When you put it that way." He really shouldn't look at her like that. Like a boy fascinated by a new invention. It made her belly warm and tingly. . .and she liked it.

She retreated to the kitchen. What was she doing consorting with the enemy? Not just consorting but serving. Woolgathering. But then, the barbaric picture her father had painted of lumberjacks didn't fit Benjamin Colfax. In fact, with his strong, capable hands and genteel heart, he was becoming more and more like a hero in the novels she dearly loved. Except, she was the Beth March of this story, not the Elizabeth Bennet.

Ben opened the screen door for her as she prepared to step outside. Once both feet hit the porch floor, she handed him the tray and pointed to the lighthouse. "I need to light the lamp."

He fumbled with the tray. "I'll clean up before I leave."

That wasn't necessary, but she didn't know what to say. She couldn't very well ask him to stay and keep her company, no matter how much she wanted to. Hands clasped behind her back, nerves humming, she gave him an uncertain smile. "Be safe, Benjamin."

He nodded, and she escaped to the tower.

Chapter 7

By the flashing beacon of the lighthouse, Ben walked back around to Ava's front porch after noticing her meager woodpile. Surely, she planned to restock. Michigan winters were brutal. And long. And in her situation, he guessed, lonely. The idea of Ava up here by herself for months on end made his chest squeeze. Why she'd come to mean so much to him in such a scant amount of time he didn't know, but she had.

He remembered a summer evening much like this one when he was fifteen and restless and had ambitions to marry Suzette Dunigan, heiress of Dunigan Mills, where Ben and his father had been employed. She was three years his senior and made eyes at him every time she visited the mill. Ben's mother had followed him to the barn that night, sensing that a war raged inside her son between the child left in him and the man he was meant to become.

She'd placed her gentle hand on his shoulder. "When you meet the right woman, there will be no doubt. Being separated from her won't be an option." She kissed his cheek. "She's out there somewhere, Benjamin, waiting for you. Be patient."

Those words had stayed with him while he watched Suzette marry Allan Scott, an executive of Standard Oil's Ohio refinery and a man old enough to be her father. A dozen other women had turned his head since, but Ava. . .stubborn, quick-witted Ava. The thought of spending the grueling winter in the woods, close yet so far from her, made his stomach hitch.

A shadow inside the house passed by the open window. He cleared his throat to give her warning. "Ava?" He knocked.

She came to the screen door and fingered the strand of white wildflowers he'd tucked in the handle after he'd cleaned and dried his plate. "I thought you'd gone."

That grin, the way she ran her fingertips over the petals, was why, after a long day of cutting down trees, he walked two miles to the lighthouse to work some more.

"Does the lighthouse commission supply your firewood as well?"

She set the flowers aside. The last sliver of daylight revealed a softening of her features he'd never seen before. Oh, so beautiful.

"No. Why do you ask?"

He gave the direction his thoughts were going a mental shove. "You've barely a rick left. That won't last you a month, let alone the winter."

"I'll. . .take care of that soon."

Except, he guessed, she was only now realizing the need. "We've left plenty of stumps behind. I'll bring you wood as I can."

"I don't expect you to—"

"In exchange for borrowing a lantern to see my way back to camp." Since darkness was creeping in, he kept his voice light to reflect his teasing.

"Of course." She walked away. A few moments later, a light appeared in her open window and then moved closer. She held a lantern out for him.

His fingers scraped over hers in the exchange. Their gazes locked, and he swore the earth shifted beneath him. "It may be a week before I'm able to bring this back. I have to see a shipment to Chicago by rail."

Was her frown the result of knowing she wouldn't see him or her regret from missing the lamp? "I don't want to leave you short if you'll be needing this." He held the lantern higher.

"I have another."

"I'll bring you a load of wood when I come."

Something scraped along the floor inside, then she lowered to a sitting position. She leaned her upper body forward and rested one of her elbows on the windowsill. A gesture that looked much to him like she was preparing to stay awhile.

"Thank you for your kindness, Ben. Despite my behavior being less than welcoming."

He set the lantern on the milking stool she'd occupied earlier and eased into the rocking chair beside the window. "Less than welcoming?"

"All right, I was downright horrible." He could hear the smile in her words.

"I believe I used the word *prickly*."

She chuckled. "Ah yes. 'Prickly as a desert cactus.'"

And as he'd guessed, she was a rare beauty once she allowed herself to bloom. He couldn't say as much in the intimate setting without scaring her away. They'd come too far since their first meeting to risk her retreating now.

She sighed. "When my father took this post a year ago, he told me of a whole other breed of men who swung from trees and scalped the woods for profit. I admit, some of the stories scared me."

He leaned back and stretched his legs, crossing his ankles. "Logging is a different way of living, but it puts food on the table."

Her hand curled around the window frame. "I mean no offense. I only mentioned it to say that you don't fit his description at all. I think he was trying to scare me to protect me."

"That's what a father does. With six sisters, I've seen it often enough."

"Six?"

He grinned at her surprise. "Ten children altogether. My father was a logger too."

"Was?"

"No matter how careful you are in the job, there's always risk. A tree fell the wrong way despite a perfect cut. It crushed both of his legs."

"He's alive then?"

"And ornery as ever."

"I'm glad. With so many mouths to feed though, why take the risk?"

"It pays better than most jobs in the area. He sacrificed for his family."

A beat of silence passed. "You wanted to honor your father by going into the same profession?"

Now she was trying her hand at fishing. And she'd hooked him in the softest part. The part where a man's dreams, his self-worth, resided. "I'm the oldest son. Someone had to work when Dad couldn't."

The flash of light from the tower lit her face enough for him to distinguish the small O shape of her lips. He rushed to add, "I'm not all that honorable."

"You replace roof shingles, deliver supplies, mend chicken coops, and stock wood for a person you barely know. That sounds honorable to me."

Now was when he'd like to take that reverence a little further and ask to court her properly. Under normal circumstances he'd ask her father but. . . . He pivoted the rocking chair to face her and leaned forward on his knees. "How is it you've come to be alone up here? If I'm not mistaken, that pretty accent is southern."

"South Carolina." She sat straight, creeping back into the darkness of the house so that he couldn't make out her features. "My father felt it best we move north. In April, he went fishing. On Tuesday, as normal. There was an accident. He got trapped beneath his boat. The doctor wouldn't allow me to see him after. . . He returned his clothing."

The chair creaked a bit, and he imagined her relaxing against it. "Silly, but a part of me has always wondered if they made a mistake. Sometimes I imagine him pulling his johnboat up to our dock and everything returning to the way it was."

"Not silly at all."

She leaned against the windowsill. His lantern light flickered across her face. "But I know he's gone. I feel it, here." She placed a palm over her breast. "Somehow I managed to coerce the lighthouse commission to let me stay on a trial basis with the intent of making this my permanent station. Even if the job comes with a few prickles."

And because she had nowhere else to go. He wanted nothing but the best for this woman. He opened his mouth to say as much when her chair scraped across the floor once again.

"With that, I must get back to my duties."

He'd worn out his welcome. But she'd made strides in her trust of him tonight, and that's what mattered. "I'll see you when I return. Good night, Ava."

Ben couldn't make the trip to Chicago and back fast enough.

Ben had lain awake all night, yet his mind had never been clearer. He breathed in the foggy air of dawn and the loamy scent of earth, and a sense of right coursed through him. For the first time in years, he knew what he wanted and he was going after it. When Christopher had met him in Saginaw a few weeks ago, he'd offered Ben a position as foreman on his crew, building churches and multilevel immigrant houses from Carnegie steel. At the time, he couldn't envision himself overseeing construction. He was a logger, not an architect.

But Ava had changed everything.

He'd taken his time walking back to camp last night, going back over their conversation, savoring every word. The glimpse of her youthful, untamed spirit combined with her tender refinement made his head swim. His mother had been right. He knew Ava was the one he'd been waiting for.

They would never live like the Vanderbilts, but Ben could offer her more than she had now. Protection, a partner to walk through life beside her and take care of the big things. Love. A modest home in New York City filled with a beautiful woman he loved and a few children sounded all right by him. It sure beat a future in a logging camp with a bunch of smelly men.

He was getting too far ahead of himself. Ava hadn't even agreed to let him court her yet. He hadn't even asked. However, that spark of attraction between them had blazed last night, and he was confident she wouldn't turn him down. Though, knowing Ava, she'd make it difficult and he'd have to persist.

The mule, already hitched and waiting, brayed. McGurdy emerged from the trees on the west side of the bunkhouse, tugging at his drawers. Ben waved his hand to gain the man's attention. "Yates is overseeing the north fork while I'm gone. Your men are on cleanup."

McGurdy's lips folded in a frown. "Cleanup?"

"Removing stumps, burning brush. . .you know, cleanup." Ben checked the saddle then swung his leg over.

McGurdy's cheeks bunched as if Ben had lost his mind. "Why?"

"The land commission is selling this property as farmland once we're done. Cut the stumps and split them into firewood. Burn the brush."

"Firewood?" The man shook his head. "We always leave things as is. Farmland or not."

"Not this time, Gurt. We have a customer."

"Who?"

"The she-spirit."

Ben kicked his heels and left McGurdy to scratch at his graying whiskers.

Chapter 8

Ava curled her fingers around the railing of the parapet and looked down at the treetops below. Or what she could see through the gunmetal fog hovering over the green mounds. She licked her parched lips and closed her eyes against the ache in her head and chest. The early morning sun warmed her shoulders, bringing both comfort and more pain.

She was glad Ben wasn't here to see her like this. Her health had taken a downturn the day he left, solidifying her resolve to keep him at a distance.

She'd come so close to giving in to his vivid blue eyes, to the very man who contradicted everything her father had told her. But she would not be drawn in again only to be rejected, and that's exactly what would happen when Ben discovered she had tuberculosis. She had no future with Ben. Or any man.

As soon as he returned, she would thank him for his kindness, offer him a wage for his work, and send him on with his life. The risk of the townsfolk or the lighthouse commission finding out her secret was too great. She had to keep it hidden as long as she possibly could.

Her upper body swayed over the railing. With a couple of well-placed steps, she wouldn't have to suffer anymore. No struggling for breath, no skin sores like she'd read about in a medical journal at the Charleston Library back home. No spending her final days in a sanatorium, alone.

A cough racked her body, sending her back against the glass panels of the lantern room. Each breath held a wheeze and a prayer. Tears slipped down her cheeks. Why had her mind taken such a dark path? Life and death were controlled by the Lord and weren't meant for human tampering. Yes, she was scared. Terrified of what lay ahead. *Though I walk through the valley of the shadow of death, I will fear no evil: for thou art with me.*

Crossing over into heaven with a new and perfect body wasn't the dilemma. The trouble was what would happen to her until she reached that golden shore.

Ben's kind eyes materialized in her memory. What a profound effect he'd had on her in such a short time. Then again, she'd been living alone for five months with virtually no human contact. Would he have warmed the frozen parts of her heart under normal circumstances? She didn't know, and it didn't matter. These weren't normal circumstances. She had to let Ben go.

She stood, gripping the windows for balance as she made her way back to the lantern room. Another cough stole through her. Her pulse throbbed in her temples. Sweat trickled down her face. With a quick glance at the wick to make sure the flame had been exterminated, she sat down on the top step and scooted down the spiral on her bottom.

The feat seemed to last an hour. If she could just get to the house and boil her lemon, ginger, and honey tea, she could crawl into bed and pray for a swift exit. Forcing one foot in front of the other, she bypassed the kitchen and collapsed beneath her blankets.

Ben stepped out of the river and dried off, shivering. Night sounds chorused all around him. It would be dark soon. He preferred not to wait this late to bathe, but the grime of travel and coal dust were marking his skin, and sleep wouldn't be pleasant if it lingered. Scrubbing the towel across his wet hair, he replayed his conversation with Christopher over the telephone at the Chicago Woldendorph Hotel. Talking into a cone attached to a box on the wall was something Ben doubted he'd ever feel comfortable with.

The position at the New York Machinery and Construction Company promised better wages and a modest home in a safe, gas-lighted neighborhood in upper Manhattan. Ben had accepted the job. A thrum of possibilities lay before him.

First, he had to convince Ava to share his new life with him.

He dressed, regretting not arriving early enough to fit in a visit to her before dark. The lantern he still needed to return lit his path back to camp. The flicker of fire was the first thing to catch his notice, followed by the slur of a bow across fiddle strings and clapping in time to the rhythm. Two nights in the hotel had been peaceful but vastly different from what he was used to.

Stumps sanded to a smooth plane made tables for the men to play cards. Saturday nights were quiet in Presque Isle. No brothels, gaming halls, or other seedy places to fall into mischief, which was fine by Ben. So, the men created their own entertainment the best they could. As long as they were sober, rested, and ready to work come Monday morning, Ben left them to their own devices.

"Boss!" Gentry raised his mug in salute then pointed to the empty spot across from him. "Help me regain my dignity."

Terrell laughed. "What he means is, help him win back the five dollars he just lost."

Gentry waved off Terrell's comment. "I let you win. That way you'd have enough money to go into town for a bath and a good shave."

"You'd been better off saving it for your own hygiene." Terrell added coffee to whatever else was in his mug. From the smell of it, it was something strong. "Whole camp's talkin' 'bout how bad you smell."

Ben turned down Gentry's offer of cards and left the men to their insults. He settled in front of the fire, his back against a log. Fingers linked behind his head, he closed his eyes and thought of Ava.

His eyes snapped open. Something wasn't right. He scanned the group of men. The darkened edge of the woods. The horizon.

There.

The flashing beam of light that brushed the treetops every night wasn't there. He squinted, waiting for the rotating beam to make its way around. It never came. A boulder materialized in Ben's gut. Ava staked her life by that light. Something had to be very, very wrong.

He jumped up, grabbed the lantern, and took off toward the lighthouse. The fiddling slurred to a stop. "Boss? What's wrong?"

The men began stirring.

"Nature calls," Ben shouted over his shoulder. That should keep anyone from following him.

Not long into the journey his lungs began to burn. The flame in his lantern flickered with his movements. No matter what, he couldn't stop now. Had she been injured? Attacked? The thought of either one made the meat loaf dinner he'd had in town sour in his gut. He hadn't realized until that moment how comforting her light was in the night sky. Like being near her when he couldn't be.

He reached the lighthouse after what seemed like an eternity. His fears were confirmed—no lights came from the tower or the house. "Ava?"

His voice echoed in the black night.

With the lantern held high, he crept toward the front door. Ava's boots rested on their sides, as if kicked off without care. The screen door allowed the night air to circulate inside the house. All was silent. "Ava, it's me, Ben."

Nothing.

His hand hovered over the handle. Should he go inside? His intentions were only to make sure she was safe, but getting caught in her home, uninvited, could change her opinion of him forever. But that boulder in his gut wasn't going away. Her well-being was worth the risk.

The screen door creaked against the motion. His boot met the hardwood floor with a groan. His first instinct was to call again, but what if she had been attacked and her attacker was still here? He certainly didn't want to give the scum any warning.

The lantern cast little illumination around the room. From what he could tell, everything was in its place. He wished he had his pistol. Adrenaline had overpowered his good sense. Though he carried it mostly to protect against panthers in the woods, it would be most convenient now.

A noise came from the back of the house, followed by a cough. He eased his way down the hall until the noise grew louder. To his right, a door lay open, allowing the wheezy noise to escape. Ben lifted his lantern. A lumpy shadow lay on the bed.

"Ava? It's me, Ben." No reply. He took a step forward. "I'm not here to hurt you. I noticed the lamp in the tower hadn't been lit, and I—"

The words died on his tongue. Her ashen face lay against the pillow. Even with her eyes closed, he could tell they were swollen and red. Her lips dry. Sweat beaded her forehead and soaked her hairline.

For a moment all he could do was blink. She'd had a cough, yes, but the woman before him looked to be at death's door.

He set the lantern on her bedside table and took her hand. She stirred but didn't look at him. He touched her cheek. Like hot coals. He grabbed the lantern, searched the house for matches, a bowl for water, a cup, and a rag. He lit the oil lamp he'd found in the kitchen, bathing the room in gold. Each labored breath made his heart squeeze.

In a calm voice he was far from feeling, he spoke to her while he plunged the rag into cool water and then laid it across her forehead. She shivered. Her eyelids fluttered open. She stared at him as if unsure if this was a dream or reality. He sat on the edge of her bed, dunked the rag again, then dabbed at her cheeks, her neck, her lips. The intimate gesture was lost in the direness of the moment. He repeated his ministrations several times until she began to rally.

"The lamp," she whispered, barely audible.

"It can wait. You're burning up. I need to get you cooled down so I can fetch the doctor."

She shook her head. Or maybe it was another shiver.

A cough unlike any he'd ever heard before had her struggling for several seconds. He helped her drink. Most of the water dribbled out the sides of her mouth. He wiped them with the rag.

She swallowed. Gasped for air. "The lamp." She tried to push herself up but couldn't.

"Rest, Ava."

"Merchant ships coming." She exhaled a wheeze. "People might die."

Yes, if the lighthouse wasn't operating, there was a chance lives could be lost. But if he left her to save those lives, her life might be the cost. He knew nothing about sickness, but he knew this was serious.

119

He plunged the rag again. Her hand, weak and warm, touched his arm. "Please. . .Ben."

Like he could deny her anything.

He took a deep breath, saddened that he could breathe so easily while she fought. "I'll do my best."

"Thank. You." Her eyelids fell, and her breaths, though still loud, evened in sleep.

Blast. He snatched the lantern and hurried through the passageway that went from the house to the tower. The metal spiral stairs bonged with each heavy step as he raced to the top. He had no idea what he was doing; he just knew he couldn't let her down.

He entered the small room beneath the huge lens where Ava had asked him to put the supplies the day he'd delivered them with the wagon. His fingers brushed over the gears and pulleys of the mechanism while his eyes followed their path. There might not be enough oil in the lamp to burn all night, but it should last long enough to fetch the doctor.

He struck a match and held it to the wick. It ignited, and he squinted against the blazing light. The crank turned easily in his grip. He hoped this was the level the lamp needed to be in order to shine its brightest.

Ben was halfway down the stairs when he realized he'd left the traveling lantern behind. Swallowing a groan, he raced back up, grabbed the lamp, and hurried to the house. Ava's condition was no better when he returned. Not that he'd expected it to be. She needed a doctor and needed one fast.

He soaked the rag once more and kissed her forehead before covering the spot where his lips had been. Lips warm from her fevered brow. He turned to go.

"Ben," she whispered.

He leaned over her.

"Thank you."

"Don't thank me yet."

Chapter 9

I have consumption." Ava bowed her head. Tears dropped onto her nightgown. How had she gotten into her nightgown? All she remembered was extinguishing the lamp and then falling into bed. Her lungs burned and her head threatened to explode.

"Hmm." The doctor rummaged in his bag and pulled out a brown bottle of liquid. He pointed at her handkerchief. "Have you expectorated blood?"

"No."

"Have you ever?"

She shook her head and instantly regretted it.

"When were you diagnosed?"

"Almost two years ago." She didn't want to talk. Didn't want to rehash the details, the pain, the inevitable.

"But no blood?"

"No."

He scratched his chin. "Does the cough ever go away?"

She leaned back into her pillow. "Sometimes it goes away almost entirely." And for a time she'd feel like a normal woman again with youth and energy and dreams. She coughed, and her lungs burned like fire. "Then it returns, and I'll cough for two, three months straight."

She hacked for several minutes, the conversation too much to handle.

"Cool, dry air is the best environment for those with tuberculosis. It makes it harder for the bacteria to spread."

She inhaled. Her breaths sounded like marbles rattling in a jar. "I nearly freeze in the winter from keeping windows open."

He sat on the edge of her bed. The mattress shifted with his weight. He wasn't much older than her, but gray threads peppered his temples. "Does woodsmoke aggravate the cough?"

She thought for a moment. "Yes."

He opened the bottle and poured a spoonful. "Here."

She swallowed the medicine. Horrible.

"It'll make you sleepy, but it'll open up your lungs enough to rest."

"Thank you for coming." The words scratched against her throat. And thank God for Ben.

The doctor laid a brotherly hand on her shoulder and gave it a pat. "I'll be back to check on you."

The covers came up to her chin. Her vision blurred. The burn in her lungs eased. In her head, she sent another grateful prayer heavenward for Ben before the bliss of sleep overtook her.

Ben's head came up at the sound of the doctor emerging from Ava's room. He hopped to his feet. "How is she?"

The man tucked a hand into his trouser pocket while the other wrapped around the handle of his bag. "Convinced she has tuberculosis."

Ben's throat ran dry. "Does she?"

Doctor Hoffman stopped by a high-back chair, put down his bag, opened it, and retrieved two bottles. "May I inquire as to the nature of your relationship with Miss Ryan?"

Ben stuttered. "Miss Ryan and I became acquainted last month through an. . . occupational agreement."

"And yet you happened to be around last evening to know she was in need of a doctor."

Ben's face heated, not only from embarrassment but from anger at what the man was implying. "I was in the logging camp when I noticed the lamp wasn't burning. I knew something was wrong. Ava would never abandon her post or endanger the lives on those ships. Knowing she lives alone, it's my duty to check on her."

"You know Miss Ryan quite well then?" His eyebrows rose over gold spectacles.

Ben took a step forward. "My crew isn't the only company out here. A single woman, isolated, with hundreds of lonely men surrounding these woods, means trouble. I came to ensure her safety. Nothing more."

The doctor stared at Ben, seeming to glimpse into his soul. After a few moments, he said, "I believe you." He approached Ben, both bottles extended. "That woman in there is too sick and speaks too highly of you for anything else."

Ben's shoulders relaxed. "Does she have consumption?"

"Her symptoms are similar, but no, I'm not convinced she has the disease."

Ben's spirit grew buoyant but sank again when he reminded himself that if it wasn't tuberculosis, something else serious plagued her.

"I'd like to continue monitoring her. With her consent, even take a sample of blood when she's feeling better. Then we'll know for sure. In the meantime, give her this when the cough becomes unbearable." He pointed to the brown bottle. "It'll relax the bronchial tubes and help her sleep. This one"—he pointed to the bluish bottle—"is camphor. Put a few drops on a dry cloth and have her inhale it. If the fever gets out of control, send for me."

He turned to leave, but Ben stopped him. "Is there a woman in town, a nurse maybe, who can stay with her? With all due respect, I have a crew to manage, and it wouldn't be appropriate for me to stay long enough for her to recover."

A slow smile curled up the side of the doctor's mouth, twitching his brown mustache. "With all due respect, Mr. Colfax, propriety is no longer a concern. Your presence here overnight has already compromised her reputation."

He held up a hand as Ben's mouth opened to retort. "I know you're both innocent. But Mrs. Harris, the owner of the boardinghouse you awoke last night, doesn't. She gets word around town faster than the *Gazette*. She knows you stayed the night here while I was at the Grandy farm delivering a baby."

The man looked at the mantel clock. "I'd say everyone in Presque Isle knows by now."

Ben's throat constricted. "That's crazy. She needed help." His fists clenched, so he flexed his fingers. "Sometimes a situation calls for human compassion above proper etiquette."

The doctor closed his bag and nodded. "I agree. But sometimes human compassion still lands us in the judgment seat. Just ask Jesus."

Air escaped Ben's lungs.

Truth hit him square between the eyes.

The doctor grasped his bag and walked to the door.

"What do I do?" The last thing he wanted was for Ava to lose her reputation. Why hadn't he knocked on every door in town until he found a woman willing to care for her?

Doctor Hoffman's hand curled around the door handle. "There's a pretty young woman in there you're fond enough of to check on during the night. A young woman who will be shunned from polite society while you move on to the next town. I guess the question is, how deep does your compassion run?"

Ben closed his eyes and pinched the bridge of his nose.

The doctor cleared his throat. "I suggest you marry Ava. Take a few days off and care for your bride. I doubt your boss will fault you for that."

Ben heard the door open then close with a soft click.

So much for courtship. What if she refused him? Could she afford to? If word of what didn't happen reached her superiors, she'd lose her position. If she lost her position, she'd be forced onto the streets. She might find someone to take her in; she might not. Marrying him was her best option.

He moved to the high-back chair and sank onto it. There was no doubt in his mind he wanted to spend the rest of his life with this woman. But did he want her marrying him because she had no other choice?

No.

Minutes passed into hours as he paced the parlor. A photograph beneath the lamp caught his eye. He lifted the picture and nearly choked. The mudslide last spring, the man he couldn't save, stared back at him. Though the man's features had been unrecognizable that day, though Ben had let others take the body into town while he dug out some of his own men, he knew by the way his gut turned over that this was that same man. He knew by the *R* embroidered on the oilskin cap. *R* for Ryan.

Bile burned his throat. The man had been Ava's father.

The battle of indecision in his mind was over. He may have failed to save Mr. Ryan that day, but he would not fail the man's daughter.

Heavy coughing had him returning the picture to the table. He trudged to the kitchen and made tea as the doctor had suggested. While it steeped, he rummaged for a cloth and then dropped the liquid from the blue bottle onto the middle. With a deep breath and a silent prayer, he went to Ava's bedroom and knocked three times before entering.

She was propped against the bed, but her head was heavy against the pillow. Her dark locks, usually tamed, were wild and loose around her shoulders, the threads near her scalp wet from fever. Flushed cheeks. Pale lips. Bloodshot eyes. Beautiful as ever.

"The doctor left. He said when you woke to have you drink some of this tea and breathe the camphor on the rag."

At the sound of his voice, her head turned slightly to face him. The hazy look in her dark irises cleared. She pulled the blankets up to her chin, but not before he noticed the delicate lace at her throat. The same lace that trimmed her sleeves. Her cheeks grew even darker.

He set the fragile cup on her bedside table, near a chair with her dress draped over it. Oh. He swallowed. How had he failed to notice that Ava was in her nightdress the whole time?

This was going to make what came next even more awkward.

She sucked in a raspy breath. Coughed. "What are you doing here?"

He swallowed. "I came to ask if you'll do me the honor of becoming my wife."

Chapter 10

Ava was a bride. Something she thought she'd never be this side of heaven. Especially when the ceremony took place while she was in bed, in her plainest dress, hours past a fever.

Pastor Jack finished his prayer with an "amen" and reached for Ben's hand. "Congratulations, Mr. Colfax." He patted her arm. "Mrs. Colfax."

She fought the urge to roll her eyes. Ben, despite what a fine figure he cut in his suit, was insane. He'd insisted on marriage despite her diagnosis. Everything in her rejected the idea, but he was right. A tarnished reputation would destroy her position here, ruin all she'd worked so hard for. This illness was just a precursor of what was to come. His presence would, no doubt, be helpful.

Ava offered a weak smile at the pastor. The blond mustache that almost covered his top lip lifted. "I'll see my way out."

The pastor's footsteps grew fainter until she and Ben were left in silence. A silence so heavy it coated the room like molasses. What did she say to a husband she'd had little choice but to marry?

Ben shifted from one foot to the other. "Now that you're on the mend, I should get back to work. Do you need anything before I go?"

Her heart sank. Apparently he didn't know the right words either. "No."

Good heavens, she squeaked like a frightened mouse.

He ran a hand over the back of his head. "I'll return around dusk."

She chewed her bottom lip, sore from dryness.

He nodded, opened his mouth as if to say more, then closed it and backed out of the room. The boyish glint in his eyes had her fighting a grin despite the horrid circumstances surrounding this day. They'd come to an unconventional agreement, however, both promising not to expect anything from the other when it came to duties or love. Ben realized a simple kiss from her would be deadly. It wasn't hard for a man to accept the terms under those conditions.

She coughed until she saw stars. Ben returned with a cup of steaming tea. He'd changed into brown trousers that were thinning and torn in spots and a tan shirt rolled to his elbows.

He handed her the cup. "I left the kettle on the stove to warm in case you want more while I'm gone."

"Thank you," she wheezed. The liquid traced a path down her throat and into her chest.

"Well, good-bye. . .Ava."

Her name melted on his lips as if savoring it like one of his New York candies. She smiled. That seemed to be enough for him, and he left.

She drank the tea, her mind swirling. How quickly a person's life could change with one moment of time. First with her diagnosis then again with her father's death. Today, with the vows she'd spoken before God. Oh, how she wished her father were here now. And how she wished her husband had married her for love and not out of obligation.

Ben tethered his mule by the logging wagon for the first time as a married man. He still couldn't believe it. When he'd proposed, Ava had gaped and sputtered and mumbled something about the fever causing hallucinations. He'd given her time to think on it, then asked again, hours later, when he brought her broth and more tea. He'd listened to her excuses. She'd listened to his logic. They'd both agreed on fetching the preacher.

Still, he was torn. Given time, they'd grow to love each other, he had no doubt. But the courting, the ceremony, none of it had turned out like it should. Specifically, his wedding night. He'd go home at dusk, tired and dirty, to a wife he couldn't touch.

Ben had visited the doctor with more questions when he'd gone into town for Pastor Jack. The man was wise in his field, according to the certificate on the wall from Boston University School of Medicine. He'd answered Ben's questions with patience and declared he still wasn't convinced Ava had tuberculosis.

Ava was convinced, however, so Ben would spend his nights in her father's old bedroom, alone, praying the doctor's hunch was right.

A forceful slap hit his shoulder. McGurdy smiled, revealing the space between his front teeth. "You really get hitched this morning?"

"I did." He couldn't help but grin.

Other men nearby heard the exchange and started toward them.

James, who didn't look a day over fifteen, scratched his chin. "What are you doing here then?"

Ben pulled his lunch box and canteen from his pack. "I've been gone for three days."

"But it's your wedding day." James's twisted mouth said Ben had clearly lost his mind.

"I've a job to do." Ben walked toward a stump and sat. He'd been too nervous for breakfast and now his stomach protested.

Terrell propped a dirty boot on the stump Ben had just vacated. "Did no one explain things to you? Your job is to—"

McGurdy stopped Terrell's next words with a none-too-gentle push to his chest. "Not to worry. Ben'll be announcing a wee bairn before we know it."

Fire ignited Ben's face and roared to his ears, his neck, his chest. His gut.

He wouldn't dare hope for such things. "Get back to work. Let me eat in peace."

His words came out gruffer than he'd intended. The men looked at each other then filed away, some shaking their heads, others whispering God only knew what. All except McGurdy, who was never one to let things drop. They'd worked together far too many years for that.

"Who is this woman who's appeared out of nowhere? Is she a gal from home?" Always suspicious. And nosy.

Ben swallowed his bite of cheese sandwich. "Ava Ryan. The lightkeeper."

McGurdy's hat came off, and he scratched his head beneath thinning hair. "How did you. . . ?" He straightened. Slammed the hat back onto his head. "The she-spirit."

Laughter rumbled from deep in Ben's throat at the bug-eyed shock on McGurdy's unshaven face. "The very one."

Ben explained about Ava gathering supplies from the old lighthouse. By the time he finished revealing the haunting attack, tears dripped from his eyes and his stomach burned from laughter.

A string of Scottish expletives ensued. McGurdy swiped the last of the sandwich from Ben's hand and ate it as he stormed away. He'd calm down after a few days. The man never stayed mad for long.

Now, to get this workday over with so he could go to camp one more time, gather the last of his belongings, and get home to his wife.

Not to brag, but her biscuits smelled like heaven. Ava's stomach growled as she spied the light, fluffy disks baked to golden perfection. All she'd eaten for days was bone broth, toast, and honey-ginger tea. She had an appetite the size of Lake Huron, and if Ben didn't come down from the tower soon, he was in danger of not getting any breakfast.

The mere thought of him turned her hunger into butterflies. At first, she'd been too sick to think much about the marriage. As her strength returned, however, as her strength grew, so did her awareness of him.

Though tall and strong, his gentle nature and the tenderness with which he'd cared for her during her illness endeared him to her more. Every evening for the past week, he'd come home, washed up under the well pump outside—the very one she could see through her bedroom window—and brought their meals to her room. He sat in a chair next to her bed, and while they ate, he'd ask her questions. Questions about her childhood, her parents, what books she liked to read. She asked him about his siblings and his favorite meals.

And then, after working all day, he went up to the tower and lit the lamp for her.

Today was the first day she felt like getting out of bed, and she was determined to show her gratitude by fixing him a nice meal. That was all the further she could go with him. If she gave him anything more, she might fall stupidly in love. And that wouldn't fare well for either one of them.

The hallway door that led to the passageway between the house and the tower opened and closed. Two thumps indicated Ben's boots coming off. She poured two cups of coffee and turned to set them on the table.

Ben walked in and released a mighty yawn while rubbing his eyes. When he spotted her, he blinked. "What are you doing up?"

"If I lay on that mattress any longer, I'll stick to it." Her voice was still raspy, and the fluid in her lungs still caused a cough, but she'd greatly improved. The doctor confirmed she wasn't contagious right now and had encouraged her to take a new blood test that would determine for sure if she had the disease. She'd promised to consider it.

Ben inched closer until their toes met. The whites of his eyes were red. "Some of your color is back." He craned his neck to see over her shoulder. "Your hair looks nice down."

She'd forgotten to pin it up. After a bath to wash away the grime and sweat from fever, she realized how late it had gotten and rushed to dress and make breakfast. Unsure how to react to his twitching fingers and the appreciation in his eyes, she returned to the stove.

"I hope you like sausage and eggs. And biscuits, I made them too. If you prefer milk over coffee, let me know." She busied her hands by dishing the food.

"I'll be satisfied with whatever you offer."

She gulped. Good thing her back was to him.

Chair legs screeched against the floor. Willing her hands to remain steady, she carried the plates to the table and placed one in front of him.

"Thank you." Was his voice always this husky?

On trembling legs, weakness left over from the fever, and nerves, she settled in the chair across from him. He reached across the table, palm up. She looked at it, at him, then at his hand again.

"Grace."

Of course. How silly of her.

She placed her palm in his, and his warm fingers curled around her hand. She bowed her head but didn't hear a word. All she could do was marvel at how big his hand was compared to hers, and how the rough texture of his calluses soothed her worries. When his thumb rubbed circles on her knuckles, she lost all concentration.

"Ava?"

Her head jerked up.

"Are you all right?"

He must have ended the prayer and she'd missed it. She yanked her hand away. "I'm fine."

"I retract my earlier statement. Quite a bit of your color is back."

Oh, the man. He chuckled then dove into his food.

When he stood to retrieve seconds, she decided to retract her earlier statement too. No matter how starving she was, she could never out-eat him. "Can I bring you more?" he asked over his shoulder.

"No, thank you." She'd barely finished five bites.

He returned to the table. "I sent a letter to my parents yesterday, letting them know we were married."

She downed her coffee. She had no idea what it was like to come from a large family, but she imagined they were protective of Ben and would probably despise her for trapping him into a marriage guaranteed to make him a widower.

He waited for her response.

"Your family sounds lovely. It's a shame we couldn't tell them in person." She didn't really mean it. That would be terrifying.

"I'm glad you said that." He worked on his sausage. His Adam's apple bobbed in his thick neck as he swallowed. My stars, why did she notice that?

He shifted in his seat. "I've had a job offer from New York Machinery and Construction Company in New York City. As soon as I wrap up work with this crew at the end of September, we'll be moving to a nice place in upper Manhattan. You can meet my family then."

The room swayed. "Moving. To New York?"

Ben nodded, smiling as if he'd done something to be proud of.

"Moving."

Her thoughts must've played on her face, because he set down his fork and pressed his back against the chair. "Uh. . .now that we're married you needn't be burdened with the upkeep of the lighthouse. I'll take care of you, Ava. The job pays better than I make now, and I'll make sure you're provided for."

The food before her may as well have been rotten. She pushed away from the table and retreated to her bedroom. No matter how hard she tried to hold them in, tears broke through anyway. She'd gone from dying to married in a matter of days, and now they were moving? He hadn't even asked her thoughts on the matter. She was just expected to obey and go. Well, she wasn't strong and brave like Sarah or Rebecca from the Bible.

"I didn't mean to upset you." Ben's hands cupped her shoulders.

"I can't go." She dabbed her cheeks with the back of her hand.

"I know you're used to taking care of yourself, and you've done a fine job, but let me take over now. We won't have servants or a vault full of gold, but I've saved some money, and we'll have a nice home."

His arms moved to her elbows, and he leaned to meet her at eye level. "They have gas-lighted neighborhoods. Can you imagine? There's an ice cream shop nearby we can walk to whenever your heart desires."

He talked about their future as if she were going to live. As it was, she couldn't be around other people for fear of spreading her disease. Besides, from what she'd read in the newspaper, parts of the city were already full of consumption.

She'd buried her father here. She'd planned to be buried next to him.

"I'm not moving to New York."

Chapter 11

Ben thought she'd be pleased. Relieved that she no longer had to carry the burden of providing for her own needs. She'd have a loving husband, a home with modern conveniences close to doctors should she need them. Instead, she was angry. Seething. And more desirable than ever. Which was maddening, since she'd barely spoken to him in a week. Now that her illness had subsided, that fiery spirit he loved about her raged.

He tossed the last of the split logs into the wagon bed. August was winding down, cooling the temperature to a comfortable level. He was looking forward to not spending another winter in these woods. Though it might be more tolerable than spending it with a contentious woman. In fact, he was pretty sure there was a Bible verse on that.

Ava stood by the mule, drinking deeply from her canteen. Fool woman insisted on coming with him. Not because she wanted his company. More like she wanted to do her share of the work so she'd be less beholden to him. He wished his father were here to give advice. God knew Ben needed it.

He retrieved his own canteen from the pack, missing the camaraderie they'd shared only weeks ago that night on the porch. Only this time, he wouldn't be confined to the outdoors. His fingers still itched to plunge into her long dark hair. Hair she'd made sure to pin up ever since his compliment. "Stubborn."

"What?" Ava turned. The dark green skirt pinching her small waist pronounced the curve of her hips. Something he was free to appreciate now. His fingers started twitching again, so he concentrated on untethering the mule.

In the few seconds it had taken him to do the job, Ava had climbed into the wagon and settled herself on the seat. *Stubborn* wasn't a strong enough word.

He followed suit, making sure he sat close enough that their thighs touched, just to irritate her. Her spine straightened and her nose rose in the air. He suppressed a grin. Before he could flick the reins, she stole them from his hands. Fine, if that's how she wanted to play.

She mimicked his gesture for setting the mule in motion, but the animal didn't budge. She tried again. Her lips pursed, as if determined to keep from asking for help. The next time she tried, he made a kissing noise that set the beast to plodding. The jolt threw her back against the seat and into the curve of his arm resting along it.

She stiffened. Put several inches of space between her body and his arm.

His parents were always touching, teasing, kissing. Which explained ten children. Had their relationship started this way? Would Ava ever relax enough to let him love her?

At the crest of the hill, the mule slowed to a stop. Ava glanced at him, brow furrowed. She flicked the reins. Did so again, imitating his kissing noise. Nothing. She tossed the reins down and climbed out. Her skirt caught, ripping the hem, as she stomped toward the mule. She looked down. Frowned. Fists clenched, she faced the mule, gripped the harness, and tugged.

Nothing.

Her cheeks grew redder with every attempt. "Oh, come on. . .you." She glared at Ben. "What do you call this thing?"

"Ava." Ben cleared his throat. "I call her Ava."

If he thought he'd seen her mad before, he'd been mistaken.

"May I?" He held up the reins.

"Go ahead. I'm walking." Chin raised, she started up the hill, the ends of her shawl flapping behind her. The mule obeyed him without protest, and Ben couldn't help thinking the beast behaved better than his wife.

They moved along, side by side, for several minutes before he spoke. "I'll stop whenever you'd like to get back on."

"No thank you."

At least she was speaking to him. "Have you given any more thought to the blood test?" The fear of contracting tuberculosis was the only thing holding him back from kissing away her ire.

"No."

He huffed. "Why are you being thick-skulled about this? And about moving? I don't understand."

She increased her speed.

So did he. "Blast it, Ava. We're married. We've got to start talking things through. If you tell me what you're thinking, maybe it'll help me understand."

She stopped and whirled toward him. "I don't want to waste my time when I already know what the test is going to say."

He stopped the mule.

"My doctor back home has been seeing patients for almost fifty years. He treated thousands of soldiers during the war. He's seen consumption more times than he can count." Tears streamed down her cheeks. "I can't begin to explain what I felt when he told me I had tuberculosis. Everything inside of me died. I lost my fiancé. My home. All to travel to some remote place to carry out the rest of my days.

"I lost my father." Her chin quivered. "I refuse to allow even a spark of hope that I don't have the disease to fill my heart, only to be told for a second time that I'm dying. I can't go through that again."

A sob escaped her lips. Ben stood to make his way out of the wagon but stopped when she threw out her palm. "My father is buried here, Ben. I'm not leaving him. And when it's my time. . .I want to be laid right beside him."

She lifted her shawl and dabbed her cheeks. "If New York means that much to you, go."

Ben lowered back to the bench and watched her walk away from him, his heart twisting. He'd had no idea the turmoil she'd carried with her the past week. He'd only wanted the best for her, but maybe his best wasn't what she needed.

The spark of hope that she might have a chance at life wouldn't be silenced within him though. What if she didn't have consumption? What if the illness she had could be managed or cured? Then she could be on the road to living. They could travel that road together.

The angry thunderheads rolling in from the north said everything Ava was feeling in her heart. She stood on the parapet, hand gripping the railing, watching the ships slice through the water. She'd gotten little sleep after they unloaded the firewood. She shouldn't have exposed so much of her soul to this man she barely knew. Her wounds were raw once again.

There were worse things than a life in New York City. But it could never hold for her what it did for others. Not when she was confined socially.

Then, there was Ben. She wanted to open up to him completely, wanted the freedom to fall in love and become everything a wife should be, but not only could she not risk her heart, she couldn't risk his life.

Restless, moody, and disappointed, she welcomed the cold rain pelting her body.

She went inside, praying for the sailors' wisdom and for the protection of all lives aboard the ships. The shelter of the watch room gave her little comfort. She lifted the can of kerosene to fill the lamp, only it had already been filled. Despite her nastiness toward Ben, he continued to be kind. Guilt churned her stomach.

The iron stairs vibrated with heavy footfalls. She whirled away, busying her hands with restacking the already stacked cans of kerosene. The loose bun at her nape came undone. Too late to mess with it now. Ben entered the small room, and she needed to concentrate on making sure the cans were in perfect lines.

He didn't speak. He didn't need to. His hulking presence was palpable. The scent of him, all pine and earth and sweat. Her back burned with the intensity of his gaze she couldn't see but knew was there. The goose bumps on her arms told her as much.

His breaths came slowly, deeply. If he didn't leave soon, he might fog up the lenses. Then she noticed the quick rise and fall of her chest. Or maybe she would. She placed a hand on her fluttering stomach. His big warm hands rested on her shoulders. She jumped. Did she want to run away or lean into him? She held her breath, doing nothing.

"I'm sorry." His voice held such regret, such tenderness, it caused the air she'd been holding to release.

He sighed. "I didn't try to see things from your side. What you've been through... and losing your father. I never meant to hurt you."

Tears pushed at the backs of her eyes. She had never heard such a sincere apology. Her brain failed to form a reply. Then a pin slipped, and her hair fell down her back. His fingers untwisted the knots. Her scalp tingled. And she thought she had goose bumps before.

Something soft yet firm touched the left side of her crown. His cheek?

"I'm sorry," he whispered.

She closed her eyes, unable to tolerate the sadness in his tone. Before she could stop herself, she relaxed against him. He kissed her temple, his whiskers poking. She needed to end this while she still had the strength.

Not trusting her voice, she cleared her throat. "I accept your apology."

Instead of retreating, his hands settled on her hips. Oh my.

"I said I forgive you." *Now please go before I do something foolish.*

He turned her to face him. His eyes were as vivid blue as the center of a flame and radiated as much heat. One hand cupped the side of her neck. His thumb stroked her cheek. Once. Twice.

She shivered.

He grinned.

What would it be like to have the freedom to press herself close and give in to him? They were married. And he roused feelings deep inside her that Matthew never had.

His thumb brushed her chin, her lips. Her eyes slipped closed. When they opened, their noses were almost touching. He was going to kiss her. They couldn't.

She turned her face away. He guided it back with fingers on her chin. "I was trying to kiss my wife."

"You can't." The words escaped on a whisper.

His brow knotted as he stared at her lips. "I know the risk, Ava, but if you think I can be married to you for years and never get a taste of you, you're crazy."

Sweat trickled down her spine. The heat between them burned hotter than the lamp at her back. Ben was right. They couldn't go on like this or they'd both turn to ashes. "I'll. . ." *Breathe.* "I'll take the blood test."

The tension around his eyes softened, and he placed the sweetest kiss on her forehead then her cheek. His whiskers tickled. "I'll take you to town first thing tomorrow."

"You're working."

"The next day, then."

"You work all week."

"Then I'll pay the doctor extra to do it after hours." He winked then turned to go.

She took a deep breath to clear her head. "Your supper is warming on the stove. I'll be down to eat with you shortly."

"Take your time." He looked at her over his shoulder. "First, I'm going to take a swim in the cold creek."

Chapter 12

Ava's skin flushed hot and the room spun. "What did you say?"

Doctor Hoffman smiled so wide his teeth glowed beneath his woolly mustache. "You don't have tuberculosis."

Ben's hand squeezed around hers. Bliss filled her limbs, making them weak. Before she let it reach her heart, however, she had questions. "But I have the symptoms. How can you be sure?"

"Your symptoms are consistent with tuberculosis as well as a dozen other illnesses." He walked to the bookshelf behind his desk, removed a thick title, and thumbed through the pages.

His shoes clicked along the floor as he closed in on her other side. He held the open book out for her to see. "This is the blood of a person who hasn't contracted the disease." His finger pointed to the opposite page. "This is the blood of a person who has. They carry a purple-colored bacillus bacteria, tuberculosis. Your blood is free of bacillus."

Ava swallowed. "You're certain?"

The doctor patted her shoulder. "Quite."

An emotion so overwhelming she couldn't describe it warmed her through like a Carolina sunshine. Tears of joy poured from her eyes. Ben's arms clamped around her waist and squeezed then lifted her off the ground. Through blurry vision, she looked at him and smiled. He set her back on solid ground and covered her face in kisses.

He stopped to look at her. A sheen of joy glistened in his eyes. That's when she became aware of his hand pressed into the small of her back, sealing them together. Her own hands had somehow found their way to the sides of his neck. His pulse pounded beneath her thumbs. When his gaze flicked to something behind her, she remembered the doctor, and they sprang apart.

Doctor Hoffman chuckled. "News to celebrate." He tucked his hands into his trouser pockets. "However, there is cause for concern."

Ben's grip tightened around her waist.

"I believe you have chronic bronchitis. It too is an illness of the lungs, easily mistaken for tuberculosis, especially by a physician who isn't following the growing knowledge of such diseases.

"Chronic bronchitis is a breakdown of lung tissue, which causes inflammation of the mucus membrane. The cells then dilate, creating shortness of breath and, at times, the lungs to fill with mucus fluid."

She leaned into Ben. "Am I contagious?"

"Surprisingly, no." Doctor Hoffman rocked back on his heels. "This disease only affects the individual."

"What caused it?" Ben's voice commanded the room.

"I can't say just yet. One colleague believes it's triggered by smoke, which would explain your episode last month. With the logging crews burning old stumps and rotten leaves, mold spores and a hundred other things could've triggered inflammation."

He retrieved another bluish bottle from his apothecary cabinet and handed it to her. "I want to continue monitoring your condition. Keep using the camphor and pay close attention to what's going on around you when a bout comes on. It might help us determine a cause."

She nodded. "Is this fatal, like tuberculosis?"

"Under the wrong circumstances, anything can be fatal. I worry most about your ability to breathe when an episode comes on. That's why you need to see me immediately when that happens."

"We will," Ben said, extending his hand. The doctor shook it then patted her elbow.

"Thank you, Doctor." She pulled her handkerchief from her sleeve and dabbed at her eyes, her mind a tornado of feelings.

Ben rubbed circles on her back. "If you'll wait outside, I'll settle up."

She left the sterile environment of the office and walked into the autumn sunshine. The leaves on the trees were just starting to turn, their colors more vivid than when they had arrived an hour earlier. Suddenly, everything was full of life. Like her.

She stepped from the dark dungeon of the past two years. Now, she was free. Free to live. Free to hope. Free to love.

Her cheeks burned. The wedge that kept them from becoming true husband and wife had been removed. This new journey was both thrilling and terrifying. Would he expect certain duties from her right away, or would he give her time to acclimate?

The door opened, and Ben emerged. His gait held the same assured confidence it had that day he'd found her by the shore, barefoot. He stopped in front of her, paused, and then offered his arm. She slipped her hand in the bend, amazed at the raw strength lying beneath the folds of flannel.

He kept her pace as they walked around the building to where he'd hitched the wagon. She started to release him, but his other hand covered hers. "I'm happy for you, Ava. I know it wasn't easy, but I'm glad you found the courage to do this."

"Me too." The boulder she'd been carrying had been lifted, and she felt as weightless as a cloud.

His gaze moved to her lips. Her heart stuttered. A corner of his mouth curled upward. He moved his arm and helped her into the wagon. The sudden changes were making her unstable.

The wagon creaked with Ben's weight. A sudden shyness crept in as his leg settled against hers. She clasped her hands in her lap, searching for words to break the silence. She failed. He set the mule into motion. Before long, they were on the rutted road that led home.

Ben bumped her elbow with his. "What is it?"

"What do you mean?"

"You keep opening and closing your mouth. If there's something you'd like to say, I'll listen."

She opened her mouth. Closed it.

Ben chuckled. "The Ava I know never has trouble speaking her mind."

The mule reared her head back and brayed.

They laughed, and the tension hovering over her vanished. "You've been good to me in many ways. I want to become a good wife for you. I guess I'm hoping you'll continue to be patient with me. In *all* things."

She studied his profile. His jaw worked, as if he were chewing what she'd said. Finally, he nodded. "I was hoping you'd agree to let me court you for a while, since we never got to do that part."

Courting. "I'd like that."

He offered his elbow, and she took it once again. "Just so you know." He glanced at her. "I intend to keep my promise about that kiss."

She smiled and snuggled closer.

Ben switched the fistful of flowers to his other hand and crested the hill. The lighthouse towered in the distance against a purple-and-orange dusk. Ava would be in the tower now, lighting the lamp and recording the weather. He imagined her in the lantern room, an open book splayed in her palm, pencil tapping against her chin. The way he'd observed her almost every evening the last few weeks. And what a pleasure it had been.

But with every new thing he learned about her, every flirtatious look she gave him, every new touch she allowed, the guilt pressed harder and heavier. Before he could become the husband she needed him to be, he needed to confess the truth about her father. Apologize to his own father. For years, he'd felt trapped by his father's injury that forced him into becoming a lumberjack. Mourned the loss of forgotten dreams. Now that he had Ava, he realized it wasn't a new profession he'd been missing at all, but a family of his own. A home.

The lighthouse lit up and flashed its beacon around the peninsula. This was home.

He kicked off his boots at the door, shrugged out of his coat, and went in search of something to bind the bundle. The kitchen turned up nothing. He scoured the other rooms until he came to hers. The door was open, revealing her pink and floral quilt tucked perfectly around the mattress. He hated to go in without permission, but surely she wouldn't mind when she discovered his motive.

He eased in, large and clumsy in the feminine space. The only other times he'd been in here were when she'd been in bed sick, and he'd been too concerned about her then to notice the room. An oval mirror hung on the wall above a bowl and pitcher on a small table. Thin curtains covered the window. Surely, she owned a ribbon or two. In fact, he'd seen her wear them.

The dresser was the only place he hadn't searched yet, and with darkness closing in, he wouldn't be able to see in here much longer. He riffled through the top drawer. His rough fingertips grazed against silky fabric and lace. His mind wandered in directions safe to travel in their marriage, but unsafe until they concluded their courtship. If he didn't burst into flames first. He found a strip of red ribbon the perfect length for binding flower stems and searched his brain for the perfect words to woo his wife.

He worked quickly and left the room. The flowers made a nice addition to the kitchen table, but food would make it even better. He walked to the stove and grabbed a mitt to see what was in the warmer. He didn't recognize the dish, but it smelled like heaven and. . .was that pie?

Flowers weren't enough. He should have gone to the general store for chocolates too.

He soaped up at the well, wincing at the freezing water. The days and nights were getting colder. When October arrived next week, he'd have to skip his baths in the creek on his trek home and haul buckets of water to the copper tub in the next room.

His fresh change of clothes smelled better than they ever did when he'd washed them. The soap had a faint flowery smell, but he didn't mind. The rip in his sleeve had been repaired too. He worked the buttons down his torso, ran a hand through his damp hair, and grabbed the flowers, hoping to coax Ava into joining him for dinner.

When he reached the covered passageway, his concern vanished. Ava stood inside, holding a lantern to the pictures that lined the wall. The faces of past light-keepers here. Particularly, her father.

Ben's gut knotted. "Now you can add your picture."

She startled but didn't take her eyes from the photo. "I don't think I will."

"Why not?"

Her sigh echoed in the small space. "We'll be leaving for New York soon. I should have told Mr. Pickett so he could be searching for a replacement."

"We're not going to New York."

She twisted to look at him. He stepped closer. "You've worked too hard for this. Congratulations."

He held the flowers out to her. Mouth open, she set down the lantern and accepted his gift. "But I thought—"

He silenced her with a shake of his head. "I've grown fond of the place. And its keeper."

She smiled into the white, star-shaped blooms. Before he could blink, her arms circled his neck in an embrace. He didn't remain stunned for long. His hands trailed from her waist, up her back, and down again, memorizing every line, every curve. Her hold tightened, pressing more feminine curves against him.

Her body fit just right against his. He couldn't wait to live life together. Make life together.

Her arms loosened around his neck, but there was no way he was letting go. He held on with one hand and held her cheek with the other. Her gaze flicked to his mouth. That was all the invitation he needed.

His lips touched hers as soft as a whisper. He lingered, giving her a chance to pull away. She dug her fingers into the folds of his shirt and pulled him closer. She was even sweeter than he'd imagined. His fingers dove into the thick threads of her hair. Their lips danced a lively rhythm for several minutes before they broke away for air.

She stayed latched on to him, breathing fast, eyelids hooded. He'd planned for their first kiss to be thorough, and he wasn't quite done making good on that promise yet. She rose on tiptoe in expectation. He obliged her again, but this time when he closed his eyes, all he could see was her father's face the way it looked in the photograph. The feel of the oilskin hat he'd found after they'd dug out the last body, the one he'd gripped in his fist to keep from shouting at the sky.

He had to confess this secret between them so they could move forward as husband and wife. And, boy, did he want to move forward.

He broke the kiss.

She looked up at him, half-dazed. "Why did you stop?"

His spirited Ava. Fierce in all things.

He inhaled a sober, steadying breath. "You need to add your picture next to your father's."

Her brow wrinkled. She stared at his lips for a moment then turned her head and gazed at the picture.

"He'd be real proud of you."

"He. . .he would've liked you. Despite your being a tree-swinging baboon." Her finger traced his chin from one side to the other.

It was killing him not to kiss her all the way to his bedroom. He clasped her hand in his and held it to his chest. "There's something I need to tell you."

She leaned away to look into his eyes.

"My crew is quick and efficient. We clear a lot of land in a short amount of time. I won't deny that we leave the woods in desolation. Most of the time it doesn't matter. Sometimes it causes disaster.

"Last winter, we cleared the land near the head of Sugar Creek. We were finishing up when a nasty spring storm rolled in. It rained for three solid days and nights. As soon as it stopped, we went out to float what logs we could to the river. A man passed through that afternoon in a johnboat."

The dread in Ava's eyes and the way she started shrinking away from him nearly made him sick. "There was a mudslide minutes later. On the other side of the creek."

"No," she whispered.

Ben swallowed, fighting the screams that still echoed in his ears at the memory. "Most of the men got to safety. We lost a few horses, some equipment. I remembered the man on the creek and ran to warn him. By the time I got there, it was too late."

Tears flowed down the cheeks he'd caressed minutes ago. He broke his hold on her.

"I. . ." He blew out a breath. "The man was your father."

Sobs tore through the walkway.

"I tried, Ava. I tried so hard." His voice cracked on the last word. Between the logs and the mud, he just hadn't been strong enough.

She swiped beneath her eyes. "How can you be sure it was my father? I know I told you about his death, but how can you be sure? Lots of men fish in that creek."

Ben turned away. "The man's face, I'll never forget it. It's the face staring back at me now."

Another round of sobs ensued. He wanted to hold her but knew it wouldn't be wise. When her crying quieted to hiccups, she slid down the wall to the floor. "Why are you telling me this now?"

He knelt in front of her. "We've married, we've courted. I'm ready to take you as my wife, but I don't want to go there with secrets between us."

141

"Secrets?" She dabbed her tears with the cuff of her sleeve.

"I've known it was your father since the day I asked you to marry me. I saw his picture on the parlor desk."

Her intake of breath was like a knife to his chest. "I'm sorry."

The fire in her eyes turned to ice. "Me too."

She pushed against the wall and stood. Her hands brushed off her skirt, and she moved back toward the tower.

"Let me help you tonight."

She turned gracefully, despite such a moment. "No, Ben. You've done enough."

Chapter 13

Pain yanked Ava from sleep. She forced her sore and swollen eyelids open, wincing against the sunlight. Groaning, she straightened her cricked neck. The sun was high on the horizon, and the lamp still burned. She threw off the blanket she didn't remember putting on. What a waste of fuel.

She extinguished the lamp and stretched her aching back, guessing it to be around ten o'clock. She'd never fallen asleep on watch before, even on her sickest days. What was wrong with her? Pieces of the night before flooded her memory. She leaned against the glass wall, wishing for the blessed numbness of slumber.

She coughed, sending her mind reeling even further. Ben had been there when her father died. Ben, the type of man her father had warned her against. Ben, whose occupation and crew caused the mudslide that had taken her father's life. Ben, the man who married her out of obligation because he felt guilty over her father's death.

Ben, the man she'd fallen desperately in love with.

She didn't blame him for the accident. She knew him well enough by now to know he'd never purposely hurt a soul. But she did blame him for holding on to the truth. For making his proposal sound like he was fond of her and concerned for her reputation. Not because he was riddled with guilt.

She sighed. Was her motive for marrying him to save her reputation any better than his? No. They'd both done what they thought was best at the time, and they both cared for each other. So, why was she angry with him?

Because she loved him.

Her weathered copy of *Sense and Sensibility* was propped in the corner by the blanket. She picked it up and ran her fingers over the worn title. "Sorry, ladies, but I have to let you go."

Holding the book to her chest, she turned and pressed her palm against the window, chilly now that the lamp was out. Her breath fogged the glass as she stared over miles of treetops speckled with red, gold, yellow, and green. Her husband was down there somewhere. A man who'd convinced her to take a chance at life, a man who'd captured her heart so completely, a man who mere hours ago had set her on fire.

Fire.

She jerked to full alert and ran onto the parapet so fast the door banged into the glass. There, in the distance, maybe ten miles away, black smoke billowed among the trees. Not a puff, like from a brush fire, but a thick black cloud. Flashes of orange flickered from within.

She lifted her skirt, tossed the book onto the blanket, and raced down the spiral stairs as fast as she could. Winded by the time she burst into the house, she stopped in the parlor for a breath. She'd need to put on warmer clothes to make the four-mile journey to town. She wished Ben had left the mule, stubborn as it was.

She hurried through the house, tugging on wool socks, adding a sweater over her blouse, and putting on her coat and boots. A wildfire at that distance could blaze to town in a matter of hours. She had to warn them.

Ben's shirt from the night before hung on a rack by the door. The sleeve was ripped. Her heart squeezed. Her husband was in the path of that blaze. Did he know it was headed their way? For a moment, she debated which direction to start. If she warned him first, she would have to travel on foot and had no guarantee of finding his crew in time.

Petitioning God to save her husband, she ran to her safety bicycle, straddled the seat, and left to warn the town.

More birds than Ben had ever seen at one time soared overhead. All heading west. He frowned and sniffed the air. The loamy scent of earth and sawdust had given way to woodsmoke and heat.

The fine hairs on the back of his neck stood on end.

"Boss!" John barreled through the woods on horseback. He reined in the animal so hard it reared. "Wildfire, headed this way."

Ben hesitated for only a moment to pray this was some wretched nightmare then sprinted into action. "McGurdy, Terrell, Gentry—fire!" He pointed east. "Get what you can save and head back to camp!"

The men scrambled to action. Ben helped unhitch the horses and mules, all the while keeping his eyes toward the east. Smoke permeated the trees. No flames were visible yet, but the roar and the pop of wood sounded in the distance. The wagons loaded with logs would be a loss. They'd never get them out in time.

He grabbed two mules' reins and led them back toward camp at a jog. He'd gotten a quarter of a mile when John raced back on his horse. "There's homes over yonder." He pointed northwest of the blaze. "We need to warn them."

Ben looked in the direction of the lighthouse. He needed to get to Ava. Inhaling smoke from a fire of this caliber might kill her. Losing her would kill him. Doctor

Hoffman would be swamped with patients. Ben needed to protect his wife.

Camp was nothing but chaos. Men scrambled with buckets of water, soaking everything they could find. Others were gathering what they thought they could save and packing belongings onto the horses and mules.

Ben yelled to get their attention. He split the men into groups, giving each a specific task. While Terrell and John were warning surrounding homes, he and Orbin would caution the town. "Once you've carried out your orders, meet at the fork on the edge of town. May God be with you."

And with his sweet Ava.

Ava couldn't decide which burned more, her legs or her lungs. Now that she'd alerted the town, she had to find Ben. Her front tire hit a hole and sent her teetering like a top. She threw her legs out for balance, but her skirt caught in a spoke. The bicycle pitched to the left. Her body smacked the ground, stealing her breath.

She coughed and gasped. Safety bicycle, indeed. She crawled from beneath the contraption. Dirt coated her hands, her arm, her clothes. All she wanted to do was find Ben, but her legs shook worse than a lone leaf on the eve of winter. Desperation rose in her chest and poured from her eyes.

Ben.

She needed to tell him how wrong she'd been about everything. That she loved him.

Pounding hoofbeats sounded behind her and grew with intensity. She turned in time to see a lone rider rein his horse and jump off before the beast had fully stopped. The figure dropped in front of her and grabbed her shoulders. "Ava!"

Her face smashed against a hard chest.

"Oh, thank God." Ben held her close, running his hands up and down her body to check for injury.

Sobs caused her wheezing lungs to tighten more, but she managed to speak her thoughts. "I love you."

Hands cupped around her face, he pulled back to look at her. Awe lit his blue eyes against a sooty face. "I love you too."

His lips came down upon hers for just a moment. His kiss tasted like coal, but it was the sweetest they'd shared yet.

Ben stood and gathered her into his arms. He carried her to the sweat-lathered horse and set her upon the saddle. She gripped the pommel as he mounted behind her. He hooked an arm around her waist and kicked the horse to a canter. Things were burning to ashes around them, yet she'd never felt safer.

"Where are we going?" The effort to speak made her cough.

"As far away as we can get." He kissed her cheek.

They rode for several miles in silence. Her breaths came easier the farther away they traveled. She'd started to doze when Ben stopped the horse near a creek. She blinked and sat forward.

"We need to give him a break before he collapses." He patted her arms, slid off the horse's back, and helped her down. Holding her hand, he led them to the water. The sun was lowering, dropping the temperature by several degrees. A dark haze marred the horizon.

The horse drank while they washed the soot and dirt from their skin. The icy water made her hiss.

"Cold?"

"Freezing."

He turned to face her, a smear of black still lingering under his right eye. "We'll camp here for the night. As much as I hate to, I'm going to have to build a fire. I managed to grab two blankets from my bunk. We'll have to share."

Another shiver stole through her. She nodded.

While he gathered kindling and anything else they could use for warmth, she spread the blankets far enough away that the smoke shouldn't affect her breathing. Once the fire was blazing, they shared the miniscule amount of jerky he'd packed. At least it would stave off hunger.

He rubbed her upper arms. "Let's get you warm."

He led her to the pallet she'd made beneath a white pine. The layer of needles beneath the wool blanket should offer some cushion. He eased under the top layer and waited for her to join him. Her stomach twisted in knots. Inhaling a deep breath that was blessedly clear, she wrapped her shawl tighter around her shoulders and sank to the ground. She lay next to him and buried her face in his chest. The blankets cocooned them. His warmth soaked into her, and she knew she'd never sleep another night away from her husband.

His Adam's apple bobbed along her forehead. "When you weren't at the lighthouse, when I couldn't find you. . . I've never been that scared in my life."

She shifted to look up at him. "I felt the same way. I'm sorry for my behavior last night. I was selfish and shocked and I—"

His lips, greedy and warm, toyed with hers. Neither one had to worry about the cold night air. They had plenty of warmth.

He pulled her closer. As the night passed, they fell deeper in love beneath the Michigan moon.

Candice Sue Patterson studied at the Institute of Children's Literature and is an active member of American Christian Fiction Writers. She lives in Indiana with her husband and three sons in a restored farmhouse overtaken by books. When she's not tending to her chickens, splitting wood, or decorating cakes, she's working on a new story. Candice writes Modern Vintage Romance—where the past and present collide with faith. Her debut novel *How to Charm a Beekeeper's Heart* was a 2012 ACFW First Impressions finalist and made INSPY's Longlist for 2016.

Safe Haven

by Rebecca Jepson

Chapter 1

Rose Miller tried to silence her grandfather's warning, but it kept whispering in her mind, an echo that seemed to fill her wintery world with peril. It had been their tradition, watching the moonrise from the lighthouse tower on New Year's Eve. The lake always shone silver, illuminated by the thousands of stars that twinkled in the northern night sky. Now those same celestial lights cast shadows that crept toward the shore like malevolent intruders.

Before she'd learned about the child-sized footprints in the sand, the hair ribbon caught in the bushes, her lakeside dwelling had been a sanctuary. Whether enveloped by nighttime shadows or sunbursts at dawn, she'd known nothing but wonder as she stood at her grandfather's side and gazed through the decagonal windows at the sparkling lake below.

Only a few weeks ago, she'd watched as the government agent, sent by the US Lighthouse Board after receiving her telegram, buried her grandfather. *Or rather, the man I thought was my grandfather.* Her very kinship with this windswept shoreline, her sense of belonging, had suffered a blow that day. A fact that did nothing to lessen her longing for the security of his presence. He'd stood guard between her and. . .something.

A soft breeze ruffled the frost-covered bushes below. Rose craned her neck, as though if she looked hard enough, the footprints would appear. But that was absurd. Not only would they be buried under feet of snow, any traces of the past had long since been swept away by wind, rain. . .time. She reached into her apron pocket, found the hair ribbon, and ran her fingers over its embroidered pink roses and sparkly golden edges.

Someone knows about all this. They must. She couldn't very well have been delivered to the lighthouse as an infant by storks. A person had left her there.

A child.

A chill swept through her at the thought.

By habit, she stepped away from the windows and checked the Fifth Order Fresnel lens in the center of the tower. But it remained unlit while ships were safely in ports for the winter. No need to light her corner of Lake Michigan when ice made it impassable.

How merry these winter evenings used to be. Free from manning the light and watching for ships in distress, her grandfather spent more time downstairs, often reading to her from his big Bible or telling her stories, his deep baritone a musical cadence in her ears. *If only he'd told me the story about finding me on the lighthouse steps.* At least then she wouldn't have been bewildered by the news just before his death. The shock of losing him wouldn't have been compounded by the questions that plagued her, one in particular. She wasn't his granddaughter, so had he ever truly loved her?

Deep within, she knew he had. When he finally told her about her origins, he added that he'd had no choice but to keep her. Something about being flummoxed by a wrinkled wee fist grabbing his sleeve and clinging to him for dear life.

Remembering a certain soft shine in the man's eyes whenever he smiled down at her, Rose believed him. She also believed that he'd searched diligently for the owner of those footprints in the sand, and that he'd had his reasons for pursuing the trail no further after that day.

"There's trouble bound up in your past, girl. I can feel it."

His ominous words, spoken in an earnest but fading voice, weren't easily forgotten. But Rose didn't have time to dwell on them, for a sudden crash from below jarred her back to the present. Her heart did a flip-flop in her chest. Had the sound come from the barn? Perhaps it was the animals, frightened by an approaching storm.

She whirled around and peered out the windows. The naked treetops barely moved. The sky was completely clear, the moon shining brightly over the lighthouse grounds.

Her collie, Tucker, began barking sharply, alerting her to danger. Though he had his own swinging door in the back entryway and could venture outside whenever he pleased, he rarely did so at night. But something had prompted him to investigate.

Thoughts spinning, Rose knelt and fumbled with the hatch at her feet. She clambered through it and descended the near-vertical stairs as quickly as she dared. The second staircase wasn't quite so steep, and the third was easily traversable. As she hurried down the steps, she attempted to slow her pace, to calm herself. *It's probably a coyote again, trying to get to the chickens.*

She arrived at the main floor just as a second crash reverberated through the air and Tucker's barks turned frenzied.

She gasped.

Someone's here.

The realization sent dread through her limbs. She sped down the narrow hallway to the front door. *Oh please, dear God, let it be locked.* She raised trembling fingers to the latch and found that it was indeed fastened.

Rose sagged against the door, her forehead pressed against the solid, comforting wood. What would she do if the intruder tried to break in? She knew where her grandfather kept his gun, not far away in the office trunk. *Do I have enough time to fetch it?*

Before she could even finish the thought, she heard boot steps crunching along the hard-packed snow toward the house. Tucker growled as if he was about to rip a villainous foe to shreds. The intruder paused.

Rose held her breath.

A desperate voice rose above the collie's barks.

"Charlie, call off your dog, man!"

A wave of recognition flooded Rose's consciousness. With it came the realization that she had never, in all her life, been so glad to welcome Captain Nathan Perry to the lighthouse.

Rose opened the door to admit the captain, followed by Tucker, who quivered with hospitality now that he knew their visitor wasn't a stranger to his master. He could hardly be blamed for not remembering the steamship captain. The man's comings and goings were unpredictable, his stays long or short as suited his fancy. *It's very reckless of him to be traveling in such bitter cold.* Ice crystals covered his heavy wool overcoat and fur cap, the latter of which hid his short sandy curls from view.

His whole body wagging profusely, Tucker hurried down the hallway, his wet tail thumping against the knotty pine walls. Rose knew he was looking for his latest treasure, a deer bone he'd found in the woods.

Captain Perry's gaze followed the dog and he smiled a rueful smile. "I'm sorry to cause such a stir. My horse crashed into a barrel in the barn and—"

"Oh no, she wasn't hurt, was she?" Rose had always loved his beautiful, spirited horse, Ginger.

He shook his head. "No, just spooked. She's snug as can be now, munching on your grandfather's hay."

Rose shut the door behind him and slid the latch into place. Out of the corner of her eye, she saw him look her briefly up and down. The moment passed so quickly she almost didn't notice the unreadable flicker in his eyes. She didn't recall seeing such a look in them before, and wondered what he was thinking.

He glanced past her, farther into the hallway. "Is your grandfather at home? I've come to hear more of his tall tales about rescuing sailors in dire peril."

His simple query caused something inside Rose to crumple. The fresh awareness of her loss caught her off guard, though goodness knew it shouldn't have. She'd been coherent enough when the stoic-faced government agent dug her grandfather's grave. She heard the ring of the man's pickax against the hard December ground, knew its heartbreaking purpose. Just before he left, she woodenly answered his many questions about keeping a lighthouse. Apparently, her replies satisfied him for, not much later, she received a letter from the lighthouse board offering her the position as the new keeper. She'd accepted. The weight of the responsibility hadn't sunk in yet.

Until now, neither had her grandfather's death. She wasn't sure if she could really tell someone that he was gone—someone who'd truly cared about him.

She squared her shoulders and faced Captain Perry, only to find that his grin had faded. His palpable empathy told her that her inner turmoil hadn't escaped his notice.

"Come in and have some tea," she offered hurriedly.

After waiting for him to hang his coat and hat on the peg by the door, she led the way to the kitchen.

He seated himself at the table while she put the kettle on the cookstove and stoked the fire. *He must be freezing.* His hands were chapped and red with cold. He kept folding and unfolding them, fidgeting with the tablecloth, and in general behaving like a man out of his element.

Once the tea was ready, she filled their mugs, handed him his, and set the kettle on the cooler side of the stove to simmer. She sat across from him and breathed in the steam wafting up from her mug. It smelled of cloves, cranberries, and holiday good cheer, all rolled into one.

He took a sip of tea. "This is good." He traced the long handle of his mug. "When did it happen?" he asked softly.

She felt her lips tremble. "Three weeks ago. The doctor said it was his heart." *I had no warning.* "It was sudden."

He winced, eyes regretful. "I wish I could have been here. He was always kind to me."

"Yes, he was kind to everyone." *Even a baby he found on his front steps—a baby he wasn't obligated to keep.*

"And the lighthouse? Who will be the new keeper?"

Rose drew herself up. "I will."

He gave her a look, opened his mouth as though to protest, and closed it again.

They sipped their tea, Rose more aware than ever of the emptiness inside her. A mocking chant kept repeating in her mind. *He's not really your grandfather, not really your grandfather, not really your grandfather. . . .* The words almost drowned out the memory of the man's affection for her. Perhaps it would help to talk about it with someone.

At that moment, more insistently than before, she heard her grandfather's warning. What had been a remembered whisper in the lighthouse tower was now a stern command.

"My girl, don't tell anyone what I've just told you."

Rose glanced at Captain Perry and felt the hair on her forearms prickle. Why was he really here? It had been years, maybe three, since she'd last seen him. He seemed amiable, good company for her grandfather whenever he visited, but how well did she really know him?

The creeping shadows she'd seen from the tower now lurked in the kitchen. They changed shape in the flickering lantern light, sometimes growing, sometimes ebbing, like the ripples of surf on the shore on a windy day.

"It's been awhile since you last visited," she heard herself say through the strange hum in her ears.

"Yes, I captained a ship in the north for a time. This past shipping season was my first year back on Lake Michigan."

"Where's your ship now?" she pressed.

"I left her docked in Grand Haven for the winter."

He'd traveled all the way here from Grand Haven? "Isn't that a pretty long trip?"

"Yes, but I stopped at inns along the way, and it didn't snow too often."

Why did you come here? She couldn't bring herself to voice the question.

"A man gets tired of his own company, sometimes," he said gently.

She gaped at him. Was she so easy to read?

He took a final swallow of tea and stood. "Nevertheless, I should go. Without your grandfather present. . ."

Her forehead creased in puzzlement. "He would've wanted you to stay, especially on so cold a night."

He nodded, avoiding her gaze. "Again, nevertheless. . ."

He has nothing to say to me. Her grandfather was the only reason he'd ever come to visit. Why that should matter now, alongside much darker suspicions, she didn't know. Perhaps the overwhelming emotions she'd experienced lately were converging on her all at once. Whatever the reason, her eyes swam with mortifying tears. *He'll think me a child.* "I'm sorry if my company seems unsuitable to you," she whispered.

He met her eyes evenly, something in his steady blue-gray gaze making her understand why his crew might obey orders without arguing. "Your company suits me just fine. I was merely concerned for your reputation."

Dawning comprehension caused a dreadful flush to rise in her cheeks. How stupid of her. Of course he couldn't stay the night, not without a chaperone. "Certainly. Forgive me."

He shook his head. "Please don't concern yourself." He set his mug on the table and started toward the front door.

She trailed after him down the hallway, watching in a strange daze as he donned his coat and cap and settled the fur flaps over his ears.

He paused, hand on the door handle. "Allow me to say once more how sorry I am, about your grandfather."

Tears clogged her throat. "Thank you."

He opened the door and a whoosh of frigid air burst inside. The shocking gust awoke Rose from her daze.

Oh, this man was *not* leaving this house in such weather. Her grandfather would have been appalled. For a recluse who'd loved his solitude, he valued hospitality very highly. He always kept the porch light on for Captain Nathan Perry.

"Wait," Rose said.

He turned. When he glanced at Rose's hands, firmly on her hips, a faint, reluctant smile appeared at the corners of his mouth.

"You'll sleep on the sofa," she ordered. "Just as you've always done." Without another word, she spun around and strode down the hall, fully expecting him to follow.

Chapter 2

Nathan rose early the next morning to care for Ginger, afraid that if he didn't, Rose would. He stopped in the back entryway to put on his boots, pausing when he heard a loud *thwack* from outside. With one boot on and the other hanging from his grasp, he opened the door and squinted against the rising sun that glittered on the surface of the snow, temporarily blinding him. As his eyes adjusted to the brightness, he saw just what he'd expected to see—Charlie Miller's wisp of a granddaughter in the barnyard, struggling to split wood with an ax bigger than she was.

Nathan shoved his foot, bunched-up stocking and all, into his boot and hurried down the path toward her. Several other crisscrossing pathways led through the snow to various outbuildings, including a well house, privy, and summerhouse. From the front of the property, the lighthouse looked like a white country church with a light tower in place of a steeple. Here in the back, it appeared more like a plantation or farm.

Rose's back was to him. She tried in vain to wrench the blade from a log, her breath coming in short gasps. Knowing he'd startle her if he took the ax away from her, which was his first impulse, he spoke quietly instead.

"That ax is too heavy for you."

He might as well have shouted. She jumped and dropped the ax, her dark blue skirt a blur of motion as she whirled to face him.

"Easy," he soothed.

"You scared me."

"I can see that. I'm sorry."

Her chin rose just perceptibly. "This is the only ax I have. I've been using it for weeks now. Cumbersome as it is, I can manage it."

Nathan bit down on his tongue to keep from commenting. If that meager mole-hill of chopped wood he'd almost stumbled over in the barn last night was her idea of managing, she was in for a very cold winter. Of equal concern was the stack of not-yet-split logs heaped against the barn wall. It wouldn't last until spring.

A knee-bobbing uneasiness had been his companion since last night. He'd nearly choked on his tea when Rose announced her plan to be the lighthouse keeper in her grandfather's place. Nathan knew that women had filled that role on these northern shores for many years. Quite capably. He'd heard more than one captain talk about being rescued by a female keeper. But that didn't change the fact that Rose was too young to be living alone on this frozen peninsula.

"This shouldn't be your task." He gestured toward the ax.

"That's my decision, not yours."

A fair point, or would have been, if she hadn't been glaring up at him, her expression that of a mulish cabin boy. The comparison ended with her stony glare.

The last time Nathan visited the lighthouse, Rose had been a dreamy-eyed adolescent, still engrossed in her woodland wanderings and reading her fairy story books—or whatever kind of books a girl might bury her freckled nose in.

The freckles were gone now. He'd noted their absence last night when he first entered the house. In the flickering lamplight, her hair shone like glossy chestnuts, her dark-lashed brown eyes holding all the mystery of womanhood, her figure everything that made men look twice.

He forced his thoughts into safer territory. *Focus on the matter at hand, man.*

Realizing that anything he might say right now would only irritate her more, he resolved to let her be the next to speak.

The silence dragged on, him with his mouth clamped shut, her still looking daggers at him.

Slowly, her rigid posture lost some of its starch. Her voice, when it emerged, was barely audible. "Grandfather always encouraged me to try new things, even if they weren't considered women's work."

Ah Charlie, what a void you've created by leaving this world, and her alone in it.

"I've no doubt that he did." Nathan hesitated. "But imagine how he'd have lit into me if he knew I stood by like a no-good laggard while his granddaughter tried to wield a. . .barbarian's battleax."

A hint of a smile turned her lovely lips upward. At the sight, his resolve wavered. A wayfaring ship's captain who spent his days in the company of rough sailors couldn't expect many opportunities to see a smile that charming.

Still, he couldn't surrender without a fight.

He risked a terribly forward use of her given name. "Rose."

Her startled gaze jerked to his.

"Just let me chop the wood."

He didn't wait for her reply but brushed past her and reached for the ax. One yank of the handle, and he had the blade out of the log. He repositioned the log flat end up, aware of Rose turning on her heel and disappearing into the barn.

He tested the weight of the heavy tool in his hands, appreciating its simplicity.

Iron and wood. Elemental things, like the coal that powered his ship.

He swung the blade through the air and brought it down with precision, splitting the log in half. He straightened with a groan. Everything hurt. That sofa in the lighthouse sitting room was shorter than he was by about a foot. Why hadn't he just stayed at an inn in the village last night or made the trip to Charlie's cabin? The man owned a wooded parcel of land not far south of the lighthouse and had built a cabin on it a few years ago. *I could've lit a fire in the hearth and bedded down with the mice.*

But Nathan knew exactly why he hadn't ridden into the village or stayed in Charlie's cabin. The reason was currently in the barn, avoiding him.

Truth be told, the desire to pull her into his arms and comfort her last night had scared him. He might have hoped that living almost exclusively among men since boyhood would've quelled such an instinct. But no, he possessed it in full measure. So much so that he'd done his level best to hightail it back to the below-freezing outdoors, just to escape his own weakness. Rose's innocence didn't help. She'd clearly been confused at first, when he pointed out the need for him to sleep elsewhere. *Ah, that lovely flush in her cheeks when my inference became clear to her...*

His breath got trapped in his lungs at the thought. If only for an instant, she'd regarded him as a man, one she shouldn't be alone with, rather than merely her grandfather's friend.

Yes, Nathan was scared. But that didn't change the fact that at this moment, he had a job to do—one that required him to actually breathe.

He tapped on the open office door and waited for Rose to look up. She was sitting at her desk, jotting something in a ledger. On closer inspection, he saw that it was a logbook, probably used to record weather patterns and her daily activities at the lighthouse.

He removed his cap. "May I come in?"

She set down her pen and nodded, her gaze still on the logbook.

He stepped into the room, the pine floorboards squeaking under his boots. There was nowhere to sit but a dome-shaped chest, complete with an iron lock that could surely survive the apocalypse. So he remained standing.

Rose raised her eyes to his, her expression guarded.

They hadn't spoken since this morning. After he'd finished splitting wood, Nathan had hauled water for Ginger, grateful that Rose hadn't tackled the demanding chore herself. It was enough that she'd fed the horse, mucked the stall, milked the goats, watered the chickens...

Restless, Nathan spent the rest of the day inspecting the lighthouse and grounds. He tapped loose boards and wiggled skewed fence posts, his tongue sticking out the corner of his mouth, much like his leadman's did whenever he used his lead line to gauge the depth of the lake.

"I'm staying the winter in your grandfather's cabin," Nathan announced without preamble.

Rose blinked, once, twice. "Why?"

He pointed out the window. "There's a fence outside that needs to be repaired, shingles that need replacing. The chimney needs to be cleaned, and your store of meat is running dangerously low." Among other problems.

"I'll be seeing to all of those things."

The answer failed to satisfy him. "When?"

"Probably when it isn't twenty degrees below zero."

He sighed. "Do you realize how quickly this house could go up in flames if the chimney caught fire?"

Her dark eyes flashed. "Of course I do."

Beautiful. Her eyes were beautiful. Nathan rubbed sweaty palms down the legs of his trousers and tried again. "I'll fix the chimney and take care of the other repairs, since I'll be living close by."

Rose shook her head with no little vigor. "I can manage on my own. I'm not a child."

"I'm very aware of that," he said frankly, trying not to pair the words with a lingering look. "But these things simply cannot be put off."

Even more urgent than the chimney were the provisions. Her supply of meat wouldn't last the winter, any more than that stack of wood in the barn would. Charlie had always been vigilant about cold-weather preparations, which made Nathan wonder if his old friend's strength had been waning during his final months. *He must have gone to great lengths to hide his failing health from Rose.*

"I don't wish to be a burden to you or anyone else." She lifted her pen and poised it over her logbook as though declaring the conversation at an end.

Nathan thought he might drown in his frustration. Couldn't she see that it was no trouble? That even if he wouldn't do it for her, he'd do it for Charlie?

"How do you plan to survive the winter with no one to hunt for you?" he demanded. "Lay traps? Haul wood?"

She abandoned her pen with a clatter and raised her heated gaze to his. "Don't patronize me. My grandfather taught me how to do those tasks if necessary. He knew how hard life on this isolated shore can be." The strength of her words couldn't hide the tremor in her voice. She turned away from him and looked out the window at the lake, but not before he saw a faint shimmer of tears in her eyes.

He berated himself for adding to her distress, even as he searched for a way to make her understand. How he wished life had better equipped him for times like

these, when the occasion called for more than the ability to navigate a narrow channel or survive the raw elements. What did a man say to someone who'd just lost her
only family?

The longer he stood there mutely, the more he felt like he was letting down
an old friend. *I'm sorry, Charlie, that you're gone, and there's no one here to console her
but me.*

A pang struck Nathan in the chest. He'd been raised by a drunken fisherman,
an unruly crew of sailors his primary companions. He couldn't pretend he wouldn't
miss the gentlemanly lighthouse keeper who'd shown him a better way.

Perhaps *that's* what he should say.

He decided to risk it.

"I'll miss him too."

She didn't turn, just sniffed and wiped her eyes.

He tried one more time. "Let me stay and help you, just for this first winter."
He choked on his next words, finding them to be painfully true. "It's all that I can
do for him."

After a moment that seemed to stretch into eternity, Rose nodded her assent.

Chapter 3

Rose wandered through the woods on an unseasonably warm morning, Tucker nipping at her heels. Come spring, she'd be asleep from dawn until early afternoon, having tended the tower light all night. For now, she fully intended to enjoy her morning stroll. She breathed in the scent of warm pine needles and watched the fluffy chickadees hop about amid the evergreen branches, signs of life in an otherwise dormant world. Her gaze traveled deeper into the forest, finding a brave winterberry bush, its glossy red berries the food of dryads and elves—or so she'd fancied as a child.

A sharp whistle rang out from the direction of the lighthouse, and Tucker's entire body froze in hopeful anticipation. He stood stock-still, his nose no doubt confirming what his ears had heard. With a glad bark, he bounded off toward the clearing.

Rose noted the contrast between his greeting today and his greeting on that cold New Year's Eve. Captain Perry's presence had become an almost daily occurrence, his whistle for Tucker now a familiar sound. When she went to the barn to do her morning chores, he was often already there, seeing to the heavier tasks for her. Once he finished them, he'd set about making repairs, the ring of his hammer resounding throughout the day.

Rose arrived at the lighthouse backyard to find him standing knee-deep in snow beside the well house, laughing at a wildly excited Tucker, who repeatedly licked his sleeve, his wrist, anywhere within reach.

Ginger made her presence known by whinnying from the hitching post nearby, and Rose turned to see that the horse had a pack strapped to her back. *Is Captain Perry leaving?*

Before she had time to ponder the question, he looked up and saw her standing there. She knew he'd seen her by the way he sobered, just a little. *We still aren't at ease with one another.*

He moved past Tucker and came to stand before her. "I stopped by to tell you that I'm leaving for a few days. Thought I'd take advantage of this warm spell and do some hunting."

Sensible enough, provided the fair weather held. "Blizzards can appear very suddenly in the north," she stated, unnecessarily.

"Yes, I know." His voice betrayed amusement.

She deserved that, but nobody liked to be made fun of. "Blizzards are no laugh—"

"It'll be all right." *I'll be careful,* his eyes assured her. Or perhaps he was reminding her that he was capable of fending for himself. He wasn't a big man, but there was no denying the hardness of his chest or the strength of his arms. To add to his obvious physical attributes, her grandfather had once told her that captaining a steamship required keen intelligence. No ordinary sailor could hope to attain such a position unless he could prove himself alert, efficient, even educated.

"I'm taking Ginger along, as you can see, so you won't need to trouble yourself with tending to her." The captain inclined his head toward the barn. "The barnyard fence is repaired, so if you let the goats out, they won't wander off. I filled the wood-box in the back entryway for the cookstove fire, but if you run short, you'll find more in the buggy shed rather than the barn, which I'm afraid is overtaken by the larger logs I hauled in from the woods. I haven't had a chance to work on the cellar yet, so be careful not to trip on that cracked bottom step. I'll fix it when I get back."

He sounds as though he were taking leave of a helpless child.

"Stay warm," he said, in parting. He tipped his cap in her direction and took a pivoting step backward, his attention already turning to Ginger and the task before him.

As he crossed the yard toward the horse, Tucker began to whine and looked up at Rose with anxious brown eyes. She patted his head and spoke briskly over his cries. "Come, Tucker, there's much to be done on so fine a morning."

But there wasn't.

Or at least, there didn't seem to be, due to the aimlessness that plagued her. No chore seemed urgent enough to undertake when all she could think about was the extraordinary silence that surrounded her. Solitude had never bothered her before. It was just her and her barnyard pets, the soaring gulls, the smoke-chugging steamboats. She'd spent hours envisioning the distant shores of the lake, from bustling docks to lonely lighthouses on reedy dunes.

In the wake of her grandfather's death, she no longer relished being left alone with her thoughts. She felt like an explorer wandering in a vast wilderness, her origins a shapeless, hazy unknown.

And then Captain Perry arrived.

Her mysterious past was easier to ignore when she could hear him whistling a sailor's rhythmic chant as he went about his work.

But this morning, not even the floorboards creaked, nor did the cookstove fire crackle.

Rose plopped her mixing bowl onto the kitchen counter. It was no use trying to bake anything with her mind in such a state. She wondered if the lighthouse had been this silent all those years ago when her grandfather found her on the front steps. For the hundredth time, she asked herself why a child would leave a baby at a lighthouse. But perhaps that was the wrong question. What adult would send a child on so weighty an errand?

Lost in thought, she drew the hair ribbon out of her pocket and stared unseeingly at it. Was it possible, even slightly possible, that the child had sent *itself* on the errand?

The ribbon came into sharp focus. The embroidered roses in the center, the sparkly golden threads marked the object as feminine. Shocked that it hadn't occurred to her before, Rose hit her palm against her forehead. *I might have been left at the lighthouse by an older sister.*

Slowly, like the ice on the lake thawing in springtime, the possibilities formed in Rose's mind. She could have had a sister. Or a brother, or father, or mother. Somewhere, at some point in time, at least one of those had existed. A father might have been absentee, even deceased, when Rose made her appearance. But one thing was certain. At the time of her birth, she'd had a mother. That fact shouldn't have been a profound revelation, but somehow, it was. *What kind of mother deliberately leaves her baby to be raised by a stranger?*

A throbbing ache arose in Rose's stomach and persisted even after she remembered something that might help answer her question. She recalled reading about a character in one of her books—Esther in *Mary Barton*, by Elizabeth Gaskell. Esther probably would have left her baby to strangers, if she'd had a baby. The woman had been desperately poor, her profession disgraceful, her situation incompatible with bringing up a child. Doubtless, she would have felt that she had little choice but to give her baby up.

Could there have been a woman like Esther in the vicinity of the lighthouse twenty years ago? *Maybe a fancy-house girl at one of the taverns in the village.* Of course, it wouldn't be seemly for Rose to visit such an establishment. But surely those women had contact with the outside world on occasion. If she could just talk to someone who might have known her mother, someone who could shed some light as to her current whereabouts. . .

What type of person might have had contact with one of those women? A priest? A physician?

Her grandfather's warning asserted itself once again. *"Don't tell anyone what I've just told you."*

Those words were even more powerful than Rose's desire to solve the riddles of her past. She couldn't easily dismiss the final admonition of the man who'd raised her.

And yet. . .

There must be something she could do, some way of digging into her origins without arousing suspicion.

Perhaps a trip to the village was in order.

Rose's first two attempts at sleuthing met with failure. She'd wanted to visit the minister and doctor, but both of them were away making house calls and weren't expected to return before nightfall. To discover this information, she had to trek a goodly distance, since the men worked on opposite ends of the village.

By the time she arrived at the general store, her feet were sore and her legs itchy beneath her plaid woolen town skirt. The shadows were beginning to lengthen. This must be her final stop. If anyone could help her find answers, it would be the proprietor, George Lardie. As a longtime resident of the area, he'd no doubt be privy to some of its oldest secrets.

Rose opened the front door to the merry ring of a cowbell. She entered and ducked her head to see the cash register counter through the pots, pans, baskets, saws, snowshoes, and every other conceivable dry good that could possibly be hung from a wooden beam. Her heart sank when she realized that it wasn't Mr. Lardie who stood behind the counter. *I hope the man hasn't sold out and left town.* Judging by the youthful appearance of the bow tie-clad individual who stood in his place, Mr. Lardie had merely hired help.

The young man spied Rose and strolled toward her, his hands in his pockets, a cheerful smile on his face.

She made a pretense of looking at the bolts of cloth on a nearby shelf. *He must be new to town.* She would have remembered meeting him, she was sure. His smile illuminated his entire face—not one crinkling corner remained unlit.

He arrived at her side and gestured toward the shelf. "May I help you find anything, Miss—" He stopped and grinned apologetically. "Let me introduce myself. I'm Jimmy Sullivan, the new clerk."

Up close, she saw that he was older than he'd first appeared. "I'm Rose Miller." She fished for something else to say. "I like the new bell on the door."

He brightened. "Do you? It was my idea. Makes the place seem friendlier, don't you think?"

She nodded.

"Rose Miller, is it?" His dark brown eyes twinkled down at her. "The name suits you. I like a name that suits." He switched topics abruptly. "But I haven't helped you a bit, have I? Anything in particular you're looking for?"

Yes, your boss. "Not really, I just thought I'd drop by and see if Mr. Lardie had gotten any new fabrics in since my last visit to the village. I'm the lighthouse keeper up at the point." She glanced casually around the store. "Is he here?"

He shook his head. "I'm afraid not. Perhaps there's something I could—"

"No, thank you." She gnawed on her bottom lip. These inquiries of hers were supposed to be subtle, nonchalant—seemingly offhand. Despite his airy manner, she doubted the new clerk lacked common sense. Mr. Lardie wouldn't have left him to tend the store alone if he did. *He knows I'm not here looking for fabric.*

"Have you been working here long, Mr. Sullivan?" she asked.

"No, my sister and I arrived here this past autumn. We came from St. Joseph, where work in my profession had become scarce. I have a fair amount of clerking experience, and thankfully, Mr. Lardie was in need of help just when I was in need of a position." His eyes twinkled again. "I owe the man. I'll be sure to tell him you stopped by."

No, please don't. She tried to sound calm. "There's no need."

He studied her for a moment. "Very well," he said with a shrug. "I'll be silent as the dead."

She felt her limbs weaken with relief.

He regarded her again, this time in a more chipper way. "I wonder, Miss Miller, if you'd like to meet my sister? She'll be here soon, on her way home from the inn where she works." He followed Rose's gaze to the darkening sky outside. "I'd be glad to take you home in my sleigh afterward. It has a lantern, and the moon is bright." He must have noticed her hesitation. "Don't worry, Dinah would accompany us."

Rose recalled her grandfather's warning, an ever-present reminder that things weren't always as they seemed. *But I wouldn't tell them a word about my past, not a word.* And the young Mr. Sullivan looked so trustworthy.

"We've hardly met anyone our own age here," he went on. "It would be such fun for Dinah to have a friend. I've felt pretty badly, dragging her along to keep me company when there aren't—"

Before he could finish the sentence, the cowbell rang once again.

The door opened, and into the store came a black-curled, merry-eyed girl who could only be Jimmy Sullivan's sister. She stopped short when she saw Rose, whatever news she'd been bursting to share halting on her lips.

"This," Jimmy announced with a flourish, "is my sister." He gestured in Rose's direction. "Dinah, this is the lighthouse keeper, Rose Miller. I'd wager she might be willing to become better acquainted with us if you can keep from chattering her to death, which I doubt."

His sister turned a deeply dimpled smile on Rose—and within seconds, fulfilled her brother's prediction.

"Oh, I just know we'll be good friends!" she exclaimed. "You've no idea how dreary it's been, having only Jimmy to talk to, when I want someone I can discuss recipes and the latest fashions with. He's all right for fetching things from high shelves of course. Brothers are useful for things like that. But for the rest, one wants a girl."

Rose soon discovered that she needn't do much more than smile and nod, for Dinah kept the conversation up on her own. The girl seemed without reservation. As the night wore on, Rose found herself forgetting hers.

Chapter 4

Despite the biting cold of the midwinter air, sweat trickled down Nathan's forehead. For the past hour, he'd been splitting wood faster than Rose could stack it. Thick gray clouds amassed on the horizon, and he hoped to beat the approaching storm. Thankfully, his hunting trip had been a success. The summerhouse, which he'd converted into a larder, now contained three rabbits and a wild turkey, plenty of sustenance to outlast a blizzard. Once the wood was split, the wind could howl as it pleased.

"I think we have enough now," she called to him from the buggy shed, where she'd been stacking the wood.

With a swift downward swing, he buried the ax in a stump and went to stand in the doorway beside her. Breathing heavily, he peered into the shed. His startled gaze flew back to her. The stack nearly skimmed the roof, much higher than she could reach.

"How...?"

She shrugged demurely, as if to say a girl must have her secrets.

He grinned and stood looking at the wood a moment longer. Then he started back toward the ax, saying over his shoulder, "The kindling still needs to be cut, and after that's finished, I'll need to see to the broken—" He stopped short at the altogether new sensation of her hand on his sleeve.

"A rest wouldn't hurt, Captain Perry."

He vowed he could feel her touch through his coat, his shirt, his cotton union suit, and the thick hair on his forearm. He wouldn't show it though. It wouldn't do for her to know how powerfully she affected him.

She removed her hand.

"You need to stay warm," he stated. "I should keep working."

She shook her head. "I might not possess the strength of a Viking, but I do know how to swing an ax."

Yes, she was accustomed to inhospitable weather and all the work that went with it. Perhaps she even found a good storm enjoyable at times. He knew he did. The very memory of shouting orders aboard his ship amid a sideways torrent of rain made his veins surge to life. It wasn't that he took his responsibility as captain lightly. Far from it. An entire crew of men and the shipping company he worked for depended on him. Yet he wouldn't trade life on the lake for anything.

Perhaps that was what drove him. Perhaps his sense of urgency to beat this storm was his way of reliving the exhilaration.

But he knew the truth. A man couldn't summon this half-barmy degree of concern for a fellow man, or even an army of men—only for a woman.

He released a resigned breath and leaned against the outer shed wall, arms crossed over his chest. He noted that Rose's hands went to her stomach, fluttered to her side, and returned to her stomach. *Do I make her nervous?* A very difficult question for a man not to investigate further. And he would, except. . .

He assumed a casual tone. "You've been spending a lot of time down in the village."

She nodded. "Yes, the Sullivans have been very kind to me. Did I tell you that Dinah and I are making a quilt to send her mother for her birthday?"

It was his turn to nod.

"And Jimmy plans to order some fabrics with little flowers on it—we specifically told him little flowers."

Ah yes, the young clerk, whom Rose had once described as *tall*. Hence, Nathan's reticence. Yet he wasn't sure exactly why he was uneasy about her friendship with the Sullivans, other than the obvious imprudence of a girl spending time with a young man she barely knew. That definitely ate at him. But his other concerns weren't so easy to define. Perhaps they had to do with the restlessness he'd observed in her lately. She seemed ill at ease, even brooding, neither of which could be solely explained by her grandfather's death. Her trips to the village, the diversion of this newfound friendship of hers, seemed evidence of an almost feverish need to fill the hours. From what was she escaping?

Nathan took great pains in flattening a splinter against the doorframe. "I do hope you're being careful."

Her brow furrowed. "Careful about what?"

"Careful about you and Jimmy being together. I assume you're ensuring that his sister is always present."

Her expression cleared. "Oh, that. Don't worry about that. We're all three of us good friends." But her gaze studiously avoided his.

Well, that was certainly convincing.

She started to say something but didn't finish it.

"Yes?" he prompted.

She still wouldn't look at him. "I don't see how my friendship with Jimmy is any of your concern."

Confound it, her heightened color and defensive tone were confirming it. *She does care for him.* "You cannot be too careful about your reputation."

Her eyes narrowed. "You're not my father."

Well, thank goodness for small mercies. He kept the thought to himself. It would hardly be appropriate to inform her that he viewed her in precisely the opposite way a father would.

He decided that his respite had come to an end. A coward's way out, but if he stood beside her any longer, he might act on his errant impulse to clasp that stubbornly lifted chin of hers and see if her skin was as soft as it looked.

He straightened and brushed his palms against each other. "Just promise me that you'll be careful." Bits of wood fell from his hands to the snow without a sound, a contrast to her deafening refusal to answer him.

Rose stood in the middle of the Sullivan's weathered, wood frame house and looked up at a portrait Jimmy was hanging on the wall. "No, tilt the right side up more."

"And then the left," Dinah added.

Jimmy's disbelieving gaze went to his sister. "That doesn't make any sense," he mumbled around the nails in his mouth.

"Well, we have to do something different," Dinah reasoned. She looked at the portrait sideways. "I think you lowered the whole thing last time, because it suddenly seems too close to the sofa."

Her brother dropped his arms to his sides and let the portrait dangle from one nail. "Is that more to your liking?"

"Try again," Dinah ordered.

He rolled his eyes upward, as though beseeching the heavens for patience, but good-naturedly did as he was bidden.

After much rearranging and deliberation, Admiral Abraham Sullivan was securely affixed to the faded gray boards of the sitting room wall. Rose and Dinah stood back and admired the effect of the portrait next to a smaller painting of a warship.

"And look, Rose, I only just now noticed how the red in Great-Grandfather Sullivan's cravat matches the red in the braided rug."

Jimmy gave his ancestor a conspiratorial wink. "I think you would've had more peace in the trunk, old boy." He ignored his sister's disapproving stare and walked away, his hammer slung over his shoulder.

For the past few days, Rose had been helping Dinah unpack a large trunk of family heirlooms her mother had sent her. It was full of special things. . .enviable things. Rose didn't gaze wistfully at the treasures because they were pretty, but because they mattered. The only thing that mattered to her was the hair ribbon in her pocket and her grandfather's Bible. She could still hear his low, resonant voice as he read to her from it every night. *Without fail, for as long as I can remember.*

She grew aware of Dinah's scrutiny.

"Let's go see if that bread has risen yet," her friend suggested.

Rose had learned this was Dinah's way of cheering her up. *"Roll up your sleeves and get busy, and then you'll forget your troubles."*

They went into the kitchen, and Rose pulled out a chair at the work table, sure she'd soon be recruited to slice, puree, mix, or mash. She sat down and watched Dinah bustle about making supper, her cheerful presence filling the lamp-lit corner of the house with as much warmth as the yeasty aroma of rising bread. She chattered on about everyday matters, not pausing when she dumped a load of potatoes from her apron to the table and handed Rose a paring knife.

"Between my wages at the inn and Jimmy's extra shifts at the store, we should be able to afford improvements on the house next spring." Dinah whisked flour into the meat drippings that sizzled in an iron skillet. "This house is dreadfully small. Luckily, Jimmy is clever with building things and other mannish tasks." She gave Rose a look fraught with meaning. "You know how handy that can be. Captain Perry, or whatever his name is who's always around at the lighthouse, sounds like he's pretty clever too."

Rose peeled a potato in a long spiral. "I suppose he is."

Dinah's eyes turned dreamy. "Is he handsome, this captain of yours?"

Taken aback by the question, Rose paused to consider it. It hadn't occurred to her to wonder whether Captain Perry was handsome or not. She recalled his average height and slim build, his ordinary brown-blond hair. His eyes, if she remembered correctly, were the color of the lake on a cold November day. "He isn't *my* anything. But he does have a. . .good face."

He did. His features were even, his skin fair, and his chin covered with a hint of blond stubble. Come to think of it, he was rather good-looking.

Rose resumed peeling.

"What's he like?" Dinah asked.

For this, Rose had a prompt reply. "Like a man who doesn't need to raise his voice to command a ship." *Though he's too modest to say so.* But reading between the lines of her grandfather's versions of Captain Perry's stories, Rose knew she'd answered Dinah truly.

"I wonder what it's like, being a ship's captain." Dinah stirred her gravy absently. "I'll bet he looks so dashing in his uniform."

Rose shrugged. "He doesn't wear one on land."

This deflating bit of news only dampened Dinah's enthusiasm for a moment. "I don't know how you do it. If I spent as much time as you do with a good-looking ship's captain, I'd behave like a smitten schoolgirl for sure."

Rose grinned. "That would be fun to see. But he doesn't think of me in that way."

Dinah's brows rose. "Oh? Why is it, do you suppose, that he stayed the winter in your grandfather's cabin? A steamship captain must be in sore need of respite after spending months on end on the lake, and he isn't likely to be much refreshed by chopping wood, filling water troughs, and whatever else keeps him busy at your place."

He does work hard. Had she ever thanked him for all he'd done? She feared not, just as she'd never really shown an interest in his work.

"He stayed on for my grandfather's sake," she said evenly. "They were friends." She recalled the night of Nathan's arrival, when she wondered if some evil intention had brought him to her door. *I've certainly long since abandoned those fears.* He'd come to see an old friend, nothing more.

Rose peeled a piece of potato she'd already peeled. "I don't know anything about his work, whether he needs a break from it or not."

Dinah gave her a scrutinizing look. "Do you know, a freshly baked apple pie can work wonders?" She winked. "Not that I have much experience with such things. It's my mother's trick for loosening a man's tongue. She employed it when my father was still with us." Dinah's father had died when she was twelve years old.

Rose surrendered to the eagerness in her friend's eyes. "There are some dried cherries I can revive in my cellar. Would a cherry pie do?"

Chapter 5

Rose stood outside her grandfather's cabin in an agony of indecision. The cherry pie was baked, a fragrant offering both sweet and tangy. It now seemed a terrible idea. She stalled, trying to distract herself by taking in the beauty of the twilit evening. The creeks were beginning to thaw, the forests filled with the musical sound of dripping water. The ice on the lake creaked and groaned, an indication that the shipping season would soon be upon them. *Captain Perry won't be staying much longer.*

If she didn't do this now, she wouldn't do it ever. Yes, she wanted to thank him, but it suddenly seemed silly, baking a man a pie. *The sort of thing a little girl would do. Or worse, a grandmother.*

Rose had just made up her mind to turn and flee, when she heard footsteps approach from inside the cabin.

No, don't open the door, don't open the door, don't open—

But he did. He filled the doorframe, a long-barreled rifle in hand. When he saw Rose, he immediately lowered the weapon. "I could've shot you!" he exclaimed, his eyes wide.

She thrust the pie blindly toward him. He took it awkwardly in one hand, his manner justifiably bewildered.

"It's cherry," she said in a rush. "To thank you for staying here and helping me this winter. I'm very grateful." She spun sharply and started down the path, obeying her earlier impulse to flee.

"Wait!" he called.

She paused but didn't turn around. *He's going to be patronizing about this, I just know it.*

"That's very kind of you," he said.

She turned.

"Truly," he added. "Won't you come inside and help me enjoy your generous gift?"

She hesitated. He was probably just being polite. And despite the many times she'd found herself alone with him, tonight seemed different. They weren't busy working, preoccupied with filling hay cribs, cleaning stalls, stacking wood. She'd have to actually talk to him.

He opened the door wider.

Stop behaving like a timid child on her first day of school.

Rose went inside and Nathan followed suit, shutting the door behind them.

After hanging his gun on a rack over the door, he lifted the red-checked cloth from the pie and sniffed the rising steam appreciatively. "I hope you won't mind if I serve this by the hearth. It's so much warmer there than at the table."

Moments later, they sat across from each other before the crackling fire, she in a creaky old armchair and he on a wooden bench he'd pulled over from the table. In such cozy surroundings, Rose was able to converse with surprising ease, speaking of the weather, the animals tucked snugly in the lighthouse barn, the ice on the lake and when it might melt.

She found herself relaxing. She even agreed to his suggestion to remove her drenched shoes and let them dry beside the hearth. Of course, she quickly tucked her feet up beneath her skirt so he wouldn't see her ankles.

"Do you miss being aboard your ship?" she asked around a flaky morsel of pie.

He nudged the blackened wood with a poker and watched the flames leap to life in the cavernous hearth. "At this moment?" He gave her one of his frank looks. "No."

Her stomach fluttered, a new sensation.

He set the poker down and leaned back in his chair, his legs stretched out in front of him. "The truth is, I do think about being back on my ship sometimes. I always look forward to spring, when I give the 'full speed' order after being land-locked all winter." He shook his head in wonder as he gazed into the fire. "She's a real beauty, the *Liberty*. Bulk freighter, steel hull, screw propulsion. Two hundred and eighty-two feet long. Three-cylinder, triple-expansion engine—" He stopped and glanced sheepishly at her. "But I didn't mean to make you regret asking the question."

"No, I've wondered about your work. You rarely mention it."

"I could say the same of you."

"Well, I'm not sure what to think of it yet," she admitted. "I haven't performed the primary duties of a lighthouse keeper for very long. The lake iced over so soon after. . ." Her grandfather's death was still a painful topic. Did this tight grip of grief ever ease?

"I'm certain your grandfather taught you well," he said gently.

Her throat tightened. There was so much she should have asked the man before his passing. Not about keeping the lighthouse, but about her life before she arrived on his doorstep. *It wouldn't have mattered. He didn't know.* She heard Captain Perry's voice as though from a distance.

"I shouldn't have mentioned him."

"No, I'd rather talk about him with you than anyone else." Suddenly, Rose longed to pour out the whole story to him. To tell him about the footsteps, the ribbon, the basket left on the lighthouse steps.

"My girl," she heard again, *"don't tell anyone. . . ."*

Rose uncurled herself with a yawn and reached for her shoes. "I do believe they're dry enough for the trip home now."

He began gathering up their empty plates. As he carried the dishes to the table, she laced up her shoes in relative privacy, her back to him. She berated herself for dreading this visit. None of the underlying tension she'd often detected between them had been present tonight.

He returned and walked with her to the front door. With one hand on the handle, he turned to face her. "I'll be leaving for Grand Haven tomorrow morning."

Though she'd expected the news, a pang of disappointment filled her. "Thank you again for all your help this winter, Captain Perry."

He released the door handle and forked his hand through his hair. It stood on end like a tousled little boy's. "My crew calls me that."

"Calls you. . . ?"

"Captain Perry."

She was still at a loss. "I imagine they do." She could think of nothing more to add except, "Is that so terrible?"

"Well, no. It's just that now and then I find myself wishing to leave the uniform behind. There's something about being on land, in villages, among families, children. . .with a woman." He shrugged. "Sometimes a man wants to simply be a man."

She wasn't sure what to say. "I do apologize, Mr. Perry."

"Ah, but that's worse." His voice dropped to a murmur that caused her stomach to flutter all over again. "Formalities between us make me feel like I'm a stranger to you." A flush arose in his cheeks, the first Rose could recall seeing there. "But I shouldn't expect you to remember or, for that matter, to really *know* my given name—"

She interrupted him softly, boldly. "I know your name, Nathan."

His gaze met hers. Fairly tangled with it.

With a curious, feminine wisdom that nobody had taught her, Rose realized she was about to experience her first kiss.

He stepped closer and tentatively, slowly, reached up and brushed a lock of hair from her eyes. He halted for the space of a heartbeat before lowering his head and touching his lips to hers.

His mouth fit hers like a kid glove, his coarse blond stubble creating shivers down her back. He smelled of sunshine and lake breezes in summer. She inhaled deeply and lifted her palms to his chest, feeling the softness of his plaid flannel shirt and the hardness of muscle beneath it. *Hold me, Nathan. . .*

He abandoned his reserve and pulled her to him. Somewhere in the midst of his kiss, she became aware of a strange, enveloping sense of calm. No longer was she the lost girl from no one knew where. She was the woman Captain Nathan Perry was kissing.

The glorious, safe sensation lasted for several uncountable seconds. Though she couldn't mark the time precisely, she knew exactly when it ended—because shortly thereafter, everything changed.

At first, she was too self-conscious to look him in the face once he straightened. When she finally did, she detected an unmistakable shadow of regret in his eyes. Unbidden, tears sprang into her own.

"Don't cry, Rose, please." He rubbed his jaw, looking as uncomfortable as it was possible for a man to look. "I'm sorry. Honestly I am."

Overflowing tears still being a very real threat, she didn't reply.

He buried both hands into his hair and left them there. "Please don't be upset. It won't happen again, I promise."

Why? Was kissing me such a terrible experience?

Fearing the answer, she remained silent and did the only thing that sprang to mind—hurry past him before she could say something mortifying.

The air outside, damp and chilly as it was, brought relief. Cold reality seemed preferable to a beautiful dream that could end so cruelly.

Chapter 6

Rain drummed onto Nathan's Stetson and dripped off the brim in rivulets. The campfire sizzled and struggled, shrouded in a cloud of steamy smoke. The forest sounded like it was being pummeled by a thousand stomping feet.

He drew his mackintosh tighter over his shoulders and sat down on Ginger's hard-as-a-brick saddle. He'd dumped it unceremoniously onto the ground after tying the horse to a nearby tree. *A pile of pinecones would be more comfortable than this.* He reminded himself that the journey would be worth it, that he'd soon be reunited with his beloved ship. He'd listen to the reports of his boatswain and chief engineer and watch his ditty-chanting crew prepare the ship to leave port.

But tonight, the memory of Rose's face after he'd kissed her crowded out any anticipation he felt about the future. Wounded—that's how she'd looked. *As if a man she trusted had betrayed her.*

He kicked a nearby rock and it shot off into the woods, startling Ginger.

"Easy, girl." He rose and stepped over to the canopy of trees where she pranced nervously about. As he stood there in the rain, stroking her back and whispering words of comfort, his mind drifted into the past.

More than once on a rainy night at the lighthouse, he'd stayed awake until dawn, probing the depths and mysteries of heavenly affairs with Rose's grandfather. Nathan, self-educated after learning the rudiments of reading and basic arithmetic in grammar school, had studied the Bible on his own. He knew all the books in order and could recite the Ten Commandments, the Twenty-third Psalm, the Lord's Prayer. But the more time he spent with Charlie Miller, the more he longed for those words to mean something to him too. So Nathan searched and agonized and prayed until he found the Jesus who lived in his old friend's big black book. *I should have told Charlie about the difference he'd made in my life before he died.*

Nathan's eyes stung, and from more than just the smoke. He returned to the dying campfire, heedless of the rain. He stretched out on his back beside the last of the sputtering blaze, his head resting on the firm leather saddle.

He'd acted impulsively, inviting Rose into the cabin. His only thought had been to assure her that her gift was welcome. She'd been so flustered about it. *She needn't have been.* In his entire life, no one had done something so nice for him. His mother died when he was too young to remember her, and his father would have burned the house down if he'd tried to boil water. According to the sailors who'd known Eli Perry as a young man, he hadn't always been a drunk. Reportedly, before Nathan's mother died, he'd been an efficient captain's mate, on his way to better things.

At any rate, a tasty domestic offering such as Rose's wasn't something Nathan would dream of turning down.

Still, I shouldn't have asked her inside. He'd realized it later, while warm and relaxed beside the hearth, having just glimpsed her shapely ankles before she whisked them heartlessly from view. By then it was too late. Her lovely face was still visible in the firelight, her shining-eyed radiance more desirable to him than any ship on any lake. He conveniently forgot that a steamship captain had no business getting himself involved with a woman, no matter how charming she might be. Spending weeks on end at home alone while he ran off to navigate the lakes was no life for Rose.

Never mind every other perfectly good reason he shouldn't have kissed her, chief among them being loyalty to her grandfather. *If the man knew how I'd behaved toward his granddaughter in that remote cabin, he'd have strung me up.* Nathan had been a little surprised when Rose herself didn't cast up his previous lecture about never being alone with that clerk fellow, Jimmy.

Now why did I have to go and think of him? No good could come of brooding over Rose's true feelings for the boy, or from stewing over the way she'd so carelessly attached herself to a near-stranger.

Sometime just before their kiss had ended, Nathan felt a sting of conscience. Yes, he'd endured weeks of forgetting to breathe whenever she was near, weeks of battling his natural impulse to draw her into his embrace, to comfort her over her grandfather's death. But that didn't excuse his actions. First and foremost, he was a man of discipline, as any good ship's officer must be.

Ah Rose, would you believe I want nothing more than to kiss you again? The warmth of her irresistible smile, the sweetness of her ladylike spirit had enveloped his every sense. He couldn't forget them. He couldn't forget *her.*

Nor could he pursue her. He could only pray that the merciful oblivion of sleep would come quickly.

Rose shut the summerhouse door and braced herself against the pounding rain. She hurried toward the back door, holding her shawl protectively over the jar of kerosene in her arms. Before he left, Nathan helped her carry the new shipment of kerosene out to the summerhouse, which he'd commandeered as a meat larder during the winter. Hanging fresh game there wouldn't be wise now that the warmer weather had arrived. *Although it would probably freeze solid today.*

Rose squeezed through the back door alongside a soaking Tucker, who was clearly eager to be indoors. *A fair-weather companion indeed.* She would've laughed at him, if she'd felt like laughing. The evening was so dreary, and it wasn't only the rain. Her last day with Nathan had been uncomfortable, to say the least. Still emotionally raw over his hurtful response to their kiss, she'd avoided his gaze like it might singe her. In return, he'd acted stiff and formal, leaving her certain he'd rather be anywhere else. But like the stoic ship's captain he was, he hadn't shirked his duty. He went over the lighthouse and grounds with her in great detail. Even more irksome, he asked her to repeat his instructions back to him more than once. *As if I couldn't understand how to operate a new milking station or use a fire poker to check a chimney for soot.*

Rose twisted her way out of her clingy wet shawl and hung it up beside the door. Leaving her puddle-creating boots in the entryway, she took the kerosene and proceeded through the house to the staircase, intending to continue up to the tower. Any lighthouse keeper understood the grave importance of keeping the lamp full. Lives depended on the light, and the light depended on kerosene.

Rose wouldn't dream of neglecting so vital a task. But she found herself groaning at the thought of all those stairs, each set steeper than the one before it. She'd practically skipped up them as a child, all but the last, which was unskippable, even for a nimble young girl.

Where had her energy gone?

With a heavy sigh, she plunked the jar of kerosene on the bottom step and plunked herself right down beside it.

How quiet the house was. With Nathan gone, every rustle of curtains or creak of wooden beams seemed ominous. They'd seemed so before his arrival, but never before she'd learned her grandfather's secret. That revelation made her feel like a tree pulled up by its roots. While her grandfather was still with her, Rose hadn't minded her lack of father, mother, sister, brother, cousin, aunt, uncle. . .family. He was her roots.

It occurred to her that Captain Nathan Perry had been her one link to the man named Charlie Miller. No wonder she took solace in Nathan's presence, despite his insufferable insistence on treating her like a helpless newborn lamb. He was one of the few people who'd known her grandfather—and her grandfather was the only human link to her past. *Well, not the only link. I simply don't know who the others are.*

With the thought came the urge to throw her former caution to the wind. She wanted—no, needed—to find her family. This wasn't just a faint yearning but an ache that had begun when she realized she had a mother who'd quite possibly given her away on purpose.

"There's trouble bound up in your past, girl. I can feel it."

The words echoed the uneasiness Rose felt in her own spirit. She shoved it aside with a strength she hadn't known she still possessed.

Come tomorrow, she would return to the village and resume her inquiries. Only this time, she wouldn't stop searching until she found answers.

For now, she had a lamp to fill.

"I couldn't say as I spoke to any ladies of an—er—fallen nature." A blush appeared on Reverend Bergmann's ruddy, whiskered cheeks. "I couldn't have, you see, because I wasn't the minister here at the time. Reverend West was, and he passed away just before my arrival fifteen years ago." He gripped the sturdy pew in front of him and leaned forward to peer at Rose with quizzical blue eyes. "Are you sure this young woman who'd made the contribution to the lighthouse had a—storied past?"

Rose could practically feel her knees quaking. Had the man somehow guessed the nature of the aforesaid woman's "contribution"? *But it's true enough, isn't it?* A baby in a basket could be considered a contribution. . .of sorts.

She forced her shaking limbs to grow still. "I suppose I could be mistaken," she said truthfully. As far as she knew, her mother might have been a saint, never missing a Sunday in this very place. But a fallen woman was more likely to resort to desperate actions than a saint.

The minister tapped his chin and stared at the carved oak pulpit that loomed before him. "The fact is," he said, his gaze returning to Rose, "your questions have brought something to mind that I'd forgotten. There was a woman buried in our graveyard during the time you spoke of. To be blunt, I don't know how she came to be there. She wasn't a member of our church, and her presence in our plot is a mystery that I'm afraid Reverend West took to his grave. The inscription on her headstone indicates the right year though."

Somewhere in the midst of the minister's narrative, Rose's mind finally grasped its meaning. A task that shouldn't have been difficult. But of all the places she'd imagined finding her mother, a graveyard hadn't been among them. *If she's gone, I can never ask her why she gave me up.* Rose's shoulders sagged, unable to bear the weight of her sinking hopes.

The minister gestured toward a door to his left and said gently, "It may be of little help to you, but you're welcome to go outside and have a look if you like. It's the grave in the far right corner of the plot."

Rose murmured a thank-you, said good-bye, and trudged toward the door.

Once outside, she saw that the churchyard was shrouded by a thin, wraithlike fog beneath an overcast sky. She spied a fenced-in little graveyard not far from the road. As she crossed the yard to the rickety wooden gate, she cried inwardly, *Why? Why would I bother doing this?* There was no possible way to identify a woman whose name she didn't even know.

Rose entered the graveyard and found the grave in the back corner. It lay beneath a slender oak tree and obviously hadn't been tended to in a long while. A brown tangle of underbrush, still brittle from winter, almost hid it from view. She stepped over to the headstone and swept aside the brambles.

"Stella Lawrence," she read. "1853 to 1872."

Rose sank onto the carpet of leaves beneath her feet. *Nineteen. She was only nineteen when she died.* No hint as to the woman's history presented itself in her stark epitaph, not even a "beloved mother" to suggest an infant being part of her story.

Inhaling the earthy scents around her, Rose tenderly touched a shoot of green grass that poked up between the dead leaves. She reached up and traced the engraving on the headstone. Even if she memorized every curve and hollow of the name inscribed there, it wouldn't come any closer to meaning anything to her.

Yet inexplicably, she found herself settling in beside that forgotten grave. Taking an unhurried moment to commune with the misty evening and the God who'd made it.

Chapter 7

Rose approached the Sullivans' house on her way home from yet another failed investigative journey and a brief, tranquil visit to the final resting place of Stella Lawrence.

Dinah won't mind if I stop by unannounced. She was in sore need of good cheer, and this was the place to find it.

She knocked on the front door and Dinah answered, poking her head cautiously out, her messy black curls tied up in a faded blue handkerchief. She exhaled fervently when she saw Rose. "Thank goodness, it's only you."

"Spring cleaning?" Rose teased. "Battling a wild ox?"

Dinah wrinkled her smudged nose and reached to straighten her skewed handkerchief. "Much worse, actually. I've been blackening the stove. Let me wash my face and tidy my hair, and then we'll have tea. I could use a break."

Rose nearly laughed. *She doesn't know how to take a break.*

The thought proved true about a quarter of the way through their tea, which Dinah served in the sitting room.

Rose squirmed under the reproachful gaze of old Admiral Sullivan. "I don't know how you and Jimmy came to have such a dreadfully stern relative."

Dinah glanced up at the portrait and shrugged. "Mother's people inherited all the jolly traits, I suppose." Without so much as a pause, she exclaimed, "Speaking of Mother, I know just the thing! We can work on her birthday quilt while we're visiting." She scarcely waited for Rose's answering nod before hurrying across the room to her sewing cabinet.

Rose watched as her friend rummaged through the bottom cupboard of the cabinet. Staring idly at Dinah's back, Rose was suddenly seized by a cold grip of paralysis.

It couldn't be.

But it was.

Just visible around the curls at the nape of Dinah's neck, awash in the afternoon sun streaming through the muslin curtains, was a duplicate of the hair ribbon in Rose's pocket. There could be no mistake. Those girlish pink roses and glistening gold border were distinct.

Sweat began to form on Rose's forehead. She thought of the small footprints in the sand, the imprints left behind by a child. . . . *It couldn't have been Dinah. Could it?*

Rose's heartbeat increased perceptibly. Dinah hadn't been raised anywhere near Old Mission, had she? Her hometown was Saint. . . Something.

Wasn't it?

And she's scarcely older than I am.

Wasn't she?

Rose had trouble sorting out her fragmented thoughts and gathering her scattered wits. Before she could do either, Dinah returned to the sofa, her arms full of vibrantly colored quilting squares in many shapes and sizes.

"Can you believe how short this stack is get—" She broke off abruptly. "Whatever's the matter, Rose? You look as if you've seen a ghost."

Indeed, I have. Not a living one, but a ghost nonetheless. Rose almost spilled out the all-too-revealing questions that consumed her. But her grandfather's warning cast its dark shadow even here, in the Sullivans' sitting room. She attempted to turn her lips upward. "I'm all right. I promise."

"Then please inform your eyes of it." Dinah sank weakly down onto the edge of the sofa.

I must ask. I must.

"Dinah," Rose asked slowly, "how long have you had that ribbon that's in your hair?"

Dinah's brow furrowed. "My hair ribbon? I've no idea." She reached back to feel the aforementioned article and twisted her head so Rose could see it. "It's sparkly, isn't it? With pink roses?"

"Yes." Rose's every muscle tightened as she awaited Dinah's reply.

"I can't remember *not* having it. Why do you ask?"

Think, think. "Um, well—" Rose's thoughts tumbled over each other, no safe answer to be found among them. "Do you have any idea where you might have come by it?" she asked finally.

Dinah shook her head. Then she hesitated. "Well. . . Perhaps I might know. There was a mercantile in St. Joseph, stocked with one-of-a-kind items. Handmade wood carvings, pottery, beadwork, and such. Jimmy used to work there, but the building burned down, and the owner couldn't afford to rebuild. That's when Jimmy and I came here to find work. I wouldn't be surprised if my mother got the ribbon from there."

Dinah's answers seemed forthcoming enough, but there was a flicker in her bright black eyes that indicated she was calculating, pondering Rose's interest, trying to connect the ribbon to anything significant.

Think back, Dinah, Rose pleaded.

Desperate, she asked, "I wonder, did your family always live in St. Joseph?" *Isn't there any chance at all that you lived in Old Mission as a child?*

"I only remember the house in St. Joseph." Dinah spread her hands to the sides, a gesture of bewilderment. "*Should* I have lived elsewhere?"

At her friend's obvious confusion, Rose's entire being slumped. "No," she admitted, "I don't suppose you should have."

The truth was, if Dinah Sullivan had ever left a baby in a basket on lighthouse steps, she was unaware of it. Further, it stood to reason that a particular batch of hair ribbons, unique as they might be, could have been sold in more than one store.

The *tick, tick* of the ancient grandfather clock on the wall marked the passing of time.

Rose felt Dinah's small, warm hand cover hers on the sofa cushion.

"Whatever's troubling you," her friend said softly, "it's best to turn it over to the good Lord."

An onslaught of emotions deluged over Rose, somehow more encompassing than the barrage that preceded it.

Dinah squeezed her hand. "I've seen for weeks now that you're holding on to something, Rose. And I can't help thinking you should let it go. Entrust your dearest hopes to the all-knowing wisdom who made us both, and return to the business of living your life. Joyfully." Her deep dimples flashed in her rose-hued cheeks. "It's hard work, you know."

Rose smiled a wobbly smile. She must have nodded, for after one last squeeze, Dinah released her hand and returned her attention to the quilting squares.

That night, Rose sat on the lakeshore, her grandfather's Bible tucked against her chest, her gaze fixed on the horizon. The lighthouse light revealed the curling smoke of a passing steamship. Was it Nathan's?

She couldn't get the conversation with Dinah out of her mind. It brought to light an awareness that had been growing inside her for weeks. As fervently as she longed to find her family, perhaps she wasn't meant to. *Did I ever actually ask God whether I should begin this quest in the first place?*

Impatiently, Rose tossed a handful of sand into the shallow surf that lapped against the shore. It was an easy mistake to make. After all, what kind of Maker wished for His creation to live without a family?

She wanted to rail, to demand answers from above. *Why would You provide others with a sense of belonging and not do the same for me?*

She heard it again, her grandfather's resonant voice, only this time, he wasn't uttering a dire warning. He was reading to her from the very worn book she now held in her arms.

"*Where wast thou when I laid the foundations of the earth?*"

It was a question for Job, long-suffering servant of the Almighty in the Old Testament. In response to the many understandable cries of *why* from the man who'd lost his children, his riches, his health, God finally answered out of a whirlwind. Rose couldn't recall His exact words, but they went something like this:

Where were you when I laid the foundation of the earth? Who set its measurements, since you know? On what were its footings set, or who laid its cornerstone when the morning stars sang together, and all the sons of God shouted for joy?

Or in this case, the evening stars. Rose rubbed her chilly arms and breathed in the tangy scent of the lake. She looked up at the sky. How lovely it was, the stars like a canopy of diamonds winking down at her. *Anyone who could make such a beautiful night simply must be good.*

God hadn't answered Job, not in the way she would have expected. Instead, He reminded His agonized servant of the splendor and glorious triumph of His creation.

Rose had never understood that ages-old reply to Job before. But sitting here tonight beneath a canopy of stars, she finally understood. This night was a gift. The earth itself was a gift, a reminder of the God who didn't change. Every day that the sun rose in the east and set in the west, every turn of the seasons, bore witness to His faithfulness to mankind. His faithfulness to *her*.

Yet could she truly give up her plan to unearth her origins?

The very thought of her desire never being fulfilled caused a terrible, chill-inducing tremor to sweep through her.

I can't. I can't let it go.

Nor could she hold on to it any longer. Such dogged determination all but eroded her joy and exposed the weakness of her faith.

After one last powerful struggle, Rose hugged her grandfather's Bible all the tighter. . .and surrendered her quest to her Lord.

Chapter 8

"The jingle of the harness makes a merry end to a merry evening," Rose said as she and Jimmy rode toward the lighthouse in his two-seated buggy.

He nodded absently and craned his head to look down at one of the front wheels. "I need to oil that right wheel—all but have to shout over the rattle."

They bounced along the rutted road, feet sore from dancing the evening away at the dock warehouse. Rose had attended the village festivities reluctantly, yielding to a pleading Dinah, who'd assured her that Jimmy would drive her home in plenty of time to light the lighthouse light.

"Do you suppose Dinah will dance until morning?" Rose asked.

Jimmy's reply was made in utter confidence. "Yep."

Rose smiled reflectively. "She looked lovely tonight, didn't she?"

Jimmy held the reins with one hand and loosened his tie with the other. "You both did."

Rose smiled again but didn't reply right away. His attempt at gallantry couldn't fool her. *He didn't notice his sister or me tonight.* Everyone knew he was smitten with the innkeeper's daughter, Abigail, who worked alongside Dinah.

"Jimmy," Rose said at last, "how do you make it seem so easy, courting Abigail?"

He gave her an inquiring glance. "What do you mean?"

She wasn't entirely sure herself why she'd asked. "Well, I've seen you dance with her, fetch her a glass of lemonade without being asked, banter back and forth so effortlessly with her. . ." She shrugged. "I've wondered how you do it."

He quirked a dark brow. "Why? Is there some village fellow you have your eye on?"

She shook her head.

"Because if you do, you'd better ask Dinah about all that." He puffed out his chest in a theatrical fashion and winked. "In case you haven't noticed, I'm a man. We don't give advice to you women. It isn't safe—we're sure to make a mess of it." He turned the horse onto the lighthouse drive, where the branches of an overgrown lilac bush hung over the road. Rose reached out, letting her fingers trail through the blossoms. She reveled in the way they perfumed the air and lent the night a dreamy quality.

The dream didn't last long.

They rolled into the lighthouse yard with a creak of buggy wheels at the precise moment when the barn door opened to reveal a strong, lean figure standing in the doorway. He stepped out into the barnyard and crossed his arms over his chest as Rose and Jimmy approached.

A series of knots formed in Rose's stomach. *Nathan.*

In addition to the shock of seeing him again—this man who'd kissed her, held her in his arms—she was very aware of the rigidness in his manner tonight.

Jimmy halted the horse and came around to help Rose from the buggy. She took his offered hand and clambered to the ground without looking at Nathan.

Jimmy introduced himself with a cheerful, "Jimmy Sullivan. I assume you're the ship's captain I've heard so much about?"

At Nathan's curt nod and cursory "Pleased to meet you," Jimmy looked from Nathan to Rose and back to Nathan again. A knowing grin lit his face. But he merely tipped his cap in their vague direction and leaped back up into the buggy. After lifting the reins and clucking to his horse, he shot Rose an impudent look over his shoulder, his mischievous eyes resembling two gleaming blackberries.

She ignored him and waited until the buggy was a dot in the distance before turning to Nathan. She saw that his arms were still crossed over his chest, his posture stiff.

"You've been busy while I was away," he said.

Rose made herself hold his unflinching stare. She'd done nothing wrong—nothing. "I always keep the tower light burning at night and the lamp sparkling clean, if that's what you mean." *I don't owe him an explanation.* "What brings you back to Old Mission during the heart of the shipping season?"

He unfolded his arms and shrugged, the thinness of his cotton shirt over his chest causing her to remember, with unwelcome clarity, the warmth of his embrace. She looked away.

"My ship is at the shipyard in Grand Haven for repairs. Not wishing to wait idly at her side, I hitched a ride with a captain friend of mine, who happened to be coming this way."

Genuine sympathy filled Rose. "What happened to your ship?"

"In essence, one of the boilers exploded." At her gasp, he quickly added, "Nobody was injured. It's a common hazard of the trade, I assure you." He tilted his head and ducked as though attempting to get in her line of vision. "I'd thought to come pay a visit to my old friend's charming granddaughter, but I see another man already had a similar idea."

Her pulse leaped. What was he saying? That he'd come to see her in the same way he assumed Jimmy had been seeing her? But no, caution was needed. In addition to recalling the heavenly warmth of his kiss, she also recalled being left near to tears once the blissful moment had ended. "My grandfather's door is always open to you, Captain Perry. I think you know that."

"And young Mr. Sullivan?"

"He's always welcome too."

Nathan nodded, his expression musing. "He seems a nice enough fellow, from what little I saw of him. Still, you've only known him a short while, and it's"—he looked around at the vast lake on one side and thick forests on the other—"awfully isolated up here. You really ought to think twice about permitting a young man to accompany you to the outskirts of civilization."

His officious words made her suspect, once again, that he still viewed her as a child. *No wonder it appalled him when we kissed.* She said icily, "I think I know enough of Jimmy Sullivan not to fear for my life every time he's kind enough to offer me a ride home."

Nathan seemed to struggle with that for a moment, indecision in his eyes. Finally he nodded. "Of course. Forgive me."

She didn't answer right away, and then decided not to answer at all. *He deserves to stew.*

The silence between them grew palpable.

"Rose. . ." He spoke her name in a pleading murmur, like the balmy breeze that sighed in the treetops. "Please don't be angry with me." He reached up and rubbed his face with both hands. "I don't know how to behave when you grow bristly on me—don't know how to make you understand. I'm simply trying to look out for you."

It's all you ever do. "Can't you just be happy that I have two such good friends?"

"I am happy. Or I will be. Once I'm certain that their intentions are honorable." His tone resumed its usual straightforward quality. "If you'll permit the intrusion, I must stay until tomorrow, when my friend's ship passes through this way again." He gestured toward the barn. "The animals are fed for the night, and I know my way to your grandfather's cabin. I won't trouble you any further this evening."

She hesitated, remembering that the cabin was currently overrun with mice.

His gaze cut through the twilight to her. "I've no notion of repeating my performance of the night before I left, if that's what's worrying you."

Heat crawled up her neck at the mere mention, however indirect, of their kiss.

"No," she blurted out, "you can't stay in the cabin. It has mice." What a terrible thing to have to admit, just when she longed to assert her independence.

There was a glimmer of a grin in his eyes. "I've braved worse."

Is he laughing at me? The thought made her want to kick him—or to cry. Where had this changeable, fragile state come from?

His amusement faded as he observed her. "Don't be upset. I'll see to the mice tomorrow."

"You needn't bother." She knew her shaky voice betrayed her crumpling composure. "I'm perfectly capable of purchasing a cat." She inclined her head toward the lighthouse tower. "Now, if you'll excuse me, I have a lamp to light."

Chapter 9

Nathan anchored a fallen limb to the ground with his knee and wrestled a mess of stiff pine needles to the side. He'd noticed the limb in the path yesterday and determined to remove it first thing in the morning. It blocked the trail to the privy, a tripping hazard, especially if Rose were to use the privy after dark.

As Nathan sawed his way through the thick limb, his hands grew increasingly unsteady. Chills shook his body. He couldn't help wishing that dawn's cold early light would hurry up and become a respectable blaze, or that he could return to bed. He'd slept terribly last night, and not because of the scurrying of a few harmless mice. He'd been afflicted with the same illness that had recently befallen his crew.

In truth, it had been a difficult past few weeks. Everything had gone wrong at once. Just when he felt ready to bow under the strain of finding it necessary to limp his crippled vessel to the nearest port, several members of his crew were stricken with raging fevers and a terrible soreness in their throats. The nurse tended to them aboard the ship, and when they arrived on shore, a reputable doctor took over their care. Nathan didn't leave Grand Haven until they were on the mend, in spite of his compelling urge to see Rose.

He hated the way he'd left things between them, before. It nagged at him. *Though come to think of it, this isn't much better.* He'd somehow upset her last night with his amusement over the cabin mice.

He abruptly stopped sawing and pitched aside the large hunk of wood he'd just cut. The effort caused a wave of dizziness to sweep through him. *I need to finish this before I leave for the docks—and then there's the mice.* All at once, the tasks before him seemed Herculean, too overwhelming to even contemplate. *But I must get back to my ship.*

Despite its current decrepit state, his handsome vessel was blessedly straight-forward. It operated on machinery, rules, order. . .things a man could understand. *Unlike certain women.*

Nathan recalled the way Rose had blushed when he mentioned their kiss. Ah, the very idea that she might be affected by him in that way, might be remembering the moment with anything resembling interest, filled him with a wistful ache that no ship could hope to vanquish.

And yet. . .

Commanding a vessel was more than just his livelihood; it was his life's blood. He'd scampered across the decks of ships almost every day of his life since childhood. But now his love for his work, specifically plying the great waters of the north, stood as yet another barrier between him and Rose.

Torn, Nathan cried out in a desperate prayer, *God, why must I be so reluctant to reside on the shore?*

Even if he weren't, there was still the matter of that Sullivan fellow. Rose had referred to him as her friend, but Nathan suspected women could be coy about such things. He longed to ask her outright, "Do you care for him?"

He *could* ask. After all, he could hardly be expected to carry on like this much longer. But he couldn't bring himself to ask the question for fear of hearing the words that might break his heart.

Coward.

What he needed to do was focus on his labors. He couldn't go anywhere until he removed this infernal tree from the path.

Nathan forced his hands to stop shaking and resume their sawing. With any luck, he'd be fit as a fiddle soon, and could escape this whole miserable situation.

Instead, it took every ounce of strength he possessed to heave the last of the limb to the side. After that, he managed to stumble through the lighthouse back door, intending to look for some bait so he could lure the mice into the traps he was determined to fashion before he left.

He made it no farther than the back entryway before his head swam and a red film appeared before his eyes. *Maybe I'll lie down, just for a while.*

Sometime later, he awoke to a blurred image of Rose approaching the sitting room, where he'd somehow come to be, lying on the sofa at an awkward angle with both legs hanging over the side. Her gaze fell on him, and an alarmed look filled her eyes.

Before his world went dark, he sensed her soft hand reaching for his forehead. He thought he heard her murmur, "You're burning up," but he couldn't be sure.

Rose scarcely left Nathan's side that day. At his delirious insistence, she slipped away just long enough to hurry to the dock with a message for his friend, Captain Volcov. The message contained word of Nathan's illness and was to be taken to his chief engineer in Grand Haven.

During the night, she descended the tower stairs several times to look in on him, keeping an eye on the lighthouse light through the downstairs windows. Using her grandfather's method of pulverizing white willow bark and making a lukewarm tea of it, she succeeded in cooling his fever a little. But he still vacillated between huddling in the bottom corner of the couch to sweating profusely and tossing off all his covers.

Clearly, it pained him to swallow. She winced every time she watched him try. *Dear Lord in heaven, help me help him.*

Sometime around 2:00 a.m. Nathan's fever rose to dangerous new heights. More delirious than ever, he spoke six words that struck her like a hammer's blow.

"Keep her safe," he muttered under his breath. "It's a secret."

This means something, Rose told herself, deeply troubled.

But she wasn't able to ponder the mystery for long. Graver concerns filled her mind. She sat beside her patient's shaking form until dawn and beyond, desperately wishing she could do more for him. She cooled his forehead with a damp cloth and stared down at his flushed face. Something about his closed eyelashes, so golden and long, made him appear childlike. The sight made her realize how greatly she'd come to appreciate his strength, even as she often bristled at his overprotective ways.

Please, please get better. On the heels of the pleading thought came a new awareness, one that seeped into her slowly.

She loved this man.

She didn't know when it happened, or how, only that it had. She loved hearing him laugh at Tucker's lively antics, loved the way his tongue protruded out the corner of his mouth when he worked with his hands, loved his devotion to his crew, loved his gentlemanly courtesy toward her.

Unfortunately, this realization did nothing to ease her distress. *He doesn't think of me like that. He can't—not when he regretted kissing me so much.*

Throughout the next day, Rose cooled Nathan's brow as best she could and kept an anxious eye on his fever, which to her relief tapered off and didn't rise quite so high again.

More than once, he repeated his mysterious words.

"Keep her safe," he'd mumble restlessly while tossing about on the sofa. "It's a secret."

Rose wondered what it all meant.

Three days later, he sat up in bed, clear-eyed and alert. Though still weak, he seemed much improved.

Rose went to get him some warm broth from the kitchen. Upon her return, she saw that he was pushing aside his covers and attempting to swing his legs onto the floor.

"Just what do you think you're doing?" She set the broth on the little table beside him and placed a prohibiting hand on his chest.

"I need to get back to my ship."

"Oh no you don't. What you need to do is drink some of this good broth."

"But I can't, I—"

"Barney Hopper from the dock brought a telegram for you earlier today from Grand Haven. Your engineer wrote that repairs are taking longer than expected, and there's no need for you to hurry back." She gently shoved Nathan back against the cushion. "So you might as well drink some broth."

To her surprise, he did.

Chapter 10

The following afternoon, Nathan found Rose in the kitchen, laboring over yet another batch of steaming chicken broth.

"You do know I can eat other substances now," he teased as he slid onto a seat at the table.

She flipped a lock of silky brown hair over her shoulder. "Until I see some color in your cheeks, this is what I'm feeding you." She ladled a bowl of soup and set it before him. "There now, see if that doesn't go down easier than. . ." She appeared to be searching for the right terminology. "Hardtack."

He chuckled. "Is that what you think I eat on my ship? Stone-solid biscuits? This isn't the days of the Mayflower, you know." *But my travels seem that long, Rose, when they take me away from you.* He couldn't say that. He still didn't know where he stood with her. Although. . .

Did she seem softer toward him since his recovery? She was still guarded as a cornered rabbit whenever he stood close to her, but her manner didn't seem hostile. And *soft* wasn't the right word. *Settled*, perhaps?

She tilted her head sideways and lifted her hair. A little sigh escaped her lips when the breeze swept over her neck. He tried his best not to think about the soft skin of her exposed throat.

"Nathan," she began. She hesitated and colored slightly. "Captain Perry."

"Nathan," he corrected. He drummed his fingers on the table, soup forgotten. *Just talk to me, Rose. I won't eat you.*

She toyed with her hair, her gaze flitting away from his. "While you were sick, you—you said something that struck me as a bit odd."

He felt his chest begin to tighten. What had he gone and done? *Let this not be anything to do with how I feel about her.*

He summoned a casual tone. "Oh?"

She still didn't look at him. "You said, 'Keep her safe.' And, 'It's a secret.'" She finally met his gaze. "What do you suppose you meant by it?"

His heart dropped, heavy as a steel ball in his chest. This went much farther back than his recently awakened feelings for her. Much, much farther back. He'd never told a soul about that basket filled with precious cargo, about that midsummer-night errand he'd been sent on. Not the authorities, not the fishermen, not Charlie Miller. . .not even his own father. *Dear God above, I've kept my secret for these many years, just as she asked. How do I escape this?*

Looking into Rose's entreating eyes, he realized he couldn't. That fact, coupled with a sudden undeniable peace that flooded him, brought him around to the truth.

It was time.

Rose could scarcely hear Nathan's voice over the jogging of his knee as it bobbed up and down against the table.

"Perhaps you should sit down," he said.

She did as he asked, her pulse thudding.

"When I was about eight years old," he began, "a woman purchased passage on my father's fishing boat."

She didn't find that particularly astonishing. "Did it happen often?"

He shook his head. "She must have been well-to-do, for my father didn't hold with hauling 'pesky females' on his boat. Doubtless she made him an offer he couldn't refuse, especially considering the fact that she was frail—and had her infant daughter with her."

The thudding of Rose's pulse grew louder, rivaling the *thump, thump* of Nathan's still-drumming knee. *A woman who was frail. A woman with a baby girl. . .*

Nathan went on. "We fished our way up the coastline, stopping at various ports along the way to take our catches to market. Before long, it became plain that the poor woman's health was declining." His knee went still abruptly. "Father was too drunk to see it. She didn't trust him or his crew, and who could blame her? I learned how little regard she had for the lot of them one day when I brought her a glass of water from the galley, and she said something about suffering greatly from dropsy, and to please, please not tell anyone. She was terrified that my father and the crew might assume it was infectious and drive her off the ship."

Why was she so desperate to stay aboard? Rose couldn't find her voice. *And what about her baby?* She realized that she was clutching the edges of her seat in a death grip.

"We docked at Old Mission late one evening," Nathan said. "My father and his crew went down to the village for a night of drunken reveling in one of the taverns, and while they were gone, the woman's condition worsened." He stared unseeingly at his bowl of broth. "I'd seen a dying woman once before, when we lost my mother, and I knew I was seeing one again. Anyway, she called me down to the hull, where I helped her arrange some blankets in the bottom of a basket. She laid her baby

195

carefully inside it. Then in the most pleading voice I'd ever heard, she asked me to take the baby to shore and leave her someplace friendly. I distinctly remember her saying that—'someplace friendly.' She spoke so wistfully." A distant look appeared in Nathan's eyes, as though he were mulling over something. "She was a motherly sort, through and through. Her every thought seemed to be for her baby, and yet somehow, she had room in her heart for a motherless eight-year-old boy too. Often, I would find her eyes on me, and they were practically wellsprings of empathy. In spite of being so ill, she took me under her wing from the very first day." He paused. "But back to that night. Just before I left with the baby, she caught me by the arm and begged me to keep her baby safe. 'It's a secret,' she said—more intently than you could even imagine."

The familiar words jolted through Rose like steam rattling a teakettle. Her thoughts whirled, unable to settle on any one aspect of this incredible story until finally they found their center. The baby. *The baby was the secret.*

Nathan gave her a wan smile. "You might have guessed by now that I left the baby at the lighthouse. And you were the baby."

Nathan was the child. The little footsteps in the sand had been imprinted there by him. His younger self, in search of a friendly place, had arrived at the lighthouse and found what he'd been looking for. He'd laid the basket on the doorstep, later to be found by kindly Charlie Miller, who'd taken Rose and raised her as his own.

"I returned to the boat just as my father and the crew arrived back from their drunken excursion. They were accompanied by a stranger, who turned out to be your father. Apparently, he'd been searching up and down the lake for your mother for quite some time." Nathan's mouth flattened into a straight line. "I don't blame her for telling him that the baby, whom he knew to have been exposed to scarlet fever back home, died of it along the way. Or for saying that she'd buried the baby in the lake. Thankfully, neither my father nor the crew contradicted her story. I guess they decided her business was her own."

"But why?" Rose whispered. "Why would she lie to my father?"

Nathan rubbed his jaw with seeming reluctance. "I'm sorry to have to add this, Rose, but if you'd seen your father's eyes, you wouldn't need to ask the question. Never had I seen such cold eyes in a human face."

Amid her overwhelming cacophony of emotions, a profound sadness emerged within Rose. Her mother was gone, lost to her before she'd even found her. *And my father, he was. . .*

"I never forgot that little baby," Nathan said thoughtfully. "In the back of my mind, I always wondered what had become of her. So after my father passed away, I secured a job as a cub pilot on a steamship and disembarked one afternoon at Old Mission. I found myself walking along the shore toward the lighthouse. I met

Charlie on the beach, and we struck up a friendship. He later introduced you to me as his granddaughter."

The words washed over Rose but didn't quite sink in. So much had been shared, so much that she'd wondered about, pondered over, agonized over. Long-sought answers were now hers. Instead of being glad about them, she could barely comprehend them.

"Why didn't you tell my grandfather the truth?" she asked finally.

Nathan traced the rim of his soup bowl. "The two of you seemed so happy together. It seemed right to leave well enough alone. And there was the problem with your father. It was clear, even to a man as young as I was, that you were better off with Charlie than with him." He shrugged. "But the biggest reason, I think, was that I'd been told all of this was a secret. A child takes those words to heart. They became a part of me, intricately woven with my view of you, of my role in your life."

Rose swallowed, hard. "My mother is. . .gone?" It didn't need to be said, yet somehow it did.

Nathan nodded. "I'm sorry."

"I didn't even know her name."

"It was Stella—Stella Lawrence."

Chapter 11

Nathan left the next day to return to his ship. Rose accompanied him to the dock, using the excuse that she could do with a walk, to which he nodded and murmured, "Little wonder, what with the way you've been cooped up nursing me back to health."

Or so she thought he said.

She couldn't trust herself today. Not when she didn't know how long it might be before he would be back, this man who'd known her since infancy. Not when there were many things she wished to discuss with him, and time was rapidly slipping away from her. Too soon, he'd be on his way to Grand Haven aboard Captain Volcov's ship.

Other than telling him about the overgrown grave in the churchyard and relaying the fact that Stella Lawrence was buried there, Rose hadn't spoken much about her past and all that he'd told her.

The past wasn't the topic she longed to talk about. *The future. I want to talk about our future.*

Instead, she walked by Nathan's side in silence, no Tucker dogging their steps to distract her from the unspoken tension between them. She'd thought it best to leave the dog behind so he wouldn't be underfoot of the dock workers. As they walked, Nathan kept sending her nervous little glances, starting to say something but not finishing it. *What?* she longed to shout. *Tell me.*

The dock was crowded as usual, and noisy, crammed with milling passengers, sailors pushing clattering carts down the gangplank, gulls crying, tugboats whistling, waves splashing against the pier. Rose and Nathan stood in the midst of the chaos for a moment before he said, "Captain Volcov's ship is waiting for me."

He made no move to follow his words with actions, just stood there looking somewhere over the top of her head, a tight muscle visible in his jaw.

Bolstered by the possibility that he was reluctant to leave her, Rose reached out and softly touched his forearm.

He glanced down at her fingers. "It pains me to see you grieving for your mother so."

She bit her lip and shook her head. "I'm not, not really."

"Perhaps if I hadn't told you about her—"

"Shh. I'm glad I know. Truly."

He stole her hand from his arm but didn't release it. *Nathan Perry is holding my hand. . .in public.* She cast a furtive, self-conscious glance around to see if anyone had noticed.

"No one's watching," he murmured. After a brief hesitation, he threaded his fingers through hers.

Her ability to breathe failed her.

"You have the traps for the mice?" he asked, his thumb rubbing lightly against her hand.

She nodded.

"There are more down in the cellar by the potato bin, in case you should need them. But I think I vanquished most of the varmints for now."

Her every sense was trained on the movement of his thumb.

"You know to pull the wire tight before setting the cheese down on the—"

"Yes, you showed me." Unbidden, she remembered their kiss that night in the cabin—the first part of it, before he'd pulled away in dismay.

Something of her thoughts must have shown in her expression, for he groaned just audibly and lifted his free hand to her jaw. He cupped her face and tilted it toward his. "Rose, please be careful while I'm away. Don't go poking around for trouble. I mean, concerning your father."

That's what's been on his mind? My father? She felt her soul shrink in despair. "I heard you when you told me of your dire observations about him."

"Yes, I know you did. But I've been worried you might seek the man out at some point, nonetheless."

She shrugged. "I never knew him."

"I suspect he doesn't deserve to know that you're alive."

She squeezed Nathan's hand, attempting to reassure him. "I have no intention of looking for him. Rest at ease."

His hold on her jaw, already gentle, turned even more so. He paused for a second before narrowing the gap between them. *If you kiss me good-bye, Nathan, I'll be incapable of watching you walk away.*

He stopped short. "If you should need anything, leave a message for me here at the docks. I'll stop by every time we bring freight in this direction, even if we're not making a delivery here. Though I probably won't be able to steal away long enough to come see you often."

"No, of course not." Her brave words concealed the wrenching in her heart. She couldn't let him see the love she harbored there. She had no real assurance that he felt the same way.

After a lingering stroke of his fingertip along her jaw, he stepped back. "Take care of yourself, Rose."

He turned and walked down the gangplank, his canvas bag slung over his shoulder, a bleak symbol of his constant leave-taking.

That night in the lighthouse tower, Rose rested her elbows on her newly polished black windowsill and gazed down at the lake, remembering another moonlit night she'd spent here. New Year's Eve, the first she'd endured alone after her grandfather's death. Oddly, though she knew about her past now, he seemed more like her family than ever. And the work he'd passed on to her was so very worthwhile. Lately, she'd found new joy in seeing to the daily tasks this dear, humble man had done so ably before her.

In the stillness of this particular tranquil midsummer's eve, the lake was quiet, illuminated by the mighty beam of light that revolved across it for a span of thirteen miles. Rose ran her finger over the sparkling lamp, mounted so securely on its pedestal stand, tiny shards of glass amplifying its power, its mechanisms functioning precisely as they ought to.

Tonight, just as it had on New Year's Eve, the light cast shadows over the lake. But they no longer seemed malicious to her.

She wondered why that was. She'd felt exposed back then, threatened by the solitude. Nathan's arrival had helped, yet it hadn't changed everything. What had?

Perhaps it was the knowing. Her past wasn't a mystery anymore, a tenuous unknown that filled her mind with ominous possibilities and her heart with painful questions. Learning of her mother's devotion to her had healed a wound inside her. If Nathan's memory could be trusted, her mother had given her away out of a desperate love, and there was comfort in that.

There was also comfort in. . .Nathan.

Just Nathan.

As a child, he'd lugged her down an endless stretch of shoreline, all the way to the lighthouse. He'd made sure to leave her somewhere safe. And in the process, he'd surely rescued her.

Rose smiled softly. She now understood his continual fussing over her safety, and it no longer upset her. As he'd said, a child didn't soon forget such a weighty admonition.

Yet he wasn't the cause of her kinship with this shadowy night. He wasn't the reason that this lakeside tower seemed a serene sanctuary once again. How could he be? He wasn't even here.

The change had come after her talk with Dinah, when her friend encouraged her to surrender her tightly clasped will to her Creator. Beneath a starry sky, Rose had done exactly that. Letting go of her quest to find her family hadn't mended everything. Often, she still felt a painful twinge at the knowledge that she lacked the one thing so many people seemed to take for granted. But the world around her, the earth fashioned by her Lord—a gift to a man named Job and now to her—had endeared itself anew to her. She never tired of wandering through the woodland pathways beyond the lighthouse clearing or walking along the pebble-strewn shore in the pink light of sunset.

Did I ever even tell Dinah how much she helped change things for me?

No, Rose realized, she hadn't. *I'll tell her, and soon.* First, she had a grave to visit, some overgrown brambles to clear away, and a bouquet of wildflowers to lay in their place.

It was late afternoon when Rose approached the churchyard. The sun's rays streamed through the tree branches of the little fenced-in grove, the light catching on a glistening object in the far corner—precisely where she intended to lay her bouquet.

Had someone been to her mother's grave?

Rose unlatched the gate and hurried to investigate. Once she arrived, she saw a dainty bouquet of pansies, neatly tied together with a shimmering yellow ribbon. The brambles had been removed from the grave, every speck of dust swept from the headstone, and the flowers appeared quite fresh.

Rose spun around and squinted at the lane beyond the churchyard. Not terribly far away, about to turn the corner onto a building-lined street that would hide her from view, was a woman wearing traveling clothes.

Rose wasted no time in setting her flowers on the grave and scrambling toward the gate. "Wait!" she called out.

The woman continued walking.

Rose fumbled desperately with the latch and repeated her cry more loudly. "Wait!"

This time, the woman stopped and glanced back. She turned toward Rose—who found herself suddenly voiceless.

The woman's heart-shaped face and something about the pointed curve at the corners of her mouth bore a striking resemblance to. . . *Someone.* But it was her eyes, or rather the expression in them, that Rose *knew* she knew.

And yet, she'd never seen this woman before.

"May I help you?" the woman asked.

"Well, I see that someone has been thoughtful enough to put flowers on one of the graves." Rose gestured toward her mother's grave. "That one there, under the little oak tree. Was—was it you?"

The woman peered past Rose at the grave. "Why, yes." She gave Rose a curious look. "Why do you ask?"

Rose heard her own reply as though a stranger was uttering it. "Because the person buried there matters a great deal to me."

The woman shielded her eyes against the sun and stared at Rose. She approached the gate, her back erect. As she drew nearer, her face grew white as a bed sheet.

Why is she looking at me like that? A tingle swept through Rose, a strange awareness that she stood on the precipice of some sort of epoch in her life.

The woman extended her hand. "I'm Stella Lawrence's sister, Hattie."

Rose took the woman's offered hand, only to release it limply an instant later. "Her sister?" *I have an aunt.* She gripped the gate, tried to restore her balance. Everything around her spun, from the dusty narrow lane to the golden-washed graveyard. *Unreal—this is unreal.* Except for the woman, Hattie. She seemed very real, this aunt of Rose's who had all but materialized out of thin air.

"My eyes don't deceive me, do they?" the woman asked softly. "You're the very image of her." She jerked trembling palms to now-flushed cheeks. "You're Stella's daughter, aren't you?"

Rose nodded.

The woman's breath left her lungs in a whoosh, and she reached both hands to cover Rose's where they still clutched the gate. "What a blessing this news is, dear girl." She shook her head, eyes alight with wonder. "Your father told us you were dead. He arrived home and reported that my sister had succumbed to her many ailments shortly after he found her, that he buried her in Old Mission at the church nearest the docks. You, he said, had been lost to them. Scarlet fever. They laid you to rest in the lake." Perplexity creased her aunt's forehead. "I simply don't understand why he would tell us that."

"Because my mother told *him* that. Apparently, she didn't wish him to know that I was alive, and he believed her."

An edge hardened her aunt's voice. "Oh, he believed her, all right. Vic Lawrence wasn't known for surrendering what he considered to be his property." The words were scarcely out of her mouth before she shot Rose a contrite look. "Forgive me, child. It cannot be pleasant to hear such things about one's own father."

Rose shook her head. "I don't fault you for telling me the truth."

"No, it's never any use to hide from the truth." Her aunt's perplexity returned. "But your mother wouldn't have surrendered you into another's keeping any more than your father would have. My sister treasured you more than all the gold in Midas's kingdom. What happened, that the two of you came to be separated?"

Rose relayed everything that Nathan had told her. When finished, she asked, "Why did my mother leave my father?" She knew that the answer would be unpleasant to hear but needed to hear it anyway.

"He drove her away, I'm afraid. He was a dangerous man, your father. As a successful banker with a reputation to protect, he was also a careful man. His violence toward my sister was always hidden, her body bruised only in places others couldn't see. She endured his cruel treatment until you came along, and then she had to flee in order to save you from him." There was a faint sheen in her aunt's eyes. "I thought it brave of her." She pressed her lips tightly together. "To his dying breath, Vic had people believing him to be the most respectable, fair-dealing of men."

"Dying breath?"

Her aunt squeezed her hands gently. "He passed away last week. Stricken with cholera."

The statement, tragic as it was, fell over Rose like a serenely falling snow. From her earliest days, God in heaven had been carrying out His plan for her, one that clearly didn't involve her earthly father. *First, He gave my mother the courage to leave the man. Then He warned my grandfather not to dig into my past, and my grandfather warned me.* Now her father was beyond hurting her.

All at once, it occurred to Rose that her aunt would probably be leaving Old Mission soon. *Wherever she lives, I'll visit her, no matter how far I have to go.* She had no idea how she would accomplish such a feat—certainly not during the shipping season when she had a light to shine.

Rose waved her hand in the direction of her mother's grave. "Did you come here to Old Mission for this?"

Her aunt shook her head. "No, not only that. I've come to live with my children. They traveled this way ahead of me, planning to send for me once they got settled." She brightened. "Oh, you must stay and meet my daughter. She should be passing by here any minute now, because as I recall, she told me that this church is on her way home from work." Her aunt looked into the distance, where a petite, black-haired figure could be seen walking toward them along the lane. "Why, here she comes now."

Rose beheld the figure with a jolting shock of recognition.

Their approaching visitor, Aunt Hattie's daughter, was Dinah Sullivan.

Chapter 12

That evening, the Sullivan household was filled with a jolly confusion. The babbling interruptions, everyone's words tumbling every which way, nearly burst the seams of the house. Though Jimmy had rebuilt and expanded the place to accommodate the addition of their mother, it was still quite small. Rose thought it perfect. It didn't matter to her that the braided rugs on the floors had frayed edges, that the paintings on the walls were chipped and the quilts on the beds faded. These items were family heirlooms. *Her* family's heirlooms.

At the graveyard, when Hattie told Dinah all that had transpired between her and Rose, Dinah had burst into tears.

"We're cousins!" she cried, dancing and hugging Rose nearly to suffocation. "That's practically sisters!"

Later, Jimmy's reaction assured Rose of his joy as well. All evening, he whistled his most jovial of whistles and grinned his broadest of grins.

Their mother prepared a simple supper of cold bread and butter, with a crock of wild honey she'd brought with her from St. Joseph. Rose found it difficult to swallow the delicious fare around the lump in her throat. *Dear God, You've been so very gracious to me.* She'd relinquished her hope of finding her family, and He'd led her to them after all.

Sometime during supper, Rose asked her aunt about the hair ribbon her grandfather had found in the bushes near the lighthouse steps. She drew it out of her pocket and held it up so her aunt could see. "Do you recognize this?"

The woman didn't need to look at the object for long. "Certainly. Although come to think of it, Dinah may be able to tell you about it as well." She glanced over at her daughter, who was returning from the kitchen with a pie she'd baked for dessert. "Dinah, do you remember making that ribbon?"

Dinah squinted at the ribbon. "No, but I have one just like it."

"Yes, there are two of them." Her mother returned her attention to Rose. "When Dinah was only four, she insisted on helping me sew two identical hair ribbons, one for her and one for her soon-to-be-born baby cousin—you." A fond, faraway light appeared in her eyes. "She smeared glue all over her new dress trying to make that golden glitter stick to the borders just so. Every day, she would ask me when you would be born. Once you arrived, she was dismayed to find that you were rather bald and unable to wear the ribbon. So she asked me to sew it onto one of your baby blankets, thinking that you and she would match that way—at least, in a manner of speaking."

Dinah and Rose exchanged smiles. Rose found it difficult to swallow again. *What a sweet story.* "My mother must have tucked that blanket into the basket my grandfather found me in," she mused. "Then the blanket must have hung over the edge of the basket, and when Nathan carried me up the lighthouse steps, the ribbon got caught in the bushes."

Never far from her thoughts, Nathan stole into them once more. She yearned to tell him of this new development, this blessing that had befallen her. How she missed him! She might be able to bear his absence better if she had some assurance that he missed her too. *Does he, God? Even a little?*

The heavens didn't reply.

Yet so many of her prayers had been answered, so many of her desires fulfilled. Looking at the beaming faces around her, Rose's heart was full.

"Doesn't that girl you fancy live around here, Captain?" asked one of Nathan's deck-hands, Lenny, as they stood on deck watching the ship cut through the water toward Old Mission.

Now, who told him that?

Nathan nodded but didn't elaborate.

Lenny shot him a sidelong glance. "You gonna see her today?"

Nathan felt the tension building inside him, a raw strain that had been present since he'd parted ways with Rose weeks ago. She'd filled his waking thoughts and robbed his nights of sleep. He gripped the rail as though to bore handprints in it and shook his head. "There isn't much cargo for Old Mission this time, and we've a schedule to keep."

"I reckon your freight crew could drag the delivery out some, just this once. They're capable of lollygagging with the best of 'em, given the chance."

"I should hope not." Nathan reached up and rubbed his tired eyes, his hands not quite steady. He held them out before him in disgust. *I'm practically trembling with longing for her.* "Like I said, we've a schedule to keep."

Lenny emitted a sound more like a snort than a laugh. "Being late would be a small price to pay."

Nathan glanced sharply at him. "Pardon?"

Lenny ducked his head. "You'll excuse me for saying so, sir, but we're all getting a little tired of your moping and mooning over that girl." He winked. "Go on, go and see her. It'll do us all a world of good."

Cheeky fellow. Not many of his crew members would dare say such a thing to their captain. But at the moment, with his every nerve frayed, Nathan found himself without defense. "And the delivery process could truly be delayed?"

Lenny grinned. "Oh, the freight can be unavoidably set back, sir. Whole boards of cargo tipped over on the gangplank, contents spewed everywhere. I'll tell the crew to see to it."

Nathan slowly released his grip on the rail. So. He was going to see Rose.

Ten minutes later, he sped on foot across the shoreline toward the lighthouse, only one thought prevalent in his mind.

I can't do this anymore.

He'd missed Rose when he'd been away before, but now, after that agonized parting at the dock, he felt ready to crack under the weight of his yearning for her. Yet he still couldn't ask her to share his life, not with him gone all the time. *She deserves someone who sticks around and keeps her company.*

Maybe—just maybe—he wouldn't be gone all the time. If he couldn't be a ship's captain and love Rose at the same time, was it possible that being a ship's captain was no longer his truest calling?

Deep within, he already knew the answer. Had already made the decision. He'd finish out the shipping season and then, come winter, he'd resign his post. He had no earthly idea what he would do with himself after that, but at least he'd have Rose.

Presumably.

He was probably presuming too much. There was still a handsome store clerk to contend with, still the matter of Rose's adverse reaction to his kiss that night in the cabin.

It didn't matter. *I'll say my piece, and she can choose her course as she sees fit.* A decision that was easier made than carried out, which his suddenly sweating palms could attest to.

Rose swept the bottom step of the daunting staircase at long last. She whisked the dirt into a pile, nearly dropping the dustpan at the sound of Tucker's sudden barks. She identified them as the kind he reserved for his gladdest of welcomes.

I wonder who that can be. She'd been expecting Dinah for a visit today, but not until evening.

She set the dustpan on the stair and hurried to the front door. She opened it—and her heart nearly stopped beating at the sight of Nathan standing in her yard. His sandy hair was dampened by the mist from the lake, his laughing gaze on

Tucker, who was riotously circling his legs in ecstatic greeting. He gave her a helpless shrug and moved forward as best he could with the zigzagging dog in the way.

He climbed the front steps. "The goats raised a ruckus a moment ago. I'm surprised you didn't hear them."

"I was in the stairwell, where it's hard to hear." She hoped she didn't sound as breathless as she felt. He stood close now, just on the other side of the doorway. "I didn't expect to see you so soon."

"So soon?" he repeated. "My crew would beg to differ. I think they were on the verge of throwing their pathetic captain overboard."

What does he mean by that?

He offered no explanation.

Tucker, who'd squeezed past Nathan into the house, resigned himself to being ignored and plopped onto the floor with a heavy sigh.

"Won't you come in?" Rose asked.

Nathan shook his head. "I wish I could, but I can't stay long." He gazed at the two sides of the doorframe and then the narrow hall behind her. "I remember standing in this doorway with you some eight months ago, on a frozen New Year's Eve."

Unaccountably, her pulse began to speed. "Yes, you looked like an icicle that night."

"And you looked like an elfin queen, capable of bewitching anyone."

Her eyes widened in disbelief. "I was wearing an old work dress and my hair was straggling over my shoulders like a mop."

He smiled and tilted his head. "I recall the matter quite differently." He grew pensive, even sober. "Your grief over your grandfather was a terrible thing to endure without being able to comfort you. I wanted to hold you, to somehow absorb your pain."

Warmed by his kindness, she said quietly, "I'm not sure I would have stopped you. I was too distraught."

His gaze departed hers, and he plucked at a loose nail on the doorframe. "Is that what you must be, Rose, to welcome my embrace? Distraught?"

The husky query caused a flush to invade her cheeks. *No, you're the one who was distraught after we kissed.* The memory stole away the warm glow she'd felt seconds earlier. With a wrenching twist in her stomach, she stared at the floorboards. "Sometimes I think you don't realize I grew up."

She replayed the words with humiliation. They'd emerged from nowhere and certainly did nothing to prove her maturity.

"Oh, but I assure you, I do." He braced his hands on either side of the doorframe, almost as though he were keeping himself distant from her with great effort.

His damp hair smelled of sunshine and cold hard steel. *Probably from the metals aboard his ship.* Equally appealing to her was the growth of stubble covering his jaw, which glinted golden in the daylight, a fetching sight indeed. She ignored the powerful pull and summoned her courage. "You mentioned my being distraught. That would be a charitable description of your reaction to—to our shared moment that night in the cabin."

In the silence that followed, she felt like her chest was trying to crush her ribs.

"You think I regret kissing you?" he clarified.

She nodded.

Something in his tone told her he was treading carefully. "If I had any regrets, they would involve fearing I'd betrayed your grandfather's trust in me. Given the situation and the remoteness of our location, I shouldn't have invited you inside."

"You wish you hadn't," she whispered.

He blew out a forceful puff of air. "What I wish is that I could understand the look on *your* face afterward. You seemed so. . .injured."

She stiffened. "Well, you must admit, your reaction wasn't very flattering."

"I thought that injured look was evidence of your feelings for someone else."

Does that mean he. . . ? She could scarcely breathe, could scarcely dare to hope.

He reached up and rubbed the back of his neck. "The whole truth is, impropriety wasn't the only reason I shouldn't have kissed you. My line of work being what it is, I had no business leading you on." He gave her a pleading look. "But that doesn't matter anymore. I can fix all that, if only you can tell me whether—" He clenched and unclenched his hands. "To be honest, I was also frustrated. Frustrated all hollow, because I wanted to kiss you again more than I wanted my next breath, and I thought you were falling for another man."

She could hardly believe what she was hearing. *Does he really, truly care for me?*

Without thought, she stepped forward on tiptoe and lightly brushed her lips against his cheek. She froze, realizing what she'd just done.

He stood completely still for a moment. Then with a strangled sound, he turned his head and kissed her briefly on the lips. Too briefly. His mouth lingered on hers only an instant before he drew away. He slid his hands up the back of her arms, gently tugging her away from him. "Are you going to marry Jimmy?"

She blinked up at him, her senses muddled. She was spellbound by the stroking movement of his fingers on her arms. "Whatever do you mea—"

"Just answer the question."

"N–no. Of course not. Jimmy's my cousin."

His brows shot upward. "I beg your pardon?"

Forcing her brain to function and her mouth to form coherent sentences, Rose told him how she'd met her aunt at the graveyard, had discovered that Dinah and

Jimmy were her cousins.

By the time she'd finished the story, Nathan's shock turned to wonder. "That's amazing, Rose. Truly. I couldn't be happier for you."

"Nathan," she ventured shyly, "what did you mean when you said that you could 'fix all that'?"

He didn't hesitate. "I meant that I'm quitting the ship-captaining business."

She gaped at him. Had she heard him correctly?

"I can't in good conscience ask you to share a life in which your husband is away all the time, so I'm resigning my post."

The word *husband* lingered in the air, veritably squeezing the breath from her lungs, but in the most wonderful way possible. *But he lives for his work.* "You can't do that," she said.

He set his jaw. "It's decided."

In spite of herself, she felt her lips curving upward. The man standing before her loved her. She knew that now, more surely than if he'd announced it from the rooftops. *Thank You, God—he loves me!*

Unable to help herself, Rose again raised her lips to his cheek.

Shaking his head slowly, he reached out and spanned her waist in both hands. He drew her closer, but to her dismay, he paused and held her at bay once more. "Tell me you'll marry me, Rose. Only then will I permit myself to do what I've wanted to do every day for eight months—kiss you properly." His disarming blue-gray gaze, trained on hers, spoke volumes.

A flood of happiness broke over her in waves, as bright and welcome as a sunbeam bursting through a storm cloud. "Of course I'll marry you, Captain Perry."

His eyes lit with soft wonder.

"But I'd never let you surrender your profession for me," she added.

"The choice is mine. My first priority is your happiness."

She held his gaze steadily. "Yes, and mine is yours. I could never be happy, knowing that you'd given up the work you love for me." She cupped his face in her palms. "You were born to be a ship's captain."

"I know," he groaned helplessly, his hands reaching to cover hers. "But I can't bear the thought of leaving you alone in that lighthouse, when you could be with someone who'd stay at your side."

I don't want him, whoever he is. "I want you," she blurted out. The shameless declaration caused heat to flood her cheeks.

He grinned broadly. "Do you now?"

She nodded. "I know it won't always be easy. But please believe me when I say that I thrive on being home alone. I adore taking long walks in the woods, sitting on the shore and gazing out at the lake." She searched for the right words. "It's my haven, created by God just for me. I'm content with Tucker, my books, my work as a lighthouse keeper."

Still, he hesitated. "I'll be away often."

"I know. And I'll be waiting for you when you return."

An unabashed tenderness filled his gaze. "I surrender."

Then at last, he lowered his head and kissed her. True to his word, he did a proper job of it, his kiss infused with a passion she'd never known. She could feel every bit of his desire in the warm pressure of his mouth, every bit of his love in the restrained strength of his arms. He surrounded her, sheltered her.

In that moment, Rose's joy was made complete.

Rebecca Jepson is a homebody who loves a good book, a cup of freshly ground coffee, and all things autumn. She is the author of *A Highbrow Hoodwink*, a novella included in the ECPA bestseller, *The Lassoed by Marriage Romance Collection*. In addition to writing, she works as a paralegal and volunteers in various ministries at her church. She lives in Reno, Nevada, with her husband, Mike.

Love's Beacon

by Carrie Fancett Pagels

Dedication

To Ruth Hill, a special choir teacher, baton twirling coach, and now friend! You've made an impact on my life!

And to the friends of my childhood and youth in Newberry, Michigan, in the beautiful Upper Peninsula. May God bless you all!

Acknowledgments

I thank God that He has allowed me to write this story despite my infirmities. Thank you to Pegg Thomas for heading up this collection and inviting me to contribute.

Thank you to my wonderful critique partner, Kathleen L. Maher, a true blessing. Much appreciation to my family, who support me and my writing—Jeffrey D., Clark J., and Cassandra R. Pagels. Thank you to all my friends who've allowed me to use their names in this story, in a fictional manner, especially Valerie Fillman and Paul Sholtus, my heroine and hero.

There'd be no collection without the team at Barbour Publishing. Special thanks to Rebecca Germany, our acquisition editor, and Laura Young, a gem. My agent, Joyce Hart, and Linda Glaz of Hartline Literary Agency deserve thanks for their efforts for this collection too. Thank you to Ellen Tarver, my editor for this novella, for all your diligent work. With much appreciation to Mary Jane Barnwell, the owner of The Island Bookstore, and manager Tamara Tomac, for their support of books set on Mackinac Island.

Thank you too for being a Christian fiction reader! Where would we authors be without our readers supporting our writing ministry? Many blessings to you!

Author's Notes

There are two lighthouses in the Straits of Mackinac nowadays. At the time of my story, only Round Island Lighthouse (brand-new at the time, built in 1895) existed. The Round Island Passage Lighthouse was built later. Visitors to Mackinac Island recognize the iconic "schoolhouse" design of the Round Island Lighthouse. It is one of the most photographed of all the Great Lakes lighthouses.

When I worked on Mackinac Island as a teenager in 1975, a fund-raiser to save and restore Round Island Lighthouse was launched. I believe I paid a one-dollar donation for a button to wear, showing I proudly supported this effort. Who'd have thought that one day I'd be writing a story set at this very lighthouse?

Clarke Historical Library at Central Michigan University has a wonderful "Life in a Lighthouse" article available online at their website. The Round Island Lighthouse Preservation Society also has a very helpful website, including a virtual tour, history, and a brochure. Since the Round Island Lighthouse isn't normally accessible to the public, I found the information at the Old Mackinac Point Lighthouse, open for tours through the Mackinac State Historic Parks, to be very helpful.

I met Joyce Shimonski Jeruzel on a trip to Mackinac Island. She shared with me about her orphaned grandmother being raised there at a Catholic orphanage until she came of age to leave. This was the inspiration for the heroine in this story, which is fictional.

If you haven't yet read *The Sugarplum Ladies* in *The Victorian Christmas Brides Collection* (September 2018) from Barbour, you may wish to do so before reading this novella. There are important characters from that story who play a part in this novella. Those who have read *Dime Novel Suitor* in the *Seven Brides for Seven Husbands* collection will recognize cameo appearances of some of those characters too.

Prologue

Mackinac Island
September 1897

Standing alone in the Island Pharmacy, Valerie's hands shook as she removed the scrap of paper from her reticule. How strange to be here alone. If Ma and Pa weren't so desperately ill, they'd never have allowed her to travel by herself from Round Island. She'd pleaded with them only days earlier to allow her to get medicine, fearing the worst for Mary and Tim. They'd refused.

"May I help you, miss?" The young man behind the counter gazed at her, concern reflecting from his dark eyes.

Niggling anxiety nipped at her as she thrust out the list. The scent of camphor mingled with beeswax and a hint of bay rum. Alone here, her senses seemed heightened. The jingling of the doorbells startled her. She pressed a hand over her hammering heart as the clerk turned and went to the back to have the pharmacist fill her order.

A pretty blond woman entered, holding tight to a toddler's arm. The child looked up, hazel eyes shining. Attired in a fashionable bonnet and matching coat, the young mother smiled at Val, and she realized she'd been staring. Val averted her gaze.

The clerk returned. "Mrs. Swaine, good to see you. I've got something for little Robbie's sniffle." After pushing his black sleeve garters higher, the young man bent and retrieved a paper-wrapped parcel from behind the counter.

"Thank you."

No payment was exchanged, which seemed odd. Perhaps the woman had an account.

The mother turned and faced Val, her blue eyes darkening. "Don't I know you?"

"My father is the lighthouse keeper, ma'am." Val cast her eyes downward, as her mother had drilled into her.

The toddler looked up at Val and held out his hands. Something in her longed to have someone reach for her like this. Just as Val was about to pick him up, the child's mother lifted him onto her hip.

"I have never met Mr. Fillman. But I know I've seen your face somewhere."

For a brief instant, Val again met the beautiful young mother's gaze. "We do come on occasion to the island." The very rare occasion, and never unaccompanied.

The toddler sneezed.

"Oh my!" His mother leaned away.

"Bless you." Val pulled a handkerchief from her reticule. "This is clean." She wiped the child's nose.

"Thank you." Arms full, the young mother headed out as a tall man entered, holding the door ajar for her.

The pharmacist stepped to the back again and returned with several brown bottles. He quickly wrapped them in paper and then placed them gently in a bag before tying the parcel with twine.

Val accepted the medications and headed out to the docks for her return to Round Island. A stiff chill wind swirled her wool skirts even higher than their already short length. She swiped at the coarse fabric, pushing it down toward her ankles.

As she reached the mooring place for the lighthouse boat, she spied the lighthouse inspector, Mr. Dardanes, arguing with Jimmy, the boy who'd promised to help her sail back to the island.

As she neared them, she caught his words. "Miss Fillman can't return and that's settled."

She took several steps closer, clutching the medications to her chest. "What's going on?"

The lighthouse inspector grabbed Valerie's arm firmly and turned her away from the boatman. "You'll need to stay ashore."

"I need to get these back to my family. They're relying on me."

Mr. Dardanes shook his head, his hat remaining firmly in place. "I've received word from my assistant just now that. . ." His dark eyes softened, but he still steered her away from the dock.

"What is it, sir?" She hugged her shawl closer around her shoulders as the wind increased.

Perspiration dotted the man's wide brow, but he didn't stop walking toward the boardwalk. "It would be best if you stayed at the parish house tonight."

"Until they're better?" They must be highly contagious, which was as she'd suspected. Only Val had withstood the onslaught of the vicious illness. The brief recollection of a smooth pale hand, so unlike Ma's, stroking her brow, flitted across her memory and she almost tripped on her torn skirt hem, but righted herself with a little assistance from the inspector.

"Until further notice you'll remain under Sister Mary Lou's supervision."

"Oh." A little jolt of happiness swept past her apprehension. "I've never been away from my family."

"Not even for a night?"

Valerie wasn't normally allowed any separation from her family. Today was the first time she could remember. As a young child she'd had ongoing nightmares of being taken away from her family.

Mr. Dardanes gestured to the boardwalk where carriage taxis parked in a long line. "Do you mind walking, Miss Fillman?"

"Not at all. It feels good to stretch my legs more than I'm able to on Round Island."

"I have a daughter about your age." The inspector smiled down at her and patted her hand, tucked in his elbow now. "You must be about twenty or so?"

"I, uh, yes." Val blinked rapidly. "We've never celebrated my birthday."

"You can't be serious."

"I am." She moistened her lips.

"My nineteen-year-old daughter gives me a list well in advance of her happy day."

She bit her lip as she considered when last she'd had a truly happy day.

For a moment she allowed herself the old fantasy—that somewhere out there were parents who truly loved her. A family where she was allowed to be a child instead of a servant. Valerie closed her eyes and pushed aside the uncharitable thought. Of course her parents cared for her. They needed her. Hadn't they told her so many times?

"Who will help my parents if I don't get this to them?" Valerie held up the package.

Mr. Dardanes's dark eyebrows drew together. "All I know is that you shall not return."

Sleep shrouded Val in misty visions. Her mother, father, sister, and brother reached out to her, but she couldn't clasp their hands. They were slipping away from her. She had to reach them. Had to get on the boat to see Grandfather. But she had no grandfather, did she? Her family members' faces were changing, shifting so that she couldn't recognize them. She should go. No! They should stay.

"Miss Fillman! Valerie!"

Val awoke, finding herself not at the lighthouse but at the island orphanage. The sweet nun, Sister Mary Lou, shook Val's shoulders. "Oh!"

Sister Mary Lou fished a handkerchief from her black habit's pocket and handed it to Valerie. Taking it, Val wiped her face, which was wet from tears.

"Thank you, Sister Mary Lou."

"You're welcome." She settled on the chair next to the bed. "You received quite a shock last night."

"Yes." The inspector's assistant had left it to the priest and nun to break the news to her. Tears welled up again. Her entire family had perished only one day after she'd desperately left Round Island to obtain medication. A cold numbness trickled through her soul. How had God allowed this? Why had Ma and Pa refused to let her go when she'd first offered, five days earlier?

"This vicious flux has taken many lives in our parish." The nun patted her hand. "We're going to have to trust God."

Trust? Had Valerie ever trusted someone? No. Perhaps long ago. Maybe that was God she'd called upon as a child. But He'd never answered her prayers.

Chapter 1

The priest's office empty, Val went inside to wait, as she'd been bidden to do. Outside the far window, some of the children, led by her new friend, Susan Johnson, played in the yard. A half-dozen boys and girls lay in the fresh snow making snow angels while others constructed a snowman with coal for eyes. The frozen "man" looked at her with his empty soul-less eyes and Val shivered. Wasn't she just as cold inside as that snowy creature? So much loss. Susan turned and waved at her. Val waved back as her friend tossed a snowball at the window. Val laughed. She'd also gained so much since coming here. Freedom, friendships, genuine care, and love.

Father Joseph's gentle shuffling walk announced his arrival. Val dipped a curtsy and he waved her toward the settee, an uncharacteristic frown puckering his forehead. He sat down behind his desk instead of in the wing chair adjacent to the settee and tea table.

Sister Mary Lou joined them, shutting the office door behind her. "Sorry I'm running a little late. We had one child who couldn't find a pair of boots. But all is well now." She offered Val a tight smile before sitting beside her.

Father Joseph's dark eyebrows arched high. "I'll get right to the point. We'd like to share some concerns we have about your parents."

The priest and nun exchanged a long look. "Father and I suspected, early on when your father took his post, that something was very wrong with your mother."

"Very secretive." The priest shook his head.

"And very odd-acting with you and your brother and sister." The nun rubbed the knuckles of her left hand. "We grew concerned about her outbursts too, when she came to the island."

Her mouth dry, Val nodded. She knew all about her mother's nature.

Children's hoots of laughter outside didn't distract Father Joseph. "You know Mr. Dardanes delivered what belongings were salvaged. A great deal had to be burned."

Val's gut clenched. "Of course." They'd had to replace all her belongings—her clothing, bedding, and cloth items for the entire family—with items from the mission bin and some things that her friends, the Christys, had gifted her with.

Sister Mary Lou gazed past Val, presumably to watch the children, whose voices continued to carry. "Then Father and I went through the belongings, one by one."

As Val had asked them to do. She'd been in too dark a place to manage the task.

"Mr. Dardanes brought us a box of papers." Sister Mary Lou leaned forward.

Father Joseph nodded gravely. "While there were birth certificates for your brother and sister. . ."

"God rest their souls." Sister Mary Lou and Father Joseph made the sign of the cross.

"There was no record for you." Father Joseph ran his thumb over the teacup rim. "And by our reckoning, Dorcas Woods—you did know that was your mother's maiden name?"

"No. She never said."

"Well, she would have been perhaps fourteen or fifteen when you were born."

"We sent a letter to her sister, Lettice Woods—there was a London address and a card from her in the box." Sister Mary Lou clasped her hands in her lap. "We didn't want to tell you what it said. We wanted confirmation first."

"Which we now have." Father Joseph pulled open his desk drawer.

A shriek of joy from outside sounded, startling Val. "What did the first note say? And this one?"

Sister Mary Lou ducked her chin. "Mrs. Fillman's sister wrote her, asking about the third child in the picture she'd sent, and why Dorcas claimed that was her daughter."

"Claimed?" Val's head pounded.

Sister Mary Lou took Val's hand. "Dorcas Woods had a stillborn child years ago—per her sister's note. A little over two years later, Dorcas reunited with her lover, John Fillman, in New York. Lettice assumed the child in the photograph was his from a former relationship."

"After Lettice asked who the girl in the photograph was, Dorcas cut off all correspondence with her sister." Father Joseph tapped a thick folder on his desk. "There is nothing dated after that letter from Lettice. Not that we could find, anyway."

Val sat up straight. "My mother never spoke of having any kin."

"We sent inquiries about Dorcas's family to London and are awaiting a letter back." The priest tugged at his collar. "But we fear, dear girl, that you may not be the Fillmans' own child."

"I see." She didn't.

"But we'd like to keep working on this mystery." Sister Mary Lou patted her hand. "We want to help you."

"Thank you."

"I always fancied myself becoming a Sherlock Holmes." Father Joseph gave a soft laugh, breaking the tension. "And Sister Mary Lou can be my Watson."

"Perhaps I was adopted? Could that be it?" But somehow she doubted it.

"Perhaps. But there were no papers." He opened the file. "I've logged every item and every date."

"Maybe some other young girl gave birth to me and my mother took me in and raised me?" She'd read of such things in her books.

"We'll need your help. How about let's go through what we do know." Father Joseph dipped his pen in the inkwell. "They were working in New York, in the city."

"Yes." Her mother had told her very little about that time other than how difficult it had been.

Sister Mary Lou cocked her head. "Valerie, the year of their marriage was 1882. And you're how old?"

"I'm. . ." Truth be told, she wasn't quite sure. "I think I will be nineteen in February." But she'd always been told she seemed older. Perhaps twenty in February.

"You don't know?"

She shook her head, tears spilling down her cheeks. Everything she thought she knew could be wrong. A life based on lies.

Sunlight shone through the window, and Val turned to see the children playing happily outside, Susan chasing them through the snow. Here were orphans seemingly happier than she'd been in her entire life.

"We're going to trust God to help us with this, Valerie." Father Joseph penned a check mark at the top of the inside folder. "We've more material to filter through, but let's start on what we have."

"It might help if you write down some of your nightmares too, dear." Sister Mary Lou handed Val a small pad of paper. "There might be some truth in them."

Palo, Michigan, February 1898

"Where's my mama?" Three-year-old Sofia, nestled in Paul's arms, patted his cheeks. Longing constricted the muscles in his chest as he rocked her. His daughter asked this question every time she was around other children, like her cousins, whose mothers were present.

Everywhere his eyes settled in the parlor were little reminders of his wife. From the afghan covering his daughter's tiny legs to the cross-stitched pictures hung on the walls, his home was occupied by a woman no longer with them. "Your mother's in heaven."

"Where's that?"

Paul sucked in a breath, knowing that any explanation was beyond his daughter's understanding.

Heavy footfalls on the front porch were followed by a stamping of feet to rid someone's boots of snow. A quick knock sounded on the paneled door before it was opened.

"Well, you got your wish, Paul." His older brother waved an envelope embossed with a lighthouse insignia.

"What?" He swallowed hard. The mail was delivered to the main house on the family farm, a home his brother occupied. But that didn't give Ronald the right to open Paul's mail. "Let me see it."

Instead of handing it over, Ronald held the letter out of reach, like he used to do when they were both much younger. "When were you going to tell us?"

"I applied. And it's none of your business." Paul leaned over and picked up Sofia's doll from where it had slipped to the floor, and handed it to his daughter. "Run upstairs and put dolly to bed."

With eyes as wide as saucers, Sofia glanced between her uncle Ronald and her daddy but then hopped from Paul's lap and did as she was bid.

"It's all of our concern if you run off and leave your child with us."

Paul scowled. "I wouldn't do that."

"And who would you have perform your farm work if you leave?" Ronald finally handed him the letter.

"Come back later." Paul made a shooing motion, but his brother crossed his arms, the fabric of his heavy wool coat straining across his broad shoulders.

Paul had dreamed of becoming a lighthouse keeper as a young man. He'd wanted anything but farm life and had tried his hand at many things. Each time he left though, he felt the tug of his beautiful childhood sweetheart, Annabelle, tugging him home. Living on the family farm had been her dream, not his. She'd wanted to be close to her parents, who lived in Ionia. Despite the chill in the room, sweat broke out on his brow. Paul opened the letter and quickly read the offer of employment. The compensation was good—more than good. He drew in a steadying breath.

His brother cleared his throat and Paul looked up. Gone was the accusation in his eyes, replaced by concern. "If you could have Annabelle back, you'd trade that coveted lighthouse position in a heartbeat, for her, wouldn't you, brother?"

Unable to manage a response, Paul dipped his chin and blinked back the moisture in his eyes. Of course he'd want his wife back. His first and only sweetheart.

From upstairs, the tinkle of Annabelle's music box played a sweet tune. Sofia must have gone into his room and gotten into her mother's things again.

Ronald sighed. "You know Grace and I would keep Sofia if you need to go. If you need to get this out of your system once and for all."

Out of his system? He'd responded to the advertisement because he needed to get away from everything that reminded him of Annabelle. That he'd always wished to man a lighthouse was simply a bonus. But what about Sofia? How would this affect her? Still, he'd never planned to leave her behind. "I can't leave my daughter."

"Why don't you go up there and see if you can get a woman to come in and help you with her?"

Paul located the salary amount again and the extra benefits. "I should be able to pay someone to help."

"Do what you need to do, little brother." Ronald tapped his booted toe. "But we'll be praying you tire of the lighthouse quickly and come back home."

With his mother, father, brothers, and sister all on the family farm, a lighthouse might be a lonely place. But as his eyes lighted upon his wedding picture in its ornate silver frame, he knew what his answer would be. "If I can't find help for Sofia, I won't accept the position."

He had to leave here though. Come spring, he'd accept his friend Louis Penwell's offer of a train ride up to Mackinaw City on the new railroad line. But instead of traveling for an excursion to get away, as his friend had offered, he'd use his time to seek out a housekeeper on Mackinac Island. An older woman, perhaps a widow, who'd watch Sofia too. He could picture her now—someone a lot like his mother. Matronly, sweet, kindly, and a wonderful cook.

Yes, that's just what we need.

Valentine's Day. Val waited in Father Joseph's office, which she'd just finished tidying up. In the five months since she'd arrived, she'd banished every speck of dust. Was this her birthday? She'd always suspected it was, despite her mother never saying for sure or celebrating her birth. Was the priest, even now, bringing some surprise? Her heart warmed at the thought.

Father Joseph entered, clutching a flat rectangular metal box. Sister Mary Lou pushed a tea cart into the room. Small cakes, covered in frosting, were placed atop assorted china dessert plates, mismatched donations to the church. Tears pricked Val's eyes. They had thought of her.

Sister poured the tea. When Val approached to help serve, the nun waved her away. "Have a seat and relax a moment, will you?"

Sister Mary Lou handed her a floral-embossed teacup on a matching saucer. "Thank you, Sister Mary Lou." Val inhaled the familiar scent of orange pekoe tea.

Sister Mary Lou returned to the tea cart and served Father Joseph. Then she brought Val a pretty pink-and-blue floral plate upon which sat three petits four, all with thick white frosting and sugar roses on top.

Father Joseph took a bite of a cake, tiny crumbs scattering onto his desk. Who would keep this room clean when Val left? She knew they had created a position for her and wouldn't have funds to keep her on. "Any luck with a possible summer position, Valerie?"

"Mr. and Mrs. Christy offered me a room in their home, above their tea shop, but don't have funds to employ me." She could accept a job cooking at a lumber camp. But as sheltered as she'd been all her life growing up in lighthouses, she couldn't imagine it, so she dared not say the words aloud.

"With your permission, we'd like to ask the parish members to consider you for employment." Father Joseph plopped a sugar cube in his tea.

"Certainly."

Sister Mary Lou set her tea and cake on the table. "We want to keep you at some job in the area."

"We're not done sleuthing, Valerie." The teacup the priest held looked so tiny in his broad hands. "In fact, we have something you might help us with."

"Yes!" Sister Mary Lou's pretty face flushed with excitement.

As he lifted the metal case aloft, Father Joe's eyes brightened. "This was found under a floorboard at the lighthouse."

The priest reached into the box and retrieved a small gold-papered box. He came around his desk and handed it to Val.

Sister Mary Lou's pale eyes lit with question. "Do you recognize this, Valerie?"

"No."

"Open it." Father Joseph sat down in the wing chair next to her.

Complying with the priest's request, Val lifted the unsealed top. Inside rested a rosewood jewelry case about two inches square. She opened the tiny wooden box, the feel of the wood smooth and cool on her fingertips. Inside lay a small bracelet. Light streaming through the window made it glitter as Val untied the white satin bows that secured it to a flocked backing. Her heart pounded. The last time she'd seen it. . .

A pretty lady handed the gold-papered box to Val. Or was it given to another girl standing alongside Val? Tied with silver ribbon, it fit perfectly in the small outstretched hands.

Red, white, and pink paper hearts were strewn on a table covered with treats.

"Have her open it, Mama!" A pretty dark-haired girl, a little older than herself, jumped up and down in excitement, her creamy satin dress flouncing around her. On the child's wrist dangled a sparkling bracelet.

With gentle hands, the woman took the box and opened it and then another brown wood box inside it. She pulled out something shiny.

"Oh Carrie, it is lovely!" The soft voice came from nearby. Val tried to look up to

see who'd spoken, but couldn't.

Val looked over her other shoulder. A young maid in a black-and-white uniform bent over and smiled at Val. Was that her mother?

"Here, little Valentine." *Carrie stood in front of her and displayed a bracelet identical to the one her daughter wore.*

The maid knelt beside Val. "Mrs. Moore is a generous woman. You're a very lucky little girl." *The thick East London accent belonging to the maid was that of the mother who raised her.*

Val rubbed her head, where an ache had blossomed. "I don't know. It might be mine...." Her voice came out a whisper. For just a moment, she'd been in a beautiful room surrounded by laughing children and adults scented with perfume. The bracelet brought back a memory that some dark voice urged her to suppress.

A frown puckered Sister Mary Lou's forehead. "Highly unusual for a lighthouse keeper's daughter."

"I don't think I lived in a lighthouse then. That is, when I received it."

Father Joseph leaned in. "How did you come by it?"

"I don't exactly know. It was a gift though." *For someone. Had it been for me?*

"What do you remember?" Sister Mary Lou patted her hand. "I'm pretty sure that's a diamond bracelet."

"Diamonds?" Val gasped and raised the tiny bracelet higher, causing sparks of light to dance around the room as a bright sunbeam pierced the windowpanes.

"The box is from a very elite jewelry store near Detroit." Father Joseph had shared with her early on that he'd been raised in a wealthy family downstate. "We have contacted the jeweler, but we're hoping you might know something."

"Let me tell you what I remember." Val ran her finger over the gilded stamped letter on the inside lid, which proclaimed VITELLIO's. "But first, how did you know this was my birthday?"

"Is it?" The two exchanged a glance.

It was her birthday. Valentine. Valentine's Day.

"Happy birthday, darling." The lady with the beautiful voice kissed her cheek.

Val shook off the memory. "I think so."

Chapter 2

Over two months had passed and Val still had no offers of employment. The Holy Week had come and gone, but her renewed sense of peace had not. Valerie hummed as she dusted the orphanage's parlor thoroughly. Then she attacked the windows with a solution of vinegar water aided by newspaper sheets. As she wiped the acrid solution from the mullioned windows, she spied a stranger walking toward the building. Attired in work clothes, the ginger-haired man sported a matching neatly trimmed beard. He tilted his head back to look up, presumably at the upper stories of the imposing structure. The sun illuminated his handsome features, and she sucked in a breath and pulled back lest he see her staring at him. One of the newspaper sheets fell to the floor, and she bent to retrieve it. The social section featured a picture of a salt-and-pepper-haired woman in fine attire and surrounded by her equally well-dressed adult children. MRS. CARRIE BOOTH MOORE TO VISIT HER SISTER ON MACKINAC ISLAND THIS SUMMER read the headline.

Carrie. That had been the name of the woman with the bracelet. Val squinted at the grainy image of the woman. There was some resemblance to the lady in her memory. Could it be her?

Sister Mary Lou entered the room, the scent of incense surrounding her. She glanced at the newspaper page. "Mrs. Moore is a lovely woman and a great benefactress."

"And blessed with many children, it appears. Wouldn't it be lovely if the matron's grown children would adopt some of the orphans?"

"Oh yes, and well they can afford them—although I suppose it isn't kind of me to say so."

"Sister Mary Lou, you're always kind. You keep your temper despite all the pranks the children play." Should she mention that Mrs. Moore might be the Carrie of her memory?

Father Joseph's baritone voice echoed from the hallway, followed by another man's response. Perhaps the handsome stranger she'd seen entering the building.

Sister Mary Lou gestured for Valerie to sit down on the rose velvet settee and then took a seat beside her. "We have returned the lighthouse association's library

228

books to Mr. Dardanes."

Those had been her treasures. Her escape from the multiple isolated lighthouses she and her family had inhabited. But all had been on loan. Their only "owned" book was the family Bible. And Ma had only pulled that out to read when she was in one of her frenzies. Then she'd hold the Bible between herself and Valerie and blame her for the fit she was having. Everything had always been Val's fault. But not the illness that had taken them. Tears slipped down her cheeks. Her brother and sister, both afflicted with infirmities, were now with the Lord.

"We need to speak." Sister Mary Lou pushed her glasses up onto the bridge of her nose. "Mr. Dardanes advised us that he's selected a new lighthouse keeper from the candidates."

"Oh." The interim one no doubt needed to move on.

"The federal government will do the final hiring." The nun adjusted her habit. "And of course, the gentleman would have to accept the position."

"Of course." Val shivered. That poor man would have to go where her family had died. "I wish there were more jobs available here on the island for me so that I didn't have to rely upon your charity, Sister Mary Lou."

"Valerie, we've wanted you to stay. Both Father and I."

Val dipped her chin, tears threatening. "I'm very grateful."

"We've asked the entire parish for help in placing you. . ."

Val held up a hand. "I understand. Even my friends, the Christys, still can't give me a job right now."

"Because of the country's conflicts with Cuba and Spain, the business owners are nervous."

Perhaps if war was declared, the summer vacationers and cottage owners wouldn't come. "I understand. I can start looking elsewhere."

"No!" The nun's word came out unnaturally curt. "I'm sorry, I didn't mean to sound like that. It's just that, well. . ."

The parlor door swung in and Father Joseph entered, followed by the stranger. This close, the man was even more handsome than he'd first appeared. Taller than the priest by half a head, the man's red-gold hair curled around his high collar. He clutched a smoky-colored bowler hat in his broad hands, his work-roughened knuckles suggesting he was a laborer. Sadness was etched across his high cheekbones and around his light green eyes that spoke of loss.

Father Joseph rocked back and forth on his heels, a nervous habit of his. His black cassock swayed as did the tassels of his cincture. "This is Mr. Paul Sholtus, a candidate for the Round Island Lighthouse position."

Mr. Sholtus nodded curtly.

"Mr. Sholtus, this is Sister Mary Lou, who is in charge of the orphanage."

Sister Mary Lou smiled at the man.

"And this is Miss Fillman, who has been with us a few months. The young lady I was speaking of."

The handsome stranger's lips parted and his eyes widened. "Miss Fillman?" He clamped his lips together and frowned.

"Mr. Sholtus needs someone to help him at the lighthouse."

Val shrugged. "He'll have relief workers."

"But he's unmarried." Father Joseph announced this fact as though the potential lighthouse keeper was helpless. Or was he implying something?

A strange sensation of both dread and fascination shot through Val. She'd read of mail-order brides going out west. Was Father Joseph suggesting Val should marry the man so he'd have help at the one place she wished never to return? And why was she jumping to this conclusion?

"I am actually a widower." His mouth drew into a thin line beneath his neat mustache.

She was sorry, but not sorry enough to marry a stranger—not even one as handsome as this one. Not that she'd been asked. In fact, Mr. Sholtus spoke as though saying he was a widower meant that he was yet married.

The lighthouse keeper applicant stepped forward, light suddenly piercing through the clouds outside and filtering through the windows. "Miss Fillman, I have a young daughter, and she's the reason I'm here."

Had he sensed her misgivings? Could he have any notion of the thoughts running through her mind? Heat seared her cheeks.

Sister Mary Lou patted Val's hand. "Could you imagine being out at the lighthouse again?"

No wonder her friend Susan and Father Joseph had both asked her the same question the previous day. She'd thought they'd wanted her to take another look around the place. Susan had suggested that being there might help her remember something more in the quest to learn her true past. Sister Mary Lou had given Val a letter from Lettice Woods in East London, confirming Dorcas's background and also giving a brief history of where she'd gone in America and her first jobs before reuniting with John Fillman.

Father Joseph clasped his hands at his waist. "Let's leave the two to discuss Mr. Sholtus's situation, shall we?"

This beautiful young woman was definitely not the kind of matron he'd had in mind for his daughter's care. Sweat broke out on Paul's brow, and he wiped it with his handkerchief before sitting down across from her.

"Do you like to fish, Mr. Sholtus?" Miss Fillman clasped her hands so tightly together that her knuckles grew white.

Was he so frightening? Paul swallowed. He would never want Sofia to be in the situation this woman now faced. "I do. But, being a farmer, I haven't gotten to as much as I'd like."

This elicited a smile and a curt laugh. "You'll have plenty of opportunity if you come on as keeper at Round Island."

"I hope to teach my daughter to fish too."

"Yes of course." Miss Fillman glanced toward the window. "A fun pastime for both boys and girls. It would be lovely if the orphans could come out sometime."

Paul's eyebrows rose. "I have many nephews and nieces whom Sofia will miss. Perhaps she could be allowed to visit here at the orphanage from time to time also?"

"Certainly. And the children would appreciate it if you'd bring some whitefish with you, I'm sure."

"A regional favorite, I hear." So said any local working-class man he'd encountered on his trip.

"Indeed." She sat silent, staring at her work-reddened hands.

So far, he'd only learned that the former lighthouse keeper's daughter had a somewhat limited education. But she had cared for her two younger siblings, both of whom suffered infirmities. And she knew the ways of a lighthouse. But would she really be willing to return to the site of the tragic demise of her family?

Miss Fillman leaned in. "I enjoy repairing nets too, Mr. Sholtus, and can teach your daughter as she gets older."

He laughed. "My great-grandfather, who sailed on the Great Lakes, taught me to make nets. I enjoy working with ropes too. I find it relaxing." Not quite as comforting as tilling the earth and inhaling its loamy scent though. This would be the first year in his life that he'd not be there for the planting and the harvest. Might never be again. He drew in a deep breath.

She offered him a tremulous smile. "You might ask the island library to stock a few more picture books."

"The lighthouse board assured me they'd send us young-children's books and a few sporting books for me." Paul brushed hair away from his eyes.

"Good."

Miss Fillman's eyes were so pretty—a blue-violet color. "And I'll request some women's literature that a wife would enjoy. That is. . ." He couldn't help staring at her. What had he just said? He blinked rapidly.

The young woman's cheeks turned pink. Did she expect more than a position providing childcare? He had no plans to remarry. But Sofia could benefit from a mother. Why was he even thinking these things? Why had he said such a thing?

"That is, Miss Fillman, ladies' books and magazines that my daughter's caretaker would enjoy."

Paul exhaled a slow breath as Miss Fillman stared at a piano that dominated a corner of the room, the expression on her face a tug of emotions.

"I can't play any instruments." Her voice came out forced and slightly higher pitched than it had been. "But I can teach her how to sing some songs."

Thank goodness, she'd changed the subject from a wife at the lighthouse. He forced false cheerfulness into his own voice. "I sang to my cows." He arched an eyebrow at the pretty young woman and was rewarded with a shy smile.

The smile slipped from her face. "If I take the position, I will be able to come to town, on Mackinac Island, by myself, won't I?"

"Yes. Of course. The days my substitute mans the light, you'll be free to come and go."

"Good." She exhaled in obvious relief.

"But for safety, I'd prefer that we travel together, Miss Fillman. If you take the position, that is."

She flushed and averted her gaze. "Of course."

So, she'd not even started the position and already she was thinking about getting away from him? Still, she seemed a good fit and the only candidate who hadn't added on a dozen other requirements. "There are two boats, a canoe, and a row boat, and we'll have access to a small sailboat during full season. But I expect you already know that, don't you?"

She nodded but said nothing.

He needed an answer today. If not this pretty young woman, then he'd have to pass on the opportunity he'd waited so long for.

Miss Fillman gazed directly at him. "Could you give me until the hour before the last ferry leaves?"

Paul exhaled in relief. She was willing to discuss the position, to consider it. "That's more than fair. Especially considering. . ." Considering that she'd lost her entire family on Round Island. But he definitely didn't need to point out what she was certainly already struggling with herself. She'd have to be an exceptionally brave young woman to go back and face her losses. And here he was running from his. What an unlikely pair they'd make if she agreed to take the position. *God, You know what I need, and what she needs, but this certainly wasn't what I was asking for.*

Val sat on her narrow bed beneath the window, darning a hole in her stockings.

Susan sat on hers, across from her. "Father Joseph and Sister Mary Lou want you to stay. I know it has to be important for them to ask me to help."

"Yes, it is." Val glanced down at the letter from London. Should she share it with her friend? Susan Johnson was loyal and trustworthy. And her first ever true friend her own age. "You see, I may not have been the Fillmans' daughter."

"What?" Susan's blue eyes widened. "Were you adopted?"

"We don't think so."

"You mean Father Joseph and Sister Mary Lou don't believe so?" Susan stood and paced the square of floor near their paneled door. "Were you taken? Stolen?"

"Maybe."

Susan clutched her hands to her bosom. "That's so romantic!"

Her own eyes widening, Val stopped darning her sock and began to laugh. "Leave it to you to think that's something good."

Her friend plopped down on the bed beside Val. "It could be! How many children in this orphanage imagine that another set of parents are out there searching for them? And yet, you really may have a mother and father looking for you."

Val hadn't truly thought of that. She'd been so absorbed in her loss, her grief, and the shock of her family background that she'd not considered what her real parents would have suffered.

A knock on the door announced Sister Mary Lou.

Susan rose, bobbed a quick curtsy to the nun, and excused herself. Valerie clasped a hand to her pin-tucked bodice embellished with embroidered roses—a donation to the orphanage from an anonymous donor and the right size for her. If she was going to live at the lighthouse, she'd need to go through her limited wardrobe and see what she could take with her.

Reaching into her pocket to retrieve something, the nun entered and then waved a missive in the air. "We've a letter back from Vitellio's."

Val straightened. "That's good. What does it say?"

"They had only seven custom orders for this specific bracelet." Sister Mary Lou held back a smile that twitched at her lips.

"And?"

Grinning broadly, the nun raised the letter high. "Only one person who commissioned them."

"Who?"

"Mrs. Carrie Booth Moore."

Shivers coursed over Val's arms and she rubbed them. "She's. . .she's coming to the island. I saw it in the newspaper."

"And you, my dear, will be here." Sister Mary Lou nodded slowly. "If you accept the lighthouse position."

"Will you send her a letter?"

"Sherlock Joseph is putting ink to paper as we speak." She winked.

Val stood and stepped forward into her friend's open arms. She was blessed with more than one friend now. "Thank you."

"Don't worry, we'll get to the bottom of this. Trust God to help us."

Trust? Since being at the orphanage and seeing the children who'd left for homes, she'd hoped they'd been put into good placements. But had she trusted God with that? No. Valerie sniffed and took a step back.

Sister Mary Lou held Val's shoulders. "What do you think of Mr. Sholtus?"

"He seems very kind."

"And handsome too, eh?" Sister Mary Lou arched a fair eyebrow.

"Yes, he is handsome." Not that she'd had much experience in the world. Yet in her dreams, she'd seen dozens of men, women, and children who were attractive, well-dressed, and well-mannered people. There was one, especially, a handsome man the others in her dreams called Percy. Who was this Percy? "I'll be speaking again with Mr. Sholtus before he returns home. I'd hate to be the cause of him not taking this position."

The nun nodded solemnly. "And I'd hate for you to be elsewhere when Mrs. Moore comes to the island."

The afternoon passed quickly. Once again, Val had attempted to help with baking duties and was shooed from the kitchen when her shortcakes burned. So she'd returned to cleaning up the classrooms.

She'd just moved on to Father Joseph's office when the clock chimed the last hour before the ferries would depart. Soon the schedule would be longer, as flocks of summer vacationers swarmed the popular vacation spot. She and Mr. Sholtus could speak privately here. It wasn't long before Father Joseph escorted Mr. Sholtus into the room.

The priest lingered in the doorway and looked at Val over the top of his spectacles. "I shall be right outside, should you need anything."

"Thank you." Her words came out almost a whisper.

Mr. Sholtus stood there, twisting his bowler cap in his broad hands. *Heavens, if he keeps that up, he'll ruin it.* Val took several strides toward the man, grasped his hat, turned, and hung it on a peg, then gestured for him to sit. "That's a nice hat, Mr. Sholtus, no need to ruin it."

He laughed, a rich baritone that rumbled from deep in his chest. "I see you are not the shy wallflower I was led to believe you are." He sat in the chair.

"Hardly." Not after what she'd been through.

He splayed his fingers and held his hands up. "Tell me what I could do to help you make a decision about working for me."

She sat at the end of the settee. "Could I have my own room back?" She had shared the room with Mary, but no need to mention that.

"Of course." He frowned. "But I'll warn you, Sofia gets frightened and sometimes will crawl into whatever bed is convenient."

"I remember doing that with my mother." A vision of a frightened young Ma surged in her memory. They'd huddled in her bed in the squalid New York City tenement building until finally Pa had taken them from there. They'd gone on to Michigan. What a long train ride that had been. For a moment she was a tiny girl, shivering as they were jostled along, periodic puffs of coal dust coming through the windows and making her eyes tear up.

Mr. Sholtus cleared his throat. "Was your father gone often, then?"

She had no idea about that early time. Was it possible that she'd been illegitimately born? Perhaps her "mother" had stolen that diamond bracelet. Had Val watched as Mrs. Moore presented the gift to another child in the household?

She closed her eyes for a moment, trying to force herself to focus. "No, but my father did have a lot of duties to perform at each lighthouse that kept him from us."

"I'm sure you understand that children are not allowed up by the light, so that would be your primary responsibility."

"Oh yes. Their fingerprints could really cause a problem. My mother made sure we understood that." And had beaten Tim and Mary the few times they'd managed to sneak up the stairs toward the light when they'd been very young. Val had never lost her vigilance after that. Tim's leg had never healed properly afterward.

How could she force herself to accept this position?

The only way forward is back. The thought came suddenly, as if a voice whispered to her heart. Trust was new. Such a fragile thing. She recalled the baby robin she'd rescued when she was a child, binding its tiny leg until it could fly again. And when she set it free, off it flew. To its family?

"I'll accept the job."

Chapter 3

Paul unpacked his silver-framed wedding photo and propped it on his bedside table. He ran his thumb over the image of Annabelle's face. The dull ache in his chest that had thrummed all these years had begun to quiet. Outside his window, seagulls squawked and swooped and dove into the water. A gentle breeze rustled the Swiss Dot curtains that his mother had sent with him—a reminder of home. But he'd come here to forget. So why had he brought the picture and the curtains? He huffed a sigh and sat down on the bed.

"Daddy?" Sofia stood in his doorway, index finger in her mouth.

"Aren't you taking a nap?"

Quick steps announced Miss Fillman. "I'm sorry, Mr. Sholtus. I thought Sofia had settled." Her stricken face seemed out of place for the severity of her perceived crime.

He opened his arms to his daughter and she ran to him. He scooped her up. "Don't worry, I know this little rascal's tricks."

Sofia leaned away from him and poked his cheeks, grinning. "Made you smile."

"Yes, my little love." Indeed, his daughter was one of the few people who had been able to get a grin out of him in the past few years.

"I'll put her back down." Miss Fillman's tone was dubious though. She'd mentioned the previous evening that her younger sister never napped after the age of three.

"How about we all go down and work on the nets?"

Miss Fillman smiled gently in apparent approval.

Paul set Sofia down.

She looked up at him with wide violet eyes so much like her mother's. "Go wading?" she pleaded.

"It's cold water in the straits." Miss Fillman feigned shivering. Excitement seemed to bubble up in her, and he was once again surprised—no, shocked—at how well she could adjust to being here where her entire family had perished.

Sofia crossed her little arms. "Grandmom says I've got warm blood." Which was why she'd strip off her day clothes and into her thin sleeping gown even for naps.

"My child has been known to run outside in a snowstorm attired just as she is now." Paul gestured to Sofia's cotton sleep dress.

"Not barefoot!" His daughter lifted her foot and wiggled her toes.

Paul raised his hands in surrender. "True. You had the sense to put your boots on."

Ducking her chin, Sofia gave an impish grin.

"It's settled then." Miss Fillman took his daughter's hand and led her from the room.

"I'll be down in a moment." Paul glanced back at the picture of him and his wife. Annabelle hadn't even had the opportunity to hold their daughter in her arms before she'd died. What kinds of things would they have done together with Sofia, had Annabelle survived childbirth? He wiped away the wetness from his cheek, recalling the haunting poem by Edgar Allan Poe, "Annabel Lee."

It was many and many a year ago,
In a kingdom by the sea,
That a maiden there lived whom you may know
By the name of Annabel Lee;
And this maiden she lived with no other thought
Than to love and be loved by me.

I was a child and she was a child,
In this kingdom by the sea,
But we loved with a love that was more than love—
I and my Annabel Lee—
With a love that the wingèd seraphs of Heaven
Coveted her and me.

He and his Annabelle had been childhood sweethearts. They were so young. And now she was gone. Forever young, while he continued on. What would Annabelle say if she were here now?

Val laughed so hard at Sofia's antics in the water that she feared she'd tear a seam in her too-tight gray plaid work dress. She pressed a hand over her mouth as the child jumped over waves, twirled like a ballerina, and then imitated a seagull. The child was so free. Free. That was something she'd not been in years. When Sofia once again attempted a pirouette in the chilly water, her father lifted her up and held her high overhead.

The streaming sun from behind them darkened their image, and for a moment

Val could feel the arms of a very tall man holding her. The scent of cigar smoke, strong tea, and something spicy clung to him. She frowned as the memory surged over her. Suddenly dizzy, she leaned back on the rocky beach. But John Fillman was average height, didn't smoke, drank only strong black coffee, and smelled mainly of lye soap. And the only time she remembered him carrying her was when her mother had chased after her, intending to. . .

"Valerie? Miss Fillman?" Mr. Sholtus set his daughter down and they came up on the beach.

"Yes?" She sat up again and pressed a hand to her brow. "I was dizzy. But I'm all right."

The handsome lighthouse keeper cocked his head, frowning. "You look like you've seen a ghost."

"No ghosts, I assure you." But she shivered. Her family had died here. "I don't believe in such nonsense." She might not yet be fully conversing with God again, but neither had she abandoned the beliefs she'd developed by reading the Bible on her own and attending church.

"Good." He patted his flat stomach. "I've worked up an appetite for tea and cookies."

"Cookies!" Sofia clapped her hands. "Grandmom's, please."

Val sighed. "I'll have to learn to bake her favorites. And not burn them."

"No need. Mrs. Christy and I have an arrangement." Mr. Sholtus winked at her. "Oh?"

"The tea shop will provide us baked goods each week if we bring them whitefish, bass, and so on. Her husband is too busy with work at the Grand Hotel to fish."

"You've only just arrived!" She laughed. "You work quickly, don't you?"

"It was the first place I stopped." He patted the top of Sofia's curly head. "Happy girl—happy daddy."

She shrugged. "If only life could be so easy. If only a cookie solved our problems."

Sofia ran off toward the lighthouse, and they both followed her. Mr. Sholtus stopped just outside the entrance. "Miss Fillman, may I please call you by your Christian name? I'm a farmer. Was a farmer anyway." He ran a hand through his thick hair. "And I'm used to keeping things simple. Please call me Paul."

A niggling of unease was accompanied by a chill breeze from Lake Huron. "Very well, Paul. You may call me Valerie—but only when we are here alone. People might misconstrue our arrangement."

When she looked into his green eyes, something warm chased away her chill. He squeezed her hand. "I have only respect for you, Miss Fillman. . .Valerie."

He released her hand. Why did his words leave her wanting more than respect? They were becoming friends after only five days at the lighthouse. She crossed her arms. She had friends on the island. That had to be enough for her in her station in life.

"Don't forget to make a list for tomorrow, for when our relief worker comes in." Paul gestured to the bigger of the two boats. "We'll take that one over. I'm hoping Sofia won't be too scared. She's never been in a boat other than coming up on the steamship with me on our one trip here."

"I'll hold her tight and I'll tell her stories while we cross."

"Thank you." Paul ran a hand over his neat beard. "I don't know what I'd do without you."

Val's trust had been rewarded. Paul had allowed her to separate from him and his daughter once they'd arrived on Mackinac. Val walked down the boardwalk, alone. Giddy exhilaration bubbled up in her. She nibbled her lower lip. Was it wicked to be grateful to be free to walk alone without her mother guarding her every step? Without the restrictions she'd been brought up with? She shook her head as a wind from Lake Huron rose and then fell. She clutched her hat for a moment, gazing out at the sapphire-blue water. For the longest time, water had been her enemy—keeping her isolated. But it hadn't truly been the Great Lakes—it had been her mother's iron will ruling them all. Except for the days when Ma had medicated herself into a stupor. Those were the blissfully quiet days. A lone tear trailed down Val's cheek as she opened the door to the Christy Tea Shoppe, where Susan was to meet her.

The proprietor and her daughters were waiting on customers at the counter, so Valerie took a seat at a table and waited. She pulled her gloves off, a gift from Father Joseph. Val marveled at the feel of the soft kid leather. A sudden recollection of pulling at similar cream-colored gloves sparked through her and she stopped tugging. She'd never owned any gloves as fine as these. Why then the memory? She must be going mad, as Dr. DuBlanc had said of her mother. Or rather, the woman who claimed to be her mother. Maybe this was a real memory.

Once the other customers had chosen their treats—muffins, scones, and cookies—and departed, Mrs. Christy called out to her. "Welcome, Valerie! Should I bring your favorite?"

"Yes, thank you!" She grinned, the wonderful warmth of this newfound familiarity and friendship a blessing. Both Garrett and Rebecca Christy had visited with her at the orphanage throughout her stay there. They'd brought her English breakfast tea, and on occasion, she'd been allowed to take some of the orphans to the shop for tea. Sofia would love this place.

Rebecca carried the creamy teapot imprinted with tiny flowers to the table and poured Val's tea. "Miss Johnson said she would be by at half past the hour."

"I'm glad she had off today." Susan had begun summer work as Mr. Foley's photography assistant.

Rebecca shook her head. "You must have a strong constitution to be able to go back out there."

"To the lighthouse?"

"Indeed. I don't know how you did it." Rebecca took a seat beside her. "But that keeper is a fortunate man that you did."

Valerie stirred honey into her teacup with a filigreed silver-plated spoon. "He's very kind and. . ."

"And handsome too, isn't he?" Rebecca laughed softly. "And he sure knows how to work a deal, doesn't he?"

"Yes, he does." Valerie lifted her teacup to her lips. "I had to smell that fish he's swapping with you all the way on the boat ride over here."

They both laughed. "It's good seeing you looking better, Valerie."

Paul and Sofia—father and child—they'd brought about this change, but Val wasn't about to confess that. Not yet. "And good to see you looking rather glowing. If I might say so."

Rebecca's cheeks grew rosy. "Garrett and I are thrilled, but at this rate we quite wonder where we'll put all our children."

"Maybe do like the nursery rhyme and have your very own master craftsman husband build a large shoe?" Val laughed again at the idea of all the Christy children peeping out from a big lumberjack boot.

"We're probably going to accept a larger one of the Craftsman's cottages from the Grand."

The shop owner leaned in. "Five bedrooms!"

"How nice." Val nibbled on an oatmeal cookie. "And well deserved."

Rebecca beamed. "I hope little Sofia will enjoy the cookies I've packed up for her."

"No doubt." What were Paul and Sofia doing right now? Val sipped her tea. The fragrance and the sweetness lifted her spirits further. A little part of her felt empty though. Sister Mary Lou had assured her that God would fill the emptiness in her heart that her family had left. But this felt different.

The door opened and Val turned, half hoping it might be her employer and his child. Instead, an older, well-dressed woman, who looked familiar, entered, followed by several pretty young women. With fashionably styled upswept hair, clutching trim leather reticules, their shoulders covered in fur stoles, the ladies were the epitome of elegance. Val averted her gaze and glanced down at her threadbare dress. She had enough money for fabric. Should she make herself a new dress, as Mr. Sholtus had suggested? Val had found a pretty ensemble she liked in *The Delineator*. She'd order the pattern and one for a new church dress for Sofia.

The tallest of the young women pointed toward the case. "Mother, look at that beautiful tray of muffins. Your Sugarplum Ladies in Detroit would love those."

"Indeed, they would. Why don't we ask for a sample?" Why did the woman's voice seem so familiar?

Val took another sip of her tea, fighting the urge to flee.

Rebecca shot Val a concerned glance. She rose and went to the counter, tugging at her lacy apron.

"Do you accept advance orders, ma'am?" That voice again brought back a misty recollection.

Val shifted in her seat, stealing glances. In all of her existence, she'd known only a handful of women other than her mother, who wasn't at all social. That's why Susan, whom she'd met at the orphanage, had become such a special friend. When the lighthouse inspectors' wives would make visits, Val had always been instructed to keep her tongue in her head "lest it be cut off." She shivered at the recollection. Having observed what her mother had done to their first cat, she'd remained silent during any visits, unless spoken directly to by the adults.

"Might you be able to make us up a tray of assorted baked goods for tomorrow? We're staying at a cottage by the Grand Hotel."

"Certainly. My husband works at the Grand and could even carry the tray up to you." Rebecca was so proud of Garrett and his work there, and Val could hear it in her voice.

"Wonderful."

The young women tittered and laughed.

Rebecca took out her notepad and a stubby pencil. "Who is this for and where should it be delivered?"

"This would be for the Moore family staying at The Canary. The cottage belongs to the Swaine family."

The young woman Val had seen in the pharmacy.

"But we're family friends and will be staying there."

Carrie Booth Moore. The woman whose daughter had a diamond bracelet like hers. The woman who had commissioned all those child-sized bracelets. Val directed her full attention to the woman. What she saw was a dark-haired woman with kind eyes and dimples in her cheeks. A woman in her thirties. But when she blinked, she clearly saw a matron in her fifties or so, with silver-streaked hair. When the woman's dark eyes met hers, Valerie averted her gaze quickly. Hands shaking, heart beating rapidly, she took steadying sips of her Earl Grey tea. She should say something. But surely Father Joseph and Sister Mary Lou hadn't known of her arrival or they'd have sent word. Heart beating louder in her ears, Val could barely hear her own thoughts.

She forced herself to relax and took in the details of the group. All were in their mid- to late twenties, one likely nearer thirty.

When the Moore women had finished conducting their arrangements, the younger women, apparently the daughters, moved toward the door. Val caught snippets of their conversations, about motor cars, an orchestra, and a beau who was on the island. Their mother lingered behind.

"Go ahead, girls, I'll catch up!" The matron stopped at Val's table and stared at her.

Val looked up, and the woman pressed a hand to her ample bosom.

"Ma'am?"

"You look so very much like a friend of mine." The woman's words almost warbled. "Or rather, like her daughter."

Heartbeat ratcheting up, Val braved her question. "Who?"

"Well, I. . ." The society matron's gaze quickly covered her. "I shouldn't say. But may I ask your name?"

Had Mrs. Moore received the letter from the priest? If so, wouldn't she have gone to the orphanage and summoned her there? "My name is Val. . ."

The woman's eyes widened.

"Valerie Fillman." But maybe it wasn't.

"Oh, I see." The matron drew out the last word, as though she struggled to check her reaction, her brow furrowed. "Sorry to trouble you."

Carrie Booth Moore once again eyed Valerie before she departed. Val sat there, staring after her.

I don't know who I am.

Rebecca came back around. "Do you know that woman?"

"I might. I'm not sure." Val rubbed her wrist. A sparkling bracelet had been wrapped around her wrist. Somehow, now, she was certain this woman had given her the gift.

"Do you want to talk about it?"

Paul clutched Sofia's hand as they wove through the tourists on the boardwalk, while he held the whitefish package in the other. He'd spied Valerie practically racing away from the tea shop that she'd recommended to them. What had happened? He picked Sofia up and moved faster, dodging folks coming in and out of the many shops between them and Sofia's caretaker. He watched as she approached a newsstand and plucked coins from her reticule. He had also planned to pick up copies of the latest papers, and used that as his rationale for chasing after her.

He waited until a dray loaded down with crates overflowing with early tomatoes, green beans, and cabbages passed by. Then he jogged across the street, dodging horse manure as he went.

The youth at the newsstand handed Valerie the *Island Herald*. "Here you go, miss."

Before she could put her coins down, Paul interrupted. "Miss Fillman, let me pay for that."

Valerie whirled to face him, eyes wide. "Oh! You startled me."

"Sorry."

"Valerie!" Sofia raised her arms toward her pretty caregiver.

To his surprise, Valerie eagerly took his daughter into her arms, pressing a kiss to Sofia's cheek. "There's our missing girl!"

Was that moisture in her eyes? "Not missing—right here with her father."

"I. . .I know." Valerie blinked rapidly and clutched Sofia closely. "I meant. . .I missed her."

"Already? What has it been? An hour?"

Valerie swiveled away from him, facing herself and his daughter toward the Straits of Mackinac. She pointed. "There's the lighthouse!"

Paul quickly selected the other newspapers he wanted and paid.

The young man touched his fingers to the brim of his straw hat. "You must be Mr. Sholtus, the new lighthouse keeper."

"Yes."

"I run this stand and own another down around the bend."

Eyebrows rising, Paul grinned. "An enterprising lad."

"Aye. And I was promised a good tip if I can get you to give Mr. Ben Steffans an interview."

Paul shrugged.

The vendor leaned in, light whiskers on his cheeks revealing he was older than he appeared. "And if you can get Miss Fillman to give him a scoop, I bet he'd reward the both of us."

Straightening, Paul shook his head. "If and when Miss Fillman chooses to discuss her tragedy with a journalist—that is her business."

"What about you though?"

"Let Mr. Steffans know that he's welcome to come out anytime." Paul arched an eyebrow. "To speak with *me*."

"Yes, sir. I'll let him know."

Valerie turned and crooked a finger at him. When he joined her, she put Sofia down and pointed to the Indian Curiosity Shop. "Let's stop in there for a moment. But then I've got to go on to the orphanage."

He shouldn't push. Shouldn't intrude on her free time. He knew he shouldn't. But the words spilled out. "May we come to the orphanage too?"

Hesitating only a moment, Valerie stared at him with those big eyes of hers then lifted Sofia and kissed her head. "That should be fine."

Paul raised his whitefish package. "I have to drop these fish at the Christys'."

She waved him away. "Go take them then, and meet Sofia and me at the orphanage."

Bossy woman. Wasn't that one of the things he'd loved about Annabelle? She'd grown up with him and was never afraid to express her mind. She wasn't like the young ladies he'd met when he worked at the hospital in Battle Creek. Their opinions always swayed to however he thought about things. And if they did express an interest in something, it tended to be about fashion and who was courting whom. His heart had been left behind in Shepherd, with Annabelle, so none of the young ladies he'd met had any chance.

Valerie's eyebrows pulled together and she motioned to him, again, to go on. Little Sofia imitated the gesture and then the two laughed. At him! His ego might take a beating if those two teamed up too much.

Chapter 4

When Val stepped outside the lighthouse, she spied the supply boat as it skimmed along the water toward Round Island. Sunlight illuminated its full white sails, and her heart skipped a beat. A giddiness she'd always felt at the boat's arrival welled up. The suppliers brought news and books, which made her feel more connected to the outside world. But the intense, almost desperate, elation was different now. A little softer. All because Paul had made her world safe. Had made the lighthouse a place of comfort and. . .home. Like a real home could be.

Paul followed Val outside the lighthouse. He held Sofia's hand as she waved to the crew of two. "The mail has finally come." Val knew he'd waited on word from his parents and other family members.

She turned and bent down to Sofia. "That means our books have arrived too!"

Paul released his daughter's hand. Valerie scooped her up and twirled her around.

When the child's squeal began to sound like distress, Val set her down and patted her shoulders. "I didn't mean to scare you."

"Dizzy." Sofia patted her strawberry-blond curls. Val had wrapped the child's hair in rag rollers the night before and pinned them until they dried. Perfect ringlets framed her gamine face.

Val tweaked her nose. "You're a pretty little girl even if you are dizzy."

Sofia made a face and then plunked onto the ground.

"I'll go and get our deliveries." Paul headed off toward the short pier.

Knowing Mr. Haapala never stayed for tea, Val didn't offer to make any for him. But she kept a watchful eye in case, for once, the older man had changed his mind. She suspected he didn't stay because of his heavy Finnish accent, which made conversation with him difficult. One of these days she'd simply bring him out a basket of cookies, made by Rebecca of course, and not her own, which could still break teeth. But she'd bring him a mug of tea too, which she could brew to perfection. The thought made her smile. Next delivery by Mr. Haapala, she would do it.

Sofia picked up her stick and began practicing drawing a straight line, as Val had been encouraging her to do. Those lines would eventually turn into the number one and also the letter *L*. Just as she'd helped her younger brother and sister with their numbers and letters. She frowned in concentration as a dim recollection overcame her. A pretty auburn-haired girl in pink muslin and lace dress had stood Val beside a small blackboard. *"Write a* V, *Valentine! That's the first letter of your name!"* She shivered, as the girl's gentle laugh echoed in her ears. Her older sister. That memory, that girl, was her older sister. But who was she? Tears pricked her eyes.

She blinked, and Sofia stared up at her, head cocked. "Sad?"

Val wiped her eyes. "I'm okay. I was thinking of someone."

Sofia dropped her stick, took Val's hand. "Mommy?"

Not of her mother. She'd not yet had a memory of another mother. "My sister."

"Come on inside," Paul called over his shoulder as he carried the large crate into the lighthouse living quarters.

Once in the parlor, Paul set the crate down in the center of the braided rug then headed off toward the kitchen.

"Open the books!" Sofia dropped to the rug and patted the box.

"Patience, my little love!" Paul rejoined them and produced a knife. He cut through the twine and then carefully sliced through the heavy oilpaper covering the wood crate. "Nailed shut. Let me get my pry bar."

Both Val and Sofia leaned closer, peering through the slats. Val pointed to the top book. "I see Thumbelina."

"I see fairy wings." Sofia pointed to a cover embossed with tiny fairies.

"Oh my, that's very pretty, isn't it?"

"Yes! I want it."

"All right, just a moment." Val sighed when she spotted Emily Dickinson's name. "I see a poetry book."

Sofia clapped her hands. "I see a book with a doggy!"

"But I asked for a cookbook for girls who love pancakes." Val cocked her head at the child. "It has only recipes for panny cakes in there. Can you believe it?"

Her tiny eyebrows drew together. "You're fibbing."

Val laughed. Sofia would eat pancakes morning, noon, and night if her father allowed. And they were one item Val didn't often burn.

"You're right. But there is a cookbook in there. I can see the letters."

"I'll learn letters soon."

Val sat down beside the little girl. "Yes. Let's sing our ABC's until your father gets back."

Although a little off tune, they commenced singing and had gotten through their ditty twice when Paul finally returned.

Soon they'd oohed and aahed over each book until the lighthouse keeper picked up the last—a large tome covered in grass-green cloth. A pucker formed between his tawny eyebrows and his lips parted. *Farming in Small Spaces.* Paul opened the book and a slip of paper fell out. Mr. Dardanes's even script was easily identified.

"What does it say?"

"Tell us, Daddy."

Paul drew in a deep breath, the furrow between his brows relaxing at last. "The inspector suggests we start another garden on what little land we have here. They'll be bringing in soil amendments soon for us since we're basically living atop rock."

Wrinkling her nose, Valerie knew what that meant—manure and fish remnants and other stinky stuff would soon be unloaded. Tending a garden had been one of the joys of her childhood though. "I love digging in the dirt and planting vegetables."

Sofia wrapped her arm around Valerie's shoulder. "Can I help?"

"Of course you'll help, you little cookie!"

"Not a cookie. I'm a girl."

Val pressed her nose into the child's curls. "You smell sweet as a cookie."

Sofia stood and raised her arms to her father. "Tell her, Daddy."

Laughing, Paul pulled her up and he too inhaled the sweet scent of his daughter. "You do smell like a sugar cookie."

"It's vanilla," Val confessed. "She asked for perfume, and I put a dot of vanilla essence in her hair."

"Not perfume?" Sofia leaned back and looked at her father, her lips in a pout.

"That's little girl perfume, Sofia. Didn't you know?"

"Oh." Apparently placated, she grinned and wiggled to get down. Her father lowered her.

"Get up." Sofia pointed at Val.

No one had to tell her twice. Val sprang to her feet, feeling color drain from her face. Only once had she not immediately obeyed this directive, and she could still remember the sting of the switch on her bare legs. She flinched. But this girl was just a child. A girl who simply wanted Val up off the floor.

"Are you all right?" Paul touched her arm briefly, sending reassuring warmth through her.

She gazed up at him. What a lucky woman his wife had been. Such a handsome and intelligent man and a wonderful, loving father. What kind of woman had Annabelle been? Val swallowed hard, averting her gaze from that of the handsome lighthouse keeper.

Although it was nine in the evening, the sun still streamed through Paul's window in his room overlooking the Straits of Mackinac. Sitting in his chair at the desk, he tucked his parents' letter into his Bible. What strange questions they'd asked. Had he found a new wife? Would she be a good mother for Sofia? What was Valerie like?

Annabelle and Valerie were about as different as two women could be, other than their tendency toward bossiness. When Paul thought of his wife, he remembered constant laughter, frequent hugs given to anyone in her path, much teasing, and devotion to dedicated quiet time spent savoring and reflecting. Annabelle was sentimental to a fault, while Valerie seemed a pragmatist to the core. And although she was gentle and affectionate with Sofia, Valerie seemed to shy away from him or flinch even at his lightest touch. The woman never stopped moving, doing, and occupying herself until, late at night, her violet eyes haunted, she finally went off to sleep. He'd looked forward to lighthouse life, which he'd read had offered plenty of time for quiet. She was beginning to make him feel like a sluggard.

Something was not right with Miss Fillman. When she did laugh, it was like something bursting forth, and almost childlike. Suppressed joy that remained restrained. He saw it when she engaged with Sofia in play and didn't realize he was observing. There was a childlike innocence, wonder, and joy that emerged during those times. And although she accepted affection easily from Sofia, when she was with her friends in town and they reached to console her or hug her, she would go almost limp. As though someone had hurt her. What had happened in her life with the former lighthouse keeper and his wife?

For some reason, lately, Paul's thoughts returned to the time when he'd worked at one of the Kellogg sanitariums. He'd met so many tortured souls there. But one stood out. One who resembled Valerie. He rubbed his forehead trying to recollect her name. Employees had been instructed to keep all information learned there private. And normally the attendants used only the patients' first names. But the young woman had received visits from a wealthy Detroit matron. A dark-haired lady who'd kept her maiden name as a middle name because she was from a distinguished family. It would come to him. Lord willing.

He thumbed open his Bible, which had gotten more use in the past month than it had since he'd become a father. He'd been deep in his grief and had less time to spend in the Word with taking care of his daughter as her only parent. After finishing reading his chapter in Luke, Paul knelt on the rag rug alongside his brass bed and prayed. He leaned his head against the quilt his mother had sent with him and inhaled the scent of lavender, which Valerie had used in the rinse water. *Lord, help me assist this young woman. I don't know what to do, Lord, but You do. Guide me. Be with me now. With us, Lord. In Jesus' precious name, amen.*

Chapter 5

Legs crossed, Sofia sat on Valerie's quilt-covered bed and pointed to the mirror. "You look pretty."

Ceasing in her efforts to pin her hair into what she hoped was an elegant coiffure, Val examined her reflection. Her new pin-tucked Batiste shirtwaist fit beautifully, as did her cadet-blue linen skirt. She fingered the cameo at her neck, a gift from Rebecca. With the shawl knit by Sister Mary Lou and the glittering hairpin from Susan, she looked. . .

Movement behind her distracted her, and Paul's image filled the mirror, his face reflecting a longing that pierced her soul. His eyes seemed to say that he loved her. Something inside her broke. Tears pricked her eyes and she turned from the looking glass.

"You're beautiful."

Sofia jumped down from the bed and ran to her father. "You're peeping!"

"Peeking," Valerie gently corrected. She blinked back the moisture in her eyes.

Paul lifted Sofia overhead until she could touch the ceiling. The child giggled until her father lowered her to the rag rug–covered floor.

"Regardless, you two fine ladies are served notice of departure." Paul adjusted Sofia's hair bow and kissed her forehead.

"We'll be down in a moment." Val glanced to the wooden box on her chest of drawers, tempted to bring the diamond bracelet and allow Sofia to wear it.

Soon, they'd all boarded the skiff and had departed for Mackinac Island. Paul focused intently as he maneuvered the boat around the lane traffic. So many boats and ships of all kinds came in and out of the area, and today was no different. When a passenger ship blew its horn, Sofia shrieked and Val wrapped her arms around the child. Sofia's warm little body felt so right in her embrace. What would it be like to be her mother? Val cast a glance at Paul, his handsome profile making her smile and sending a different kind of warmth through her.

After they'd moored, a dock boy assisted Valerie and Sofia from the boat as Paul secured the vessel in an area reserved for smaller craft.

On the wharf, Sister Mary Lou sat on a long bench, her head bowed. Porters pulled carts of luggage toward the long line of drays and carriages parked streetside.

Paul gestured toward the nun. "You should go see your friend. We'll catch up with you later at the Tea Shoppe."

"All right." Val wove through the throng of disembarking passengers and toward the bench by the ferry ticketing building.

As she reached her, Sister Mary Lou rose. "I need to speak with you privately."

Had her friend discovered something important? Val glanced around the crowd. She spied a wide swath of open green and benches in the park where the fort's garden used to be, and she pointed toward it. "Let's sit over there."

"I'm fairly certain of what I'm about to tell you. But there's more to know." Sister Mary Lou linked her arm through Valerie's and patted her hand.

Valerie's heart beat rapidly. "Did my mother steal that bracelet?"

"No."

Val exhaled in relief.

"But she did work for Mrs. Carrie Booth Moore."

"She did?" As they passed a fudge shop, Val sucked in a breath, the scent of sugar permeating the air. Through the window she watched as a man pushed hot fudge back and forth with a huge paddle across a large marble-slabbed table.

"Yes, but..." Sister Mary Lou's lips pulled in tightly. "It's somewhat complicated."

Soon they'd found an empty private bench in the park. Robins warbled nearby. The white limestone of the fort gleamed as sunshine broke through the fluffy clouds overhead.

They both sat, turning in to face one another. "What did you find, Sister Mary Lou?"

The pretty nun averted her gaze to the nearby side street, where bicyclists and carriages competed for space. "My dear, it's a mystery what exactly happened, but..." She shook her head.

"What is it?"

She exhaled sharply. "Mrs. Moore did employ Dorcas Woods, but Dorcas left."

"Why?"

"Mrs. Moore never knew. But she was told it had to do with a man."

"My father?"

The nun's eyes widened. "Yes, Mr. Fillman. But he wasn't your father."

"Are you sure?"

"Dorcas, the woman who raised you, was employed by Mrs. Moore. She didn't have a child."

Seagulls squawked and circled overhead nearby, and Sister Mary Lou glanced up.

"How did Mrs. Moore know that?" Val's hands began to shake.

"As a servant, Dorcas Woods lived in the Moore home, upstairs."

"And the bracelet?"

Again, Sister Mary Lou sighed. "A gift to another child, not Mrs. Moore's child."

Val's hands began to tremble. Was she that child? "Who?"

"A friend of Mrs. Moore's. To her friend's daughter, Mrs. Moore's goddaughter."

Suddenly light-headed, Valerie gripped the bench.

"Mrs. Moore wouldn't tell me any more than that, Valerie."

Her mouth dry, Val could barely manage her question. "Why not?"

"Because her dear friend has been bitterly disappointed in the past, looking for her lost daughter."

"Lost daughter?" Was she that lost daughter? Her stomach clenched.

Children's laughter rang out as several girls in sailor hats raced by, chasing a fluffy white cat.

"Yes, my dear. You must be patient. But I believe you were taken from your real parents."

Who would do that? What kind of person? Someone like the bitter disturbed woman who had raised her. No, Dorcas hadn't raised her. If anything, her father— rather, the man who had raised her—had performed that job. And Val had helped raise their two children, who weren't her siblings at all.

It was like the jigsaw puzzles that she and Paul put together at night. Except that someone had broken the pieces all apart. And had thrown them in the air. And now they'd settled, mixed in with another puzzle—the pictures of both puzzles intermingled but incomplete. How would this all be straightened out? Val had the feeling the process would not be as enjoyable as assembling a picture puzzle with Paul was.

"I think it explains the nightmares you have." Sister Mary Lou patted Val's shoulder.

"Yes."

"Perhaps they're memories."

Val took a slow breath. "I believe so. And I have other memories that come to me. They flit. . ." She pointed to a cardinal. "They flit like that bird does."

Her friend rose and brushed the wrinkles from her black habit. "I have to get back to the orphanage, but I will keep you updated if I hear anything."

"Thank you."

"I know it's a lot to take in. But at least you now know your fears of going mad aren't true in the least."

Valerie couldn't help chuckling as a lone tear coursed down her cheek. "Yes, that's a blessing." But who was her true mother, if the madwoman who'd made her life miserable was not?

"Mrs. Moore promised to contact her friend, but she wouldn't give me any specifics."

So once again, Val would have to trust God. Hope bloomed in her heart. Trust was coming easier now. "Thank you, Sister Mary Lou, for your help."

"I thank God." With a smile, she departed.

"Let me down!" Sofia kicked and struggled until Paul set her on the grass in the small park overlooking the straits' harbor.

Unsure of whether the area was part of the Michigan State Parks, which owned much of the island, or a private domain, Paul watched in consternation as Sofia ran toward a picnic table. A silver-haired woman attired in a flowing creamy muslin gown more suited to a younger woman presided at a table. She was surrounded by children ranging from near Sofia's age to a youth in his teen years. All held a book.

The matron ceased speaking to her group and watched as Sofia ran toward her, calling, "Grandmom!"

Sofia neared the woman, suddenly stopped, and began to wail. She turned back to face him. He cringed. Somehow his daughter had believed she'd found her grandmother here. Now that Mother was finally free to spend time in her own home, with Father, she no doubt was getting the rest she deserved—although her letters professed how she wished they were there.

Paul knelt and opened his arms for his child. Sofia returned and flung herself at his chest. He bent his head over hers, as her tears saturated his cotton shirt. "My poor girl." He patted her silky head. "You're missing your grandmother."

Her sturdy little body shook with sobs. "Want to go home."

He didn't have to ask to know she meant their family farm and not the lighthouse. When he and Valerie had assembled his puzzle, Sofia kept insisting they should go "home" and jabbed at the image of a large farm. Paul drew in a fortifying breath and stood, lifting her up.

The silver-haired woman joined them, her blue-gray eyes gentle and her smile lighting her face. She was a handsome woman of about sixty. "I may not be your little girl's grandmother, but we welcome her to join our library book readers' group for children."

Sofia swiveled around from his chest, wiping at her eye. "Libry?"

The scent of lemon verbena soap wafted from the matron, who nodded solemnly. "Indeed. We have children from three to thirteen who visit with us on Wednesday mornings."

Sofia's eyebrows pulled into a slim auburn line. "I'm three." She held up three fingers.

"I'm Paul Sholtus, the new lighthouse keeper." He pointed toward Round Island, where the lighthouse was now being supplied by his relief man.

"Would you like to leave Sofia with us for a while, Mr. Sholtus? We're sharing about the books we've read this week."

"Val read me *Thumbelina!*" Sofia gestured to be put down.

Paul complied. "I guess it would be all right." He could keep an eye on her from a distance.

The librarian offered her hand to Sofia. "Noon then, right here, for pickup."

Paul stood there, watching, as his baby girl eagerly clutched the stranger's hand and left him. She was growing up a little more each day. As much as his family had helped him, he'd never left Sofia and gone anywhere by himself to do anything other than work. Guilt had prevented him from ever asking for more than his parents and siblings had already done for him.

He often felt it was his fault that Annabelle had died. He knew it hadn't been. But she'd been his childhood sweetheart, and her parents had shunned him after her death. They'd been married only one year when Sofia had been born. And then Annabelle was gone. Sweat broke out on his brow. Painful memories of his in-laws' hurtful words brought back the pain of that time. They'd not once come to see Sofia. Strange how people could be so self-absorbed in their own pain that they couldn't see the needs of others.

Valerie Fillman clearly had her own demons with which to wrestle. How could he have been so selfish to have brought her back to the very place where her family had perished? Desperation, pure and simple, had motivated him. Desperation to have his way and to escape his own pain. But there was no escaping it; there was only the moving through it. Pastor McWithey had spoken on that very topic the week before—how if God could restore Job, then He could help anyone.

Valerie. A breeze carried the scent of the abundant roses edging the small park, which must be part of the library. *God, help me ease Valerie's pain.* Her muffled cries in her sleep had drawn him to her door repeatedly. But her repetition of "Don't take me! Stop!" and other protestations left him perplexed. When he'd looked in on her, lamp aloft, she was always asleep.

A tall man sporting a straw boater strode toward him. When he reached Paul, he held out a broad hand. "I'm the journalist, Ben Steffans. One of our newsboys pointed you out to me."

Paul shook his hand. "Paul Sholtus. Good to meet you." How strange to be interviewed about a job. No one interviewed farmers unless it was about crop predictions.

"Might now be a good time for an interview?"

Paul glanced toward Sofia, who was staring in rapt attention as a boy of about ten held up his book and spoke animatedly. "That's fine."

Steffans gestured to a nearby table. "By the way, welcome to the Straits of Mackinac!"

Paul pointed to the Round Island Lighthouse. "She's awfully pretty, isn't she?"

"*Ja*, that *schön* lighthouse, that beautiful light, has been a blessing."

The two men sat down on the rustic wooden bench by the table. Steffans scribbled something on his notepad. "What brought you to the position?"

"I've always wanted to be on the Great Lakes in some capacity." *Or anyplace besides the farm.*

"How are you enjoying it so far?" Steffans offered an easy grin.

"I. . ." Paul shrugged the tension from his neck. "It's different." It wasn't all he'd imagined it to be.

"Oh?"

"The water is lovely. The work is busy, but lighthouse tending is far from the grueling work of farming."

"I'd expect so."

"On the other hand, I still haven't gotten accustomed to working through the night and sleeping during the day."

"What can you tell me about your background?"

Soon the journalist had filled up his notepad. He laid his broad hand flat on the table. "Off the record, I'm hearing something you're omitting."

Paul shrugged. He'd been missing his family something terrible. But if he returned, he'd have to face all those memories again. *What a coward.* Look how Valerie faced up to her own demons. He swallowed hard. "I did leave out my work at the Kellogg Institute. I was there as an attendant for only six months." From late autumn until planting time. Until Annabelle told him she'd not move to the city with him. That her life was there in their farming community and not in Battle Creek.

"That must have been interesting."

"And difficult." That case he'd thought about a few days ago still haunted him. A beautiful young socialite, addicted to alcohol, blaming herself for the loss of a sibling whom she'd been watching over. Not watching closely enough, apparently. Paul glanced toward the library matron's table. His daughter's tousled head was missing. He stood and glanced all around the children's table, heart hammering. Where was Sofia?

He ran toward the assembled circle, frantic to lay eyes on his daughter.

Chapter 6

Sofia popped up from behind the table, a large tabby cat clutched in her arms. Paul stopped, midstep, sweat gathering in his beard and at his collar. He'd not experienced a panic like this since Annabelle had died. With family all around them, all the time, he'd never worried about Sofia being carefully watched. And while he was vigilant at the lighthouse, he trusted that Valerie would protect Sofia.

He wiped his brow. The librarian lifted her hand in a brief wave, one eyebrow quirked. Feeling foolish, he returned to the reporter. But what if Sofia had slipped off? What if she'd been taken? That brief moment of panic was so intense, so overwhelming. Was this how the Kellogg patient had felt? The name of the pretty young addict came to him—Georgina. She was from a wealthy old Detroit family. He'd been a young child himself when Georgina's sister was supposedly abducted. He'd never been sure if the patient's comments to him were true or not. She'd asked him to sneak in whiskey for her and had told him a sad tale of her sister having been under her watch and having been stolen away, possibly killed, but never found. A chill came over him as he recollected what she'd called her sister—*"My little Valentine."* Maybe that was the child's name, albeit unusual. He'd believed, at the time, that Georgina was using a nickname. And Valerie's birthday was on that day, he thought she'd said.

"You all right?" Mr. Steffans frowned. "Your little *Tochter* was just hiding. Daughters can be *schelmisch*—mischievous."

"Yes." Paul rubbed his beard, which needed a good clipping at the barbershop. "By any chance, Mr. Steffans, would you humor me and let me ask a journalistic question?"

"Sure."

"Did you ever read of a missing child from the Mott family?"

"Ja! That was one in the first newspapers I sold as a child on the streets in Chicago. *Sehr traurig*—very sad story." Steffans shook out his shoulders, as though the recollection disturbed him. "That story resurfaced when I moved to Detroit. By then, I think the family resided mainly in England though. The Gladstones, I believe. The mother was a Mott, inherited her father's holdings."

"So it's true."

When the reporter's eyes lit up, Paul cringed. He should have kept his mouth shut. Steffans leaned in. "Why?"

Paul shrugged and averted his gaze to his child. Sofia clapped her hands, along with the other children. She was safe and sound. But Steffans's words meant that Georgina's tormented story was likely true. What if Valerie was the missing Gladstone child? If so, she'd come from a wealthy family. And if she was reunited with her family, would he lose her forever? "It's nothing. Just remembering someone I knew in an old job."

"You can't tell a journalist something like that and leave it dangling." Steffans made a notation on his pad. "Would you promise to give me the story if and when you decide to share it? Or should I dig deeper?"

"Some of this I can't tell you because it is confidential, from previous employment."

"How about you tell me what you know?"

It might mean the end of a romance that had finally sputtered to life. If Valerie left him, he'd have lost love not once, but twice. "Yes, but will you help me find out some things too?"

Val scrubbed dishes, lost in thoughts of her supposed parents, as Paul played his accordion for them. What a far different scene this was from when she'd lived here before. Her mother so often would be lying down, her brother and sister taking down clothes from the line and folding them after dinner while Valerie cleaned up. Father—no, not her father—would be up tending the light. It was her job to make sure that neither Mary nor Timothy went up to the Fresnel lens light. Children's greasy fingerprints could wreak all manner of havoc if they got on the precious light that guided ships through the precarious Straits of Mackinac. Poor Tim and Mary—they'd not had much happiness in their lives. At least they'd had their books and she'd read to them every night. She'd had to read slowly and clearly because Mary had lost her hearing in one ear from Dorcas having boxed it so viciously for a minor infraction. Val had comforted Tim and Mary. She'd sung for them. Taught them during the times they weren't able to go to school.

Val had not been able to attend but a few years herself. She'd been a precocious reader though. How? She strained for a memory to come. She'd read at a very young age and had been able to learn much, reading on her own. Her so-called father had instructed her in math and other topics. But Mother. . .no, the pretender always acted as though Val was simply supposed to know things.

Val had cherished the quiet times when Dorcas Woods Fillman had been kind and rational. And even though she didn't direct her affection toward Val, she'd been grateful for the kindness Dorcas had lavished on the other two during those brief and intermittent times. What had tortured the woman? Was it guilt over what she had done? *She stole me.* But how?

Paul, who also seemed lost in his thoughts, stopped midway in his polka refrain and looked at her. "What's wrong?"

She stopped washing the blue-speckled enamel pot she'd boiled potatoes in earlier. "Let's take a walk before you go up again to the light."

"All right." Paul set his accordion back in its case. "I have something I've wanted to ask you."

Her heart skipped a beat. Could it be that he wished to ask her to marry him? Now, just when she was discovering who she might be? Although she, Paul, and Sofia felt like Val imagined a real family could be like, if she didn't address where she'd really come from, how could she feel whole?

When she'd finished the dishes, the three of them went outside and strolled on the Round Island beach. They circled the lighthouse twice, and then Sofia settled on the sand and began pulling rocks up to make designs, one of her favorite activities.

Paul stepped closer and took Val's hand in his. She felt her eyes widen, and she opened her mouth to protest, but the warmth of his hand and his firm grip felt right. *So right.*

"Tell me what is bothering you." He stroked the top of her hand with his thumb, sending a frisson of electricity through her. "Is it being out here, where they died?"

She shook her head. "No. Not truly. It's more that I don't know who I am anymore."

"What do you mean?" He pushed a windblown lock of hair from her brow, the sensation pleasant. What would it be like to be loved by this man as his wife? To be cherished?

"I. . .I have learned that Mrs. Fillman and her husband were not my parents."

"They weren't?" He squeezed her hand and took another step closer as a breeze lifted and ruffled her hair.

"I don't know much, not yet." She chewed her lower lip and averted her gaze. "But Mrs. Fillman was employed by someone at about the time I would have been a very young child. And Mrs. Fillman had no child, according to her employer."

"Is this woman reliable?"

Valerie looked up into Paul's eyes. "She's a society matron and has no reason to lie."

"What is her name?"

"Mrs. Carrie Booth Moore."

"From Detroit?"

"Yes."

His brows furrowed together, then he whistled. "Does she have any more information for you?"

Inhaling a deep breath of fresh Mackinac winds, Valerie nodded. "Yes, but she's contacting the people she believes may be my parents. Sister Mary Lou told me."

Paul stepped closer and drew her into his arms. This felt so right. It felt like a real home in his arms. But then he kissed the top of her head as he often did with Sofia. As though she were a child. She shivered. Perhaps the handsome lighthouse keeper was merely offering her comfort as a father might. Maybe he had no real feelings for her. Not like those she had for him. He hadn't asked her to marry him.

She broke free. "Excuse me." She headed toward the lighthouse, knowing he'd soon follow, with Sofia. And then she'd put her to bed. *The caretaker. Not the child's mother. Not Paul's wife. Not the Fillmans' daughter. Nobody.*

"Mine. You are Mine. Always Mine, and I am here too."

Val shivered and hugged herself. She didn't need to escape God. She needed to let Him embrace her and bring healing. *Oh God, I know You're there. Let me be the child You wish me to be.*

"Valerie, I need to tell you something."

She turned to see Paul staring down at the rocky beach, his face a mask of confusion warring with sorrow. She took several steps to rejoin him. "What is it?"

"There was a child who was taken from her family many years ago. From a prominent Detroit family."

"I think. . .I'm fairly sure, I was taken in New York."

"Really?"

"I have memories of a tenement in New York City and of traveling to Michigan. And we know Dorcas lived in Detroit. However, she didn't have a child with her there."

A chill wind penetrated Val's thin cotton work dress. "But what was the family's name?"

"Gladstone."

She shook her head and shrugged.

Paul seemed to exhale in relief.

A cooing sound distracted her. Val turned to spy two doves very close to her, yet not startled by her. They were joined by a third. The sun dipped behind the cumulous clouds overhead, casting a shadow on the trio. Then, in a flash, the three flew into the heavens. Something marvelous coursed through her, as though she'd had a heavenly visitation. She pressed her hand to her chest, heart beating rapidly as tears streamed down her face.

Paul took her elbow. "They were so close to you, Valerie."

Sofia held out her arms for Val to take her. "Birdies were visiting you!"

She accepted the child into her embrace, her heart full to overflowing.

"Valerie?" Paul wrapped an arm around both of them. "Wouldn't we make a nice family?"

Was that a proposal? She didn't know. But the intensity in his green eyes reaffirmed his words.

Chapter 7

Day by day, more shiploads of passengers departed the island and sailed out past the lighthouse than had sailed into port. Strange that he didn't think of the Round Island Lighthouse as "his" lighthouse, as the inspector called it upon his recent visit. The summer was passing so rapidly. Harvest was coming back home on the farm as well as a harvest of answers that were needed for Valerie.

He waved at a group of pretty, well-dressed young women who clung to the White Star Line ship's rail as it moved farther out into Lake Huron.

Paul lowered his hand and patted his pocket, where a letter from his mother seemingly burned a hole. He'd gotten his yearning for experience at a lighthouse out of his system, and now it was time to make decisions. He couldn't answer Mr. Dardanes's question as to whether he could see himself continuing in this lighthouse post. The man had told him that his lack of an answer was answer in itself. He still remembered the look on Valerie's face when she peered through the doorway at them, having overheard Dardanes's comment. She had been mighty quiet last night. No doubt wondering what her future might be. Could she imagine being the wife of a farmer? How would his parents react to her? And Annabelle's parents? He almost snorted aloud at the thought. That was their problem—not his and Valerie's.

The door to the lighthouse opened and Valerie emerged, two coffee mugs in her hands. Sofia carried a plate of Mrs. Christy's cinnamon rolls aloft, as though she carried a plate of gold. Golden goodness, that was for sure and for certain.

"Breakfast with the gulls!" Valerie announced.

"We need to go, Daddy." Sofia's lips formed an adorable pout. "My turn to share in story time."

"Today?" Paul accepted the steaming mug of black coffee that Val offered him, the brief touch of her fingertips warming him more than the cup had.

Valerie smiled up at him, a blush tingeing her cheeks. Had she felt the effects of that brief encounter as he did? When he looked into her eyes, he knew she did, and he couldn't help grinning.

"Today, Daddy!" Sofia set the rolls down on a boulder and pulled one free for herself. "I'm telling about the Ginger Man."

"Ginger Man?" Paul laughed as he too grabbed a roll. "I believe you mean the Gingerbread Man."

"No." Valerie's cheeks looked even more rosy than usual. She raised her finger to her lips.

"The Ginger Man, Daddy!" Sofia cocked her head at him. "He has ginger hair. Green eyes. He saves the Lake Lady."

"Sh!" Valerie bent and whispered something in his daughter's ear.

"It's secret." Sofia bit into her cinnamon roll, frosting smearing white on her pug nose.

"A secret?" He sipped his coffee. "Is the Ginger Man handsome?"

"Of course," Valerie answered, too quickly.

"Dad!" Sofia rolled her eyes. "Of course. He looks just like you."

Was this his daughter's idea, or Valerie's? From Valerie's guilty expression, and knowing that she'd helped his daughter with the story, he drew his own conclusions—and grinned even bigger. Today, he'd stop at the island jeweler's and pick out a ring. And pray that she accepted his offer. One that might include a barn, lots of livestock, and a big farmhouse they could fill with children.

"Miss Fillman?" One of the port message boys, with blond hair like straw sticking out around his large ears, ran toward her from dockside.

"Yes?" She stopped, Paul and Sofia beside her. "What is it?"

"Message from Sister Mary Lou. She wants you up at the orphanage." The youth handed Val the note and extended his palm.

As she scanned the missive, Paul gave the boy a tip and he ran off.

"I'll need to head up there now, Paul."

"Should we go with you?"

"No. I'll be fine."

Sofia tugged at her father's hand. "Come on, Dad!"

To Val's surprise, Paul leaned in and pressed a firm kiss to her cheek, right there in front of God and everyone as their witness. He gently touched her waist. Her breath caught in her throat. She loved him. Oh, how she wanted to shout it. But that simply wouldn't do. "I'll come to the library afterwards."

"See you then." Father and daughter strode off to the left and away from the wharf as Valerie headed toward the orphanage.

Hopefully, nothing was wrong. But as she neared the church, apprehension filled her. Sister Mary Lou was investigating for her, and Paul had revealed to her that he'd also involved Ben Steffans. What if they'd discovered something truly terrible? What if Val wasn't Mrs. Moore's friend's child at all? What if Dorcas Fillman had murdered another woman and taken her child? Given some of the cruel behavior Mrs. Fillman exhibited over the years, Valerie could imagine her doing almost anything. She exhaled a sigh and headed on.

Once inside the dimly lit building, the receptionist gestured for her to take a seat on the divan outside the priest's office. Within a few minutes, a tall gentleman entered through the side door. With dark hair generously streaked with gray, his attire bespoke wealth. Something about him drew a recollection.

He spoke to the receptionist. "Good day, miss. I'm here to meet with Sister Mary Lou."

The receptionist glanced nervously toward Valerie and then back at the man. "Lord Gladstone?"

Gladstone. The name Paul had asked about. A name that had niggled at her all through her dreams.

"Indeed." His eyes sparkled. "I'm a tad early."

He looked in Valerie's direction then, as if just noticing her there, and he frowned. His jaw slackened and his mouth dropped open. Just as quickly, he drew in a breath and straightened his broad shoulders. He turned back to the receptionist. "If you'll excuse me, I'll be back in a moment."

He departed the building, head down, just as Sister Mary Lou called out, "Valerie, we're ready for you."

She stood, wondering who this Lord Gladstone was. But then it came to her. *Percival. Percy!* "That man. His name is Percival Gladstone, isn't it?"

Sister Mary Lou frowned. "Who? Did you see Lord Gladstone?"

"He was just here." Her head throbbed. She knew him. Tears pricked her eyes as she strove to recall from where. No one had mentioned his Christian name.

They entered Father Joseph's office, which smelled of cloves, oranges, and tea. "Come in, my dear."

"I know that man, Father." Val's breath seemed stuck in her throat.

Sister Mary Lou had barely closed the heavy mahogany door when someone rapped on it sharply. She opened it, and Lord Gladstone entered, a lovely woman on his arm. With dark tresses upswept beneath a broad-brimmed hat and matching dark eyes and ivory skin, she recalled someone. She was the picture of elegance in her lacy cream-colored ensemble with matching kidskin shoes. Too young to be his wife. But she reminded Val of another beautiful woman. Her mother?

"Excuse us, Father Joseph and Sister Mary Lou, but I wanted my daughter—"

"Percival Gladstone. He's left you. Forget him. He's never coming back. He was never there for you anyway." Dorcas Fillman's hate-filled words flooded Valerie's memory. She struggled to get her breath. *"They didn't deserve you. I'm your mother now. This is your father."* Val pressed her eyes shut, as the image of a younger version of this man

came to her—clutching a leather case and rushing out the door in a large atrium, the ceiling high above, a chandelier taunting her as Val cried and someone in servant's attire picked her up. He didn't even turn around when she cried.

She couldn't manage any words. All she knew was she had to get out of here. Now.

Valerie pushed past the man and young woman and fled the church building. Once on the walkway, she pulled her handkerchief from her reticule and wiped her tears away. Sucking in a breath, she hurried on, toward the street. A frightening energy propelled her onward.

A carriage was parked there, the driver tense and the horses whinnying, tails flicking as though picking up on the nervous energy that charged the air. The door to the carriage opened and a woman called out.

"Valentine!"

Valerie hesitated, as the name jarred her.

"Valentine Rhys Gladstone!"

Val froze. Then looked into dark eyes, so unlike her own but much like those of the young lady inside the building. Her mother's eyes. She stumbled, recovered, and then spurred on by the years of angst built up in her, ran from the very woman her younger self had cried for every night until the switchings burned the tears out of her.

She didn't stop, pushing past tourists on the walkway, until she reached the library. When Paul turned from the perimeter of the group waiting for the children's reading hour, she rushed toward him. He opened his arms and took her into his embrace. *Oh dear Lord, help me* was all she could pray. Somehow, she knew Paul was part of God's answer to all the prayers she'd felt had gone unanswered over the years.

"What is it?" He stroked her hair.

This was home. In this man's arms. Back there, with her parents, was only confusion, separation, and hurt. An anger she'd not felt in years coursed through her. How could they have abandoned her? Had they though? She sniffed. She was being irrational, buying into Dorcas's lies. From what she'd learned so far, these people, her real parents, hadn't rejected her.

From nearby, the group of children began to shout. "The boats!"

Val and Paul turned to face the entrance to the harbor as two large ships sailed precariously close together, past the Round Island Lighthouse.

Paul took two strides forward. "What the devil are they doing?"

The passengers on board could be heard yelling, and the ships appeared about to collide.

Val ran toward the children. They didn't need to see this. The adults should shield the little ones' eyes from the tragedy.

In a flash, she smelled smoke and metal that wasn't there. *She stood, small and* surrounded by a mob of tall people in coats, in New York harbor. Work-roughened hands covered her eyes. "Miss Valentine, don't look."

Where was Georgina? Her sister had been holding her hand, watching over her as they awaited the big boat that would take them to England. To see Grandfather Gladstone.

"Come over here." The servant girl pulled hard.

Shrieks, shouts, dense fog, and the sound of metal on metal. But all in the past. Tears streamed down her face as Valentine shook. Where was her mother? Her father? Her brother and sisters?

"Come along now, missy." Mrs. Moore's serving girl pulled her away from the loud noises and the bad smells of the harbor.

When Valentine tried to ask a question, the redheaded girl ignored her. "I'm taking you to your real home."

Father had said England had been his home.

"Valerie!" Paul shook her shoulders, bringing her back to the present, the sky bright blue overhead.

She gasped in air, her face wet. "She took me! The Moore's servant girl. Dorcas."

Past him, the children had taken their seats again, the librarian's face pale. The two ships had continued on, the White Star liner in front and the Cadotte steamer in the back.

"What are you talking about?" Paul wrapped his arms around her.

"I was taken from my parents." She leaned into his chest.

Paul stroked her back.

Those people back at the orphanage. "The Gladstones. They're really my parents." She choked back a sob. What had the woman, her mother, called her? She'd called her Valentine, which she now remembered her childhood name being called by her family.

She drew in Paul's piney scent. If she took this course, everything between them could change. How could she give up the only happiness she'd known? She drew back and looked up at him. "Would you wait for me?"

His tawny eyebrows pulled together. "Of course I would. Where should we meet you?"

"That's not quite what I mean." But for now. . . "Come to the church."

Seated in Father Joseph's office with only her parents, Val trembled from head to toe. Even in her new ensemble, a gift from her friend Rebecca, she more resembled a street urchin than the child of these two wealthy aristocrats. She clutched the tiny diamond bracelet in her hand, a reassurance that she really was Valentine Rhys Gladstone. That she possessed a past that hadn't included only misery.

Lady Eugenie Gladstone, her mother, clutched a wet handkerchief in her hands. "We looked for you for years."

"Detectives, Pinkerton agents." Lord Gladstone, standing by the wing chair, looked as lost as Val felt.

"Then one day, I realized that if I didn't accept God's will, His help, then I'd lose my mind." This woman, her mother, had suffered, but in a different way than Val had.

"Our daughter, your older sister Georgina, has never gotten over your loss." Percival Gladstone frowned and stared down at the floor.

Seated on the edge of the velvet settee, Val felt her spine stiffen. "What happened?" She recalled the image of a pretty smiling girl trying to teach her letters and numbers, even at such a young age.

"Georgina blamed herself. Lapsed into melancholy. Then as she grew older, she turned to alcohol. And drugs."

"Opium at one point." Her father sighed.

"Oh my." Val had read of such things but never knew anyone who'd actually succumbed.

"Your kidnapping resulted in all of our lives changing." Percy Gladstone tugged at his ascot tie.

"Some good came from our sorrow though." Eugenie's cheeks flushed. "Our youngest daughter, your sister Perianne, was born."

"A pretty name."

"Named after your father and my dear friend Anne, who helped me through the devastation over your loss."

"Our youngest, your sister, is sixteen now."

"I have a sixteen-year-old sister?"

"Yes." Eugenie exchanged a long look with Percy. "She has a Pinkerton assigned to her around the clock."

"Something that she's not very happy about at present." Lord Gladstone gave a soft laugh. "But that's how our lives changed."

"We were never without protection after that time." Her true mother began to sob and opened her arms for Val. "Oh my precious girl, I'm so sorry!"

Val began to cry too as they clung to each other. All the years they'd lost. Val had been caged in by her kidnapper, and her own true siblings had been hemmed in by guards.

When they finally released one another, Val's pent-up questions burst forth. "Where did I live those first few years?" From her earliest recollections, there was change. A shuffling of places and people.

"My family home, the Motts, in Detroit, is one where we spent some limited time. Your older brother, Gerald, and his family live there now."

"I don't remember him."

"He was off to school back then." Her father sat down.

Her mother patted her hand. "And you were so young."

"My Ontario home in Windsor was where we primarily stayed." Her father's voice held a mix of British and Canadian accents. There was so much she wanted to know about him. "Your older sister, Leonora, and her husband live there, and we also stay there when we're in the Dominion."

Mother squeezed her hand. "Do you remember Leonora? She's four years older than you. She has eyes very much like yours."

Val shook her head.

"It will come back to you. They are waiting to hear from us, and we'll all gather."

Two older sisters, an older brother, and a younger sister she'd never met. Val's inclination was to run from here, but she owed her family this. It would be easy to escape into Paul's arms, into his invitation to form a family. But easy wasn't always best. "What happened the day Dorcas took me?"

"We were staying in New York. We'd been visiting with my friend Carrie Booth Moore and her family. Business had brought her husband there for an extended time. So we stayed and visited with the Moores before we were to depart for England."

"For England?" She recalled the huge ship in the harbor.

"We were taking you to England for the first time." Mother fingered the strand of pearls at her neckline.

"To see your grandparents and the rest of my family."

Her parents exchanged a mournful look. "We didn't go then, after all, because you went missing."

"Georgina was watching over you. She was fourteen at the time. Something happened. Leonora and Gerald saw her talking with a young man right before the ship collision in the New York harbor."

Both parents bowed their heads briefly.

"I remember looking up at all these people around me, like a sea of tall people in jackets. Then someone, Dorcas, took me and led me away." Val unfisted her hands, which had been balled tight. "Life was never easy after that." To say the least.

Her mother embraced her again. "You can tell us all in due course. Don't worry."

Val sniffed and pulled away. "Where is Georgina now?"

Chapter 8

Detroit, Michigan

Valentine responded to the knock at her bedroom door and accepted the letter from Paul, offered on a silver salver by the butler. "Thank you."

She recalled her sweetheart's last words to her before she left. *"Will you come back to us?"* She'd promised him she would. But that had been many weeks past. She brought the missive to her mahogany desk by the wide windows. She retrieved her silver letter opener from the top drawer.

A swift rap at the door was followed by a creak as it opened. Val turned to see Perianne looking around. "The bedroom is much more interesting like this."

Val laughed. She'd hung several pictures of the lighthouses she'd lived in on the picture rails. She also preferred rag rugs underfoot, so her parents had rolled up and removed the heavy, dark wool rugs. And she'd propped on her windowsill the "rock people" she and Sofia had made. She also kept a treasured picture of Paul and Sofia on her desktop.

Of all her siblings, Val's younger sister had been happiest for her kidnapped sister to be returned. For now, Perianne wasn't the complete and sole target of her parents' attention and scrutiny.

"May I come in?"

"Certainly." Val laughed and made a grand gesture of waving her sister in.

Perianne unpinned her hair and sat atop Val's bed. She ran a hand over the patchwork quilt, which Paul's mother had made. Sighing, she kicked off her leather slippers. "I want a more grown-up hairstyle. Can you help me?"

Val would have loved to have sat down, alone, with her letter, but this girl, this sister of hers, needed attention. "I can try." Truth be told, she'd finally stopped allowing her parents to shuffle her off to appointments at the hairdresser, the hatmaker, the dressmakers, and makers of all manner of undergarments that she didn't wish to wear.

"I like that twist you do." Perianne's hazel eyes sparkled.

Val laughed. "That one is easy. But it will make you look like a working-class girl and not the young society lady that you are."

"That's what I want."

"Why?"

"I'm the replacement child, you know." Perianne got up and took the silver-handled hairbrush from Val's mahogany dressing table.

"You shouldn't say that."

"It's true."

"No. You're simply you." Val smiled at her beautiful sister. "And a more wonderful homecoming gift to me I could truly not imagine!"

"I can't believe you're really here. I thought you must have died. I had all kinds of horrible notions that you were moldering in your grave and I was your replacement on earth." Perianne shuddered.

"You have a wild imagination."

She laughed. "Yes I do. But is it truly more imaginative than your notion of living in a lighthouse again?"

Or on a farm? Val nibbled her lower lip. "I just got a letter from Paul."

Perianne squealed in delight. "Open it!"

"All right." She'd skip over any romantic comments from Paul. She opened the envelope and unfolded the letter. "Let's see. Paul has returned home to bring in the harvest. He says he wants to remain there. And he wants to see me." Her cheeks heated as she read his lines about wanting to feel her in his arms again, his lips on hers. "He asks, how about a Gladstone marrying a farmer?"

Perianne clapped her hands together. "As scrumptious as me marrying our new French chef. He's so handsome!"

Valentine's eyes widened. "Paul's good looks aren't what makes me want to marry him."

Her sister arched a blond eyebrow. "What then?"

"He's kind. A good father. He's a thinker. Makes lovely music. Makes me laugh. Loves God." *Loves me.*

"Then why are you still here?"

Why indeed? Because Georgina wasn't yet well enough to come visit, and they needed to clear the air.

"Paul!" His mother's voice carried across the wide yard where chickens roamed freely and Sofia chased her new puppy.

"Yes?" He washed up at the pump then dried his hands on a towel hanging from a nail on a nearby post.

"You have a guest."

A carriage from the train station in town pulled forward. A dark-haired woman of about thirty, attired in a wool peplum jacket and matching skirt and brown laced boots, stepped out. Paul hung the towel back on the nail. He watched as the handsome woman marched toward him. Something about her demeanor suggested she wasn't accustomed to wearing such finery. She pulled hatpins from her feather-topped hat and removed it. He felt he should know her.

In several strides, she joined him by the pump and extended a hand, much like a man would do. He offered his own, surprised by her firm grip.

"You don't remember me, do you?"

The voice was familiar. "I'm sorry, I can't quite place you, ma'am."

"It's miss, Miss Gladstone here, or Lady Georgina on the Canadian side. Lady Georgina Gladstone, if you're into titles and all that." She shrugged.

His former patient. "Valentine's sister?" Which meant Valentine was Lady Valentine Gladstone. He'd not thought of her title before.

She smiled at him and cocked her head. "And a former patient at the Kellogg Institute, as you know."

"Oh. I hope the note I sent didn't upset you." Perspiration broke out on his forehead.

"On the contrary. Your letter spurred me on to travel to Detroit."

"So, you've visited Valerie? Lady Valentine, rather." He swallowed hard.

Georgina slowly surveyed the farm. Their acreage extended far into the tree line. Between his brothers and himself, the Sholtuses owned four farmhouses, two large barns, two stables, and other outbuildings. Prosperous by local standards. Nothing compared to the Mott or the Gladstone wealth.

Georgina dug the toe of her boot into the dirt. "The last time I did something like I'm doing right now, my little sister was stolen from me."

He frowned. "I don't understand."

"The last time I escorted my younger sister somewhere, Mrs. Moore's horrid servant girl, Dorcas, snatched Valentine."

Paul nodded solemnly. Sofia ran out of the house, her pup chasing behind her.

"You've stolen her too." Miss Gladstone gave a curt laugh. "You've stolen her heart though."

Sofia stopped and looked up at their visitor. "You're not Val."

The woman bent and playfully tweaked Sofia's nose. "Nope. And you're not a puppy!" She petted the dog's head.

His daughter cocked her head at the woman. The carriage door opened again. Valentine, as she'd written him she'd prefer to be addressed, emerged from inside. Sofia shrieked and ran to her, her beagle chasing her and barking.

Tears coursed down Georgina's cheeks. "This time, I'm quite all right with Valentine leaving the family."

She'd come. His sweetheart had returned to him. To Sofia. Valentine lifted his daughter and twirled her around.

"She loves you." Georgina leaned in, early lines showing around her mouth and eyes. Maybe now she'd be able to beat back the demons of addiction that had plagued her.

"I love Valentine more than I can say." And in a different way than the almost obsessive love he'd felt for his childhood sweetheart.

"We Gladstones love her too, Mr. Sholtus." Georgina grasped his forearm. "Please don't keep her from us. I couldn't bear it again. We couldn't."

"Never." And he meant it.

She brushed away a tear. "Will you be returning to the lighthouse?"

"I don't know." He'd run from his memories. But with Valentine here, there would be new memories to make, happy memories. Why subject her to a constant reminder of all that had been taken from her? Yet the lighthouse had given something back to her too, otherwise they'd never have met.

"By the way, my parents are gifting you with their Mackinac Island cottage for your wedding."

Stunned, he wasn't sure what to say. The "cottage," as she called it, was an ornate three-story manse high on the cliffs near the Grand Hotel. "That's very generous."

Valentine held Sofia, both of them crying and talking and kissing each other's cheeks. Wetness pricked Paul's eyes.

"I'll be staying in Detroit with my parents awhile longer before traveling to England for the winter." Georgina brushed a tear from her cheek. "It's been a long time coming."

"And very welcome, I imagine."

"I'd love to have you and your daughter and new wife accompany me." Georgina gestured to Sofia and Val. "It would be wonderful getting to know my new niece and brother-in-law and to spend time with Valentine."

Certainly Valentine's family had very different circumstances than his own. Trips to England. The gift of a home.

Hand in hand, Valentine and Sofia ran toward them. He opened his arms for his beloved. Sofia reluctantly released Valentine's hand and she stepped into the place where she belonged. Always. Where God had put her.

Her tears wet his chest. Valentine Gladstone, his wife-to-be, looked up at him with a yearning he understood. He bent and kissed her soundly, not wanting the moment to end. She responded back, and he deepened the kiss. She felt so right. She was where she belonged.

From behind him, the door to the house slammed shut, and the two broke apart. His mother stood there, arms akimbo. "Well, it's about time you got here, missy! Welcome home!"

Valentine blinked up at him. "Have you decided to stay?"

He shook his head. "Not yet. But whether in a lighthouse, on the farm, or in Detroit or England, if you're with me, I'm home."

"You're my beacon no matter where you are." Val's violet eyes glistened.

"Am I?"

"You are! Love's beacon—guiding me home."

ECPA bestselling author **Carrie Fancett Pagels**, PhD, is the award-winning author of over a dozen Christian historical romances. Twenty-five years as a psychologist didn't "cure" her overactive imagination! A self-professed "history geek," she resides with her family in the Historic Triangle of Virginia but grew up as a "Yooper" in Michigan's Upper Peninsula. Carrie loves to read, bake, bead, and travel—but not all at the same time! You can connect with her at www.CarrieFancettPagels.com.

The Last Memory

by Kathleen Rouser

Chapter 1

S he struggled to maintain her grip on the splintered wood plank, the only thing keeping her from drowning beneath the roiling waters of Lake Huron. A blur of gray and green swallowed her for a moment. She bobbed, carried along by the water's current. She couldn't get her bearings as she swirled away from the sinking ship. Lightning sparked enough for her to see the last of the *Mallory* sink beneath the stormy waves.

She wanted to cry out, but her mouth filled with the foamy water. She choked and sputtered instead. This wasn't supposed to be happening. Not now. She was too young to die.

Her shoe grazed something. Was it sand? She grunted as the waves thrust her against the stony shoreline. With one more nudge from the water she lost her grip on the board. Unable to stand, she slipped. Sharp pain surged through the side of her head. The world melted from gray to black.

Cal Waterson held his lantern high from his place in the rowboat. The rain pelted him, flowing off his oilskins in rivulets. His faithful volunteer rescue crew of a half-dozen men from Mackinaw City shivered in the cold. His heart lurched at the sights around him. Nothing left of the ship but some floating boards, a man's hat, an empty barrel. No survivors.

What good was it being a lighthouse keeper if he couldn't do more for those guided by the glowing Fresnel lens? Henry MacPherson pointed as they rowed along the shore toward the beacon.

"What's that? I think there's someone on shore."

Something out of the ordinary indeed reflected in the light. A long shot, but a lone survivor may have washed up onto the beach.

Cal glanced back toward the wreckage one more time. He cupped his hands around his mouth and leaned low to be heard over the thunder and wind. "We're done here. Head for whatever that is on the shore." Having registered his command above the din of the thunder and wind, his faithful crew rowed harder to shore.

After the boat was safe along the beach, Cal leaped from the craft. Henry held up the lantern. The kerosene flame's glow reflected off shimmering pink fabric.

Cal waded, careful not to slip. Frigid water splashed over his boots onto his pant legs. A mist arose, though the rain abated. What was this draped on the sand, just above the rocks?

A young woman. His breath caught at the sight of ethereal loveliness. Dark hair framed the pale face, and he scrambled toward her. Was she even breathing? Upon reaching the still form, Cal knelt on the sand. He bent over her and touched his fingers to her slender neck. She had a pulse. "She's alive!"

He shrugged off his coat then lifted the girl to a sitting position with as much care as possible and wrapped the garment around her shoulders. As he knelt on one knee, he scooped her into his arms. She'd be lucky if she didn't die from pneumonia.

Henry took up the lantern and trudged alongside him through the sand, dark from being stirred up by the storm. "Such a pretty little gal, isn't she? And so young. What a shame. Wonder how many others like her were lost."

Cal grunted in response. Henry's ponderings echoed his own morose thoughts.

He shook them off. *Take care of the ones that survived.* He'd saved someone this night. He had to concentrate on that.

The girl lay limp within his arms. *Please, God, let her live.* When they reached the boat, he let her down gently.

Angus Brewster, the crusty old butcher from town, pulled her to the center of the boat with his firm grip. "She ain't made of china. Let's get her someplace warm before we all get pneumonia."

Cal heaved himself into the small craft. The dawn spread fingers of sunlight and revealed blood trickling over the young woman's hair. He dug his oar deep into the water with a sense of urgency. "Come on, men, move! We need to go faster."

She awoke from her dream of the crashing sea and bolted upright. She squinted as she focused on the spinning room. Searing pain engulfed her head, and she flopped back down on the pillow.

Two luminous brown eyes stared and then blinked at her. Their owner, a little girl of around six or seven, stood inches from the side of the bed. "Are you going to be my new mama?"

"What?"

"My papa says that if I was ever going to get another mama, the Great Lakes would have to cough her up." The little girl leaned on her elbows on the edge of the bed now, studying her as she would a rock under a magnifying glass. "What's your name, miss?"

"I d—don't know." Her head hurt too much to recall, her tongue was as thick and useless as sausage, and her heart beat a staccato rhythm. Panic came with her realizations. She rubbed her forehead and turned over, away from the little girl.

The child poked her arm. "You got to have a name."

"Well then, what's yours?" She-who-had-no-name turned back over to face her captor.

"I'm Lily. I was born on Easter." The child twirled one of her blond pigtails around her finger.

Mallory. The voice echoed in her head from her confusing dreams. She didn't know whose name it was or who said it, but it was as good as any.

"You can call me Mallory. How's that?"

Lily leaned against the bed. "It's pretty. I like it."

The door swung open and a tall, square-shouldered older woman lumbered into the room. Her gray eyes peered over wire-rimmed glasses, and her white hair was swept into a Psyche knot above the high collar of her starched white shirtwaist. "Come along, sweetie, you mustn't bother the lady." She waved Lily away.

"Shh, Miss Mallory just woke up." The girl put a finger to her lips.

Behind the woman, a man filled the doorframe with his height and broad shoulders. He ducked under the doorway and stepped into the room. With his golden-blond hair, piercing blue eyes, and angular jaw, his presence overwhelmed "Mallory."

Who are these people? Where am I? She pushed herself up on one elbow. Her head swam with dizziness.

The large man sized her up, concern emanating from his eyes. He rubbed his chin. "Well, that's interesting. That's the name of the ship she came from."

Pain pulsed in her right temple, and Mallory placed her head back on the pillow. This was all beginning to make sense. Or was it?

She pulled the sheets up to her chin. "Why are you in here, sir? Who are you?"

"This is my home." Cal paused. "And you're our guest. This is my aunt Ada, my daughter, Lily, and I'm Cal Waterson, head lighthouse keeper."

"What? Why am I here?" Her glance darted from wall to wall of the small room, bouncing from him to Aunt Ada and Lily.

Perhaps he frightened her, towering over everyone in the room as he did. He grasped the straight back of an oak chair from the corner, spun the seat around, and straddled it as he sat. He crossed his arms on the back. "Miss, I hate to be the bearer of bad news. You're the only survivor from the *Mallory*."

The young lady blinked. Her brows furrowed above her caramel-brown eyes as recognition crossed her face for a fleeting moment. "I dreamt about a ship. About a storm, but I can't seem to recall what happened."

Ada held Lily's shoulders, bent to whisper something in her ear, and pointed toward the door. Lily pouted and widened her eyes.

Cal tilted his head in the same direction. "Go on. We'll talk later."

Lily's shoulders slumped in dejection. Being the only child in the family, she knew more than was good for her, but she didn't need to know everything at once.

He turned back to the young woman and found her shivering under the quilt. "I have no idea. . .who I am." Her flushed face turned almost chalk white.

"Dear me." Aunt Ada made her way toward the bed, her footsteps quiet. "We've quite frightened you, haven't we?" She tucked the quilt around the young woman, who sniffled. "Cal, you're the worst. Do you have to be so direct about everything? You upset the child too." She clucked her tongue like the mother hen she was.

"Aunt Ada, she has to find out sooner or later." He drummed his fingers on the back of his chair.

She put a hand to the young woman's forehead. "But there's no use in upsetting her so soon. Maybe you'd like some broth or tea, miss?"

Mallory pushed up on her elbow as her long dark tresses fell across her shoulder. "Where is this place? Just tell me." She rubbed her temple and clamped her eyes shut for a moment.

Cal pointed to the floor. "This is the Old Mackinac Point Lighthouse." He stood, turned the chair back around, and returned it to the corner. "And I'm afraid you're stuck here until we know where you came from and, quite frankly, where you're going."

She fell back on the pillow and covered her eyes with her hand. "You've got to help me."

"We'll do our best, miss." Cal scratched his chin. "You've been out cold since I found you hours ago. Doc Reed stitched up the cut on the side of your head. My aunt did her best to clean you up."

"I'm cut? No wonder my head hurts so much." She reached for her hair.

"Leave it alone, dear. You simply must let it heal." Ada sat on the edge of the mattress and took the girl's hand in her own. "We'll help you get your strength back soon enough. As you can see, we eat well." She patted her own girth and chuckled.

Tears welled in Mallory's eyes as heartrending sobs rose from her throat.

"It'll be all right." Aunt Ada touched the young woman's shoulder. "Let it out, dearie. I'll be right here for you."

Cal closed the door behind him as he exited the room. He couldn't stand to see a woman cry, especially one so lost and afraid. Something moved, catching his eye.

"Lily, come out here right now."

His daughter came out from the shadows in the hallway, a sheepish grin spread across her face.

"Have you been listening to us, nosy girl?" Cal took her by the chin and looked into her chocolate-brown eyes. "Lily?"

"Yes, Papa."

He exhaled. "I sent you out for your own good. Besides, Miss Mallory is getting used to her surroundings. She doesn't need you bothering her right now." He let go of her chin and patted her cheek with great affection.

"I had to ask her a question when she woke up. I'd been waiting awhile." Lily clasped her hands behind her back, bouncing from one foot to the other.

"What did you have to ask that poor waif in there now?"

"Whether she was going to be my new mama." Lily smiled up at him with smug satisfaction.

"You didn't, you little monkey." What on earth was his child thinking?

She gave him a big nod of reassurance. "I sure did."

"Come with me." Cal engulfed his daughter's hand and took her down the stairs and into the parlor. He sat down in a large chair covered in brocade cloth and pulled Lily onto his lap.

She bit her lip. Her eyes were wide with fear. "Am I in trouble?" She trembled a little.

"What on earth made you ask a stranger such a question?" The weariness of the rescue engulfed Cal, but he was afraid he sounded more angry than tired.

Lily swallowed.

"No, you're not in trouble. But what were you thinking?"

She looked down for a moment, playing with the watch fob hanging from his pocket. "Papa, I heard you say I'd only have a mama if the Great Lakes coughed her up. I just wondered." She shrugged and leaned against him.

"That was just a manner of speaking. What I meant to say is that nobody can replace your mama."

"But I never knew her." When Lily gazed back up, her eyes filled with tears.

Cal stroked her hair. "Oh Lily, I know, but that's why Aunt Ada's here to help. And the good Lord is here too, watching over us."

"But I wish I had a real mama."

Cal let her cry, his shirt dampening with her tears but he didn't mind. "I wish you did too." But finding a good woman was more trouble than it was worth. And a bedraggled castaway with amnesia sure wasn't a good bet any day.

Chapter 2

Mallory had cried herself to sleep the night before. Ada interrupted her sleep several times checking on her due to her concussion. Finally, she was able to fall into a more restful sleep. But when she awoke, the darkness of the room enveloped her in despair. After rolling over onto her back, she stared up at the ceiling. Empty. Like her mind. And her life.

She released a breath. What time was it anyway? And did it matter? She had no place to go. No one to care what she did. Then again, perhaps someone would be looking for her.

Her vision cleared as light seeped in from behind the shades and curtains. That older woman, Ada, was it? Told her to ring the bell on the nightstand before she got up, but her headache was gone. She could try to get up by herself and use the chamber pot. At least she remembered how to do that.

Mallory pushed the heavy quilt off and shivered as the cool air drifted through the openings of the oversized blue-pinstripe flannel gown, and swung her legs over the side. A small bout of dizziness subsided. She could do this. Holding to the edge of the bureau, she stood on the soft braided rug. Her legs shook a bit. Once she felt confident, she used the chamber pot and set the cover atop. She moved to the gray marble-topped washstand in the corner and poured some water from the cream-colored pitcher into the matching bowl. She washed her hands with the white cake of Ivory soap, inhaling its pungent, clean scent, and then splashed her face with the soapy water. If only she could wash away the fogginess inside her head. A knock sounded at the door. Her heart pounded.

"Mallory, are you all right in there?" Ada's voice sounded through the wood.

Mallory's heart settled into a steady beat. "Yes, come in."

The door opened. "What are you doing up? I told you to ring for me."

Mallory took the towel hanging from a bar on the side of the stand and patted her face dry. "I'm fine. I had to get out of that bed."

Ada came toward her, wringing her hands. "Dear me, the doctor said—"

"Please, let me try sitting up and eating breakfast in a chair. Wouldn't that be easier for both of us? And where are my clothes? I need to get dressed." She held firm to the edge of the washstand in case the dizziness returned.

"Well, your clothing has been damaged. I simply must wash and mend it now that it's dried out. You'll be happy to know that Lucinda Brewster is bringing some clothes for you from the church box." The whole time Ada spoke she held fast to Mallory's arm and maneuvered her into a chair, then put a pillow behind her and a blanket over her.

"Are you sure you're warm enough?"

"Yes. What should I call you?" Mallory pulled her hands out from under the smothering blanket.

"Aunt Ada would be fine. Mrs. Waterson's a mouthful." Ada peered over the top of the wire-rimmed frames perched on her nose and smiled. "Cal's my nephew."

"That tall man who was in here last night?" Mallory eyed the partially open door.

"Yes, and don't worry. I won't have him bursting in here anymore."

Mallory grinned her thanks at the kind woman. "What time is it?"

Ada went to the window, drew up a shade, and chuckled. "You slept well into the day, my dear. It's eleven o'clock."

Mallory blinked, taking in the shimmering blue of the water as the reflection of the sun danced like diamonds tossed on the currents. She squinted until her eyes adjusted to the brightness, and she leaned toward the window. "What a lovely place to be. You must never get tired of it."

Ada grinned. "It's not a bad place. It's home, after all. You stay put now. Just relax and I'll bring you something to eat."

Mallory frowned. Aunt Ada had avoided meeting her eyes. What was she hiding? She swallowed hard against the thickness in her throat. "Has Mr. Waterson learned anything yet?"

Ada stopped in the doorway and sighed. "Child, let's get some nourishment in you and then, once we get you up and dressed, you can talk to Cal. But it's going to take some time before he knows anything." She pulled the door closed behind her.

It was hard to be patient when you weren't even sure what you were waiting for. A chill swept over her.

Outside on the platform, the wind cooled Cal from the heat of the Fourth Order Fresnel lens encased by the eight-sided glass lantern room behind him. He gripped the railing and surveyed the straits after cleaning the outsides of the windows. The lake churned, dark blue and moody as his mind, but still with patches of ice. What had possessed the steamship captain to push through the second full week of April before most of it had thawed? Adding a thunderstorm and heavy winds no doubt made it easier for them to wind up with a hole pierced in the ship's hull. He prayed no others would come to such a demise as the *Mallory* had.

Mallory. Interesting the dark-haired beauty resting below remembered that word and nothing else from the wreck. Was she lying? No. He shook his head at the thought. The tempest in her brown eyes showed fear and confusion.

He braced himself against the thought of further storms. He had a duty. This was his little corner of the world to stand for Christ. That was one of the things which attracted him to lighthouse service. He was a part of this beacon as much as it was part of him. His work made the Fresnel lens with its red glow shine all the brighter, guiding ships through the Straits of Mackinac. As Jesus was the Light of the World for lost sinners, the Old Mackinac Point Lighthouse lit the way for lost ships.

As spring life budded and bloomed, so did life on the straits. The *St. Ignace* and *Sainte Marie* passed one another, traveling in opposite directions between Mackinaw City and St. Ignace. Both vessels were weighted down with railroad cars and passengers as they connected the commerce of the upper and lower peninsulas. Travelers were beginning to hire boats to take them to Mackinac Island. Many of them were likely to stay at the Grand Hotel, which appeared as a white strip on Mackinac Island from where he stood. The straits only grew busier each year, but was it really progress as the peaceful village became more industrial? Cal longed for things to stay the same and for the comfort that brought him.

"Cal!" Ada called above the din of waves and wind. She huffed and puffed after climbing her way to the top step and poking her head through the doorway.

"Hmm?"

"The girl wants to talk to you."

He glanced back over his shoulder. "Once you have her dressed in some decent clothes."

"Lucinda brought something for her. I have her propped up on the settee in the sitting room."

"Very well." He stroked his chin. "Still not much I can tell her."

"I know that, but she needs to hear it from you." She nearly growled, as though Mallory were her own cub.

Cal patted her arm and made his way down the circular stairway behind her.

Light streamed into the sitting room, illuminating the girl's hair and face. Even the simple long gray frock she wore appeared elegant though a little large on her shapely form. Lily giggled, sitting on the edge of the settee and holding up a string wound around her hands.

"I hope you're not tiring our guest, Lily." His voice boomed in the relative quiet.

Mallory looked up at him and bestowed him with a demure but lovely smile. "She's teaching me—cat's cradle, is it? It seems somehow familiar, but like so many things, I can't remember how or why."

"Truly, Papa, I'm not being a bother." Lily took the string. "We were having fun, right, Miss Mallory?"

"We are having a nice time." Mallory helped his daughter rewind the string.

"How are you feeling?" Cal pushed unruly bangs from his forehead.

"Better. I have quite a bruise though." She handed the rest of the string to his daughter before she lifted the hair from the side of her face to reveal a patch of blue and green. "At least if there's a scar it will be hidden by my hair."

"A good thing, yes." He sat down in the chair across the room from her.

Mallory smoothed her locks back over the injured area.

"Does it hurt?" Lily asked.

"Not too bad." Mallory scrunched her nose, and something melted inside Cal. This stranger didn't seem to mind his child at all.

She looked into his eyes and squinted, as though searching for something. Hope, perhaps? "Mr. Waterson, have you heard any news?"

"I've sent messages to the shipping company, the Lighthouse Service, and the coast guard, but it may be a long while until we hear from any of them." He bounced the heel of his right foot. What could he tell her?

She exhaled and relaxed against the back of the settee. "So I'm stuck here until someone claims me?"

"Any day now one of the newspapers will be snooping around for more information. Those reporters are notorious for digging up stories. Who knows if somebody won't read yours and come looking for you?" He looked up when Aunt Ada swooped into the room and handed him a steaming mug of coffee. She always seemed to know when he needed one.

Aunt Ada wiped her hands on her apron. "And if not, you can place an advertisement."

"But I don't have any money for that." Mallory's voice hitched an octave higher with her concern.

"If an ad needs to be placed, it can be done courtesy of the Lighthouse Service." He sent a frown Aunt Ada's way. No sense in getting Mallory's hopes up too soon. "Would you mind if we pray for you?"

"Why didn't I think of that?" Aunt Ada tsked as though scolding herself.

Mallory's answer was subdued. "All right."

"You need to fold your hands, like this." Lily intertwined her fingers as she was taught and tucked them under her chin. She moved to the floor and knelt by Mallory's knee.

Cal connected with Mallory's bewildered gaze before he bowed his head and closed his eyes. "Heavenly Father, we ask for Your mercy on Miss Mallory here. She probably feels alone and lost. Um, please guide her family here to her and help us . . . to make her feel at home while she waits. Amen."

"Amen," Lily echoed.

"Thank you." Mallory paused. "I only hope you're right and I have some family looking for me. If they weren't all on that ship."

Cal raked his hand through his hair. What if they had been?

"Why are you squeezing your eyes like that?" Lily squinted at Mallory and scrunched her nose with the effort.

"Am I? I guess the light is a little bright. Maybe it's my concussion." Mallory rubbed her hand over her forehead and her face, covering her eyes for a moment.

"Come on, now, let Miss Mallory rest." Aunt Ada took the little one's hand.

"She's not bothering me. Truly."

"I'll be quiet, I promise. Can I draw something?" Lily looked with bright hope at her great-aunt.

Aunt Ada sighed and shrugged. "Very well. You can stay in here if you play quietly."

"Oh goody! I'll be right back. I have to get something." Lily retreated behind Aunt Ada.

Mallory turned her gaze toward Mr. Waterson, who studied her, a question in his eyes. Did he think her amnesia was a ploy? But his prayer was so sincere. Her heart still warmed from his words, that the large man was so comfortable conversing with God as though He were in the room with them.

"I'm sorry for the lack of quiet here. When you're confused, I'm sure you don't need Lily's constant chattering." He paused, his hands clasped together and elbows resting on his knees. "But I feel it's my duty to care for you here where I know you'll be safe."

The blue of Mr. Waterson's eyes warmed. Something about his solid presence proclaimed him as constant as the ticking of the mantel clock. Despite his size, as he averted his gaze his shyness was revealed.

"I don't want to rush you, miss, but anything you can tell me about yourself would be helpful." Their gazes met again.

Mallory played with the ends of her dark chestnut hair. She'd peeked in a mirror. Her eyes were brown. She was thinner than Aunt Ada and a lot shorter than this man in front of her. But that was all she knew about herself. Names, places, they'd been erased. She squeezed her eyes against the hot, unbidden flood. She shuddered. Nothing. No past. No future.

She shook her head. "I have these dreams, mostly of a storm and the ship." She twisted the ends of her hair around her fingers. "When I try to make sense of them in the morning, there is nothing. I wish I could help."

"Take your time. The doc says something will probably jar your memories. Eventually they'll come back."

"Will they? What if they don't, Mr. Waterson?"

"Too soon to worry about that, Miss Mallory. We have to trust you'll get better." He grinned at her.

A staccato rhythm took up residence in her chest as gentle heat spread through her, warring with the anxiety within. Was she mad to develop feelings for this kind man she didn't know, especially when she didn't know herself?

Chapter 3

Lily burst back into the room with a trail of butcher paper. "Look, Miss Mallory. I brought paper and an extra piece of charcoal in case you wanted to draw too." The child's grin spread across her face. Her eyes glowed with promise.

Mallory sat straighter, placing her feet on the floor. "Of course I'd love to draw with you." She reached out to push a golden strand of the little girl's hair from her forehead. How tempting to pretend this was her real life. It couldn't hurt to enjoy her time with these kind people.

"Here!" Lily held up a thinner piece of charcoal. This time her impish grin revealed an uneven row of teeth as her grown-up teeth came in.

The child hummed a little tune and sketched a stick figure of a girl with long hair. "I'm drawing you, Miss Mallory. I'm going to put a pretty gown on you."

"Why is that?" Mallory fingered the charcoal stick in her hand. It fell into a spot between her fingers and her thumb. Comfortably. Like it was meant to be there.

"I'll put a crown on you too. You could be a princess." Lily grinned.

"Why, you're very imaginative." Mallory made strokes with the charcoal and then an oval. An image formed of the little girl with her head bent over her drawing. She was wearing a ruffled white pinafore over a beige-and-green calico dress. A shame she couldn't capture the color with her drawing implement.

Mr. Waterson harrumphed and sipped his steaming coffee while his eyes wandered toward the window and the water. "Too imaginative."

Mallory ignored the comment, her attention poring over the paper. A comfort flooded over her which she hadn't experienced since she'd regained consciousness. She sensed, though briefly, that she was settled in a safe place and had nothing to worry about.

"Do you like it?" Lily held up her drawing of the stick princess covered by a billowing gown decorated with bows. Atop the swirls of charcoal making up her hair sat a large crown dotted with circles. Mallory suspected they were gems.

"It's lovely, sweetie. Even if I were a princess, I don't think I would have such a beautiful outfit."

"But I saw your pretty pink dress when Aunt Ada washed it. I never saw a gown like that. Maybe you went to a ball like Cinderella did. Or lost your crown in the lake."

"Oh." What had she been wearing when she washed ashore? Shiny pink fabric and the distant sound of screaming flashed at the edge of her mind. She closed her eyes, and a tear slipped down her cheek while her heart pounded.

"Please don't cry." Lily knelt by her side and grasped her fingers. The warmth of the little hand comforted Mallory. Her heart slowed. She wiped away the tear with the back of her hand.

"You drawed this, Miss Mallory?" The child tugged her hand.

Mallory opened her eyes to find the child pointing at her small portrait. "Yes, it's you." Even as she said it she marveled. She didn't remember drawing before, but it was a fair likeness. The little girl, with her sweet rounded face, was bent over her work. Her braids fell on her shoulders.

"Papa! Aunt Ada! You have to see what Miss Mallory did!"

Cal's reverie broken, he placed the near-empty mug on the round maple side table. His daughter brought the piece of paper to him. He sighed, not knowing what to expect after her declaration. Taking the butcher paper in his hands, surprise filled him. The quickly drawn sketch was almost as lifelike as a photograph. The woman had captured the utter sweetness of his Lily. Rather than a princess, did he have some famous artist in his home?

"How were you able to draw like this?"

Mallory shrank back. She looked down and drew her shawl tighter around her shoulders. "I don't know."

Perhaps his words had sounded suspicious, accusatory.

"All I know is it felt right, Mr. Waterson." Her shy look when she met his gaze with her misty eyes tugged at his heart.

"It's perfect, Miss Mallory. I love it!" Lily just about hopped into the girl's lap and threw her arms around her neck.

"Slow down, child. You're going to hurt her."

"It's all right, Mr. Waterson. I'm not made of porcelain." As though to prove it, Mallory hugged the girl back.

"Can you teach me how to draw like that? Please?"

"Well, I. . .I suppose, sweetie, but we're going to have to work together. I'm figuring all this out anew." Mallory took the little one's face in her hands with such gentleness.

"What's all the racket out here? Can't a woman make dinner in peace?" Aunt Ada lumbered out of the kitchen and wiped her hands on her generous white apron.

Cal handed her the paper.

Aunt Ada gasped. "Who drew this?" Her eyes darted from face to face.

Lily had turned toward her. "Well, it wasn't me." She put her hands up in six-year-old exasperation and shook her head. "Miss Mallory did it."

Though Ada could have scolded Lily for her impertinence, instead, she guffawed. "Truly, this is amazing. Think about it, girl, art must be part of your past. That's your first clue."

Mallory shrugged. Cal could only describe her wry smile as almost bitter. It was like asking a blind man what it was like when he could still see.

"I wish I knew. I can tell you how it feels." She paused. "Drawing feels natural to me. I must have learned how to draw somewhere along the line, but I couldn't tell you where, when, or who taught me." Her eyes took on that faraway look for a moment until they lost their glow and an empty desperation replaced the hope.

His aunt handed the paper to Lily. "As soon as I finish peeling the potatoes and putting them in the stewpot, I'm going up to the attic."

"Whatever for?" Cal frowned. What scheme was she cooking up now?

"You weren't even a mite yet when I learned how to draw and paint. I was considered quite a talent in our town. But then I married your uncle and got busy keeping my house. No time for other pursuits, it seemed. Wish I'd kept it up. But it's not too late for you, Mallory." Aunt Ada sighed. "Anyway, I'm sure I have some art supplies stored away. They were too expensive to throw out."

"That would be lovely. Thank you." Mallory's forehead wrinkled as her eyebrows rose.

Aunt Ada bustled toward her next task in the kitchen, humming, and Lily followed. "I want to help you find the paint, Aunt Ada!"

"If I ever find out who I am, I'd like to repay you." Mallory sat up straight and folded her hands across her knees.

"No need to worry about that." Cal picked the mug up again with the intention of taking it into the kitchen for his aunt to wash. He stared into the brown liquid in the bottom and swirled it round.

"But—"

"It's part of my job." Cal stood. "Speaking of which, I have work to do." It was nearly time to wind the weights back up in the tower so the clock mechanism would work and the faceted lens would continue its smooth turning.

Mallory's eyes trained on the handsome lighthouse keeper as he retreated from her. The way he rose abruptly when she mentioned repaying him—had she insulted him?

Somehow, as she again picked up the smooth stick of charcoal, a soothing peace flowed through her middle. She drew the coal stove then quickly sketched the table in the corner. Her lips curved into a smile.

Heavy footsteps sounded from the corner of the lighthouse. Mr. Waterson was surely heading up to the tower above for his duties. Mallory stood and ambled toward the window.

The heavy burgundy drapes had been pulled aside. She drew back the lace curtains beneath for a clear view. Echoes of the searing headache she'd had earlier pulsed in her temples, and she squinted for a minute or so. Oh! How the sight of glorious blue waters shimmering under the sunlight boosted her spirits. The sandy shoreline. The graceful swoop of birds. She could only imagine the sweeping view Cal Waterson must have from up above.

She blinked, her eyes adjusting to the warm, tastefully appointed room. The brocade fabric on the chairs, flanking the settee, matched the drapes. The settee was covered with a faded damask a shade lighter. The slight scratches on the polished walnut trim of each piece showed the furniture was well used. Treads of footsteps had worn a slight path on the green-and-gray rug with its elegant trellis pattern. The black metal stove stood like a sentry at one end of the room. No doubt the appliance kept everyone toasty on cold winter nights, but it was the kindness of the lighthouse family that really created the warmth of the home. Mallory sighed. Did she come from such a place? Or leave that kind of family behind?

Cal's breath hitched in his chest. He loosened his collar and scanned the mail on the desk. He'd hoped something would come through the telegraph office soon. Something. Anything.

He rubbed a hand over his face. That girl, Mallory—or whatever her real name was—was utterly distracting. Even the annoying Eva Jones hadn't done so well with Lily. Oh, the spinster made a pretense of liking children whenever there was an unmarried man within her grasp, but she never fooled him. Yet the tenderness with which Mallory had held his sweet daughter's face in her hands drew him into the depths of her caramel-brown eyes. She could melt a ten-foot pile of snow in ten seconds flat with one look if she were allowed. For Lily's sake, he didn't need to entangle his life with this stranger's.

She was the opposite of Lily's mother. Sarah had been a sturdy woman whose infectious laughter and spirit had won his heart. Her faded picture stared out at him from its ornate frame. He'd never expected to lose her shortly after childbirth. With Sarah's death he believed that part of his life was behind him. "No one can take your place, Sarah."

"Miss Mallory, yoo-hoo!"

She'd better return to her seat before Aunt Ada scolded her. Steadying herself, Mallory took a couple of steps while keeping her hand on the wall for balance.

"There you are! What are you doing up and around by yourself?" Aunt Ada shook a finger at her.

"I was merely admiring the view." Mallory clasped her hands in front of her.

"You didn't try to climb the tower stairs by yourself, did you?"

"I thought about it." She bit her lower lip.

"Tut, tut. You mustn't get too anxious. Your rest is important." Aunt Ada shook her head.

Mallory suddenly didn't feel any older than Lily, who came darting past Aunt Ada and threw her arms around Mallory's waist. "I'll show you around the lighthouse! I know where everything is. We're in the head lighthouse keeper's quarters now."

"Child, you must be more careful, so you don't hurt Miss Mallory. Shame on you. Slow down now." Aunt Ada marched over and pulled the girl away by the collar. "I'm so sorry, but she can be a bit wild. I do my best with her."

Mallory grasped Lily's hand. "She didn't hurt me. I really don't want her to go."

The child rewarded her with a smile and clung to her hands.

"Very well. Now come with me. I have something to show you."

Chapter 4

She followed Aunt Ada and Lily back to the sitting room and parked again on the settee. The little girl plopped down next to her. On one of the tables sat a stack of papers, boxes, and long-handled paintbrushes.

Aunt Ada bustled toward the pile and sat on the other side of Mallory. "I found a few things that may help you." She blew the sheen of dust off the small wooden box on top and unlatched it.

As though anticipating the opening of a miniature treasure chest of delights, Mallory held her breath. Inside were small cakes of colored paints, partially used. A few broken sticks of charcoal resided alongside small sheets of unused paper. When she breathed again, the scent rattled something in her faraway memories. What was familiar about this smell of colors and charcoal? Or was it only the dusty mustiness that tickled her nose? She sneezed.

"God bless you, child." Aunt Ada handed her a hankie.

Mallory sneezed again and blew her nose. Lily giggled.

"Dear me, I never meant to send you into a sneezing fit. I should have aired everything out first."

"No, no. It's all right."

"I know it's just a few watercolors, but I did find an easel too."

Warmth from the pit of Mallory's stomach filled her with a desire to grab the brushes and head outside to create a painting of the aqua-blue waters. She grasped one of the brushes and it felt as natural as holding the charcoal. "As soon as I get better, if it's warm enough, I'd love to go outside and paint a landscape of the lighthouse and the lake."

"Drawing will have to be enough for you until you are closer to being mended." Aunt Ada's voice was firm.

Lily picked up another brush. "I'll help you get better, and Aunt Ada will make chicken soup and maybe cookies. They always make me feel better."

"Shall we draw with the charcoal, Lily? You can use some of the good paper with me."

The child gave Mallory one of her endless smiles.

Mallory touched the older woman's sleeve. "Thank you, Aunt Ada. You have been too kind. At least I will have an occupation until I figure out where I belong. . . and who I truly am."

A week later, during the third week of April, men's voices drifted on the breeze from the lighthouse. Mallory recognized the timbre of Cal's voice but not the other man's. She had only caught an occasional glimpse of the other man coming in from the assistant lighthouse keeper's apartment on the way to his duties. She'd yet to have a conversation with this other fellow, as he and Cal kept busy. Knowing Aunt Ada, she had probably warned any company away while Mallory was recovering. She turned as they retreated from view, both in overalls, ready to work. Cal's shoulders were broader, the kind of shoulders anyone could lean on. He stood half a head taller than the stranger. She admired the lighthouse keeper's strength, his unflagging sense of duty.

After she turned back to her easel, Mallory dipped the brush into the can of water and then into the blue cake. She swirled a little green and then white into it on a palette before she made her favorite aqua color of the lake. With soft strokes of the brush, she layered the colors of the water and shining ripples and even the few remaining chunks of ice. A sailboat traveled westward under the brilliant sunshine. How she wanted to capture the glory of the day! She sighed.

Then a picture, like a small vignette, popped into her mind. A smallish vessel, not a sailboat, docked. Mallory closed her eyes. It was on a day like today, but where? Her heartbeat sped up and then. . .she lost the picture in her mind. Why couldn't she remember more?

Every time she picked up pencil or brush, especially when she sat out near the shore, flashes of memory, a sense of place, emerged in her thoughts and was gone as quickly. Though she'd only been there a little over a week, the amnesia had grown tiresome.

"Hello!"

Mallory stood and looked around to see a woman with light brown hair strolling toward her with a tot holding one hand and a baby slung on her other hip. Her willowy figure gave her an air of grace despite carrying the little one.

"Hello! I'm Jane." The woman drew closer. "My husband, Henry, is Cal's brother-in-law, the assistant lighthouse keeper."

"Pleased to meet you. I'm Mallory. At least I am for now."

"Dear me, I heard what happened and I'm so sorry." Jane wrinkled her nose.

"Thank you." Mallory shrugged and smiled at her new acquaintance, hoping to ease the awkwardness of the conversation. She wasn't sure what else to say.

"I've just returned from helping my mother out. My father's been ill. Not a great time to be away." She shook her head. "Good thing I'm back. Soon things will be buzzing at the park and we'll have no end of visitors to clean up and get ready for." Jane dipped her head toward the not-so-distant trees.

"Really?" Mallory tugged her shawl tighter around herself, against the breeze.

"Yes indeed. The Lighthouse Service feels we should be open to the scrutiny of the public, and tourist season will soon be upon us. People camp at the park nearby where the old fort used to be and walk over. May I look at your painting?" The baby in Jane's arms fussed as though wondering why he hadn't been introduced, while the little fellow next to her clung to her leg and stared at Mallory with big blue eyes and barely blinked.

"Of course. Your children are beautiful." Something tugged at Mallory's heart, like a desire she recognized and couldn't quite name. Did she even like children? She had been enjoying her acquaintance with Lily. What if she never found out who she was? Would it be right for her to marry and have a family? Maybe she was already married. She touched the empty ring finger on her left hand as a reassurance.

"You've really captured the water, almost as though it had a life of its own. Amazing." Jane gave her a tentative grin while the baby fussed louder.

"Thank you." Mallory poked the toe of her shoe into the sand and looked down.

"All right, we'll get you something to eat now, child. This is Clarence, and the one hiding in my skirt is Teddy."

"So pleased to meet you, sir." Mallory took Teddy's pudgy little hand and gave it a quick squeeze, eliciting a smile from the shy child.

"Teddy, what do you say?" Jane spoke louder above the din of crying and waves crashing on the shore.

"Pweased to meet you?" He looked up at his mother for approval.

"Yes, you're doing better." Jane patted him on the head. "He's only three, and Clarence is nearly one."

"I suppose it's time to pack up my paints and help Aunt Ada with dinner now." Mallory stood from the stool Cal had brought out for her and dipped the brushes in the water to clean them. The colors muddied the liquid, much like her past.

"We'll see you later then, as I believe Ada is expecting us. Do you need help with the easel?"

"No, not at all. Besides, you have your hands full."

"All right then." Jane turned to go back to her side of the lighthouse.

As Mallory dried each brush, wiping it on the apron she wore, then tucked the paints away in a box, the order of how she cared for things comforted her. She was flooded with a sense of déjà vu as she cleaned and put away each object and disassembled the easel. *I've done this before, many times. If only I could remember where and when.*

The rhythm of the waves comforted her as well, yet even as she stared out into the cold depths, trying her best to remember what happened on that fateful evening, so much was missing. *Please, God, show me my past again.* Mallory wiped the tear from her cheek, hoping no one had seen her in this moment of weakness.

"Aunt Ada, you've outdone yourself again. I'm not sure how every time I eat your apple pie it seems to be the best one I ever tasted." Cal leaned back in his chair and patted his stomach. The Watersons and MacPhersons were gathered around the expanded oak table in the kitchen.

"Pshaw. Cal Waterson, you are nothing but a flatterer." His aunt wagged a finger at him.

Everyone chuckled at the familiar scene, except Mallory, who smiled. She busied herself with washing and drying dishes. As she rubbed a towel over each shiny white plate and stacked them in the pantry, a strand fell across her cheek from the hair piled on top of her head. She pushed it out of her face with the back of her hand. The steam rising from the water gave her a delicate flush most becoming to her porcelain skin. Cal couldn't deny she'd grown lovelier over the two weeks she'd been with them. The way she lent a hand as soon as she was able, insisting she was no invalid, was admirable. Was there another man looking for her?

The last bite of Aunt Ada's flaky crust melted on his tongue.

"Cal, did you hear me?" Jane tapped his arm, bringing him back to the present.

He blinked. She held an enameled pot of coffee above his cup. "Well, do you want any more? You're in another world."

"Please." Cal tapped on the saucer, not meeting her gaze. Heat coursed up his neck. Had any of them noticed his study of Mallory? He took a swallow of the hot, bitter brew. "Thanks, Jane."

Henry cleared his throat. "Have you looked into the ship's manifest from its origin yet?"

Mallory's eyes widened as she trained them on the assistant lighthouse keeper. Cal took a deep breath. He hadn't wanted to get her hopes up until he had the information in his hands. "I'm still waiting to receive it."

"Ah." Henry forked another bite of pie into his mouth.

Mallory's head dipped, her lips in a straight line. If anyone could "wear" disappointment on their face, she did.

"And nobody has come looking for her?" Henry sounded incredulous.

"Not yet." Cal shook his head. "Though if I remember correctly, the *Mallory* riginated in Erie, Pennsylvania." When he looked toward the stack of dishes again, he had disappeared. The blue-striped towel was hung neatly on the bar above the ink.

Henry shook his head too. "I pity her family."

Jane picked up another towel and flicked it at his arm. "You men, talking like Mallory isn't even in the room. She's left now. You probably hurt her feelings."

Aunt Ada stood with one hand on her hip and the other collecting the dessert dishes. "Yes. You oafs have no manners at all."

Lily stood from her seat at the table and stomped her foot. "Miss Mallory is my friend. I wish you wouldn't hurt her. I don't want her to go."

"Sweetie, we've talked about this. . . ." But his cross little daughter buried her face in his sleeve.

She pushed closer. "Please don't make her go. She doesn't have any other friends."

"Lily, I. . ." How could he explain this to her in a way that would make sense to her six-year-old mind?

Teddy squawked when his fork was taken away, and Clarence pounded his spoon on the table until it was confiscated. He rubbed his eyes and whined.

"Jane, you should take the boys and put them to bed. They look so tired after all your traveling. I'll finish cleaning up."

"Thank you, Ada. I suppose you're right. That's very kind of you."

"Excuse me." Cal stood to leave the ladies to their conversation and tossed his napkin on the chair.

"Where are you going?" Henry stood and put his napkin down as well.

"Where do you think I'm going?" Cal stalked into the sitting room, but she wasn't in a chair or standing by the window looking out. "Mallory?" he called up the stairs before he made his way up. The last thing he wanted to do was to frighten her.

The guest room bedroom door stood open, as did the other two. Would she have climbed the tower or gone outside? He raked a hand through his hair. Why did he care? She was probably better off by herself for a bit if that's what she wanted. But the ladies had a point, and he didn't want her to feel any more alienated than she likely already did. Something in Cal's heart compelled him to look for her. He lifted a curtain. Town visitors walked along the beach, but Mallory was nowhere to be seen.

His footsteps echoed on the hardwood floor in the hallway and down the stairs. Happy voices traveled from the kitchen as Cal strode past the dining and sitting room entrances and made passing glances once more to his right. He took the hallway and turned left at the end where he walked through the reception area. He continued through the door into the small lobby where his apartment connected to that of the assistant's and a service room led to the tower.

Curiosity drew him to the tower steps. He clomped up the spiral staircase. Would Mallory even accept his apology after he was so callous toward her?

The distant echo of work boots on the metal stairway called to Mallory. She peered at the water through the rounded tower window. Despite the upper peninsula and the islands within view, to her it might have been an ocean. Her lack of memories separated her that far from her past. She shivered despite the warmth of the kerosene-lit lens behind her. Its acrid odor surrounded her. Men and women, mothers and children, held hands as they explored the shoreline in the evening, enjoying the gentle breezes off Lake Michigan.

But who were her parents? Had anyone loved her? Ever? No news had come in the passing days other than what Cal alluded to a few minutes before. Perhaps her family was glad to be rid of her. She squeezed her lids shut against the warm tears. She would do her best to help the Watersons. *God, who am I? Was I so bad that You needed to punish me like this? Did I ever know You like the Watersons do?*

The sobs that had been threatening for days racked her as she crossed her arms tight to her front and rocked on her heels.

"Mallory, why are you up here?" She turned as Cal's head popped through the opening in the floor.

Wiping the back of her hand across her face, she sniffled. "You weren't supposed to see me like this, Mr. Waterson."

"Like what? I came to apologize for the thoughtless way Henry and I spoke in front of you. And by the way, you can call me Cal." He shook his head and pressed his lips into a grim line.

"I know you didn't mean anything by it. But I don't really belong here. Or anywhere." Mallory inhaled deeply and braced herself.

"It takes awhile for communication to get through the right channels. We're a small town. The city papers may have just reported the incident."

"Now I'm just an incident." She knew Cal spoke of the shipwreck, but she was raw. So many hurts had been pricking at her heart like a woodpecker on a window frame.

"I give you credit for knowing exactly what I mean." Cal gave her half a smile, but the way he gripped the railing, with the whites of his knuckles showing, hinted at his frustration.

"Henry will be up to turn the light on for the night, but I have work to do. I'll leave you alone now." Cal pivoted. Going down the stairs to the level below where his desk sat was more like negotiating a ladder. The gracefulness the large man showed surprised Mallory.

"Wait. Please. . .Cal."

"What is it?" He blinked slowly. Surely, she tried his patience.

"All of you have been very kind. How may I help? I want to repay you."

"There's no need. Besides, you've already done a fine job pitching in. Now, just be careful coming down these steps."

"I'll use the utmost care. I promise." Mallory did her best to curve her mouth into some kind of smile, no matter how poorly given. She would find a way to help them.

Chapter 5

Saturday morning, the next day, Aunt Ada limped into the kitchen. "What's wrong, Aunt Ada?" Mallory took her elbow as she came through the doorway.

"I'll be fine and dandy in a few minutes. What are you doing up so early?"

"The sun came in my window and I couldn't sleep. I got up and thought I'd set the table and start brewing a pot of coffee. I did manage to make some slightly burned toast with jam for Lily and me. She is happily playing with her doll in the sitting room now."

She took a white stoneware cup down from a pantry shelf and poured coffee into it, placing it in front of the older lady. "I need to learn much more about cooking from you. The fact is, I don't remember much about ever cooking. Seems silly, doesn't it?" Funny how after less than two weeks she could have such affection for this woman she hardly knew. In her heart, Mallory wanted her to truly be her "Aunt Ada."

"No, not at all. I'd be glad to teach you what little I know. Dear me." She reached down and rubbed her foot through her shoe.

"You're being too modest, Aunt Ada."

"Oh child, it does me good to hear you call me that. If you never find your family, I'll adopt you." She gave Mallory a wink.

A knock sounded at the door. "I'll get it. Don't get up, Aunt Ada."

Mallory rushed to the door, wiping her hands on her apron before opening it. "Good morning, Dr. Reed. Please come in."

"Well hello, I'm just coming to check on my most interesting patient." The balding, redheaded man tipped his newsboy cap. "How are you feeling these days? Are any of your memories returning yet?"

Mallory shook her head. "I'm afraid only flashes here and there. Sometimes as I am painting or looking out at the water."

"Ah, then I would recommend you continue your art work. And being by the water is often very calming." He carried his black bag in his hand. "I would like to see if the wound on your head is healing well."

"Of course." Mallory bit her lower lip for a moment, wondering if it was her place to tell him about Aunt Ada's condition. "Doctor, why don't you come into the kitchen. Cal's aunt Ada has a very sore foot. If you have time, perhaps she would let you examine it."

"Of course, I'd be happy to, if she'll let me." He smiled. "She's an awfully stubborn woman."

"So I've learned." She returned his smile. He followed her into the kitchen.

Aunt Ada stood there, holding on to the large cast-iron cookstove. Her grin looked more like a grimace. If Mallory had to guess, she supposed the independent older woman was trying to hide her malady. Aunt Ada sucked in a breath. "So nice to see you today, Dr. Reed. As you can see, our patient is doing very well."

"No doubt with your exacting care, but I've heard you are having some problems."

"Me?" Her nervous laugh gave her away.

"Let me see, Ada Waterson."

"Oh, I'm fine." She leaned heavily against the stove before raising a hand to wave away his concern.

"Aunt Ada, please let the doctor take a look. I could tell you were suffering this morning."

The older woman shook her head.

Mallory crossed her arms. "Very well. Then I won't let him look at my head wound either."

"All right then." Aunt Ada held on to the back of a chair and then the sturdy oak kitchen table as she hobbled around the seat and lowered herself into it.

The removal of her button-top shoe and black wool stocking revealed a red bulge near the big toe of her left foot.

"It looks like you're having a flare of gout, Ada." Dr. Reed examined her foot, bending the toe gently as the older lady braced herself. "What else is bothering you these days, hmm?"

"Nothing else. I'm fine." She put a fist to her mouth.

Dr. Reed's eyebrows went up. "Too much pie and coffee, with rich cream, I'll wager. You need some rest."

"But I have so much to do—"

"You have three people depending on you, and you need to take care of yourself." He pulled his stethoscope from his black bag and leaned forward to continue his examination.

Mallory knelt next to Aunt Ada and took her free hand. "I'm sure I can help quite a bit. And I'm happy to after all you've done for me. You'll get better faster for sure if you're able to stay off your feet."

The physician chuckled. "Make sure she drinks lots of water too. Now, let's take a look at that nasty cut and bump you have." Once he'd examined Mallory's head and proclaimed her quite well enough to take over for Aunt Ada, Mallory helped the older woman back up to her room.

"This won't do at all, miss. I'm supposed to be taking care of you." Aunt Ada fussed as she moved aside the flowered quilt on the bed in the room she shared with Lily. The light lavender walls were reminiscent of lilacs. Why was that impression so strong? A flash of a watercolor painting struck Mallory's thoughts, the rhythm of the brushstrokes so strong of an impression she could almost feel the paintbrush in her hand. She suddenly itched to be outside and pulled the muslin curtain aside.

"Would you like some air in here, Aunt Ada?" Perhaps if she opened the window a crack. . .

"And catch my death? No, no. It's still too early in the season to have it open long."

"All right then. What can I get for you?" Mallory plumped a pillow behind the kind woman.

"Paper and a pen first off. Then my Bible." She nodded and held a finger up. "And while I write a list of things for you to do, you can get me a pitcher of water and a glass. You're going to learn the day-to-day running of a lighthouse quite quickly, my dear. I'm sure Jane will be happy to help you. The busy tourist season is nearly upon us."

Mallory swallowed. A swarm of flutters arose in her stomach, but she wouldn't let Aunt Ada know of her trepidations. "I wouldn't have it any other way."

She couldn't remember her own name or where she was from, let alone the running of any home. Now she'd be responsible for a lighthouse. Though she listened with care, Mallory wondered how much would sink in.

"Though Old Mackinac Point Lighthouse is our home, it belongs to the people. We serve at the pleasure of the Lighthouse Service. We must welcome them as they visit from the park nearby."

"I apologize for not helping you more. I hadn't realized you had such a burden."

Aunt Ada put her hand up. "Nonsense. You are our guest, and your task has been to heal and get back your memories."

Mallory sighed. If only she'd spent more time following Aunt Ada and learning from her instead of spending all her time painting on the beach.

"I can see you are worrying about the past. Why don't you try to start new today and look forward? Hmm? I'm confident you can do this, child." The way Aunt Ada furrowed her eyebrows even as she grinned told of her pain. She pulled the coverlet up farther, as though she'd taken a chill, and closed her eyes.

"Aunt Ada, why would you trust me when I am a stranger who doesn't even know who I am?" Mallory picked up the paper.

Aunt Ada's eyelids popped open. "My dear Mallory, God brought you here for a reason, and you've been nothing but trustworthy, despite your difficult circumstances.

I trust God will help you learn these tasks again. Maybe that will be the means of regaining your memories."

Curiosity sparked in her at the wise woman's words. "Aunt Ada, when you speak of God, my heart is stirred, as though He's been working in me, but I don't remember much." Mallory squeezed her eyes shut against threatening tears and opened her hand to the older woman's warm touch.

Aunt Ada squeezed Mallory's hand and looked her right in the eye. "I see something in you. I believe you are one of His children and your spirit knows of His work. Open the drawer there." She pointed with her other hand to the little nightstand right in front of Mallory.

When Mallory pulled the drawer open, a volume with a dove-gray leather cover sat tucked inside. On the cover, in gold lettering it said *Holy Bible*.

"I want you to have this. Go on." Aunt Ada tilted her head in the direction of the nightstand. "Hand it to me first, please."

Mallory lifted it gently from its resting place and gave it to her. Aunt Ada opened the cover, her smile wistful, the look in her eyes far away. "I had a daughter—Essie—short for Esther. She was a lovely young girl, like you, before she died of consumption. Please take this and you'll find the truth. Jesus knows who you are even if you don't. You are in the palm of His Father's hand. Read the Gospel of John and we'll talk about it."

"But I can't take—"

"Nonsense. You can, and you will as long as you promise to read John's little book." Aunt Ada placed the book between Mallory's hands and patted the one on top. "Please."

For a moment, Mallory's heart was heavy with the gravity of holding on to what must have been a treasured item of Aunt Ada's. Her deceased daughter's Bible. Mallory had wanted her own Bible to read ever since Cal had read it aloud at the table the first night she'd eaten dinner with them, but this was even more special.

"Thank you, Aunt Ada." She bent to kiss the plump cheek. She couldn't feel any closer to her if the woman were truly her aunt by blood. "I'm so sorry you lost Essie. I'll take good care of her Bible. I promise."

"I know you will. Now, you best get some breakfast ready for Cal. He was up very early to take over for Henry."

Cal yawned and stretched. The sun had come up over the straits an hour ago and his coffee had grown cold. He might as well finish up some paperwork while he waited for breakfast. Come to think of it, what was taking Aunt Ada so long? He swirled the remains of the brown liquid in his cup, as some of the grounds stuck to the sides. The last mouthful was like bitter sand on his tongue.

Sarah stared at him from her portrait. "Don't start accusing me now." He drummed his fingers on the desk. "I'm not planning on finding another wife, even if Lily wants a mama. Really, Sarah. God would have to put her right in front of me."

"I have."

The voice in his head gave a jolt to Cal's spine. He sat ramrod straight and looked around the small room just below the Fresnel lens. Had he really heard it? In the silence, his heart pounded away.

"The girl from the shipwreck."

"But. . ." Cal closed his eyes and sank his face into his hands. All he could see was Mallory. Her dark, flowing hair. Her kind eyes. Her gentle ways with Lily. But could he love again? That wasn't part of his plan.

He picked up his pen and dipped the nib into an inkwell. Scribbling in the ledger, he hoped to forget that Mallory was below, helping his aunt. After a bit, when he was caught up on his bookwork, Cal pulled his pocket watch out and clicked it open. It was much later than he expected.

He made his way to the bottom of the stairs. "Aunt Ada?" Except for a shuffling sound coming from the kitchen, his ears met with quiet. When he reached the kitchen, there was Mallory throwing up her hands and shaking her head. "What's wrong?"

She looked up and gasped. "I didn't hear you come in. I didn't want you to see the mess I've made."

"Where's Aunt Ada?" Scorched eggs and bacon sat alongside burnt toast on a plate on the sideboard. The acrid odor of the burnt toast met his nose. His aunt was nowhere to be seen.

Mallory recounted Doctor Reed's early morning visit and its result. "I promised her I would take care of things. Making toast for Lily and getting her ready for the day is one thing, but a hot breakfast for you?"

"Perhaps you didn't cook for yourself in the past. Maybe Lily is right, and you are a princess." He gave her a grin, hoping to lighten the mood.

Instead, Mallory pinched her lips together and crossed her arms. She averted her gaze. He stepped closer to her. His hand went up instinctively and he patted her shoulder.

"It will get better. You'll see." He didn't know what else to say. He was praying for her every day.

"What good am I not knowing who I am? Especially if I can't even be much help to Aunt Ada when she has been nothing but kind to me?" She stepped back and turned toward the stove.

Cal's gaze drifted to the floor as he placed his hands in his pockets. His face warmed.

"I guess I will try again with your breakfast."

"We shouldn't let that one go to waste. I'll eat it."

"No, I'll try to eat it. I won't throw it out. I'll make you something fresh."

Cal retrieved the plate off the sideboard. "With a little salt and pepper, it will be fine." He sauntered over to the table. "I would love some hot coffee though, please."

"That I can get you." Mallory lifted the enameled pot from the cast-iron stove and took the mug from Cal. A shy smile lit her face for a moment when he met her fleeting glance.

He dipped his head for a quiet blessing before cutting through the rubbery eggs with a fork and scooping them into his mouth. He would be able to get this breakfast down with enough coffee. He bit into the bacon, beyond crispy to hard, and chewed it well. How often had he just swallowed his meals down, not being thankful enough for Aunt Ada's delicious and consistent cooking? "Don't be discouraged. I'm sure your cooking will get better with practice." Cal couldn't bring himself to tell her anything else.

Mallory sat down across from him at the table. She sipped on a cup of coffee while staring down at a piece of paper.

"Aren't you going to have something more for breakfast?" he asked.

"I'm really not hungry." She shook her head, not meeting his gaze. Folding her hands in front of her on the table, she seemed tense. "What if my memories never return?"

"It's a bit soon to worry about that. Don't you think?" Cal shifted in his seat. Biting into the toast was like nibbling on charcoal. He savored the butter he barely tasted.

"I'm not so sure. I mean, I have bits and pieces that I believe are memories come to mind for a moment. . .but then. . .they're gone." Mallory opened the palm of her right hand almost as though she were releasing a bird.

"Poof. The thoughts are gone like dreams are when you awaken in the morning, other than the recurring nightmares of the shipwreck." Mallory let out a deep breath slowly. "I'm so happy to help Aunt Ada while she's ill, but eventually I need to find out where I belong. And if I can't find my family, then at least I must find a place to stay. I can't impose on you indefinitely."

Cal's fork rattled against the plate as he set it down and leaned back in his chair. He brought the coffee cup to his lips and blinked. His eyes were ringed with fatigue.

He lifted his gaze to her. "You are no imposition. Lily looks up to you. Ada is happy for your company."

Had she offended him somehow? Was that hurt that flickered in his eyes?

"I wouldn't want you to feel unwelcome. You're safe here." The cup returned to the table and he picked up his fork. It clicked against the plate as he continued to eat the horrible breakfast she'd provided him. How long would they truly want someone as useless as she was around?

All Mallory could find in herself to do was nod. "Thank you, nonetheless. I will find a way to repay you." She paused. "Perhaps Jane could give me some perspective on caring for the lighthouse. Excuse me."

The chair's legs scraped against the pine floor as she pushed the seat away from the table and rose. The handsome lighthouse keeper stood, following her with only his deep blue eyes. Eyes that often seemed to express what he couldn't say. She knew so little about this kind man. If he hadn't rescued her, perhaps she would have died. Binding gratitude filled her heart. Yet it seemed her soul was still set adrift on the waves, looking for the true Mallory and the identity the shipwreck had stolen from her.

Chapter 6

Mallory wrapped the shawl given her from the church box around her shoulders. Though clean, a musty smell clung to the faded green wrap. When she opened the door to the stoop, spring air engulfed her with its scents of sweet, thawed earth and the breeze from the lake.

Up until that morning this had been a place of healing. Mallory had pitched in when she was able, but it was an idyllic spot. When she sat on the beach with her paints, her heart soared with joy. For a little while she could dismiss that she was an unknown person, even to herself. She could, as Aunt Ada hinted, reinvent who she was. But right at that moment, Mallory was to be reinvented into a housekeeper—a worthy cause.

She trod with purpose around the front of the golden-beige brick building, glancing up. The lighthouse stood like a castle protecting the Straits of Mackinac. The lighthouse keeper's and assistant lighthouse keeper's quarters were attached to the tower. A square section jutted out from the center front. Its walls reached upward, with a battlement at the top of the three sides. The tower rose above the red pressed-metal roof at the far end and took on the appearance of a keep. Three slit-like windows climbed in a diagonal along the side. A limestone base girded the whole building's foundation. She feasted her eyes on every arch, each bit of decorative brickwork and strategically placed window.

In the morning sun, she could imagine for a moment herself as a damsel in distress, waiting to be rescued. Yet, she was not held captive against her will by some evil prince. Her rescuer also protected her. A princess, indeed! Mallory placed a loose lock of hair behind her ear before knocking on the door of the assistant keeper's apartment.

When Jane opened it, her little ones clambered around her legs and cried. "Good morning." Her curt greeting and quick grin didn't convey much pleasure in seeing Mallory.

"I'm sorry to bother you, Jane, but Mrs. Waterson has fallen ill, and I need to take—"

"Mallory, as you can see, I have my hands full here. I'm not going to be able to take over for Mrs. Waterson any time soon. May we talk later?"

Mallory nodded. As Jane closed the door, the baby's shriek pierced her ears. *Poor woman does have her hands full.* Though pressed with worry for all she needed to get done, Mallory dragged her feet as she returned to the head lighthouse keeper's side of the station.

Returning to the empty kitchen and Aunt Ada's list, she scanned it again. The older woman had scrawled something at the bottom that she hadn't noticed before: *Before you start this list, pray and read Philippians 4:13!*

Mallory slid into the chair. She touched the leather cover of the Bible she'd left on the table, which had been worn soft, and a dim picture swam through her mind. A woman with dark hair and a kind smile placed a similar Bible in her hands, small hands to be exact. Had she been a child then? And just as quickly the thought escaped her. She squeezed her eyes shut as though she could bid it return, to no avail, then opened the sacred book to the prescribed chapter. She read, *"I can do all things through Christ which strengtheneth me."* Her lips turned up in a grin. Such familiar words. Weren't they? Or was she imagining it?

"God, I feel like I know You, but something is missing. Maybe it's just me." Maybe she blamed Him for the accident and that was why He seemed far away. "I give my life, for what good it is the way I am right now, to You. If I could live for You like the Watersons do, with such kindness for others, then all this might not be a waste." She swallowed and wiped the tears from her face.

There was familiarity in her prayer. As though the Lord Himself had entered the room and reached out to her with a gentle touch, warmth spread through her.

A knock interrupted her thoughts. Maybe it was Jane coming to see her after closing the door on her with such abruptness. "And God, please help Jane with her little ones. . .and me to keep up the lighthouse well." Mallory stood before the little fish-eye mirror in the hallway. The distorted image wasn't much help, but it was better than nothing. She repinned her hair and straightened her apron. Then she patted her fingers underneath her eyes to make sure the tears were gone before pinching her cheeks. The knock grew persistent.

"Coming!" Mallory strode toward the door and pulled it open. "Good morning!" She froze at the sight of the strangers before her.

"Why, hello. I thought perhaps no one was home, which is highly unlikely in a lighthouse." A prim matron stood alongside a plump man, presumably her husband, who wore a monocle and twitched his handlebar mustache.

"H–how may I help you? Are you lost?" Mallory stammered, unsure of what else to say to the strangers. Any hope that her family had come looking for her was dashed with their looks of curiosity. No recognition lit their eyes.

"Goodness, no. We came for a tour of the lighthouse."

"Oh. Please come in then." What *were* the instructions she'd been given by Aunt Ada for that? They'd only spoken for a few minutes on the topic. And where was Cal when she needed him? *"I can do all things. . ."* She would do her best.

"Have you been here before? What would you like to see first?"

"You must be the new Mrs. Waterson? I'm so glad that nice young widower has found a new wife." She placed a hand on Mallory's arm as she ambled over the threshold.

"I'm afraid you're mistaken. I'm Miss, um, Mallory, an assistant to Mr. Waterson's aunt."

"How. . .interesting." The woman frowned. "I'm Mrs. Widley, and this is my husband."

"A pleasure meeting you, I'm sure. Please come into the sitting room and let me get you something to drink."

"We're anxious to get on with the tour. We have to be back at the Stimpson House Hotel to meet some friends at eleven." Mr. Widley clicked open an ornate pocket watch on too long of a gold chain for his portly stature. He shut it with almost as much precision as though he were winding it before tucking it in his suitcoat pocket.

"Well, then, um, where would you like to start?" The staccato beat of her heart was amplified in her ears and not in a good way. The dizziness that threatened to overtake her was much like that when she tried to no avail to delve into the blackness of her past memories. Panic, sheer panic.

Cal's steady footsteps calmed her just in time as they beat a rhythm down the stairs to the rest of the quarters and into the hallway. What a relief!

"Mr. and Mrs. Widley, what a delight to see you." He held out his hands to them both. As he passed Mallory he turned to give her a discreet wink she was pretty sure only she could see.

How he'd banished sleep from his eyes and donned his uniform so quickly was anyone's guess. Usually he wore his more practical overalls. He tipped his hat, uncovering the thick wheat-blond hair that contrasted with the tan of his skin. His gracious smile crinkled the corners of his eyes. The navy-blue uniform fit nicely over his broad shoulders and muscled arms.

Mallory's nervous heart stilled. Her dizziness turned to an unexpected lightheadedness. How was it every time she saw Cal Waterson, he grew in stature and attractiveness? She wiped her hands absently on her apron and closed her mouth, which had been hanging agape. When the Widleys gazed at her, she stopped staring at Cal and turned away, hoping to hide her burning face. She really should follow along and see how he gave the tour in case she was asked again, but. . .

Cal looked over his shoulder. "Mallory, please feel free to do whatever you need to for Aunt Ada." He nodded, his gaze tender with concern.

"Of course." She was relieved to be dismissed and trod up the stairs lightly. Soft snoring emanated from Aunt Ada's room. She peeked around the partially open door. The lines on the older woman's face softened as she was able to rest. She worked so hard to make them all comfortable. At least she was temporarily relieved of pain.

Aunt Ada's clock ticked away. Ten o'clock already? She needed to get to work and start dinner after she checked on Lily. Would she even have time to get bread baked? Time for her to stoke the waning fire in the stove with more coal too.

"Mr. Waterson, I'm afraid there's gossip in town." Mrs. Widley cleared her throat and narrowed her eyes. Cal dragged his gaze away from Mallory's dark tresses, as her delicate figure disappeared into the hallway.

"What is that, Mrs. Widley?" Cal blinked and turned his attention back to the suspicious woman who stood with her hands on her hips.

"Is it true you're housing a woman with no recall of her past?"

He wanted to smile but thought it best to school his face into a serious expression. "Yes, ma'am. She was the only survivor from a ship called the *Mallory*."

"I see."

"Which is why she's using that name."

Mr. Widley had his hands clasped behind his back. "She seems like a lovely young woman."

"But people are starting to talk, you know, dear. I just thought I should warn Mr. Waterson." Mrs. Widley fussed with her reticule and sniffed. "I had hoped they were wrong."

"People will always talk, Mrs. Widley." Cal rubbed his chin. "I feel especially responsible for Mallory, and she is safe here. I assure you there's nothing improper going on. My aunt and daughter are both here. The young lady and I are never alone." He put a hand out toward the hallway to the tower. "Shall we proceed with the tour?"

"Yes, my dear, you were in quite the hurry a moment ago." Mr. Widley winked at Cal.

"Very well," she huffed.

As Cal ushered them around the lighthouse, showing them the view of the straits from the tower, he silently prayed. The worry in Mallory's eyes concerned him. He'd kept her at the lighthouse to protect her, not turn her into a maid. Yet, there was no doubt he needed the help.

A week later, Cal wiped his mouth with a fresh linen napkin after dinner. "That was your best dinner yet, Mallory."

"Thank you." She busied herself with clearing the table, hardly meeting his gaze.

"Don't tell Aunt Ada, but the chicken and dumplings rivaled hers."

Lily piped up before dipping her spoon back into the stew for another bite. "I liked the dumplings best! Did you make cookies for dessert?"

"Sorry, no cookies." Mallory shook her head, but her eyes twinkled with mischief despite Lily's pout.

"No dessert? But I ate all the vegetables in my chicken stew." His daughter gave Mallory the best puppy dog face she could muster.

"I didn't say no dessert. I said no cookies." Mallory smiled at Lily with affection.

"Really?"

"Yes, I made cake for dessert."

"Cake? With frosting?" Lily scooted toward the table in her chair.

"Yes, boiled frosting, just like Aunt Ada makes, and chocolate cake. Now finish up."

"I hope I'll get some too." Cal feigned ignorance of her answer, hoping she would look his way.

Mallory turned away from the sideboard with a hand on one hip. "Have you eaten up your dinner, Mr. Waterson, like a good boy?"

Lily giggled. "You're silly, Miss Mallory. Papa gets to eat whatever he wants."

Cal's gaze met Mallory's. Several strands of hair had found their way free and framed her oval face. She squeezed those full pink lips together in an attempt not to smile, but the mirth reached her eyes. How he would like to push a strand of hair behind her ear, stroke her cheek, and taste those lips.

Mallory spurted a light laugh and flashed a sheepish grin his way. "And he eats every bite despite my cooking."

"On the contrary. You learn fast." Cal stood and handed her a serving dish.

She brought the prettily frosted cake to the table and set the platter down. "I had a good teacher."

"You've worked awfully hard this week." Cal shoved his hands in his pockets, feeling like a lovestruck schoolboy yet wanting to convey nothing more than a friendly manner to her.

"Cal, I've wanted to be useful to you. It's not—"

Cal put up his hand to stop her little speech short. "You've done more than one would ever expect of a recuperating guest. I think we could all use a little fun."

"What do you propose?" She sighed, as though annoyed to give up on her protests, while she sliced a knife through the cake.

Lily stood on her toes next to Mallory and licked her lips. Her pointing finger was poised to steal a bit of frosting. "Can I help?"

"I don't need that kind of help." Mallory grabbed his daughter's offending hand and kissed it. "Why don't you get some more forks out of the drawer in the dining room cabinet instead?"

"All right." A pouty bottom lip made its way out.

"Lily. What do you say to Mallory? And stop that pouting, young lady." Cal directed her to face her very kind accuser. He'd never seen anyone with more patience for Lily than his aunt before. His heart lifted and filled with, what? Had it really been under an anvil of worry and grief for so long? Perhaps it was the lightness of joy, like a spring breeze coming in after a storm, so that he could almost smell the sunshine in the air as it warmed the damp earth.

Mallory patted the little one on the shoulder as if to convey it was all right, then lifted her eyes to Cal with a question in them, perhaps not wanting to undermine him. He nodded.

"I meant, yes, Miss Mallory." Lily dipped her head as she escaped to the other room for more flatware.

"Back to your proposal. . .well, I mean. . ." Mallory glanced away.

Her cheeks reddened, only heightening their pretty color. Was she actually embarrassed by her word choice? Thought he'd assume her too forward?

"About our outing, yes. I thought if Henry and Jane would be willing to watch in case we had tourists come by the lighthouse, we could take a picnic to the park tomorrow afternoon after church. I'm sure Lily would love to play on the beach. You could take your paints."

He'd watched as she'd drawn with charcoal the night before while he read aloud to all of them, how she'd touched the cakes of pigment and picked up each brush before she rearranged them in the box. She'd not taken any time for herself to paint since she'd taken on Aunt Ada's work, yet this activity seemed to be the key to opening her up to her past again. As much as she longed to learn of her past, he yearned for her to know it too. Knowing her true identity would be best for all of them. But as soon as she knew who she was, she might leave. Already her smile, her kindness, and her way with Lily had gripped his heart in such a way that her absence would leave a hole there. But if she did belong to someone else, then wasn't the sooner they both knew that the better?

Chapter 7

As she thought of the next day's possibilities, the taste of hope filled Mallory, even as the bite of chocolate cake spread over her tongue with bitter sweetness. Each time she painted, it was like her heart lifted as the seagulls above her on the breeze, soaking in the azure of the sky. The rhythm of the waves against the shore sang words of comfort, and the colors on the paper took shape in almost miraculous ways before her eyes. Like she was meant to do this. Every. Day. Plus, the prospect of spending an afternoon with Cal and Lily cheered her.

"I would love that. Shall I fry up some chicken for the picnic?" She took another forkful, disappointed the cake wasn't quite as light as she hoped. The frosting, at least, had turned out well.

"This is so good." Lily had almost as much cake around her mouth as in it.

"Slow down or you'll get a tummy ache." Mallory chuckled. "Someone—maybe it was my mother—said that to me when I was little."

Cal's eyebrows went up. "Really?"

She nodded. "Occasionally I have these flashes of memory, like I've heard something said before, but I can't quite remember a voice or a face."

"I wish I could remember my mama." Lily stole a look at her father.

"I'm sorry you both have that in common." He finished the last of his slice of cake and leaned back in his chair, lacing his hands behind his neck. "Please don't go to any trouble for the picnic tomorrow. I want this to be enjoyable for you as well." Cal grinned at her, and she couldn't tear away her gaze.

"There is some cold ham left in the icebox, and the bread is fresh. Would sandwiches be all right with you?"

Cal winked. "Nothing could sound better."

Lily licked her fork in a most unladylike manner. "Can we take some of Aunt Ada's spiced peaches and some chocolate cake too?"

Cal wiped his daughter's mouth with a napkin. "It's 'may we,' and I believe you need to remember the manners your aunt Ada has taught you." His large hand engulfed the child's chin, yet he was as gentle as a butterfly alighting a flower.

"I wish I could take your aunt some cake. Perhaps the doctor wouldn't mind if I took her a thin slice. I would like her opinion, and I could take her some applesauce too." Mallory spoke more to herself than anyone else in the room.

Lily tugged on her sleeve. "I'll help you."

"I think Miss Mallory has had enough of your help for one day. Why don't you help me now? We'll make the rounds of the lighthouse and check on things together."

"All right. I mean, yes, Papa." Lily sat up straight and batted her eyelashes at him.

Mallory rose from the table to look for a clean plate for Aunt Ada. The days were becoming routine for her. What if there was nobody who cared enough to look for her? While the thought troubled her, being in the lighthouse was like being set in the cleft of a rock during a storm. She was protected for as long as she was there. How she looked forward to their picnic tomorrow. She wasn't going to let worry about the past spoil the time for her.

The next afternoon, Cal hauled Mallory's easel in one hand and the picnic basket in the other. He slid a glance toward her as she walked beside him with Lily's hand clasped in hers. *Why am I doing this?* A vulture of unease sat on his shoulder. The woman could be spoken for, married, have a family already. Spending time with her like this would only give them both pain once her husband came for her. The only thought that comforted him was her lack of a wedding band. Still, it was possible she'd lost it in the shipwreck.

Mallory lifted her face to the sun and peeked out from under the floppy straw hat she'd borrowed from Aunt Ada. Its golden glow bathed her china-like skin, kissing her cheeks and nose with pink. The most charming freckles had sprinkled her nose since she'd come to lodge at the lighthouse. Cal held tightly to the easel, though he wished it would be proper for him to take her arm and escort her as though he were courting her.

Lily's giggle interrupted his thoughts as she ran ahead and called over her shoulder. "You can't catch me, Miss Mallory. I'm going to find the best spot first."

Mallory started off in a sprint, and Lily ran faster and tumbled into the sand.

"Oh my!" Mallory ran to help Lily up. "Are you all right, sweetheart?"

"I'm fine." They both brushed the sand off her pinafore.

"Let's not get your Sunday clothes too messy." Cal wagged a finger at his mischievous daughter. "And I don't want you playing too near the water. It's still awfully cold, and you're not a very good swimmer yet."

They found Lily's favorite spot, near the water yet with a bit of shade to protect them from the sun.

Mallory stared out over the lake. "How can you continually live in this much beauty and not have your heart burst with joy every day?"

Cal let out a sigh, sounding as weary as an old man teetering with a cane. "Beauty, yes, but tragedy too. Sometimes man is no match for the elements." He paused. "And there is a limit to what I can do but for the grace of God, like finding you in time."

"I guess I hadn't thought of it that way." She lost her smile, and her outspread arms dropped to her sides.

"Don't let me discourage you. It's good for you to remind me of the beauty I take for granted." He went about setting up the easel for her.

Mallory stooped, somehow with grace, and stretched a blanket out on the ground. Once the basket was set down, she opened it and spread their little feast on top of the blanket. She unwrapped a sandwich for each of them and put them on the plates. Though clothed in a faded green dress from the church box, an elegance emanated from her. She was like a shiny diamond in a scratched gold setting. Her trials only polished away the dirt so that her quiet beauty shone through.

His pulse beat a little faster as their hands touched when she handed him the plate. "Thank you." He swallowed. He had to control these runaway thoughts.

Cal called Lily and said the blessing over the food. They all grew quiet as they munched away.

"What are you going to paint? You paint out here a lot." Lily spoke through the food in her mouth.

"Don't talk with your mouth full." Cal shook his head.

"Oops." Lily covered her mouth with a napkin.

"I think today I might paint a view of Mackinac Island." Mallory grinned at her. "Why? What do you think I should paint?"

"Me and Papa!" Lily sat with her legs crossed and took a sip from the cup of milk Mallory had poured for her.

"Hmm...I hadn't thought of that. It might take me too long." She smoothed her skirt over her legs, which were tucked under her to the side.

"What do you mean?" Lily stood, upsetting her cup. "Uh-oh." She placed a hand over her mouth.

Cal and Mallory grabbed at napkins to wipe the spill. Much of it had gone over the edge of the blanket, into the sand. As they both went to blot it up, they nearly collided. The back of her hand grazed his. Then Mallory lost her balance and he reached out to catch her. Her soft form collapsed into his arms until she stiffened and righted herself. But for a moment her warmth overwhelmed him as though he were ensconced in his favorite chair near the hearth on a winter evening. Yet at the same time her touch was like a lightning bolt to his soul, bringing alive all his senses. Cal was the one who needed rescuing from the sweet scent of her hair, the softness of her skin, the allure of her caramel eyes.

"Are you all right?" He still held to one of her hands. She pulled it away.

"I'm sorry. I'll be fine." Mallory stood, flustered. She patted her hair, straightened her skirt, and turned to her easel. She took her paints out of their storage. She dabbed her brush in the water and in the blue paint, spreading the wash over the paper she'd tacked to the board.

Lily pulled on Mallory's skirt. "You still didn't tell me why it would take too long."

"Well, portraiture requires some study." Mallory flashed a glance back at Cal.

He scrubbed his hand over the bottom half of his face. His chest tightened. He should probably tell his daughter the truth of it. "Mallory's family may come for her, Lily. It could happen any day. She might not have much time to draw us properly and then paint our picture." He stood, moving toward the little girl.

"But if she had a mama, she would of found her by now. Don't you want to stay with our family, Miss Mallory?" Lily crossed her arms.

Mallory put her brush down and stooped to Lily's level. "I have loved being here, Lily, but someone might be missing me, and I just can't remember them right now. Things might change. Perhaps my memory would come back if I knew who they were. But I'll never forget you. You'll always be in my heart." She pulled the little one into a hug, and Cal's throat constricted at the thought of Mallory leaving.

When Lily pulled away, she wiped her eyes, kicked off her shoes, and ran down to the shore again. Mallory bit her lower lip. She didn't want to look up at Cal and let him see how hard this was for her. It was better if she didn't get too attached to them and for them not to get too attached to her. Yet, she felt like her heart had been knit to both of theirs as tightly as the knitting stitches Aunt Ada had shown her, strands of wool looped together to make a mitten or a sock.

When she finally lifted her eyes to his gaze, he opened his mouth for a moment then closed it again before he spoke. "It's best she knows the truth. You've been awfully patient. She's gotten attached, but she should know. . ." He trailed off.

"I'm sorry for any upset I've caused. Your family is so easy to lo—care for." Could she really love him, when she didn't even know who she was?

"Mallory, I—we—wanted you here to recover." Cal closed the distance between them and grasped her hands in his.

"But it's not a long-term solution." She wanted to pull away again, but his blue eyes were like a powerful magnet, drawing her in with his sympathetic gaze, not of pity, but of concern.

He placed both of her hands in his left hand and reached up with his right, touching her cheek. His calloused fingers alighted there for a second or two before he grasped under her chin and drew her face close. She should have pulled away, but instead let his lips graze her forehead and then allowed him to draw her into his embrace. His warm chest against her cheek, his heart thudding strong and even. A tortured sigh escaped his lips.

"I wish I could paint you both and take the picture with me forever." And while her hands rested on his shirt in response, she longed to hug him back. "We both know this can't work, Cal." She pushed away.

"Look at me!" Lily called from the large stone she stood on at the water's edge. She balanced on one foot. Her pink cardigan sweater was open and flapping in the breeze.

The little girl teetered and gave them a grin that said she was quite satisfied with herself.

"Young lady, I told you not to play so close to the water!" Cal released Mallory and turned to jog toward his child.

Mallory gasped and wrung her hands. She followed right on his heels, then cupped her hands around her mouth to be heard over the waves. "Lily, be careful!"

Lily giggled. "Look, now I'll do the other foot!" But as soon as she changed to stand on the other foot, she lost her balance.

Her father ran faster, his feet no match for the shifting sands beneath them.

"Ahh!" The little girl squeaked out her cry as she slipped into the water, just beyond Cal's grasp.

Chapter 8

The spirited little girl came up from the shallow water, sputtering and coughing. "Ow." Blood trickled over her palm. "It hurts." Lily sobbed as Cal picked tiny stones from the gash.

Frigid water seeped over his shoes and onto his pant legs as he reached down and pulled her up in a strong swoop. "I told you to be more careful." Cal's voice was tinged with annoyance as he examined the cut and then held her close.

Mallory retrieved the blanket they'd picnicked on and took it to wrap around the little one. "We don't want you to get sick now, sweetie." She pressed a napkin over the little girl's hand.

Lily reached from Cal's hold down to Mallory, and his eyebrows shot up as she gathered the child into her arms and held her drenched head against her shoulder.

"Will you take care of me, Miss Mallory?"

Mallory swallowed. "Of course. We need to get you dry and have some nice tea with honey. I don't want you to catch a cold." She nuzzled the child's head. In another time, another place, perhaps she could have been Lily's mother, but Cal Waterson was an honorable man. She couldn't take advantage of his kindness forever. This wasn't fair to any of them.

A strong breeze brushed her skin as Lily shivered in her arms. Clouds scudded in overhead as though to ambush them. Rain started its wayward sprinkle like tears wetting her back.

"You go on. Take Lily to the house. I'll get everything else." Cal waved her away, and Mallory quickened her steps toward the distant castle on the Straits of Mackinac while drops pelted her ever faster.

She tightened her grip on Lily as lightning streaked the sky, seeming to punctuate the uncertainty she felt about her future. *Father, please keep us safe in the storm.*

Dusk darkened the sky from the steel gray of thunderheads to the inky darkness of night. Once Mallory settled a dried Lily, with a change of clothes, under a quilt by the fire, she went up to help Aunt Ada get ready to come downstairs after her nap.

"I see your picnic was ruined. Dear me. I was afraid you'd all catch your death out there when the storm came through."

"I think we'll be fine. How is your foot feeling?"

Aunt Ada grimaced as she used a shoehorn to help slide her foot into her shoe. "Still a little tender, but much better. I just won't fasten my shoes all the way up."

"Aunt Ada, I am concerned about something." Mallory allowed the older woman to lean on her for support as she rose from the bed.

"What is it, child?" Aunt Ada motioned for her cane.

"Lily is a treasure." Mallory paused. "But I'm concerned she is becoming too attached to me."

Aunt Ada reached for her cheek. "And you to her?"

Mallory nodded.

"And what of my nephew?"

Mallory's face grew warm under Aunt Ada's accusing gaze.

"I can't deny how much I admire him. He is a good man. . . . He saved my life." She reached for Aunt Ada's cane, which was hooked on a corner of the dresser.

Aunt Ada leaned on her cane and took a deep breath. "You have been a balm to their souls. My nephew would never admit how lonely he's been since his wife's passing. She died shortly after childbirth, so Lily has never had a mother. And I've enjoyed your company. In fact, I don't know what I would have done without you these last couple of weeks as I've been recuperating."

"But I know I don't really belong here. We don't know who I really am or where I truly came from." Mallory wrung her hands.

Aunt Ada pointed a finger at Mallory's chest. "We do know who you are by how you behave. You have a good heart, one renewed by the Savior, I'll wager." She turned toward the door, and Mallory offered her arm to her. "I can't say I haven't feared that this would happen though. Hoped and feared. I'm praying that once you get your memory back, you'll still be able to continue your acquaintance with all of us." The older woman's eyes twinkled.

"I'm not sure Cal feels the same way, and I don't want to hurt either of them."

Aunt Ada clucked her tongue. "He's probably working on the foghorn right now. Take a lantern and some hot cocoa with you. Maybe you two should have a talk."

Cal wiped the grease from his hands and took the steaming mug Mallory offered him. She'd left the door open behind her and the eerie light of storm clouds cast shadows, making the foghorn engine loom like a crooked beast. Mallory's face was waxen in the odd lantern light. The oilskin coat she wore dripped into growing puddles on the hard-packed earthen floor. *Plink, plink.*

"Thank you." He shifted his weight from one foot to the other.

"I best be getting back to Aunt Ada and Lily. They'll need supper." She graced him with half a smile.

"Wait. I was surprised Lily preferred that you carry her, and I apologize for not thanking you for taking care of her the way you did. I hope I didn't seem rude."

"No, but I thought we should. . ."

"And I'm sorry for acting inappropriately on the beach." While thunder rumbled outside, Cal's heart was crumbling like chalky stone under pressure. He knew the truth. Whatever her past was could change everything.

"No, please. . ." Mallory's lovely mouth formed words, but nothing more came out. Her eyes, shining with tears, pleaded with him.

"Mallory, what if you are married? Or betrothed? I still haven't heard the report from the investigators who work for the steamship company."

"You're right of course. Good night, Cal. By the time you come in, I'll be upstairs, I'm sure." She backed away, swinging the lantern. Her head hung as she brought her hood back up. Like a ghostly apparition, she glided through the door, closing it behind her.

"Good night!" He threw a wrench across the room. It hit a pipe and thudded to the floor unceremoniously. Its echo didn't last long in the cool building. Only the clank of machinery sounded as it chugged to life like the unbidden stirrings of his heart.

Chapter 9

It drizzled until dinnertime the next day. The distant quiet swept between them like a cold draft every time he caught her glancing at him.

A knock on the door interrupted the silence. Likely another tourist curious about the inner workings of the lighthouse. Cal snapped open his pocket watch. It was getting a tad late for such a visit. He ambled toward the door and pulled it open. "Yes?"

"Good evening, are you the lighthouse keeper?" A medium-height man with dark eyes, curly black hair, and a heavily waxed mustache stood before him. He removed his derby hat and gave a nervous shrug under his matching gray tweed suit. Something about the gentleman reminded Cal of a jittery hare. He suppressed a grin.

"I am. How may I help you?"

"I'm looking for a young woman by the name of Natalie Brooks."

"There's nobody here by that name." *Unless. . .* Cal's mouth dried.

"Please, if you could bear with me for a moment, sir, I'm looking for someone who is purported to be the only survivor of the wreck of the *Mallory*."

"I see. And who might you be?" Cal leaned forward a bit, resting more weight on his left leg. He couldn't give out information to just any stranger.

The man's Adam's apple bobbed. "You see, I'm Grover Harrison, and I'm most anxious to find my fiancée. They told me in town, at the general store, that I might find a girl who washed up on shore when the *Mallory* sank. Of course, I also heard she has amnesia." He twisted the brim of his hat.

"Pardon me?" Cold dread snaked down Cal's back. He gripped the door with his trembling left hand and leaned forward some more. "Do you have any *proof* of this, Mr. Harrison?"

The man shoved a hand through his thick, dark hair and shuffled his feet a little. Then he gave a dry laugh. "Yes, of course, you would expect that. What was I thinking? She's of a petite build, but not too short, dark hair, brownish eyes."

Cal narrowed his gaze at Mr. Harrison. Her eyes were like warm caramel and her hair a dark chestnut, prettier than the mane on any horse. How could the man claim to know her and not notice those things?

"Yes, you heard right about the amnesia." Cal crossed his arms and steadied his

319

bulk against the doorframe. He both towered over Harrison and blocked the doorway. "There was one word she remembered from the accident—Mallory—and she goes by that name now."

How could he stall? "Is there anything else you could tell me for proof of who you're looking for?"

"She is quite an artist, but I don't know if you've seen that." He shrugged.

A distant golden orange on the horizon signaled the encroaching night. The waves rolled in, a seething foam after the storm like ever-encroaching truth. His gut tightened. Would Mallory be glad someone claimed her? Or would it unsettle her new routine, the contentedness she seemed to display? Yes, Cal could lie to himself. Of course she would be happy to see a man from her past, especially someone who likely cared for her.

But deep down he knew the lighthouse was a beacon, not just for ships to find their way, but also for those who found their way to its door. He and Aunt Ada had discussed it many times. They were there to tell not just the lighthouse's story but the story of the one true Light. And because of that, Cal knew his role was not only to protect Mallory and his family but also to extend Christ's love.

He extended his right hand. "That she is. I'm Cal Waterson, head lighthouse keeper here at Old Mackinac Point Lighthouse."

Harrison nodded and gave his hand a tentative shake. Not impressive at all. "Pleased to meet you, Mr. Waterson."

"Cal is fine."

"Grover is fine as well."

"Please come in and have a seat in the sitting room. I believe Mallory—or perhaps Natalie—is upstairs with my daughter. I'll fetch her." Cal led Grover around the corner and into the hallway and pointed to the settee. How was he going to break this to Mallory? It was a lot for him to take in, let alone for her. Then again, Grover may find that the young woman wasn't his Natalie at all.

The visitor parked himself in one of the chairs flanking the settee, looking uneasy. He wiped beads of sweat from his brow with a handkerchief from his breast pocket.

"Perhaps you'd like some iced tea. I believe we have some in the icebox." Cal gave the man a wooden smile.

The visitor stood again and turned on his heel to pace. "You must understand, I've traveled quite a long way to find her."

"You can't catch me, Miss Mallory." Lily's giggles followed as her voice drifted closer.

"Oh yes I can." Mallory laughed, and their footsteps pounded down the stairs. "Slow down, now, Lily. No running in the house."

It was all happening much too fast for Cal. Lily appeared in the doorway.

"Hello." She waved at their guest. Her face was flushed with exertion and her blond hair curled in wisps around her face as she ran to hug Cal around the waist. "I came down to say good night, Papa."

"We have company, Miss Mallory."

"Oh, so we do." Mallory stopped short before entering the room all the way.

A nice-looking, well-dressed gentleman stood across the room. His dark eyes looked her over like a starving man taking in a buffet. Warmth crept over her neck and face. Who was he to gaze upon her so boldly?

"Natalie." Though his voice was barely above a whisper, it spoke volumes as to the incredulity he felt at seeing her. Whoever he was. And why did he call her Natalie? Could it really be...someone she once knew? She looked to Cal.

"Mr. Harrison here..." Cal stopped as though he couldn't find the right words. "Grover, to be exact. He says he knows you. He's been looking for you. I was just coming to tell you." Cal averted his gaze. Had she detected a hint of pain? One of his hands curled into a fist, the other went to rub his neck.

"My darling girl, I thought I'd never find you!" Mr. Harrison stepped forward and reached out as though to embrace her, then seemed to think better of it and dropped his arms to his sides when she stepped back and crossed hers. She closed her eyes, tightening her lids. Images danced through her mind. That man she'd seen in the memory of a picnic with friends. He had dark wavy hair and a mustache. Could this be the same person? Her heart palpitated. *Natalie.* And suddenly that name spoke softly to her heart like it fit, like a puzzle piece that had been missing.

"I'm Natalie?"

"Natalie Brooks, to be exact." Mr. Harrison's stance relaxed as he smiled. He reached out his hand this time and she took it. He gave her hand a gentle squeeze and bowed to kiss it before he let her go. What was the cause for this familiarity?

Cal interrupted the silence. "Let me get that iced tea for us."

Please don't leave me alone with this stranger, she pleaded with her eyes, but he looked away. Again. She reached out to Lily, who readily came to her side.

"Miss Natalie is a pretty name." Lily stared up at her with trusting eyes as though nothing had changed. Dear child. She took Natalie's hand and held it against her soft cheek.

"How do I know you, sir?" Her stomach became a leaden knot of apprehension.

"Maybe he's your brother," Lily piped up with a cheerful lilt to her voice.

"Goodness, no." Mr. Harrison chuckled. "I'm your fiancé."

Natalie's mouth fell agape at the news. She inched toward a chair and sat down. Lily leaned against her, and Natalie pulled her onto her lap. As though holding to an anchor, she hugged the precious little girl tight. *Lord, what shall I say?*

"I'm so sorry, Natalie. I didn't mean to frighten you. You don't remember me at all?" He came and knelt by her chair.

"I've had flashes of memory of a man who looked something like you. But I don't remember you. I'm sorry, sir."

"Don't worry, we'll get to know one another again. I'll be patient. You'll see. I'm just so happy to have found you. And enough of calling me 'sir.' I'm your Grover, darling. Why, we were childhood sweethearts. I've loved you for many years." He patted her arm, but the dullness of his furtive gaze seemed insincere.

She dizzied. Her gut tightened as visions burst into her head. *People laughing and clinking glasses, everyone saying, "Congratulations." That young man again, coming toward her, smiling and taking her hand. Natalie looked up and felt. . . What did she feel?*

The rattle of glasses on a tray sounded in the hallway, bringing her back to the present, and Cal came in, looking awkward with the tray Aunt Ada handled with ease. Natalie supposed now Ada would never truly be an aunt to her.

Grover moved away as Cal came around the corner. The lighthouse keeper sent a chilling glare toward the stranger. She had to smile to herself. The visitor stepped back and went to the opposite chair.

"We could all use a little refreshment, though I apologize my aunt has retired early and is not here to serve us, as she does a much more gracious job of it." He plunked the tray on the table and some of the light amber liquid sloshed out. Cal mopped it up with a napkin before handing first Natalie a glass, then one to Mr. Harrison, and then sitting between them.

Natalie gave Lily a quick kiss on her sweaty hair, breathing in the scent of the child as though she were her own. "Lily, why don't you go finish getting ready for bed and I'll come up to read to you in a little while."

"Aww, do I have to?" Lily stuck out her bottom lip.

"No sassing, Miss Mall—Miss Natalie. Go on with you." The stern reprimand from Cal sent Lily toward the stairs with head hanging low.

Natalie exchanged a glance with Cal, catching the slight knowing smile in his eyes. She could sense Mr. Harrison's eyes upon her with a strange intensity of feeling, as though he were boring into her soul. A frown passed across his face as he looked from her to Cal.

The visitor cleared his throat. "It's been very kind of you to take care of Natalie the way you have, Cal, but I'm here now." He sat straighter.

"The Watersons have been nothing but gracious. At the moment you are a virtual stranger to me, Mr. Harrison."

"And you two have been here only with the child?" Mr. Harrison's eyebrows shot up.

Natalie bristled at his insinuation. How dare he imply that anything unseemly had occurred between Cal and her! "But nothing—"

Cal put up a hand to stop her. "I assure you, my aunt Ada has been here the whole time. She retired early this evening because she's been unwell. Besides, my assistant and his family live in their quarters next door, and we have a steady stream of visitors. I take the care of anyone staying in my home seriously. Miss Brooks's reputation is intact."

"You can be sure I will find a way to make accommodations more suitable to your station as soon as possible, Natalie. While these folks have been very kind, this situation isn't totally proper."

"I'm sorry, but until I remember who you are, I'm not going anywhere with you. And these accommodations have been more than adequate, sir." Natalie clanked her iced tea glass onto the tray, bolted from her chair, and marched to the hallway. "Cal, I'll check on Aunt Ada before I retire." Who did this Grover person think he was anyway? Her stomach churned at the thought of marrying a stranger.

After checking on Aunt Ada, who was sleeping soundly, Natalie tucked Lily into bed and read the promised story to her. Then she sank into bed in the guest room, which had become her sanctuary. She turned down the lantern she'd set on the table next to the bed. Soft moonlight cast blurring shadows in the chamber. She nestled in the sheets that smelled of the lake and grass, the spring breeze and sunshine, the lighthouse and the paint on its walls.

How she would have loved to talk to Aunt Ada of this stranger who'd come to claim her. *Natalie* sounded similar to *Mallory*. Was that why she'd so easily chosen the substitute name? The present was all she had. Did she want to be this other person again? At least her affection toward Cal had not been a sin against a husband. But she'd been promised to someone else.

Father in heaven, who am I really? Am I this Natalie Brooks? I like who I am in this lighthouse. And the good people I'm with here. She wiped the tears from her face and waited in the quiet of the room.

"You're My child." It wasn't an audible voice; instead, it spoke to her heart. As she closed her eyes, visions of a picnic returned. . .an older man and woman, some younger people. . .laughing. Like a bright light, visions seared her mind, causing her head to ache. She opened her eyes and sat up. Could she be remembering? She closed her eyes again to concentrate.

Her best friend, Chloe, grasped her arm as they walked together. "What do you think of my cousin, Natalie? I'm so glad you finally met him! If you married him, we would be almost like sisters." She giggled. "It would be perfect if you marry Grover. And with your dowry, his parents would be most pleased. They need the money, and you need a husband, don't you?"

"I suppose."

Natalie's stomach had fluttered as she glanced at Chloe's handsome cousin. But the flutter was one of unease. There had been too many expectations. What were they? She reached deeper into her mind. . . .

Chapter 10

"Miss Natalie?" Lily tugged on her nightgown sleeve.

Natalie jumped as though an apparition had appeared. She gasped as she opened her eyes. The little girl appeared as a diminutive angel with her wheat-blond hair, almost white in the moonlight.

"I didn't mean to scare you." Lily rubbed her eyes.

"I'm sure you didn't." Natalie grasped the front of her own nightgown. "What is it now, little one?"

"Can I sleep by you? I had a bad dream." Her luminous eyes shone with fear.

"Of course." She helped the little girl up into the bed and placed an arm around her as they settled. Somehow, the soft cadence of the child's breathing as she fell asleep lulled her into her own peaceful slumber. *I am home.*

As much as the government expected the lighthouse keepers to paint, at least Old Mackinac Point Lighthouse was mostly brick and stone, Cal mused. Still, the porch pillars and railing, as well as the window frames, needed to be done every year. He dipped his brush in the can of white paint. Aunt Ada barely leaned on her cane as she limped toward him. Evidently, she was on a mission.

"Cal, you've been moping around this place since that Harrison fellow first came by." She poked his shoe with her wooden weapon until he turned around to face her.

"I've had a lot on my mind, Aunt Ada. A lot of work to do. What do you expect of me?" He harrumphed.

"You could be more civil." Aunt Ada paused and leaned into her walking stick with her ample frame. "You know it's important for Mallory, I mean, Natalie, to learn about her past. We've been blessed to have her with us, but she has her own people."

"I know." The thought pricked him under his collar like a thorny rosebush. Cal placed his brush across the top of the container and took a kerchief and wiped the sweat dripping down the back of his neck. The sun grew too warm for early May. He couldn't even meet his aunt's accusing gaze. Not that she made him feel guilty, but he didn't want her to see his despair at the thought of Natalie leaving.

"Cal, look at me. You're worse at hiding your feelings than you were when you were a child."

He sighed and glanced up. "I have to get back to work."

"Tell Mallory how you feel before it's too late."

He picked up his paintbrush and turned back to the window. "What do I have to tell her?"

"You know. I'm not putting the words in your mouth. It's not my business."

"No, it's not." He paused. "You want me to tell her to stay with us, and this is what I have to offer, a lighthouse on loan? Mr. Harrison probably has much more to give her. We're from two different worlds. She can't be our Mallory anymore." Judging from the other man's fine clothing, he was of a higher class. Natalie would likely have everything she needed, plus luxuries. Cal could offer her, what? Hard work, sand in her hair, calloused hands, and a lighthouse that belonged to the people. At least he didn't have to listen as Natalie and her beau took a turn by the shore. They were far enough away.

Only the tap of Aunt Ada's cane and her footsteps as she headed to a chair to watch over the couple sounded in his ears.

Grover placed the gift in her hand. "Please, take it."

Natalie blinked at the open velvet box. A lone pearl dangled on a golden chain winking in the sunlight. This was the second time Grover had tried to give it to her.

"Not yet. But thank you."

"Have any more of your memories returned?" His brow furrowed as he snapped the box shut and withdrew the gift.

"They are coming slowly, Grover." Natalie chewed on her lower lip. Gentle waves came toward shore. The delightful feel of warm sand pushed between her toes while grass tickled them.

"Where are your shoes, Natalie? If you need more, I'll buy you twenty pair if you want them." His tone pleaded.

"Don't be silly." She chuckled. "I like the feel of the sand sometimes. It's freeing." With her hand tucked into the curve of Grover's arm, she restrained herself from running down the beach like Lily would.

"Let's go over it again." He stopped and faced her. Lifting a hand to her face, he brushed her cheek and pushed a strand of hair back. It tickled, unlike when Cal had done the same thing and sent a current of warmth through her body. She bristled.

Grover pulled his hand away. Good.

"You were coming to meet some of my family in Harbor Springs. The *Mallory* was a steamship that was bringing you with your chaperone."

"Mrs. Brightworth, yes. I remember. But I'm wondering why my aunt and uncle didn't come as well." The faces of a stern woman and affable gentleman loomed on the edges of her mind, but she couldn't quite recall anything other than an unsettling feeling. She placed a hand on her stomach.

"Are you quite well, Natalie dear?"

"I'm fine, but let's talk about the past." Some of her memories hadn't added up.

Grover sighed and walked with his hands clasped behind his back. "Natalie, don't you remember? I've known you since you were a little girl. I've loved you for a long time."

She stopped and turned toward him. "How? I remember that Chloe introduced us at a picnic one summer not that long ago."

He tried to grab her hand. She pulled it away and crossed her arms.

Grover's smile didn't reach his eyes as his face grew red.

Natalie narrowed her eyes and leveled a gaze at him. "What can you tell me about my parents then?"

"Well, um, I. . . You grew up in Pittsburgh." He tugged at his collar. Then he stood a little straighter. "I'm sorry, but I know you weren't that close to your aunt and uncle. Your uncle went to England on business, and your aunt went with him while you were coming to visit us. I've sent them word. You came to them a few years ago when your parents died. Do you remember that?"

She faltered a little, and Grover took the opportunity to grasp her elbows and steady her. "Yes I do."

A rather dark room. They had just returned to her home after the funeral. Aunt Phoebe and Uncle Bertram didn't know she was just on the other side of the door.

"I'm done raising children, Bertram. I know you want to do right by your brother, but I don't want to adopt her. We have our own sons and their inheritance to think about." The woman's voice was nearly a hiss.

"Yes dear, but she is a sweet thing. It's not her fault her mother died when she was a child and my brother caught a fever. She'll be good company for you."

"But I don't know what to do with a girl. Promise me we can marry her off when she's of age."

Tears made hot trails down her cheeks and she vowed to herself not to be a bother to her aunt. She could take care of herself. She would be an artist someday.

And she had done her best. When there was no one to comfort her when she was sick or lonely, Natalie cried herself to sleep. She prayed as her papa had taught her. At least she'd been given a fine education. Her heart's desire had been to teach children, especially the joy of art and creating beautiful things.

Grover leaned a little closer and whispered in her ear as he caressed her cheek,

"I've always been here for you and always will be. I've waited so long for you to be ready to get married. Don't you remember? That's all you've ever wanted—a house, children, not just your silly drawings."

Natalie stiffened. Her memories flashed through her mind, churning like spokes on a wheel until her head nearly hurt with it all. The puzzle pieces began to fit more snuggly in her mind. She could never love such a man.

The lighthouse loomed like an old guard, a castle of stability to her right. The expanse of where Lakes Michigan and Huron met was spread to her left, like an unknown future, free and vast. *Help me, Lord, with what I must do.*

"I won't marry you, Grover."

"What on earth? We are well-suited to one another. I care for you deeply." He cupped her chin, but she grasped his wrist and flung his hand away.

"No, don't. I don't belong to you. . .or anyone." She stepped back. *My heart longs for someone else.*

"You must have a reason."

"I've remembered. This was an arrangement, Grover. You know that. Your family stood to gain a dowry. I remember now that they're in the lumber business and lost quite a large shipment. And Aunt Phoebe was most anxious to get me out of her house. She never liked me."

"All right, fine. But let me tell you something. You're giving up an opportunity." He stood with a hand on his left hip and wagged the index finger of his right hand in her face, like she was a child. "Your dowry was going to be my contribution to my family, so I could work with my father and make something of myself. We could be rich again. Chloe wanted to introduce us, and I wasn't that keen at first. But you aren't half bad to look at, so I took a chance. Your aunt wanted you to at least marry above your station and not embarrass them. Your father was nothing but a common laborer. Go ahead back to that old woman, Phoebe, who hates you. Or better yet, marry your poor lighthouse keeper."

Grover grasped at her arm to pull her toward him, lowering his face as though to kiss her. "Let me show you the opportunity you're giving up."

Natalie twisted away and slapped him soundly. "I will gladly give up such a dreadful opportunity!" She pivoted and, in a most unladylike fashion, whether upper class or not, ran toward Aunt Ada. Her temples pounded with a hundred memories too hurtful to comprehend.

"What is it, Natalie?" Aunt Ada reached out her arms to her, and Natalie bent to be engulfed by them.

"I won't marry him." And then she spilled her heart to Cal's aunt.

Chapter 11

As limp as a wrung-out dishrag, Natalie sat on the ground and leaned against Aunt Ada's chair. At least Lily was in town with Jane and her boys. She couldn't bear the thought of the little girl seeing her so upset.

"What will you do now?" Ada patted Natalie's hair with gentle strokes.

When was the last time Natalie had felt so loved? She wiped the fresh crop of salt water from her face.

"There, there, child. You may stay here as long as you like." Aunt Ada's voice grew softer than usual.

"But you know I can't." She turned and held fast to this older, wiser woman's hand. "It wouldn't be proper any longer."

Something in Aunt Ada's eyes told Natalie she held something back. "Well then, I should tell you Mrs. Brewster stopped by today. She mentioned that her brother is on the school board in Cheboygan. They're looking for a new schoolmarm."

"Truly?" Natalie felt a stirring of hope. "That's not terribly far away. I could still come and visit. Perhaps I should see what it would entail." The thought of teaching art and having an opportunity to enrich children's lives warmed her.

Cal made long, careful strokes with the paintbrush along the porch post, pretending not to pay attention as Natalie ambled toward him while Aunt Ada enjoyed a few more minutes of the lake air. He glanced up. Her grin unnerved him.

"I suppose you have an announcement to make now that your beau has left."

"It's not what you would expect." She clasped her hands in front of her and barely concealed a grin as she bit her lower lip.

"Your gentleman friend did leave in rather a hurry, but I thought he gave you something first." He glanced sideways at Natalie again, bracing himself for the news.

She took a step closer, putting herself more in his view. "Cal, I'm staying here, at least in the area. Your aunt told me of a schoolmarm position in Cheboygan. Isn't that wonderful?"

Cal wiped his hands on an old towel he'd slung over his shoulder. An eddy of emotions stirred within. So she wasn't planning on keeping her engagement with that Grover fellow. But she wasn't staying at the lighthouse with them either. How *did* he feel? He grunted.

"I see."

"Until then, I plan on earning my keep by assisting you and Aunt Ada as I have been." Her voice was nervous and breathy. Their gazes met, and Natalie's eyes widened, a question mark forming in them. "Would that suit you?"

"I don't see why not." His jaw muscles tightened. So that's how it was. She would be there to help them and then leave. His gut tightened.

"I can never repay you for everything you've done." Natalie dipped her head.

How Cal desired to grasp her shoulders—no—to hold her in an embrace and whisper into her sweet-smelling tresses that she owed them nothing. That having her there had changed him for the better.

Instead he put the brush down and wiped the sweat from his forehead again. "Nonsense, it's part of my job to make sure you are safe."

"I see. Well, it's part of my job to check on preparations for the evening meal. Excuse me." A curt nod followed her clipped tones as she swept past him, head held high. The front door slammed behind her.

"What is wrong with you, Cal?"

He jumped at his aunt's shrill tone, unusual for her. "What do you mean?"

"You know very well." She poked a finger into the chest of his dirty overalls.

He shrugged, averting his gaze.

"That girl is taking a chance by not going home. She might have had a much easier life with Mr. Harrison than here at the lighthouse."

"And she still has a chance to find someone like that." *A better man than I.*

Aunt Ada shook her head, a grimace crossing her face.

"Aunt Ada, you're here to help me raise my daughter, not to run the rest of my life."

Her mouth gaped at his disrespectful tone, and Cal shrank inside, knowing that Aunt Ada's help had meant everything to Lily and him.

"I've never known you to be ungrateful, Cal Waterson." She sniffed and turned on her heel, likely heading for a walk to cool off.

He rubbed his neck, suddenly tight. "I'm sorry." His voice fell flat on the air.

That evening, when Lily heard the news that Natalie would possibly leave, she cried herself to sleep in Cal's arms, inconsolable. The next morning, his little girl poked her spoon around in her oatmeal, not making eye contact with anyone.

"Would you like a bit more brown sugar in your oatmeal, Lily?" Natalie tapped her on the shoulder.

"No thank you." Lily barely looked at Natalie. Not even the bribe of sugar had tempted her.

Cal sat back in his chair and sipped his coffee. Natalie barely slid him a glance long enough for him to smile, to show approval of her attempts to reach out to Lily. Aunt Ada scowled at him over her coffee cup before sighing and getting up to start clearing dishes.

Why was Natalie acting so cold? He'd done his level best to stay neutral and allow her to live her life, even if it meant her moving to Cheboygan. He probably owed Aunt Ada another apology, but mostly he hurt for his little girl.

"Lily," he said, "if Uncle Henry will take over my duties for a while, how about we take a walk to the woods near the McGulpin Point Lighthouse and look for trilliums?" The three-petal white blossom had fascinated Lily since she was a tot. To her they'd appeared as "bright stars on the ground."

"Really, Papa?" She lifted her face to him, hope bright in her eyes.

"Yes, really." He smiled at her.

"Can Miss Natalie come? Please?" Lily's eyes darted from him to Natalie and back.

He met Natalie's questioning gaze. "I think this will be our special time together, just like I usually take you to pick trilliums every spring. Just you and me."

"Your papa has a good idea. Perhaps another time you and I can pick some lilacs together. All right?"

"Yes, Miss Natalie." Lily pulled out the napkin tucked in her dress collar and wiped her mouth. She got down from her chair and went to hug Natalie. "I wish you never had to leave us."

"I haven't left yet, you silly goose." Natalie tapped her on the nose and gave her a grin before she hugged her close. "Besides, I won't be that far away and I can come visit."

"Harrumph." Aunt Ada looked daggers at Cal as though to say he could change the situation if he wanted.

He shrugged in response. "Come on, Lily. Let's get ready for our little adventure."

Lily's chatter as she clung to Cal's hand kept him fixed to the task at hand as they walked through the park surrounding their lighthouse and to the west along the shoreline. He preferred the quiet of tourists enjoying nature to the din of the small town. Sometimes he wished he'd been appointed to the more remote McGulpin Point Lighthouse, but it would be a longer walk to school for his daughter.

"Papa, look, some 'jibwas!" She pulled on his sleeve and pointed.

He shaded his eyes to watch the Indians gliding east in their canoes, probably on their way back to the island. "Yes, and it's pronounced O-jibwa. And pointing isn't polite." Cal tilted his head in her direction.

"Oops, sorry."

Mackinaw City locals rowed small craft in the same direction. Both were likely returning from fishing for smallmouth bass along the shallow area of Waugoshance Point.

With Lily's company, the nearly hour walk seemed to take only minutes. Nobody answered when he knocked on the door of the lighthouse. *How unusual.* "I don't think they'll mind, as they know who we are."

Lily's step was bouncy despite navigating the downward slope of the hill behind the lighthouse. "Come on, Papa." She beckoned to him as she moved ahead. Oh, to have her energy and lightness of foot! He had to grin.

When Cal caught up, the brush ahead of them moved and a doe darted forward. "Shh, Lily. Do you want to see a mama deer? I bet there's more traveling with her."

She nodded. He held her hand again, and they moved forward to where the woods opened into a small clearing, then stopped behind some bushes, waiting. Sun shone through the treetops and white trillium surrounded the trunks of several trees. The floor of the forest flickered with playful leaf shadows dancing across the canvas of the ground in the breeze.

"My star flowers," Lily whispered, her face pink with excitement. She grasped tighter to Cal's fingers.

A doe made her cautious way into the opening, followed by two more, along with two speckled fawns. Lily gasped at the sight and then pinched her lips together to be quiet. Cal nodded his approval.

Their special moment was broken when some bushes on the other side of the clearing parted and a gunstock aimed their way. Time hung like an ominous cloud as gunfire discharged with a deafening blast.

Cal grabbed Lily and pulled her to the ground just in time. A bullet pinged off a tree trunk, just above their heads.

The deer darted from the small meadow, and Cal lifted his head as their hoofbeats grew distant. "Stop, right now!" He shook his fist and stomped into the clearing. Lily trembled, a little to his side and behind him.

A youth shuffled into the open with a rifle in his hands. "I'm sorry. Didn't know anyone else was around." He scratched his head.

"You're lucky you didn't kill someone." Cal set his jaw and balled a fist. "This is the time when city folk come up north to visit. You've got to be more careful. Did you even seek permission to hunt on this land?" Where was the boy's father anyway?

"I'm very sorry, mister. I think I'm done hunting for today." His sheepish expression as he hung his head gave Cal some assurance of a penitent attitude as the boy turned to walk in the opposite direction.

Lily sobbed and clung to his arm. Cal knelt by his sweet child and gathered her into an embrace. He kissed the top of her head. They'd come very close to one of them being shot or dying. Life was so short, like a vapor, as the Bible said. Cal worked long hours, and the sweet moments had gone by so swiftly. It seemed like only a year ago he'd lost Sarah, but it had been more than six years.

His heartbeat sped up as though seconds were ticking away more quickly than possible on his watch. He shook from the middle of his being. He'd almost lost his precious Lily.

"What's wrong, Papa?" She sniffled into his shoulder.

"Thank the good Lord you are safe. I love you dearly, little one."

"I love you too, Papa, and Aunt Ada." She was silent for a moment. "And I love Miss Natalie. Do you love her too, Papa?"

"I'm glad she's come to stay with us." His mouth dried.

"Make her stay, Papa. I want her to be my mama." Her brown eyes, still liquid from her tears of a few minutes earlier, and filled with innocence and truth, begged him.

He could only smile at his little daughter as he drew a clean handkerchief from his pocket and wiped her cheeks. The brevity of life was now as clear to him as the glass that housed the lighthouse lantern. Did he want to let go of the one woman who'd stirred his heart and treated his daughter as her own?

Later in the morning, Natalie sat outside drawing with a shawl around her protecting her from the brisk breeze. Aunt Ada had insisted she take some time for her art. She had turned the wicker chair toward the lighthouse, wanting to remember every bit of ornate brickwork, the curve of the tower, the windows. This beautiful castle on the lake had been a haven like no other for her.

Cal waved at her as he sent Lily into the house. He ran toward her, nearly breathless. Taking his hat off, he got down on one knee.

"What are you doing, Cal Waterson?" She stood and dropped her paper and charcoal with her sudden move.

"Stay with us, Natalie Brooks. Let me court you. . .properly." The words came out raspy as he ventured to engulf her small hand in his larger, stronger ones.

"Is this a joke? Just yesterday you were happy to let me leave." She blinked and tried to pull away, but his hold was firm.

"No, never." His blue eyes were filled with an ardor he'd not allowed her to see before. His sincerity was plain to her with the set of his jaw, the intensity of his gaze.

"But Cheboygan still needs a teacher." She wasn't sure why she was testing Cal, though she was a little frightened by his sudden shift in plans.

"Lily needs a mother." He stood and cupped her chin while drawing her closer with his other arm around her waist. "But more importantly, I need a wife. And after what happened to me this morning, I believe life is too brief and precious to put off things like love. . .and marriage."

Natalie lifted her face. Cal's lips met hers with a tender fusing of life and hope. He slipped his hand behind her neck, entangling his fingers in her hair. Her hands rose, touching the front of his shirt and feeling the strong beat of his heart within his chest.

She pulled away to catch her breath. "Then, yes, I will let you court me properly, as long as Aunt Ada is our chaperone."

The door to the lighthouse banged shut and Lily came running toward them. "I think we will have two chaperones for the price of one." He grinned and sealed their agreement with a kiss on Natalie's forehead.

Epilogue

Six months later

I now pronounce you man and wife. You may kiss the bride." The minister gave the decree, looking over the top of his reading glasses at them.

Natalie's face grew warm as Cal lifted the ivory lace veil away from her face. This was the second time for him. Would she measure up? His arms encircled her waist as he tugged her closer. His lips met hers with tenderness, only to trail across her cheek as he whispered into her ear.

"My love for you grows deeper every day, Natalie."

"And mine for you, Cal." A sense of peace calmed her fluttering heart.

Lily's little body pushed in between them. Natalie pulled back and giggled. Lily, now her daughter, searched her gaze with her own trusting one. "Papa said I would only get a new mother if the Great Lakes coughed her up, so I prayed the lakes would, and they did."

"I'm so very thankful you did, or your papa might not have been there to save my life." Natalie reached down to caress Lily's cheek. "And I'm so very glad to be your mama."

"We both needed you." Cal smiled like a lovesick schoolboy. Her heart pattered, and she returned his pleased expression with one of her own.

Her new husband lifted Lily into one of his arms and crooked his other elbow for Natalie to grasp before they ambled down the aisle toward the back of the church. She'd come to them not knowing anything about her past or even who she was. But none of that mattered now. Her heart had led her to her future and where she truly belonged.

Kathleen Rouser has loved making up stories since she was a little girl, a passion she believes God put on her heart from an early age. She desires to create characters who resonate with readers and realize the need for a transforming Savior in their everyday lives. A former homeschool instructor and mild-mannered dental assistant, she lives in Michigan with her hero and husband of thirty-six years, Jack, who has not only listened to her stories, but also sometimes cooks for her. Since having an empty nest, a sassy gray tabby cat managed to find herself a nice little life in the Rousers' home. Kathleen enjoys making jewelry, walking, and knitting in her spare time.

The Disappearing Ship

by Lena Nelson Dooley

Dedication

This book is dedicated to my coauthors in this collection: Rebecca Jepson, Carrie Fancett Pagels, Candice Sue Patterson, Kathleen Rouser, Pegg Thomas, and Marilyn Turk. They were very helpful while I did the research for my story. I learned way more about historical Michigan and Lake Superior than I could put in this book. I'm very happy to share shelf space with you.

And every book I write is dedicated to the love of my life, James Dooley. This godly man and I have shared more than fifty-four years together. James, I wouldn't be who I am today without your love, encouragement, and support. Every day with you is a special gift from God to my heart.

Chapter 1

Upper Michigan
Early Summer, 1902

Defeated.

The word drummed through Norma Kimbell's head as she gazed out at the pine forest rushing by the window in a blur. Riding the train always felt as if life were passing her by without noticing her. Despondency clung to her, weighing her down like the heavy woolen robe packed in her trunk in the baggage car did in the long winter months. Sometimes days went by without seeing even a peek of the sun.

That's what she needed right now, to know the sun was shining on her. But how could she believe it? Papa had encouraged her to follow her heart, and she did. Now she had failed at the only thing she ever wanted to do with her life.

After Papa died, she'd spent several years living at the Whitefish Point lighthouse station with her uncle and aunt. Because of her inheritance, she'd been able to pursue her dreams. Dreams of being a doctor. She knew it would be hard, but some medical schools accepted a woman or two, and she'd enrolled.

When she graduated at the top of her class, Uncle Charles contacted a friend who was a doctor in a needy area of Chicago. He'd agreed she could be a part of his practice. After all, he'd needed all the help he could get. But now she was returning to Whitefish Point a complete failure.

Tears filled her eyes, blurring the landscape even more, like one of those impressionist paintings she'd seen in the museum she often visited on her one day off per week. Before she could control them, they leaked down her cheeks. She grabbed a hankie from her lady's carpetbag and dabbed at her eyes, trying to stem the flow.

"Are you all right, miss?" The conductor's gentle bass voice interrupted her thoughts.

She glanced up and gave him a quick nod. "I'm fine." At least her words hadn't trembled or revealed just how much she wasn't "all right."

After lingering a moment, the man headed farther down the railroad car, checking on other passengers. Norma was so glad the train wasn't crowded. She wanted to sit as far away from other people as possible. She wouldn't have been able to carry on a conversation without sobbing. Being by herself was better.

As the train began to slow when they reached the outskirts of Sault Ste. Marie,

Norma grabbed another hankie and mopped up the rest of the mess from her face. She took a deep breath. Soon they would pull into the railway station. She faced many more miles before she'd reach the Whitefish Point Lighthouse and feel her aunt's arms around her. Right now, she needed that hug so much.

But she dreaded seeing Uncle Charles and the disappointment in his eyes. She'd done her best. Her failure wasn't her fault. None of the patients wanted a female doctor treating them. She could understand men feeling that way. *But the women?* Why didn't they want her? Much medical treatment dealt with intimate exploration of the patient's body. She would much rather have a woman examine her, but not a single one of the women who came to the clinic wanted to be seen by her. She was just a glorified nurse for the physician. She knew it wasn't his fault either. Female doctors all over the country were facing the same situation. She'd heard of a few physicians out in the far West, where male doctors were scarce, who experienced success. If someone needed medical help and the only one close enough to reach was a woman, they used her. Maybe she should have gone west instead of staying in Chicago.

As the train pulled into the station, she picked up her handbag and her black, barely used medical bag from the seat beside her. She wanted to be near the baggage car to make sure her trunks were unloaded. She'd need to find some way to reach Whitefish Point from here. She'd have to take a coach or wagon along the coast of Lake Superior to Shelldrake, or even a packet boat, then find a way to cover the last six miles to the lighthouse.

Still with so far to travel, she was already worn out. Maybe she'd stay in a hotel in Sault Ste. Marie tonight and find transportation early tomorrow morning. She headed down the platform and waited for her trunks.

Drake Logan sat slumped over his desk, checking the numbers from yesterday. They had an accountant who did most of the financial work, but he liked to check the columns himself to make sure they tallied. A knock sounded on the door.

"Come in." He leaned back in his chair and glanced up to watch his assistant, Henry Jones, enter.

"I hate to bother you, but we've received a telegram, and I thought you should see it right away." The man hurried across the cramped office and thrust the opened missive at him.

He glanced at the bottom to see who sent it. Mr. Henderson, the sawmill manager at Shelldrake.

SHIPMENT HASN'T ARRIVED *Stop* WHEN CAN WE EXPECT IT *Stop* NEED IMMEDIATELY *Stop*

Drake frowned at Henry. "This doesn't make any sense. That ship should have been there, unloaded at the sawmill, then gone on to the copper mine to pick up a load. I'm expecting it back here today or tomorrow. I don't have a good feeling about this." He waved Henry back to his desk in the front office.

Drake's father had gone to Detroit to meet with a new client and wouldn't be back for a few days. So he was on his own for this one.

How can I find out where this ship is?

He couldn't. Good thing he wasn't really on his own. Clasping his hands and bowing his head, he voiced an earnest prayer for God's intervention in his life today. "Lord." He felt the prayer ascend beyond the ceiling. "I need Your wisdom. Guide me in the direction where I can find answers."

He couldn't sit still. With his hands behind his back, he paced between his window and the desk. At the window, he glanced at the harbor. Not a single Logan ship in sight.

He heard the bell over the front door ring. Before he could reach the door connecting the two offices, Henry came back to Drake's office.

"A strange day, Mr. Logan." His assistant held an unopened telegram this time. "Here's another one."

After handing it to Drake, he went back to his own desk.

Drake ripped open the envelope.

AMELIA WRECKED *Stop* LOST IN GRAVEYARD OF GREAT LAKES WHITE-FISH POINT *Stop* ONLY SURVIVOR *Stop*

No name was attached to the message. Who was the only survivor, and where could he be?

Drake continued to pace for another half hour, plans formulating in his brain. The only thing he could do was go to the Whitefish Point lighthouse station. Surely they kept records of each shipwreck. He could search for anything that might be left of the missing Logan Steamship Line vessel.

He hurried into Henry's office. "You're going to have to hold down the fort. The *Amelia Logan* has wrecked. I'm going to see if I can find anything to salvage."

No one but he and the owner of the sawmill knew the ship carried a load of gold coins for the mill's payroll. They kept it quiet so no one would try to rob the ship somewhere along the way. The gold was in bags hidden inside a barrel of flour.

Drake needed to find the barrel with his initials carved into the side. The loss of the gold could be catastrophic to the company. They had business insurance, but the gold wasn't on the manifest. The insurance probably wouldn't pay for that loss, which was substantial.

Before the day was over, Drake left Chicago on a train heading to Sault Ste. Marie. Tomorrow he'd take the packet boat along the coast of Lake Superior to the sawmill. He had no idea what he'd find there. If Mr. Henderson had no information for him, he'd head on out to Whitefish Point to check with the lighthouse keeper.

Norma was up bright and early to board the packet boat that would take her to Shelldrake. With any luck, she'd arrive in enough time to get a freight wagon or farmer to take her the rest of the way home. She didn't want to leave her luggage unguarded at the coastal town. She didn't know anyone there, and the area had plenty of poor people. She'd seen enough in Chicago to know that desperate people would sometimes resort to stealing to get enough food to feed their families.

She glanced around and noticed a man pacing on deck. Worry wrinkled his brow, and his eyes scanned across the water as if trying to see what was on shore. Then he turned his attention to the open water side of the packet.

She liked watching people and trying to figure out what was going on with them. This man was an easy read. He had to be really concerned about something important. She hoped he wasn't carrying as heavy a burden as she was. Her life was a mess, and her bright future had dimmed. She tried in vain to put together an explanation for Uncle Charles that would keep him from knowing how hurt she was.

Even though her news wouldn't please her uncle, she looked forward to feeling her aunt's warm hug. Auntie never seemed disappointed with Norma, no matter what happened. Her aunt was the closest thing to a mother Norma had had these last few years. Her hugs felt almost as comforting as those her mother had given her when she was younger. The memories filled her eyes with tears.

Norma glanced up when the pacing man stopped beside the ship's railing in front of her. She could tell from the way he stood with his feet wide apart and his arms folded across his chest that he wasn't aware of her nestled in the shadow of the captain's cabin, where the cold breeze off the lake didn't reach.

From her vantage point, she watched him without him seeing her. By the clothes he wore, he must be a man of business. He turned his face straight into the strong breeze that gave his cheeks a ruddy hue. With his hands clenched tight, his muscles rippled, straining against the confines of premium wool.

His eyes seemed to take in everything outside the boat, but not what was on deck behind him. A fine specimen of a man. Norma tore her gaze away from him before someone else on the boat noticed how closely she studied him. For a moment, she whispered a prayer for the man and his problems. The words pushed her wayward thoughts from her mind.

The gleam of puffy white clouds, rimmed with gold from the morning sunshine, hovered over the whitecaps of the waves. So often she didn't even notice the beauty around her. But now, with all her books packed in one of the trunks, she didn't have anything else to occupy her mind. She didn't want to dwell on what she'd find when she arrived back at the lighthouse. She hoped for a resolution for her problem but couldn't imagine what it could be.

When the packet boat docked at Shelldrake, she watched the man head toward the sawmill. He wasn't carrying any luggage, and he didn't wait for anything from the hold. Maybe he was just here for a meeting and would return on the eastbound packet later in the day.

With a strong wind whipping her skirt against her, Norma stood on the dock and watched the sailors unload the hold. Her trunks must be in the very bottom. Clasping her arms across her chest, she tried to keep from shivering. She hadn't expected the wind to be so cold. After all, it was summer.

The piney fragrance of the fresh-sawed lumber permeated the area. She'd always loved that smell.

Finally, both of her trunks sat in the dirt road beside the dock. She didn't want to leave them unprotected, so she called to a young man walking toward her from the center of the small town, where unpainted wooden buildings haphazardly clustered together.

"Sir, do you know where I could get someone to take me out to the Whitefish Point Lighthouse?"

He crossed the road and stopped in front of her. "My uncle has a freight wagon. He's just finished unloading everything. Want me to ask him to come over here?" He stared into her eyes with a questioning look that matched his voice.

She smiled at him, the first smile of her day. "I'd appreciate it."

She sat on one of her trunks and waited for him to return.

The man didn't take long. "What can I do for you, ma'am?"

Even though she'd been a woman for a few years, being called "ma'am" made Norma feel ancient. "I need a ride to the lighthouse"—she waved her hand in the correct direction—"and I have these two trunks."

He studied her and her belongings then quoted what she considered a fair price. In only a few minutes, everything was loaded. The man and his nephew hadn't even complained about how heavy the trunk filled with her books was.

She glanced once more to where the man from the boat had disappeared. For some reason, she found him interesting. She had no idea why. He paid no attention to her on the boat or after they docked.

Besides, they'd never see each other again.

Chapter 2

Drake strode into the office at the sawmill. Mr. Henderson, the manager, hunched over his cluttered desk. Actually, the tiny room was filled almost beyond capacity with stacks of papers. How in the world did the man know where anything was in this mess? And the racket from the steam-powered saws would drive Drake crazy if he had to work here.

The man glanced up. A smile spread across his face, and he rose from his chair and ushered Drake out of the cramped space into the sunlight.

"Mr. Logan. I hope you have good news for me." His piercing eyes looked as if they could see right through Drake.

Drake shook his head and frowned. "I'm afraid not."

A dark grimace pinched the other man's features. "I don't mind telling you just how bad that sounds. I've never missed paying my employees on time. Of course, they can still get supplies at the company store on credit, but if it takes very long before our gold coins arrive, it could close down this mill. A lot of people would lose their jobs. You'd lose one of your best customers, and your company's reputation would be in tatters."

Every word cut through Drake like a dagger. How had this happened? Even with the dense fogs and wild winds, Logan had never lost a ship on Lake Superior. A bitter taste rose in his throat.

"I received a telegram telling me the ship was lost in the Graveyard of the Great Lakes off Whitefish Point. I'm going there next to see what records the keeper has about the *Amelia Logan* going down." He stared across the busy sawmill at the point where the logs floated down a stream into the millpond.

"I don't remember hearing about any recent shipwrecks." Mr. Henderson crossed his arms over his chest and straightened even taller. "Word usually spreads around here when one goes down. Some of the loggers help when needed to rescue survivors. You sure it went down near Whitefish Point?"

Drake took a deep breath as he focused his attention on the burly man. "That's what the telegram said. That only one man survived. The one that sent the message."

"Who was it? Don't remember seeing any strangers around here either."

The wind picked up from the north, and a gust sent the top of a large pile of sawdust swirling through the camp. No wonder Mr. Henderson was always covered from head to toe with the wood by-product.

Drake looked down at his black suit and tried to brush off some of the debris. Of course, it stuck like the down of a thistle. *Great.* He'd look like some kind of vagabond when he arrived at the lighthouse. He took out his handkerchief and covered a cough. He'd be glad when the dust settled.

"About the gold." Henderson's voice hardened. "We need that to be replaced as soon as possible. Business, you know."

Although Drake had expected some comment like that when he stopped in Shelldrake, he didn't have any more of an answer than he did when he left Chicago. He needed to search for that barrel of flour. He hoped he'd find it so he wouldn't have to withdraw funds from the company account. If he had to do that, the steamship line could have a serious financial problem.

"I'll be checking to see what I can find out about the wreck. The barrel of flour containing the bags of gold coin is much heavier than the other barrels." He swiped his handkerchief at the beads of sweat that popped out on his forehead. Even the chilled breeze couldn't cool him off. "It could have sunk to the bottom of the lake. If the wreck was close to the shore, we might be able to raise it from the water. I'll stop by here on my way back and let you know what's going on."

He held out his hand and Henderson shook it.

Drake started to leave then turned back. "Is there anywhere in Shelldrake where I can hire a horse for a day or two?"

Henderson gave him directions with plenty of hand gestures, and Drake headed toward a farm in the opposite direction from the road he would take to the lighthouse.

The sooner he finished this task, the better. A lot of work awaited his return to Chicago.

The two men were silent as they and Norma traversed the dirt road through the forest. As the wagon approached the lighthouse, she was filled with trepidation. At this time of day, no one would need to have the light on. She wondered where Uncle Charles was. Auntie would probably be in the kitchen.

The younger man who shared the wagon seat with her came alive when they exited the forest. He stared around at the buildings sitting in a meadow beside the shore of Lake Superior.

"I ain't never been out here before." He wiggled on the seat, his voice filled with excitement. "That's a lot of buildings." He turned toward her. "How many people live out here? Almost looks like a little town, but the buildings are fancier than Shelldrake's."

Before she could answer, the older man spoke up. "Are you going to the building attached to the light tower with a walkway?" Evidently, he knew plenty about the lighthouse station.

"Yes please." This would be her home for a while.

"Are they expecting ya?"

The man should have asked that back at Shelldrake if he had any concerns.

"Charles Kimbell is my uncle." She still didn't notice anyone around, not even the assistant lighthouse keepers. "I lived with them for a few years before I went away to college."

"You went to college?" The younger man's eyes widened. "Ain't never met no one who's been to college. Was it hard?"

Few people went to college, but he didn't have to be so surprised that she had. "It wasn't easy."

"What'd you study?" Maybe he was just eager to discover things.

Good for him. She took a deep breath and blew it out in a sigh. "Medicine. . .I'm a doctor."

His eyes widened even more, and she could see the white all the way around his irises. "For real?"

She nodded. "Yes." Reaching under the seat, she lifted her medical bag. "See." Everyone should recognize its purpose.

"Ain't never heard of a woman doctor neither." He crossed his arms over his skinny chest. "I wouldn't wanta go to one."

She'd heard this plenty of times. . .and she was tired of it. But he didn't know any better.

"What if you had a life-threatening injury, and the only doctor close enough to save you was a woman?"

He scratched his head. "I don't reckon it'd matter then."

She turned toward the older man. "Just stop near that door." She pointed to the one on the building that contained her uncle and aunt's living quarters. "That way, you won't have to carry the trunks so far. I know they're heavy."

"One feels like it's full of rocks." He jumped down from the wagon and headed toward the back. "Won't be easy to take it up the steps."

"I'm sorry. It contains my books."

He mumbled something that sounded like "whole library."

"I'll go let my aunt know I'm here." Carrying her two bags, she headed up the steps.

"Auntie," she called as she opened the door.

Her aunt came from the kitchen, a smile spread across her face. She threw her arms around Norma and held her close. "I didn't know you were coming for a visit."

Tears filled Norma's eyes. "It's not a visit." She choked back the sobs that had been trying to escape.

Her aunt took a step back and looked at her face, love shining from her eyes. "What's the matter, dear?"

"Where ya want this trunk?" The male voice interrupted their conversation.

Norma leaned close to her aunt's ear. "I'll tell you all about it when the men are gone."

While Auntie led the men upstairs with the first trunk, Norma meandered around the room, taking comfort from the familiar surroundings. A warm homey feeling stole over her, and a few of the tears she'd been holding back trailed down her cheeks.

Her quarters in Chicago consisted of one bedroom on the second story of the doctor's home. The room barely held her two trunks, a straight chair, and a single bed.

Most of the first floor had become the clinic where patients were seen and treated, and sometimes a couple of the bedrooms on that floor served as the only hospital rooms available for those living in extreme poverty. Although she really wanted to utilize her training as a doctor, even if only in that barren place, she was thankful she had somewhere to come home to.

When she heard the two men coming down the stairs for the second trunk, she went into the kitchen. She didn't want them to see her tears.

Auntie had been baking this morning. Loaves of bread cooled on one side of the long table, and pies lined the other.

The enticing aroma reminded Norma it had been a long time since she'd eaten. She was tempted to cut a slice of bread—or pie—but she didn't know if there was enough for her to have some. Her stomach emitted a rather loud growl. *Glad no one's in the room to hear it.* She rubbed her empty stomach.

"Sounds to me like someone is hungry." Auntie entered the room laughing. "Am I right?"

Norma nodded. "I had to get up early to make the boat before it left Sault Ste. Marie."

Her aunt went to the stove and lifted a teakettle from the back of the range and placed it on a hotter spot.

"I'll get the teapot ready." Norma wanted something to do to take her mind off her problems.

If she was busy, maybe she could keep the tears away. She set her aunt's china teapot on a trivet on the table. While she put the tea leaves in the tea ball, Auntie poured the heated water into the pot.

Norma added the infuser and slipped the chain through the notch in the lid. She retrieved cups and saucers from the cabinet and set them on the table.

"Would you rather have warm bread, butter, and jam or cherry pie?"

She smiled at her aunt.

"Cherry pie."

They both spoke the words in unison. Auntie knew her so well. Norma took out dessert dishes and forks while her aunt cut generous slices of the pie and set out some lemon slices, a pot of honey, and a small pitcher of milk. By the time they were finished, the tea had steeped just enough.

"I didn't know if your tastes had changed during your time in medical school or in Chicago, so I set out anything you might want."

Once again, tears filled Norma's eyes. She felt like a woman who couldn't control her emotions during her monthly time, but this wasn't about that. All the pressures she'd had as she fought her way through medical school, then the additional pressures of caring for people with so many physical problems. Knowing she could help them, and they wouldn't let her. All this had come down on her at once. She picked up the napkin embroidered with tiny roses to match the tea set and swiped away the moisture from her face.

While Auntie poured Norma's cup of tea, she asked, "What's the matter, dear?"

After adding milk and honey to her cup, Norma took a sip, trying to calm herself. She didn't want to cry the whole time she talked to Auntie.

"You know I graduated at the top of my class. Many of the men resented me. They didn't think women should be doctors, and I'm sure it added insult to injury when I made better grades. I was so thankful Uncle Charles helped me get the position with the medical practice in Chicago. And I loved being there. . .at first. I was learning how the practice ran. I felt useful." The cherry pie was calling to her, so she took a bite and savored the sweetness and the flaky crust.

"I know that's not what's causing you to cry." Auntie patted her hand.

Norma shook her head. "No. It's not. I've been there several months, and not one single patient has let me examine them. I can understand the men, but even the women wouldn't see me. I've just been a nurse helping the physician. That's not why I worked so hard to get through medical school. I *am* a bona fide doctor."

"Oh dear, I'm so sorry."

"I'm not wanting to move here with you, but I need a place to stay while I find somewhere I can practice my profession."

As they continued the conversation, they also sipped tea and ate their pie.

"How do you plan to do that?" Auntie's expression held love and sympathy.

"I'm not sure. Out in the West, some places don't have many doctors, and female doctors are successful there. I've considered going out there."

"Maybe when your uncle returns, he'll have another idea."

Norma glanced around. "I wondered why he wasn't here sharing this pie with us."

"He received a call from his father's lawyer. Your grandfather is gravely ill and not expected to live much longer. Since he's the only living child, he went to be with him. If Mr. Kimbell passes, Charles will likely have to stay and take care of all the legal matters. We're not sure when he'll return. He had to leave right away, so I didn't go with him. I'm the only one here to take care of the cooking and other household chores. The two assistant lighthouse keepers are sharing the station duties while he's gone."

"I'm glad you were here when I arrived. I'm not sure what I would have done if you hadn't been."

Probably just sat down and cried. And that's not what she wanted to do. Something had to go her way. She must find a place to practice medicine. . .but where?

Chapter 3

After negotiating with a farmer to rent a horse for the day, Drake mounted Haystack and headed toward Whitefish Point. *Who names a horse Haystack?* This farm animal was nothing like the steeds he usually rode for pleasure. Thank goodness the horse had been trained for riding as well as for pulling wagons and plowing.

Plodding along the dirt road through the forest, Drake met a wagon with two men heading toward Shelldrake. They took his measure before they came abreast of each other. He gave them a nod, but they didn't return it. Perhaps they thought he was a highwayman, what with all the sawdust dimming the black of his sack suit. He hoped they wouldn't lie in wait for him to return. Of course, they couldn't know he would be coming back this way any time soon.

He leaned forward, trying to see the end of the road. He had only glimpsed Whitefish Point from the deck of one of his steamships. If he remembered correctly, the area around the lighthouse was open meadow, not forest. His heartbeat accelerated in anticipation of what he might find. *Please, Lord, lead me to the barrel of flour with the gold in it.*

As he reached the edge of the forest, the trees became more scattered. He was able to study the lighthouse station as he rode toward it. He burst from between the last few trees into the bright sunlight. There wasn't a cloud in the sky. It should feel warm, but a cold wind blew across Lake Superior from Canada with enough force to create whitecaps on the waves.

A woman stepped out of the doorway at the top of the steps on the side of the building that faced him. Something about her looked familiar—the way she carried herself and the way her hand swiped the hair from across her forehead and tucked it behind her ear.

He slowed his horse to a walk. *The woman that exited the boat at Shelldrake when I did. What is she doing way out here?*

Each dainty step down the stairs brought them closer, but she didn't seem to have noticed him. She really must have something on her mind if she couldn't hear a horse and rider approaching. Or maybe the wind blew the sound away from her.

The serenity of this place contrasted with all the hustle and bustle he was used to in Chicago.

She glanced up, and a startled look crossed her face. She hurried across the bright green grass between the building and the road that curved around to meander between the edifices. Raising her hand to her forehead and shading her eyes from the bright sunlight, she stared at him.

Wonder if she saw me on the packet boat?

She stopped and stood beside the dirt road as if waiting for him to get close enough to have a conversation. Everything about her was beautiful. Her black hair waved down the sides of her head and gathered into a bun at the nape of her neck. Her skin had the creamy look of ivory. When he was close enough to see that her large expressive eyes were the color of warm chocolate, a tiny smile raised into cheeks that were the color of a ripe peach.

"Hello, sir. May I help you?"

I hope you can.

Norma watched the man dismount from the horse that looked as if it just stepped from the barn on a farm. He held the reins as he approached her. She felt the need to step back from the power he exuded, but she stood her ground.

When he stopped a few steps from where she was, she let out the breath she hadn't realized she was holding.

"Yes."

Yes, what? She couldn't even remember what he was answering. The man could really upset her equilibrium. This had never happened before, and she didn't know quite how to handle it.

"I'd like to talk to the lighthouse keeper." He answered her unspoken question.

"He's not here right now." She stuck her hands into the pockets in her apron because she didn't want him to notice how shaky they were.

A frown wrinkled his forehead. "Who's in charge when he's gone?"

"I suppose my aunt is. . .his wife. Why do you need to see someone?"

He gave his head a slight shake. "I'm sorry." He took another step toward her. "I'm Drake Logan with the Logan Steamship Line. One of our ships went down in the Graveyard of the Great Lakes out there." His gesture encompassed the choppy water of Lake Superior that spread from Whitefish Point to the west toward Munising. "I want to check to see when it happened. They do keep records of the shipwrecks, don't they?"

"Of course they do. You can tie your horse to the handrail of the steps over there. I'll take you to meet my aunt."

She led the way to avoid the chance his horse made a mess in the grass. She'd stepped in enough of that to last her a whole lifetime.

While he tied his horse's reins, she went up the steps and opened the door. "Auntie, there's a man here who wants to talk to you."

Her aunt came from the kitchen wiping her hands on a towel tucked into the waistband of her apron. "And who might that be?"

Norma stepped aside to let the man in. "This is Mr. Logan from the Logan Steamship Line." She turned back toward him. "This is my aunt, Mrs. Charles Kimbell."

Auntie held out her hand. "Welcome, Mr. Logan."

"Drake, please." He shook her proffered hand. "When I hear Mr. Logan, I usually know someone is talking to my father. Most people call me Drake."

"And what can I do for you. . .Drake?" Auntie's eyes twinkled with interest.

"I'm checking on a ship of ours that sank near Whitefish Point." He stuck his hands in his pockets.

"Follow me." Auntie led the man to the small nook where a rolltop desk and telephone attached to the wall served as an office.

Her aunt took out her keys and slipped a tiny one in the slot on the desk, unlocking it and then sliding the top up. A journal sat near the back of the desktop. She pulled it out and opened to the current date. "So when did this shipwreck happen?"

"That's the problem. I'm not sure exactly." He rubbed the back of his neck with one hand.

Norma's father used to do that when he was trying to think. For a moment, her heart hurt, even though he'd been gone for several years. She loved Uncle Charles, and he looked a lot like his brother. But her father had loved her more openly than many men did. That's what was missing from her life right now. A man who loved her unconditionally. . .wholeheartedly, the way he had.

"I received a telegram announcing the shipwreck early yesterday morning. That's why I'm here. I wanted to see if there was any salvage from the ship. One of the items in the hold was valuable and irreplaceable." He stuffed his hands in his pockets again.

Auntie looked at the list of wrecks. "The most recent shipwreck was almost a month ago. And the one before that was last year, a week before the end of the shipping season." She looked up into the man's eyes. "Who sent the telegram?"

"That's a mystery. He didn't sign his name. Just said he was the only survivor."

"Something is strange about what you're telling me. There were no shipwrecks that could possibly be your ship. The timing is wrong." Auntie shut the book and returned it to the desk. "Where should this ship be right now?"

Drake's shoulders slumped. "On its way back to Chicago with a load of copper ore."

Auntie turned back to him. "And how do you know it isn't? This could just be some kind of joke someone is playing on you."

His eyes widened. "I hadn't thought of that, but I do know it didn't make the first delivery, which was supposed to be to the sawmill at Shelldrake. I received a telegram from them just before the one about the shipwreck was delivered. The manager wondered where their supplies were. They hadn't arrived."

"And you know that for sure?"

Norma liked the way her aunt could look at a problem from all directions.

He nodded. "I talked to Mr. Henderson before I ventured out here. He really needs his delivery."

"Would you like a cup of coffee or tea, Drake?" Auntie nodded toward Norma. "My niece can make us some. We can go into the parlor and see if we can figure out a way to help you."

"Either would be fine." The man followed her aunt.

Since the water on the stove was still hot from before, Norma started a new pot of tea steeping, glad the kitchen was close enough that she could hear the continued conversation.

Drake sat in the proffered chair and leaned his forearms on his thighs, his best position for thinking. His hostess sat in the other wingback chair and waited. Evidently, she understood a man's need to figure things out in his mind.

He glanced up at the lighthouse keeper's wife. "How long is this 'Graveyard of the Great Lakes'?"

The woman glanced out the window. She had that look on her face he'd seen on students when he was in school when they were trying to work out a problem in mathematics.

Finally, she looked back at him. "Actually, it's the coastline between here and Munising, about eighty miles."

"That's interesting." He spent a minute or two mulling over the information. "The telegram said near Whitefish Point, but what if it was closer to Munising?" He stood. "I'd like to travel along the lakeshore and see if we can find any debris that could have come from the *Amelia Logan*."

Mrs. Kimbell stood. "You wouldn't be able to ride a horse very close to the shoreline in many places. It would be too dangerous."

"I hadn't thought of that."

She pulled the curtains back from the window so he could see. "The shore is cleared of brush here, and there aren't any boulders, but farther down there's lots of brush and many places have rocks or even rocky cliffs."

"But things that float could have been blown by the strong winds all the way to the shore, couldn't they?" That wouldn't help him find the barrel with the gold in it, but it would let him know where the ship went down.

"It will take a whole day to cover the entire coast, and you'd need to start as soon as the sun comes up. Perhaps you could spend the night here at the station and head out in the morning. I'll see if Alf Evenson, the second assistant lighthouse keeper, could accompany you. And there's an empty bed in his quarters, so you can spend the night there."

The plan sounded good to Drake, but he hadn't brought any luggage. He'd need other clothing and a nightshirt. Maybe it really wasn't such a good idea.

The woman's niece came in with a tray containing a teapot, cups and saucers, and a plate of cookies.

"Here, let me help you." He reached for the tray and set it on the small coffee table in front of the sofa.

"Thank you, Norma." Mrs. Kimbell poured the tea into three cups.

"What do you take in your tea, Mr. Logan? Or do you drink it without adding anything?" Norma smiled straight at him.

"A little milk." A light flowery fragrance wafted from her.

"Do you want honey with that?"

Once more, his heartbeat accelerated. "Sounds good. I like honey better than sugar."

The warmth that radiated from her face held a sincerity he hadn't often found in women. Maybe he shouldn't judge every woman by the fiancée who broke their engagement a month before the wedding. He had sworn off romantic relationships that day, and he'd kept his promise to himself until now. He didn't ever plan to break it.

He watched Norma walk toward the kitchen, a subtle sway in her hips. How could he think straight with her distracting him from obtaining the information he needed to find?

Chapter 4

In the light of a kerosene lamp, Norma dressed in long underwear under a woolen dress with long sleeves. Even though summer had arrived, on the shoreline of Lake Superior the winds were strong and often cold. Before she went to the kitchen for breakfast, she grabbed her medical bag and set it by the front door. In school they were taught to always keep their doctor's bag close by. She hoped there'd be no need for it on this excursion, but it was better to be safe than sorry, as her father used to say.

Drake sat at the table eating a stack of pancakes when she arrived. She had noticed he didn't bring any luggage with him, yet now he had on the kind of work clothes all the men at the station wore. Someone must have had some that fit him, because these surely did. Fit like a glove made just for him, enhancing the athleticism of his body. She quickly glanced away before he caught her studying him.

Auntie sat across the table from him. The conversation she'd heard from the parlor stopped when she entered.

Her aunt hurried to the stove. "Here's your plate." She lifted it from the warming shelf above the stove top. "I've got your sausage ready. How many pancakes should I fix for you? Before you left for school, you ate like a bird at breakfast."

"Not anymore, Auntie." Norma went to the cupboard to get another coffee cup. "I learned the importance of breaking your fast with substantial food. And many days at the clinic, it was the only meal we had before a late dinner. Three will be fine."

Drake glanced up at her as she leaned against the lower cabinet and sipped her coffee. "Clinic? What kind of clinic?"

Well, isn't he full of questions? She had a few of her own about this mysterious stranger. What was he really looking for? Not just some evidence of his shipwreck. He was too intense for that.

After pouring the batter for the pancakes, Auntie turned back around. "Norma is a doctor. She worked in a clinic in a poor section of Chicago."

His eyes widened so much, they looked like they might pop right out of his head. "A doctor? Really?"

He didn't have to sound so surprised, as if it wasn't even a possibility.

With a nod, she set her coffee on the table two chairs down from him and went back for her plate. Auntie had already flipped the pancakes. Now she stacked them and slid them beside the sausage.

"You want honey or maple syrup?" Her aunt smiled at her, but before she could answer, reached for the maple syrup.

Norma laughed, and Auntie joined her. "Why do you even ask?"

"I'm used to asking the other workers when they eat here. It's a habit."

Drake had put his fork down and was staring at them.

I hope he's enjoying the show.

Alf Evenson came in and glanced around the room. "Has everyone finished eating?"

"Not yet." Norma smiled at him. "We were just getting started."

He pulled out the chair across from Norma and dropped into it.

"The usual, Alf?" Auntie didn't wait for his agreement before she started pouring his pancakes on the griddle.

"You know it, Mrs. Kimbell. Thanks."

Norma slid her chair out a little so she could get him a cup of coffee.

"Go ahead and eat your food while it's hot." Alf stood. "I can get my own coffee, if there's still some in the pot." He poured a cup and headed back to the table. "Heard you were working at a clinic in Chicago. How's that going?"

Why is everyone so nosy? Oh well, maybe he was just trying to start a conversation.

Drake watched the interplay between the other three, wondering about the relationships. Evenson seemed very comfortable in this kitchen. Of course, Drake didn't know anything about how many people lived at the station and what their relationships were. It shouldn't matter one bit to him, but Dr. Kimbell upset his equilibrium. And he didn't like it one bit.

The woman was beautiful. He'd give her that. But she wasn't the kind of woman he should be interested in. He needed to find someone who was his social equal. . . and loved the Lord as he did. The very thought of her doctoring people in all stages of dress or undress, especially men and boys, was totally unacceptable to him. And yet, he felt drawn to her, stronger than he'd ever been drawn to a woman in the past. He needed to push back those feelings in light of her being a practicing doctor. It would have been bad enough if she were a nurse, but never a doctor.

Evenson finished his breakfast, wiped his mouth with a napkin, and placed it on the table. "Thank you so much, Mrs. Kimbell. It was wonderful, as usual." He rose and turned toward Drake and Norma. "Before I came in, I hitched the wagon to our horse."

"Why are we taking the wagon?" Norma asked the question before Drake had a chance. "Won't it be hard to get through the brush scattered along the shore?"

With a nod to Drake, he continued. "That's why I saddled the horse you rode in on. You can get closer to the shoreline in some places where we can't with the wagon. I thought it'd be good to take the wagon in case we find some of the things you're looking for."

"Sounds good to me."

He had watched Norma turn from one man to the other during their exchange of words.

Now she looked only at him. "There may be places where you'll have to leave the horse with the wagon and walk closer to the water. You'll just need to be very careful."

What does she think I am? An imbecile? He knew to watch where he was going, especially since he hadn't been there before.

Soon they were all loaded with food from Auntie as well as Norma's medical bag. Neither of the men seemed to notice when she put it under the seat of the wagon. They carried on a conversation while she climbed up to take her place on the bench seat.

Alf turned back toward the wagon, climbed to the seat, and picked up the reins. By the time they headed out, fingers of light painted the occasional cloud in pastels—pink, peachy orange, lavender—and the horizon was rimmed with a thin line of golden light. As they followed the faint road, the colors intensified until bright pink, orange, and purple greeted the sun as it climbed above the horizon.

She had always enjoyed watching the sunrise...and sunset as well. She couldn't even remember the last time she saw either one. The poor section of Chicago had buildings right next to each other, and many were several stories high with tiny apartments. By the time the sun rose above them, the colors of dawn had faded into direct sunshine.

As they rode along, no one seemed inclined to talk. Drake could get much closer to the shore than the wagon could. The ruts that made up the track were faint, evidence that not many people used this road. After half of an hour with him riding back and forth from the wagon to the shore, he brought the horse and tied it to the tailgate of the wagon when Alf stopped to rest the horse.

"I'm going to walk for a while. It looks as if I can get closer to the shore that way."

"Would you like a drink of water?" Norma felt hot, and he had sweat popping out on his forehead.

He stood beside where she sat in the wagon. "Yes, please. Thank you for thinking of me."

She handed him a mason jar wrapped in a towel and filled with water. "It won't be as cold as the water back at the station, but it should cool you off some."

He nodded his thanks then twisted the lid off the jar and drank half the quart of water. He finished by wiping his mouth with the back of his hand before replacing the lid. Maybe being dressed in more casual clothes made him loosen up from the first time she observed him on the packet boat. She liked him better the way he was now.

When he handed the jar back to her, his fingers brushed against hers. Strange shivers shot up her arm, making her feel almost like she was cold, but she wasn't. The contact increased the heat flaming deep inside her. Maybe she was getting sick, or maybe she would just need to make sure that kind of contact didn't happen again.

When Alf reached under the seat of the wagon to get his own drink, the side of his leg slid along hers for a few inches. Nothing like what happened with Drake occurred with Alf. Of course, she'd known Alf for a long time. He felt more like a brother to her than anything else.

He drove the wagon much slower while they tried to remain close to where the ship owner wandered. At one point, Drake stepped over the high grass and disappeared over the side of an outcropping of large rocks.

Alf stopped the wagon and hopped down. He headed toward where the ship owner disappeared. Norma followed him. Before they reached the rocks, Drake's head popped up, and he climbed over the boulders.

"Did I miss something?"

His question confused Norma. What did he think he missed?

"We were just worried that you might have fallen and gotten hurt." Alf frowned as he spoke.

"I thought I saw something, but when I got closer, I realized it was only the way the light shone on small stones in the water." He walked back to untie his horse and mounted. "I'll ride for a while."

When Norma climbed back into the wagon, she took a drink out of her mason jar. For as far as they could see up the road, tree branches met in the middle over it. It would be much cooler than riding in direct sunlight.

When they stopped to eat lunch, Norma pulled the basket of food from under the seat. Auntie had fixed quite a feast—ham and cheese sandwiches, homemade pickles, and at least a dozen oatmeal raisin cookies. She was sure there was enough food to feed twice as many people, but she was wrong. While she enjoyed a sandwich, a pickle, and a cookie, the two men devoured the rest.

Even though the men hadn't made friends during the morning ride, they spent the time between bites getting acquainted. For the most part, she just listened. She had no idea that Alf was the oldest of seven children or that he came from

Wisconsin to work at Whitefish Point Lighthouse.

Drake was an only child, the son who joined his father's firm after he graduated from college with a business degree. He liked catching a ride on one of the steamships as often as he could. He even owned a sailboat that he used when he had time off, traversing Lake Michigan from bottom to top and back.

"What makes you think your ship went down in this area?" Alf leaned against a tree trunk while he ate.

Drake stood up. "A telegram told me."

"Who sent it?" Alf sounded interested.

"That's the problem. I don't know. The person didn't sign his name." He stared off across the water.

She turned to look at Lake Superior, where the winds kicked up whitecaps on the waves. A chill ran down her spine. How could a ship and all the sailors be under that water without leaving some sign behind?

Alf got up and stood beside the two of them as they stared across the water. "I hate to say this, but maybe it was someone playing a trick on you. Why else would the person not sign the telegram?"

Drake crossed his arms over his muscular chest. "A ship that size can't just disappear into thin air. It has to be somewhere. If not here, then. . . ?"

His unanswered question hung between them. Norma didn't have an answer, and evidently, neither did Alf.

"How much farther do we need to go?" Drake looked toward Alf for his answer.

Good thing he did. Norma had no idea.

Alf stared down the road in front of them. "I'm not sure, but we're not going to make it all the way to Munising then back to Whitefish Point today. We need to decide what to do now."

Drake rubbed his hand across the nape of his neck. "Let's go a little farther before we turn around."

Norma thought about trying to return after the sun went down. She wasn't sure she wanted to do that. It was hard enough seeing the faint road in the daylight.

"No more than an hour." Alf picked up the basket and shoved it under the seat.

Drake mounted his horse and headed closer to the shoreline.

Norma was tired of sitting on the hard wagon seat. She hated to think of how she would feel even if they turned back now. Adding two hours to the time they'd already spent traveling made her grimace. If she could keep up with the speed of the horse, she would walk beside the wagon for a while.

After the meal they ate, she felt drowsy. That was all she needed, to fall asleep and fall off the seat. . .and maybe off the wagon. She shook herself and opened her eyes wide when a strange whinny and snort called her attention to where Drake and the horse hurried along.

Just as her eyes found them, the horse stepped into some kind of hole. With a wild, unearthly scream, it went down to its knee, and Drake sailed over its head. Although the wagon wasn't alongside the horse and rider, she heard the loud thud as Drake hit the ground.

Alf sped up the horse until they were as close to the spot as they could get while staying on the road. When the wagon came to a standstill, Norma yanked her medical bag from under the seat and jumped down from the wagon.

"Be careful, Norma. We don't want you to get hurt too." Alf scrambled down behind her.

Norma picked her way across the rough ground, making sure she didn't step into a hole. She dropped her bag beside Drake's limp body and knelt beside him. She conducted a careful examination without disturbing the way he lay on the ground, to see if she could find any broken bones.

She knew she wouldn't be able to move such a large, strong man without assistance. "Alf, please help me carefully turn him over."

When Drake was on his back, she lifted each eyelid then gently felt around his head. On one side of his forehead near his hairline, blood rushed from a gash. Head wounds were like that. She had to stem the flow before he lost too much blood. She noticed a sharp rock with his blood on it that his head must have hit. Drake never even moaned, and no part of his body moved. He was out cold. She had never treated anyone in this condition.

Dear God, please help me save this man.

Chapter 5

W e're almost there."

The words caught Norma's attention. Riding in the back of the wagon so she could monitor Drake's condition, she'd almost dozed off. Night descended a long time ago. Thank the good Lord, the moon was bright, and Alf was able to see the road. The trip home took so long because Norma told him to drive slowly so Drake wouldn't be jostled too much.

She raised her head and looked toward the lighthouse station. Every window was lit up like a Christmas tree. Auntie must have been concerned when they didn't return earlier.

The horse tied to the tailgate of the wagon gave a soft whinny. He must have seen the lights up ahead as well. Although the horse's leg was swollen, Alf didn't think it was broken. He told Norma he could nurse Haystack back to health.

She leaned over to check Drake's vital signs and found him staring at her. For the first time since his fall, his eyes looked clear instead of confused. Hopefully, he would heal without any lasting effects.

"Where. . .are we?" His voice came out gravelly.

Hours ago, she had used all the remaining water they had in the wagon. No wonder his throat was dry.

"I can see the lighthouse station. All the windows are lit up. Auntie probably is worried because it's taken us so long to get home."

He slowly reached his hand toward his forehead. "I have. . .a headache."

Norma took hold of his fingers before he could touch his wound. "Of course you do." She remembered them laughing while they ate their lunch about the name the farmer gave the horse. "When Haystack stepped in a hole, you were thrown from his back."

She wanted to brush his hair back from his forehead but knew that was too intimate a gesture. Yes, she'd cleaned his wound and even stitched the gash together, but now she was just a woman watching over him.

He closed his eyes and looked as if he had dropped off to sleep. After a moment, his eyes widened again.

"How is. . .Haystack? Did he. . .get hurt. . .when he fell?" His eyes drifted closed again.

She didn't know if he was asleep or if he passed out. When she placed her fingers under his nose, she felt the air as he took a breath then exhaled, and the rhythm of his breathing was accompanied by his chest rising and falling.

Just in case he could hear, she leaned close and answered his question. "Alf was afraid that Haystack had broken his leg. But he didn't. He's bruised, and he's limping along behind the wagon. Alf's really good with animals. If anyone can help him heal, it's Alf."

"Good," Drake whispered between his lips, but his eyes didn't even flutter.

Auntie must have been watching for them, because she came out the door and hurried down the steps before the wagon stopped beside their quarters. "My gracious, I was so worried about you. Alf, where are Norma and Drake?"

"They're in the back of the wagon, ma'am." He glanced over his shoulder at them. "Sure was a good thing Norma was with us. Drake needed a doctor really bad."

Drake leaned back against the pillow and sighed, glad to be out of the hard wagon bed and into a more comfortable one. Getting him to the room he'd used last night had been a real chore. Not only did Alf help him, but James Kay, the first assistant lighthouse keeper, also aided them. The two men helped him get undressed and into the flannel nightshirt he'd worn last night.

"What. . .happens. . .now?" He wasn't sure either of the two men knew, but he had to ask.

Mr. Kay shrugged his shoulders and left the room. He probably had other things to take care of, since the lighthouse keeper wasn't home yet.

Alf watched the man go. "I think Norma and her aunt will be taking turns sitting with you."

"Why? Better now. . . Can really relax. . .and rest. Better. . .in the morning." He squirmed as little as possible while he tried to get in a comfortable position. No matter how little he moved, every slight change in his position felt like a mule kick to his wounded head.

I can't stay here much longer. I have to keep looking for my ship.

A quiet knock came on his door, and it opened a slit. "Mr. Logan, would you like something to eat or drink before you go to sleep?" Mrs. Kimbell stuck her head in.

"Yes. . .please. My mouth. . .is dry."

"I'll be right back." She slipped out, and he heard her footsteps fade away.

Her return came quicker than he expected. She had a pitcher of water and a glass on a tray.

"Can you sit up at all?" Her voice held the warmth he remembered from his mother when he was sick or had one of his many accidents as a boy.

Tears pooled in his eyes. "I'm. . .not sure."

She set the water on a table beside the bed then pulled a chair close. "I can spoon water into your mouth, if it hurts too much to sit up."

The idea of being fed the water like a small child wasn't ideal, but he knew it was for the best. "Yes please."

She went back to get a spoon and once again returned quickly. After pouring water in the glass, she sat in the chair and leaned toward him. "Open up."

The cool water was a balm for his scratchy throat. There just wasn't enough of it.

Another gentle knock on the door was followed by Norma entering. "Maybe we could put water in a much smaller glass and you can hold a towel under it while I pour it into his mouth. We've done that at the clinic."

Her aunt got up from the chair. "I'll go get a towel and different glass while you check him over."

"Drake. . ." Norma leaned over him.

Even though they had been out in the weather all day, a faint scent of some kind of flower and honey clung to her, permeating the air around him. He closed his eyes for a moment to enjoy it.

"How bad is your pain right now?" That feminine voice was music to his ears.

He opened his eyes. She was so close. "Not. . .as bad. . .as in the wagon."

"I really don't want to give you laudanum, because even though you need rest, I don't want you to sleep too deeply right now. We have a rather new medication, aspirin. It's been very helpful for pain. Would you like something to eat before you go to sleep?"

His stomach answered for him with a rather loud growl that lasted longer than any other he'd ever had. He couldn't keep his lips from turning up in a slight grin. "I guess. . .that's. . .your answer."

A chuckle tried to make its way out, but laughing hurt too much. In addition to the throbbing in his head, his body started manifesting aches, and probably bruising. He was in a fine pickle. He knew Dr. Kimbell would try to get him to stay here under her care. He. Could. Not.

Mrs. Kimbell returned with a tiny glass and a towel. The two women were able to get quite a bit of water down his throat without spilling any on him. The moisture made it feel much better.

After the second glassful, Norma stopped. "Auntie, would you bring Drake some of the warm bread I smell, with only a bit of butter on it. He's hungry, but I don't think he should eat too much too soon. When he's finished, I'll give him something for the pain, and we can let him go to sleep."

As Norma and her aunt left the room, she heard snoring coming from her patient. Yes, a patient that was hers alone, and she'd done a good job of taking care of him. A boost to her confidence after all the people who had refused to see her as a doctor. Maybe after this she could find a place to practice medicine. Perhaps Drake would write her a recommendation.

"When did you eat last?" Auntie put the water to boil on the stove.

"About noon." Norma dropped into a chair beside the table. "I'm starved. What time is it anyway?"

Auntie looked at the watch pinned to her white shirtwaist. "Just after midnight. I'm sure you're starved. I could scramble you eggs and make toast." She looked in the icebox. "There's part of a ham. Would you like me to fry some for you?"

"Yes. Maybe two eggs, a bit of ham, and one piece of toast." Norma stood. "I can help you."

Her aunt placed her hands on Norma's shoulders. "No, you can't. Sit down and let me do this for you. Now, tell me about the day. Did you find anything from his ship?"

"No." As she settled in the chair, she gave her aunt a rundown of the day. "There wasn't even a tiny trace of that ship. I'm wondering why he's so intent on finding it. I know steamship lines have insurance on their vessels and the contents. Something else is pushing Drake for him to go to such lengths to find debris."

As Auntie set a plate of food in front of Norma, she nodded. "I sensed that in him too. Something's not quite right. I hope he doesn't try to leave here before he should. He needs your medical help."

Yes, he does. More than he realizes.

She needed him too. As her first patient, she wanted him to be completely well before she let him leave. Deep inside, she knew he wouldn't want to stay long enough.

And there wasn't a thing she could do about it.

When Drake opened his eyes, he saw Norma sitting in a rocking chair beside the bed. Her head leaned back against a pillow, and some kind of cover had been pulled over her. In sleep, her face looked so peaceful. Not at all like the first time he saw her on the packet ship. Worry had puckered her forehead, and she was twisting a hankie in her hands until it was almost knotted.

He didn't know what had her in such a tizzy, but he enjoyed watching her here. She looked like the sleeping beauty in the child's fairy tale. With the breathy soft snores coming from her slightly opened mouth, Norma looked like his ideal woman. After the way she saved his life on the road yesterday, maybe he could overlook the fact she was a doctor. She'd been careful of his privacy while she took care of his wounds. Maybe his first thought of a female doctor needed to be adjusted. And she was just the woman to make that adjustment for him.

With her coal-black hair in a long braid that reached below her waist in front and the dark chocolate eyes, which were closed right now, she was beautiful in a way that most of the women he knew well could never achieve with all the powder and other enhancements they used. Her beauty was more than skin deep. It came from her heart.

The tender way she took care of him touched him. Even while she put the stitches in the wound on his head, she'd whispered, "I'm sorry. . .forgive me," often while she was doing it. Her gentle voice removed part of the pain because he concentrated on her words.

She closed her mouth and opened her eyes, and her gaze connected with his. For a long moment, this visual link made the room fade away.

He sat up and pulled the covers around himself, even though the nightshirt covered him to well below his knees.

"How long have I been asleep?" Her soft voice was barely audible.

A vision of waking up every morning with her by his side flashed through his thoughts. "I'm not sure. I just awakened a few minutes ago. I don't know when you fell asleep."

She rose from the chair and stared at him. "Does your head hurt? If so, I can give you more aspirin powder."

"It's sore, but the pain isn't bad if I don't move too quickly."

She went to her medical bag and removed a couple of instruments. "Let me check your breathing and heart. . .and take your temperature. Then I'll change the dressing on your head. See how it is healing. I hope you don't have a fever. It would signal an infection."

Drake watched every move she made as she finished her ministrations to him. "So what's the verdict, Doctor? Will I live?" He hoped the joke would take the tension from the atmosphere of the room.

She didn't laugh. "Do you want the medicine?"

"Not right now."

When she left the room, he got out of bed. This injury couldn't stop him from continuing on his quest to find out what happened to the *Amelia Logan.* He was glad she'd left the room, so she wouldn't see how long it took him to get to his feet.

While helping her aunt with breakfast, Norma heard someone coming toward the kitchen. Maybe Alf was up and wanting to eat too. He'd had as long a night as she and Drake did.

Glancing toward the door, she stopped what she was doing and stared. "What are you doing up? You have a bad head wound. You need to be careful."

Drake leaned against the doorframe, his crossed arms spanning his broad, muscular chest. The bandage on the one side of his forehead made him look like a rakish pirate. *Yes, he looks healthy.* But as his doctor, she had to make him aware of the dangers that accompanied such a wound.

Auntie smiled at the man. "Come in. Breakfast is almost ready. Are you hungry?"

"As a bear." He moved to the table with a catlike grace.

"Mr. Logan—" His frown stopped her there. "Drake, you probably should eat light for a day or two at least, if not longer." She sounded like a scolding parent, and the last thing she wanted to feel about him was parental.

His masculinity captured the atmosphere in the room. She didn't need to be noticing things like that. She would probably never see him again after he left here.

Alf arrived, and the four of them sat down to a breakfast of scrambled eggs, fluffy pancakes with maple syrup and butter, and both sausage and bacon. It looked like a lumberjack's breakfast, not a meal for a man recuperating from a serious head wound.

She watched Drake pile his plate high. His gaze dared her to say something about it. She wouldn't give him the satisfaction, but she'd have a talk with him in private after the meal. And she'd make him listen to her medical concerns. She knew the conversation wouldn't be a pleasant one.

Chapter 6

I don't think you understand, Drake." Norma tried to make sure her tone wasn't confrontational. She knew he would put up a wall against a verbal assault. "The kind of head wound you sustained could have long-term effects if you're not careful."

She could see disagreement rise up in his eyes.

"You don't understand, Miss Kimbell. I really must find what happened to my hip, and the longer I wait, the harder it will be to find any evidence of the shipwreck." His calling her Miss Kimbell and his tone held a finality that told her not to make him angry.

"As a doctor. . ." She was careful not to call herself *his* doctor. He might resent that. "My professional opinion is that you will need to be under observation for several more days, if not longer. You might not realize when something is going wrong. And you'll need someone to change the dressing every day, check the progress of the healing, and take the stitches out when it's time."

This conversation was going nowhere, quickly. She'd hate to have her first real patient die from a side effect of the injury, just because he was too stubborn to follow her orders—that is, her suggestions. She knew he wouldn't accept orders from her.

"And you really should stay in bed today. Let your body concentrate all its attention on your head wound. If you're putting other strains on it, you could be inhibiting your body's amazing ability to heal."

Drake frowned through her advice. He opened his mouth as if he was going to say something then closed it again. He touched the middle of his forehead with the tips of his fingers and whooshed out a deep breath. Maybe he was feeling dizzy.

"Very well, Dr. Kimbell. I'll rest today, but I won't make any promises about tomorrow." He walked past her to get to the room where he'd spent the night.

She followed him. "Now would be a good time for me to change your bandage and check the injury."

He dropped onto the side of the bed and leaned over toward his shoes. Without touching them, he raised up and lay back on top of the covers, his feet hanging over the end of the mattress. At least his shoes wouldn't soil the quilt Auntie had made.

Now she was sure he felt dizzy. "Do you have any nausea from all the food you ate?"

He stared at her then closed his eyes. "No, ma'am. But I am feeling a little weak."

She opened her bag and took out the stethoscope and the portable thermometer. "Let me check your vital signs."

"Vital signs?" He grimaced. "You can tell I'm alive just by looking at me."

She started to roll her eyes then thought better of it. If he opened his eyes while she was doing that, it might make him doubt her professionalism.

Alf came by the room and stuck his head inside. "Anything I can do for you Norma?"

"I'm fine." She smiled at him. "I'm just checking on our patient."

A grin spread across Alf's face.

Drake opened his eyes and looked at the other man. "Thanks for all you did to help me yesterday, Alf."

The assistant lighthouse keeper moved into the room. "Glad you're doing so well."

Drake glanced at her then back to Alf. "I guess I have Norma to thank for that."

She felt a blush steal across her cheeks. She wasn't used to being praised for her prowess as a doctor. It felt rather nice.

"Say, Alf, how is Haystack today?" Drake turned so he was facing the other man. "Have you checked on him yet?"

She stood and watched the two men interact. Drake wasn't showing any signs of distress. She made a note in the mental record she was keeping on his condition.

"He's doing really well after the tumble he took. His leg is swollen, but I'm sure nothing is broken. I've put a healing salve I concocted on the knee and wrapped it with strong fabric to keep pressure on it. That should keep it from swelling any more." He ran his hand across the nape of his neck. "I'll do my best for him."

"I'm sure you will, Alf." Norma smiled at the man.

Drake had a strange expression on his face as he glanced from her to Alf and back.

Surely he didn't think there was anything going on between them besides a warm friendship. They hadn't done anything to make him think anything else. Maybe she was just sensitive because of the way other people had treated her medical expertise before.

Drake scratched his head through his thick hair. "I've been thinking a lot. Would you do something for me today?"

He still looked at Alf and ignored her. Maybe he was planning something she wouldn't approve. It was a good thing she was present to hear what he had in mind. And she would try to stop him if it was going to interfere with his recovery.

"I rented a healthy horse from the farmer, and I hate to return it in bad shape."

Alf nodded. "I know what you mean."

"Would you go see him and offer to buy the horse for me? I'll give you sufficient funds."

That sounded good, but Norma could see a problem. "What will happen to the horse when you leave the peninsula?"

He glanced at her. "I'm sure the crew here at the Whitefish Point Lighthouse could put the horse to good use when he gets well. It will be my thanks for the way all of you have taken care of me."

She crossed her arms. "We don't ask for any kind of payment from visitors."

A cross tone accompanied her words. This man was getting on her nerves. Coming here. . .taking over. . .not listening to reason. She stopped her thoughts there. After the night they had spent, she was totally exhausted too. She was going to take care of his needs the best she could right now. Then she was going to get the sleep she missed last night.

Maybe she'd be in a better mood when she awakened. At least, she hoped so.

When Drake woke up, the midafternoon sun shone through the window across from his bed. Except for the pain throbbing in his head, he felt much better. Slowly, he sat up and waited a bit to see if he felt queasy. No dizziness assailed him, so he stood. Rumbling in his stomach reminded him he had missed a meal, and he could smell something enticing coming from the kitchen.

After taking care of personal business, he headed toward that wonderful aroma. He stopped in the doorway to the kitchen and took an appreciative sniff.

Mrs. Kimbell must have heard him, because she turned from where she was removing loaves of bread from the oven and placing them on a long table by the window to cool.

"Mr. Logan, it's good to see you up again. How are you feeling now?" She wiped her hands on the towel stuck under the waistband of her apron.

He smiled at her. "For the most part, I'm much better than this morning."

"Then I'm sure you're hungry, because you enjoyed eating even then."

He nodded.

"Have a seat. I made a pot of stew, knowing some of you might be eating at times other than our regular mealtime. I kept it warm on the back of the stove." She took two thick, folded towels and pulled the stewpot to the front of the stove top.

Because of his mother's training in manners, he wanted to offer to move it for her, but he wasn't sure he was strong enough for that yet.

"Norma has been asleep ever since she took care of you this morning. Maybe she'll soon join you while you eat."

"That would be nice." *Especially since my head hurts. I really could use some of that aspirin powder right about now.*

She filled a bowl with the rich-smelling stew and set it before him. "One of the neighbors went hunting and shared some of their elk with us. I like to make a stew with elk."

He looked down into the brown gravy with carrots, potatoes, and nice-sized chunks of the meat swimming in it. His mouth watered, and he picked up his spoon.

Mrs. Kimbell lifted one of the loaves of bread cooling on the long table. "I'll cut you some bread. We have butter and honey to put on it, if you'd like."

There was no question in his mind. Butter and honey melting into the hot bread sounded delicious. With food like this, he'd be well in no time.

"That sounds wonderful." He dipped a spoonful of the savory broth and carefully tasted a little of it to see if it was still too hot to eat. It burned the tip of his tongue, so he put it back in his bowl and waited for the bread.

"That's a lot of bread. Do you make bread for everyone at the station?"

"Usually I do." She cut two thick slices and set the plate in front of him. "I love cooking and baking. It's my main contribution to what we do here."

After she went to the icebox, she brought butter to him then took a pot of honey out of a cabinet. Before she even got to the table with it, he had butter melting into the yeasty bread. Everything smelled like heaven, and his stomach grumbled again. This time not as loud as it did earlier this morning.

"Auntie. . ." Norma stood in the doorway, looking much more rested than she had this morning. "Something smells wonderful in here. And I'm hungry."

Mrs. Kimbell went to her niece and gave her a hug. "You're looking better than you did earlier. I knew you needed rest. Now you can join Mr. Logan while he eats. He likes warm bread as much as you do."

Finally, Norma looked straight at him. "How are you feeling?"

"Better." He took another bite of the stew, which was now the perfect temperature to eat.

She put her cool hand on his brow. "I don't believe you have a fever. That's a good sign. How's the pain?"

"Not too bad, but I'm ready for some of your wonderful powder."

She left the room and returned with a paper packet. "What do you want to drink?"

"Water sounds good to me." While he continued to eat, Norma got him a glass of water.

She watched him while he took the powder and washed it down. *Why do most medicines taste so bad?* At least this should soon relieve most of the pain.

While Norma took care of him, her aunt prepared a bowl of stew for her and a slice of hot bread. Just as she sat down to eat, Alf arrived.

Mrs. Kimbell welcomed him in to eat with them. "Did you get everything done?"

"Yes." He took a bite. "This is really good. Maybe I'll go hunting when this elk is gone so we can restock our larder. Are you going to join us while we eat, Mrs. Kimbell?"

She quickly got her own food and did just that. The four of them had a pleasant visit, helping Drake get better acquainted with them. When they were all finished with the meal, Alf handed over a bill of sale and the rest of the money Drake sent with him.

After counting the money, he smiled. "I was afraid the farmer might demand a large payment for the horse, but I see it was a reasonable amount."

Alf nodded. "I think he was glad to get rid of the animal. He didn't want to have to nurse him back to health with the risk of losing him if he didn't recover."

Drake looked at Mrs. Kimbell. "So now the Whitefish Point lighthouse station has another horse. You never know when one will come in handy."

"You're right." She started stacking the dishes on the table. "There have been times we really needed another one, but not often enough to buy one. Thank you."

Norma stared at her aunt as if she had grown an extra head. He was surprised she didn't say anything like she did to him this morning about not taking payment from visitors, but she kept quiet.

"Okay, Doctor, I've rested like you told me, and I'm feeling much better. I plan to leave tomorrow morning, early. I have to find out what happened to my ship."

Norma frowned, which wasn't a surprise to him.

Mrs. Kimbell put the dishes into the dry sink and came back to the table. "Let's go into the parlor and visit. I'm sure we'll all be more comfortable there."

That kept the good doctor from expressing her thoughts on what he'd said. From the way she'd been looking at him, he didn't want to know what she was thinking.

When Mrs. Kimbell, Alf, and he were seated, Norma stayed standing. "I don't agree with you, Drake. You need to stay under a doctor's care for a while. You would be leaving way too soon."

He ignored what she said. "I need to find out more about where this telegram really came from. Something doesn't feel right about all of this."

"That's what Auntie and I were talking about after we returned yesterday."

After a short silence, Mrs. Kimbell cleared her throat. "Mr. Logan, was there anything on the paper indicating where the telegram originated?"

He went into the bedroom where he'd slept and retrieved his jacket. When he returned to the parlor, he pulled the message from the pocket and unfolded it. After perusing everything on the paper, he looked up. "There is no indication on this."

"Do you think the telegraph operator who received the message would remember it?" Norma was as interested as her aunt.

He wondered what she was getting at. "I'm not sure if they keep a record of them, but they might. I often use the telegraph, since not everyone has a telephone, and the operator knows me."

Mrs. Kimbell stood and gestured at the wall beside the desk in the adjoining office area. "Why don't you call the Western Union office in Chicago and see if the operator there can tell you where it came from?"

Chapter 7

I see." The telephone call did reveal information that Drake could follow up on. The telegram had been sent from Sault Ste. Marie. He hung up the earpiece and turned around. Alf, Mrs. Kimbell, and Norma stood staring at him, waiting for a report.

He looked straight at Norma so he could see her immediate reaction. "I have to go to Sault Ste. Marie."

She gave a firm shake of her head. "You cannot go until we're sure you won't have serious repercussions from traveling."

The emphasis she placed on "cannot" was so strong, he knew he might be fighting a losing battle. But he had to follow up this information as quickly as possible.

"I'm healthy as a horse, and I must have a hard head, since the wound isn't keeping me down." He flashed his sweetest, albeit forced, smile at her.

She crossed her arms and lifted her chin at a stubborn tilt. He had to hide his grin from her. This attitude made her even more attractive. He could imagine crossing swords with her the rest of his life, but he didn't have time to pursue anything romantic until he found evidence of what happened to his ship. Besides, she might never welcome a relationship with him.

"You may be healthy, and that's a good thing, because it kept the accident from doing too much damage to you." Her serious expression gave him pause. "And I agree that you are hardheaded, in more ways than one, but I can't in good conscience condone what you're planning."

Alf and Mrs. Kimbell watched and listened intently to the conversation. The older woman whispered something to Alf, and Drake wondered what she said.

"It's imperative that I leave on tomorrow morning's packet boat." He could be stubborn when he had to. And this time, it was absolutely necessary.

Norma stared at him a moment then whirled around and headed toward the door. He felt as if she were giving up on keeping him safe. *Keeping me safe?* Now that's an idea.

"Doctor, I have a proposition for you."

373

She stopped before reaching the door, stiffened her back, and turned back around. "What kind of. . .proposition?"

A breathless silence reigned in the room.

With his idea only half formed, he answered, "I could hire you to go with me as my physician. That way, you would be there if anything happened to me."

"No!" Both Norma and her aunt spoke at the same time.

"What are you thinking, Mr. Logan?" Mrs. Kimbell continued. "No unmarried lady can travel alone with a single man. It would ruin her reputation."

Norma agreed. "That would never work. I'm trying to find another place where I can practice medicine, and it would be the final nail in the coffin of my professional life if my reputation was destroyed."

What was I thinking? Of course he knew that, but his pressing need had kept him from looking at all sides before he'd made the blundering suggestion.

Alf didn't say anything, but Drake felt his dismissal of the subject.

He didn't want to risk his life, but he also didn't want to completely lose everything on that ship. What a conundrum! There had to be a solution somewhere, but nothing came to mind. Then it hit him.

"Alf, would it be possible for me to hire you to accompany us? That would protect Norma's reputation, and I'd have a doctor in case I need one."

None of the three responded to his suggestion. They all looked dazed for a few moments. *Please agree.* He didn't feel up to much more of this lopsided discussion, but he really needed to go to Sault Ste. Marie and talk to the telegrapher.

Now Norma, Alf, and Mrs. Kimbell all started talking at once. With little success, he tried to separate what each one thought from the cacophony. Finally, they settled down.

Norma looked at Alf. Drake tried to discern whether the two of them could be involved in a romantic relationship. He didn't detect any indication. That was something to be happy about.

"Auntie, is there any way Alf could accompany us, so I can keep a close eye on Mr. Logan's head wound?"

Her aunt studied the two of them then turned toward Drake. "We might be able to arrange that, if Alf is willing."

Eagerness crept into Alf's expression. "What about keeping the lighthouse rotations going? James and I have been doing an eight-hours-on, eight-hours-off rotation while Charles is away."

"I talked to Charles earlier today, and he seemed to think he'll be coming home very soon. I've filled in before, so I can take your place in the rotation." She smiled at Drake. "I would really worry about Mr. Logan if he left here without the medical care he needs."

Drake returned her smile. "I'd be most grateful, and I will pay both of them for their services."

At least Norma had lost her strong disagreement with him leaving tomorrow.

"Alf. . ." Mrs. Kimbell nodded toward the kitchen, and the assistant lighthouse keeper followed her.

Drake watched the two of them leave. Although he and Norma could hear them talking in the other room, Mrs. Kimbell was speaking so softly he didn't understand many of the words.

"We need to see if James will agree to this." Now she was speaking loud enough. Soon she and Alf were on their way to find James.

After all the tension of working things out, he was able to relax. "I'm going to turn in early, so we can be at Shelldrake when the eastbound packet boat docks."

"Mr. Logan, first I need to change your dressing and check the healing of your wound."

"Of course." The tension that had built up in him while they were working things out seeped away. "Thank you, Norma, for agreeing to serve as my doctor while I search for my ship."

"Wait here." She left the room but quickly returned with her medical bag.

The early morning breeze blew fog from Lake Superior across the trio waiting at the dock. Norma checked the watch pinned to her shirtwaist then pulled her summer-weight coat tighter around her. The packet boat was half an hour late. Auntie had already driven the wagon back to Whitefish Point.

Because they didn't know what they would find in Sault Ste. Marie, she'd brought her medical bag and her carpetbag with some essentials in case they needed to stay overnight. Alf and Drake both carried duffel bags. Alf was dressed in his work clothes, and Drake in his sack suit. But according to Alf, Drake's bag contained the clothing he had worn when they searched the shoreline two days ago. She was sure he would want to fit in to any situation they might find themselves in.

"I see the boat." Drake looked back at her. "It's moving really slow."

She got up from the cross-cut section of a tree that served as a seat near the dock. She was tired of sitting on the hard surface. When she stood by Drake, he pointed out the vessel that looked tiny from that distance.

After the boat docked and packages and mail were unloaded, the captain welcomed them on. "Sorry we're late. Been havin' some trouble with the engine. The engineer on board finally got it runnin', and he says we'll make it back to Sault Ste. Marie, where we can get it completely fixed. Might take awhile though."

Drake, Alf, and Norma sat on a bench lining the wall in the passenger section of the packet boat. She glanced out the blurry windows across from them as the vessel cleared the dock. With the water spots mingling the colors, the landscape blurred into a kaleidoscope design. Being out of the wind helped her warm up a bit.

"Do you think the boat will reach Sault Ste. Marie without breaking down? The engine sounds louder and terrible." She wouldn't want to be stranded on a boat in the middle of Lake Superior. *Please, God, help us make it.*

Drake looked as worried as she felt. "I want to trust the captain's words, but maybe we should pray about it, just in case."

All three bowed their heads. Although Norma could hear murmuring from the two men, the loud engine drowned out their words. So she prayed quietly, knowing God could hear all three of them.

The boat limped into port right as the sun sank below the horizon. The journey had been long and worrisome for Norma. She planned to give her aunt an extra-strong hug when she returned, thankful for the food she sent with them. They devoured it near noon, and now she was once more ravenous as well as weary.

After they left the boat, Drake turned to her. "I still want to see if I can talk to the telegrapher this evening. Then we can find a hotel. Or I can take you and Alf to get us hotel rooms while I try to reach Western Union."

She was really tired, but she didn't want them to be separated right now. "You'll get there quicker if you don't take us to a hotel first." She turned to their traveling companion. "Right, Alf."

"Yep." The way he was looking all around them with great interest, she wondered if he had ever been to Sault Ste. Marie.

Drake hailed a hansom cab, and they all climbed in while the driver put their luggage in the boot. "Western Union as fast as you can get us there."

The office, which was situated right beside the train station, was locked up tight.

"It looks as if we're going to a hotel without finding out anything." Drake stared at the building across the street. "There's one across the tracks. The Hutchison Hotel looks pretty new. Want to try it?"

Because she was so tired, she agreed. So did Alf. They entered the lobby, and she liked the looks of the place.

Drake booked two rooms, one for the men and one for her. They shared a meal in the hotel dining room. Norma enjoyed the delicious fare. It tasted and felt like a family meal.

Drake thanked the young woman who'd served them and handed her a folded bill. He was right to give the woman a tip, because her service was excellent. Carrying their bags, they headed up to their rooms.

"I really need to check your injury, Drake." She left her carpetbag in her room and brought her medical bag with her to the men's room.

Alf sat in a chair and stared out the window while she examined Drake. "Do you need something for pain? Aspirin or even laudanum?"

"I've had laudanum before. I don't like the way it knocks me out. The aspirin takes the edge off the pain so I can deal with it. I'll need to be able to think clearly in the morning." He gave her a tired smile.

She removed the dressing, glad to see how much the wound was healing. After cleansing it, she put on another bandage.

"Thank you, Norma. I'm glad you agreed to come with me. I trust your healing touch." Drake walked her next door. "Lock the door, and don't unlock it for anyone but Alf or me. Rest well."

She listened for his step on the squeaky board she'd noticed between their rooms, but he didn't move until after the key clicked in the lock.

I'm glad I came with you too. Drake's words of encouragement meant more than she could express. After all the time and all the people who had refused her ministrations, she no longer doubted her ability to practice her profession.

This journey was good for her as well as for Drake Logan.

Chapter 8

After a good night's sleep, Drake rose with the dawn. While he dressed, he tried to be quiet so he wouldn't wake Alf. Staring out the window at the pastel colors slashed across the clouds as if painted by the brush of God, he prayed for success in his quest. Peace descended on his heart as he whispered, "Amen."

Alf rolled over and stared at him. "Time to get up?"

"I'd like to be finished with breakfast by the time Western Union opens."

While Alf got ready, Drake went into the hallway and gave Norma's door a tap. She had been extremely tired when they went to bed. Even though they retired early, she might still be asleep. After a short wait, he turned back toward the door to his room. The click of the key in the lock caught his attention. He went back to her door.

She exited wearing a dark brown skirt and jacket with a shirtwaist the color of rich cream. These brought out the warm chocolate color of her eyes, with bits of gold sparkling in them.

"Have you been up long?" He tried not to stare at her, but her beauty overwhelmed him, robbing him of further speech.

"I was asleep by eight o'clock last night, so I awoke awhile ago. Longer than I usually sleep, but when I'm awake, I have to get up." She sounded chipper this morning. "Are we going to breakfast now?"

"Yes." He tapped on the door of his room, and Alf joined them. "After we eat, Western Union should be open. I'll go see what I can find out from the telegrapher."

The early morning sunlight brightened the lobby of the hotel as they descended the staircase. Other guests were headed in the same direction. A hostess met them at the archway between the lobby and the dining room.

"A table for three." He ushered Norma ahead of him and Alf as the woman led them to a table by one of the front windows.

When the hostess turned away, a young woman dressed in black with a white apron and a white cap on her hair appeared with a serving pot. "Coffee all around?"

He and Alf nodded, but Norma asked for hot tea. The next serving girl took their breakfast orders. Both men's meals were hearty, but Norma's was lighter.

"I thought doctors encouraged people to eat a good breakfast to start their day."

He couldn't help teasing her. His comments brought more color into her cheeks and even more fire to her dark brown eyes.

"My breakfast is adequate for a woman my size." She clipped each word. "However, I'm glad to see you have a good appetite. I take it you're not experiencing nausea, dizziness, or anything like that."

Always the doctor with me. He wished she'd relax and be more like she was on Whitefish Point. Maybe it was because he'd hired her to take care of him. They needed to get past these professional constraints. *But how?*

"What is your pain level this morning, Drake?" She watched him intently.

She didn't ask if he had pain, just how much. That illustrated what a good doctor she was. The pain was worse than yesterday morning, but he didn't want her to know how much. If she did, she might try to make him waste a day resting instead of following up on any lead he might get from the telegrapher.

"I wouldn't turn down some of that aspirin."

She opened her handbag and gave him the small packet. "I thought you might need this."

Their food arrived, and they started eating.

After she finished her first bite, she looked up at him. "I will be accompanying you to Western Union."

Not a question. She seemed to be waiting for his reaction to her statement. He knew she wouldn't like what he was going to say.

"No you're not." He took another bite of a biscuit, and it felt like sand in his mouth. He took a quick drink of coffee to wash it down.

She put her fork on her plate and daintily patted her lips with her napkin. "And just why is that? I'm here to make sure you're all right. It's the only reason I came."

"I promised your aunt I'd protect you while you're with me." He stopped eating and leaned toward her, glad no one was sitting at the tables close by. "You are a very beautiful woman. I can't protect you while I'm following leads. So you need to stay in your hotel room. A lot of men who might do you harm are in places like this."

Her face blanched then a blush stole its way from the collar of her dress all the way to her hairline. "I will only stay if Alf goes with you."

Drake glanced at the other man and received a nod from him. "I can go along with that if you promise me to stay in your room."

Norma clenched her teeth, and her lips thinned as she looked at Alf. "Only if *you'll* promise *me* you will bring him back to the hotel if he develops any problem with his health."

"I'm not goin' to leave his side."

As they left the dining room, Drake stopped to talk to the woman who managed the dining establishment. "If I'm not back by noon, could you have one of the girls take a meal to Dr. Kimbell in her room?"

After he made all the financial arrangements, he escorted Norma upstairs. "I didn't think it would work out like this, and I'm sorry to ask you to stay here. I give you my word that if I feel worse, I'll gladly return with Alf so you can treat me."

Worry lines furrowed her forehead. "I do understand, so don't worry about me while you're gone."

He turned away to go downstairs. When he reached the third step, he heard a faint whisper.

"And please come back to me."

Then her door clicked shut, and the key turned in the lock.

Drake heaved a sigh of relief that no one was in the Western Union office besides them. He didn't want other people to know why they were there. "I wonder if you can help with some information I need."

The telegraph operator stared at him from beneath his green visor. "And what kind of information would that be?"

Although the man kept records, the person who sent the telegram had just been another client. Nothing about him stood out in the operator's memory. "He did have a wad of money. He pulled it out of his pocket and peeled off the bills needed to pay for the message."

Interesting. Where did the man get so much money if he'd just survived a shipwreck? Wouldn't he have lost everything on the ship when it went down? Drake couldn't imagine a sailor carrying a wad of bills in his pocket while on the ship.

As he and Alf left the building, Drake shook his head. "Looks like that was a dead end."

"Too bad. I know how eager you were to find out something there."

The sound of horses clomping and a very squeaky wagon drew Drake's attention to the cobbled street across the railroad tracks from where they stood. The team of horses appeared to be straining to pull the wagon laden with packing crates. Someone had been careless and loaded too much weight for them to pull. His glance continued to the hotel where they were staying. He needed to let Norma know they didn't find out anything.

Something registered in his brain, and his gaze flitted back to the wagon. He didn't recognize the driver, but he did recognize the freight. Those crates contained parts of a new piece of equipment for one of the mines near Lake Superior. Equipment he'd watched being loaded into the hold of the *Amelia Logan* just days ago.

He wanted to shout but suppressed the urge. After taking a deep breath and slowly letting it out, he turned toward Alf.

"Don't turn your head, but did you notice the wagon that just passed?"

Alf nodded. "Yes. What about it?"

Drake started casually walking the same direction the wagon was headed, and his companion took the hint and accompanied him.

"That freight came from my missing ship. I saw our markings on the sides of the crates. They couldn't be here if she sank. Things could be salvaged from the shipwreck, but they wouldn't be in the condition those crates are."

The wagon turned down another street. They hurried to the intersection, and Drake peeked around the corner of a building. He figured they would be able to follow the wagon that was going slow enough for them to catch up with it if they wanted to. They could stay back but keep it in sight.

"Let's see where he's taking the load."

They sauntered down the sidewalk, occasionally meeting other pedestrians, but never taking their attention from the wagon. Several blocks later, the wagon pulled up in front of a warehouse. UNCLAIMED FREIGHT was emblazoned across the front. The driver left the wagon and went into the building.

"He's selling the freight from the *Amelia Logan*. I'd really like to get my hands on him." Drake's fists hung by his sides.

Alf gave a grim smile. "You can, and I'll help you."

"We need to be crafty about this. I don't want just this person. I'm sure he's not the one behind whatever happened." Thoughts were tumbling through his mind. "I want to catch whoever is behind this hoax. We should follow this man and see where he goes."

Alf took out his pocket watch and looked at the time. "Don't we need to let Norma know what we're doing?"

Drake shook his head. "And risk losing him? I can't. This is the only lead we have. If you want to go back—"

"I can't do that. I promised to stay with you." The man stared into his eyes. "We're in this together."

Drake clapped him on the shoulder. "Good man. We'll have to be careful and not let this driver know we're onto him."

They loitered on the sidewalk up the block from the warehouse and watched while several men unloaded the heavy crates. It took quite awhile, so they continued talking and gesturing as if they might be in a disagreement, to keep the driver from being suspicious.

When the empty wagon left the warehouse, it went faster, but the two men were able to at least keep it in sight as they hurried in the same direction. In a few blocks, the driver left the wagon and horses at a livery stable.

"He must have rented them." Drake slipped into a space between two buildings, and Alf joined him as they watched the driver hurry back toward the train station.

He entered the station, and they waited for him to come outside. When he did, he slouched down on a bench, leaned back, and pulled his hat over his face. He had to be waiting for something.

"You stay here and keep an eye on him." Drake gestured toward the man. "I'll go in and see if I can find out where he's going. If he should get up while I'm in there, go ahead and tail him. I need to know what he's doing. I'll wait for you at the hotel."

The station was almost empty. Only one family clustered on a bench at the other end of the station. He went straight to the ticket counter.

"I've never been in this area before. Do you only have southbound trains?" He glanced at the chalkboard with times of departure and destinations on it. "I see I'm wrong. You have northbound too. I assume they take you into Canada."

"Yes, sir. We're connected by our new railroad bridge with Sault Ste. Marie in Ontario, Canada. It's become a very popular destination. As a matter of fact, the fellow who was in here just before you is headed that way."

Yes. That was easy. "My friend and I would like tickets there also. When is the next train?"

"It should be pulling into the station anytime now. You want two tickets, you say?"

Drake hurried with the transaction. By the time he finished, he could hear the train approaching, the whistle piercing the air. Hurrying outside, he found Alf watching the approach down the tracks.

The man they were watching stirred, stood, and stretched as if he'd had a good nap. Unobtrusively, Drake kept the man in his sight.

Hissing steam started before the clacking of the churning wheels stopped. Metal on metal squealed as the huge monster braked beside the platform. Drake had always been fascinated with train engines, but steamships were much quieter than railroads. The excitement and stress of the morning, along with the loud noises, had his head throbbing. Dr. Kimbell wouldn't condone what he was doing. But he couldn't stop now. He gritted his teeth and willed himself to relax.

Passengers disembarked, and the driver who'd sold the freight entered one of the cars. Drake led Alf into the car directly behind. He chose a seat where he could see all the way through the passenger car in front of them. He'd be able to see anyone who got out into the aisle.

Alf remained standing. "How about if I go into his car and keep a closer eye on him, just in case?"

"Sounds like a good idea to me."

With Alf in the other car, Drake could relax. Maybe even enough for this drumbeat in his head to settle down a bit. How he wished he had some of that aspirin powder right now. And Norma with it, he had to admit to himself. Her presence brought comfort to him...and something more he wasn't ready to name.

Chapter 9

Norma had nothing to do. When they'd left home, she thought that if they had to be here overnight, it would be a short stay. If she'd realized it could be more than that, she would have brought a book to read and more clothes. This morning, she clung to the idea that they would go home later today. But the men had been gone for hours. It was past noon, and worry crept into her thoughts as she paced from the window to the door for the hundredth—or thousandth—time.

At first, she'd prayed as she paced. For Alf. For the success of their venture, whatever that meant. For Drake. She didn't want to let her thoughts settle on him too much. She wondered if his head was hurting and wished she'd given him a few packets of aspirin powder to take with him. If he became nauseated or weak, would he just push through without even telling Alf? *Probably.* Why were men so stubborn? She should have insisted that Drake let her accompany them. She'd make him take care of himself.

The man was consistent and focused on his quest to find out about his ship. The *Amelia Logan*. She wondered if there was a woman named Amelia Logan. If there was, who would she be? His mother? His sister? She didn't want to think it, but his wife? That thought cut straight through her, slicing all the way to her heart.

She'd never felt this way about a man. What could it mean? If he was married, nothing. If he wasn't, how could she find out?

In medical school, they were warned against developing romantic feelings for any of their patients. So that couldn't be what she was feeling. It. Could. Not. Be! She would rein in her emotions.

She was about to wear a permanent path across the beautiful room-sized rug. Again, she began praying. For their safety. For them to return. For Drake not to have any lasting effects from his fall and injury. That should have been her first thought, not an afterthought.

She dropped into the chair beside the window, and tears breached the dam of her lower eyelids and dribbled down her cheeks. *Dear Father God, I think I may be falling in love with Drake. If this isn't in Your will, please cleanse these feelings from my heart.*

A timid knock sounded on her door. She grabbed a hankie and dabbed at the tears, mopping them up, hoping her face wasn't splotchy. Maybe it was Drake at the door. She didn't want him to be able to discern what she had been feeling. But would his knock sound timid? She doubted it, unless he thought she might be napping.

"Yes." Her heartbeat accelerated. She unlocked the door and opened it only wide enough for one eye to peek out. *It's not him.*

"Dr. Kimbell?" One of the serving girls stood with a tray in her hands.

"Yes." She opened the door all the way.

"I hope you like chicken and dumplings. This is the lunch Mr. Logan ordered for you." She came in and set the tray on the table beside the chair where Norma had been sitting.

In addition to the chicken dish, an assortment of fresh vegetables was on the tray and some kind of sauce nearby. A large biscuit rested on a saucer, and butter and a small pot of honey was also on the tray. Her stomach growled.

"I'm sorry to be so late bringing your food, but the dining room was hopping for the noon meal."

"This is just fine." Norma went to get her handbag. "What is your name?"

"Molly."

"Well, Molly. I want to thank you for your service." She handed her a folded bill.

"Thanks, Dr. Kimbell. Is there anything else I can do for you?"

"Maybe." A smile crept over Norma's lips. *This girl might be able to help me.* "I'm accompanying Mr. Logan, because he had an accident, and I'm his physician. My friend came with us to help however he was needed."

The girl nodded, her eyes sparkling with interest. "What do you need me to do?"

"This was supposed to be a short trip. I didn't anticipate staying so long, so I didn't bring anything to do while they are gone. Is there someplace close where you could obtain a book for me?" She hoped she wouldn't have time to finish a whole book, but she could buy it and take it home for later.

Molly squinted and looked as if she was thinking hard. "There are no stores with books near here, but my roommate just finished reading that new book by George Mcsomething, Somebody's millions. . . Oh yes, *Brewster's Millions*. She really enjoyed it. Said it was kind of crazy though."

"Have you read it?"

Molly shook her head, setting her curls to dancing. "Oh ma'am. I'm not much of a reader."

"If she's willing to let me read it, and if I don't finish before we leave, maybe she'll sell it to me. Or I can try to find a store with a copy."

"I'll ask her." Molly went out the door, and Norma locked it behind her like Drake told her to.

Sitting down at the table again, she bowed her head and thanked God for the food. And for the possibility of obtaining a book to read while she waited for the men to return. While she was eating, she pushed her worries about them to the back of her mind. The food was delicious.

An hour later, Molly returned to pick up the dishes with a book under her arm. "You were able to borrow it." Norma gave her a big smile. "Thank you so much."

After Molly exited, she stacked the pillows against the headboard of the bed, removed her shoes, and nestled down to start reading. In only a few pages, the story captured her full attention. And she agreed it was a crazy idea. How in the world could anyone spend a million dollars in a year? And with the restrictions on how he could do it, that man was in real trouble.

When she received her inheritance, she'd carefully planned what to do to make it last as long as possible. Uncle Charles had taught her a lot about handling money. It had carried her through medical school. She even had a couple of investments that brought her interest payments. But now that she didn't have a position in a medical practice, she'd have to be extra careful.

Getting back into the story, she relaxed. Soon she had a hard time keeping her eyes open, but she couldn't stop reading. Each new development brought another level of problems for Montgomery Brewster.

A knock on the door, louder this time, woke her up. She glanced toward the window. Daylight still lingered, but the sun was nearing the western horizon. *How long have I been asleep?*

Another knock sounded more insistent. *Drake. He's here.* After jumping up, she tried to press the wrinkles out of her skirt as she approached the door. She flung the door open wide and almost called out his name. Before she could, she realized Molly was standing in the hallway wringing her hands.

"Come in, Molly. What's the matter?"

The girl stayed where she was. "Oh Dr. Kimbell. We need you downstairs. One of the cook's helpers has a terrible cut on her hand, and we can't stop it from bleeding."

"Don't worry. I'm coming." She grabbed her medical bag and hurried after the girl.

Molly took her down a back staircase that was a shorter distance to the kitchen than the ornate one in the lobby. It must be the one the staff used. They approached a small room across the hall from the large, bustling kitchen. The supervisor they'd met that morning sat with a girl who had what looked like blood-soaked kitchen towels wrapped around her hand. The supervisor's soothing words didn't seem to be working, because the worker sobbed while the woman mopped her tears with another towel.

"Mrs. Wilson, this is Dr. Kimbell. Remember her from this morning?" Molly pulled Norma's arm as they rushed into the room.

The supervisor didn't get up, just kept trying to calm the patient. "Dr. Kimbell, thank you for coming so quickly. I hate to bother you, but our regular doctor is at a farm in the country delivering a baby."

Norma moved close to the two women. "What's your name?" she asked the crying woman.

After another sob, she glanced toward Norma. "Mary. Mary Norton." Her shoulders and hands shook.

Norma hoped she wasn't going into shock. She addressed Mrs. Wilson. "Just how much blood has she lost?"

"Quite a lot. That's why I sent Molly up to get you."

Norma took Mary's hand and unwrapped the mess of towels. "Please bring some hot water and more towels. I have material to bandage her, but we must get this cleaned. I will need to use stitches to close a cut this size."

An hour passed while Norma gave the young woman laudanum, cleaned the wound, sterilized it, stitched it up, applied some ointment over the closure, and bandaged it.

"She needs to go to bed immediately. Someone must watch over her now and through the night. I'll come back in the morning to check on her." She washed her hands while she was talking. "And, Mrs. Wilson, be sure to send someone for me if she doesn't sleep through the night, or if she develops a fever. She can have sips of water, and tomorrow we can start her on broth."

Molly walked Mary out of the room.

The supervisor stood by the door as she had through the entire treatment. "What do we owe you, Dr. Kimbell?"

"I'm glad I was able to be of service to you. You can pay me what you would have paid your regular doctor."

"I'll have the money for you before you leave." The woman walked her to the lobby, where Norma went upstairs.

First Drake, now Mary Norton. Was God trying to tell her that she would continue to practice medicine? *Thank You, Lord.*

When the man Drake and Alf were following disembarked from the train in Sault Ste. Marie, Ontario, they stayed far enough back in the crowd so he wouldn't notice them. He went straight to the docks. A small boat was moored at the far end of the docks. After he went aboard, the boat headed west, staying close to the shoreline.

Drake left Alf at that end of the docks, watching to see if the boat changed directions. It didn't take long for him to find a boat owner who was happy to hire out his boat so they could follow the other vessel. Keeping their distance while never letting the boat get out of sight, they followed the man for the next two hours.

Drake was about to give up when the boat they were watching turned north and disappeared into the forested shoreline. He went to the captain of their vessel.

"Can this boat go any faster?"

"Yes, sir. I was just holding her back because you didn't want us to be seen."

At the place where the other boat disappeared, there was an inlet large enough for more than one ship the size of the *Amelia Logan* to enter. Just as they spied the entrance to the channel, the sun dipped behind the horizon.

"Keep on going past this, and we'll search the area." Drake raised the captain's spyglass to his eye and focused on the waterway from inside the cabin of the boat.

There she is. He'd know her anywhere. As he watched, oil lamps and lanterns began to glow through the twilight from the deck and wheelhouse of his ship.

"That's her all right. The *Amelia Logan*. My ship that disappeared. It wasn't a shipwreck at all." Drake clapped Alf on the back. "We did it! We found her."

"So what are we going to do about it?" His companion sounded practical.

"That is a good question." Drake turned to the captain. "Are there pirates on Lake Superior?"

"None that I've heard of." The old sailor slowed the speed of the boat.

"So the ship probably wasn't hijacked." Drake didn't even want to voice what that meant. "I can't imagine my captain or crew taking her from her regular route. But someone on the ship could have mutinied. I just can't figure out how he could have gotten away with it."

The captain started a slow turn that would take them away from the shore before going back toward Sault Ste. Marie. "I'll turn all our lights off so we can't be seen from the inlet, and navigate using the stars. We'll head back on a straight course, not following the shoreline. It won't take us as long as it did to get here."

Drake stood near the porthole and stared toward the waterway where his ship lay at anchor. He wouldn't have been able to see the ship if the lights weren't lit on her.

Alf stood by the captain. "What can we do when we get to the city?"

"My brother-in-law is one of those Mounties. You know, the Royal Mounted Police. They would have jurisdiction way out there where the ship is. I'll take you to meet him. See if he has any ideas."

Finally, an idea that sounded good to Drake. He could hardly wait to get his ship back. . .and the sawmill's money to Mr. Henderson.

That is, if it was still there.

Chapter 10

Four *whole days*. The men had been gone for four days. Norma had borrowed and read several more books. With Molly accompanying her, she'd gone to a department store to buy a couple more outfits. She cared for her patient with the injured hand. But the worry for Drake and Alf was always on her mind.

While at the store, she asked for a newspaper. Had the unidentified bodies of two men been found anywhere in the area? The only reason she could figure for them to be gone so long without even trying to contact her was if they were dead. She didn't find any mention of bodies, but that didn't mean anything. Maybe they just hadn't been found yet.

She'd spent the entire morning grieving, convinced she would never see them again. If she didn't hear something by the time she went to bed that night, she would make arrangements in the morning to return to Whitefish Point.

Each time she thought about Drake, another part of her heart broke. She remembered the way his intense eyes, the color of a spring forest, stared into hers from time to time as they traveled. His blond hair had just the right amount of wave in it to maintain its shape when he combed it, but she also remembered the unruly curl that often fell across his brow when they were returning to the lighthouse after his fall. Somehow, God had not removed her feelings for this man. She was confused. Weren't people supposed to take a long time to get to know each other?

Oh, she had heard about "love at first sight." She had always thought it was an exaggeration, but her feelings had grabbed her the first day she spent with Drake, and they hadn't let go. Thinking about his death, she felt like a widow. . .which was absurd. Maybe she should have bought a black dress when she was shopping. *Dear God, these morbid thoughts aren't helping.* She shook her head to dislodge them.

A strong knock on her door captured her attention. Remembering the things Drake told her, she once again opened the door only far enough to peek out with one eye.

"Drake!" She threw the door open so fast the knob hit the wall and bounced back.

She rushed through the doorway and threw herself into his outstretched arms.

They closed around her as his head descended toward hers. Without another thought, she turned her face up toward his and welcomed his kiss.

Everything around them faded away, and she was lost in feelings she'd never imagined. Something passed between them like a connection that could never be broken. She almost forgot to breathe.

Finally, he pulled back, and as their eyes met, she read in his gaze the glimmer of the same feelings she'd been experiencing. Then she remembered she was a doctor, and he was her patient.

When she looked down and stepped away, his hand caressed her cheek. "I'm sorry. I didn't have the right to do that. But I'm not sorry I kissed you. I missed you so much while we were gone."

His cheeks were covered with a short beard. *A red beard.* She'd never seen a man with blond hair and a red beard. In this light, she could see faint red highlights in the soft curls on his head. She touched his face with her fingertips. The short hairs felt so soft. She remembered the times when her father hadn't shaved and his whiskers roughened her cheeks. This was so different.

"I cleaned up at the hotel where we stayed in Canada before we boarded the train back to the United States, but I left my mug, soap, and straight razor in my room here. The beard will be gone in the morning."

She cocked her head at him. "I'm not sure I want it gone. I kind of like it."

"All right then. I'll leave it until you get tired of it."

That sounded as if he thought they'd be together a long time. She blew out a soft breath. That's what she wanted too.

"I like the sound of that." Finally, she looked around. No one was in the hallway with them. "Where's Alf?"

"He's staying on the *Amelia Logan* tonight."

That caught her attention. "You found your ship!"

"We'll tell you all about our adventure in the morning as we sail to Shelldrake on the *Amelia Logan*. I have cargo to deliver there." He dropped another quick kiss on her lips. "And I need to talk to your aunt. . .and your uncle if he is there."

"Come in and let me check your injury. We can leave the door open in case anyone comes by. They'll see what we're doing." She retrieved her medical bag and had him sit in the chair by the window so she could use the table beside it for the things she'd use.

She wasn't sure what she'd find under the bandage that hadn't been changed for four days. She was glad to see there was no more seeping from the line of stitches, and the line of flesh had fused a lot more. She carefully cleansed it and placed a much smaller bandage over the area.

When she finished, they headed downstairs together. Drake to talk to the manager of the hotel and the manager of the restaurant, Norma to check on her patient.

When they walked into the restaurant, Mrs. Wilson noticed them right away. "Mr. Logan, it's good to see you here."

"I'm glad to be back." He shook her hand. "I want to thank you for taking such good care of Dr. Kimbell."

The older woman looked at her. "She's a real good doctor. Our doctor was on a house call in the country when we needed a physician right away. She's a marvel. Now our doctor has returned, and he checked out Mary's injury just a few minutes ago. He praised the work you did on her hand." She reached into her pocket and handed Norma an envelope.

"What's this?" Drake looked from one of them to the other.

"Her pay for Mary's treatment. It's what our doctor would have charged. We were blessed to have her here."

Mrs. Wilson made sure they had a table near a front window. The night's special was roast beef with carrots and potatoes and cherry pie for dessert, and that's what they ordered. While Norma waited at the table, Drake took care of his business with the hotel manager.

While they ate and talked, they exchanged a lot of lingering looks. Norma wondered what the other people in the restaurant thought. When she glanced around the room, no one even noticed. *How can they not notice this intense connection?*

After the meal, Drake walked her to her door. "The ship will be waiting at the docks, and we can leave as early as you are ready. We can have breakfast on board if you want to leave that early."

"I really do. Although I've been treated well, I'm tired of being in the hotel and eager to get home to Whitefish Point."

When she pulled her key from her handbag, he took it from her and unlocked the door. Her fingers tingled.

Before she went into the room, she asked, "What time should we leave?"

"Is six o'clock too early?"

She smiled at him before entering her room. "Not at all."

They sailed away from Sault Ste. Marie without a backward glance. Drake stood beside Norma at the railing at the bow of the ship, looking forward to talking to the Kimbells about his desires for a new life. He hoped they'd agree.

They soon joined Alf where their breakfast was being served.

He stood to greet them. "Norma, how have you been?"

"Worried. I couldn't imagine why you two didn't come back to the hotel. For a while, I even thought you might be dead somewhere. I had decided to leave this morning and return to the lighthouse station."

Drake pulled out her chair and seated her. "I'm so sorry. I didn't think it would take as long as it did to get everything taken care of, and I was remiss by not contacting you."

As they ate, Drake and Alf explained about seeing the freight from the *Amelia Logan* in Sault Ste. Marie, following the sailor, finding the ship, and contacting the Mounties.

Alf didn't look up from buttering his biscuit. "The Mounties found a group of sailors on the *Amelia Logan* that had mutinied."

Norma gasped. "Mutinied? Were these the regular sailors you employ?"

Drake was glad she showed an interest in his business. "Some of the sailors who usually sail with the ship didn't show up when it was time to sail. My captain understood the need for meeting the schedule, so he hired some sailors who hang around the docks in hopes of signing on for a trip."

Alf stopped eating. "That was a big mistake."

Drake put down his fork. "Yes, it was, because he didn't know anything about these men. But he needed to get the ship on the way to Shelldrake. I'm wondering why the sailors who usually manned the ship didn't show up. I'll have to check that out when I get back to Chicago."

Fascinated, she forgot about eating. "How did they get control of the ship?"

"Several of them saw the captain walking alone on deck late at night when most of the regular sailors were asleep. They waited until none of those on guard duty could see them and jumped him, tying him up and covering his mouth so he couldn't cry out. Then they locked him in the brig. Soon they had all the loyal sailors locked in there with him. The Mounties captured the rogue sailors and released the others from the brig. I had to convince a judge that we needed to deliver the rest of the freight they hadn't stolen. I'll contact my insurance company about the cartons they stole and sold." He noticed that the excitement of his tale brought high color to her cheeks.

While he studied her, his desire to taste those rosy lips again was almost his undoing. They needed to get to Shelldrake quickly. He knew the captain was making up as much time as he could. Soon all would be well. . .he hoped.

This woman had so many facets it would take him years to figure her out. Intelligent, beautiful, interested in helping others. The list could go on. But most endearing was how her inky hair fell in wavy rows all the way down her head with the rest of it gathered into a bun at the nape of her neck. Her long, slender neck that beckoned him to kiss her there. He shook that thought from his head. He had to keep his mind on other things besides her beauty until he could talk to her uncle

Charles. He hoped to gain the man's approval for courting her. And he hoped her uncle wouldn't insist on a long courtship.

He and Norma were once again at the bow of the ship as they approached the Shelldrake dock. He knew the moment she noticed the people waiting.

She grabbed his arm. "Is that who I think it is?"

"I certainly hope so. I sent a telegram before we left Ontario, letting them know when we'd be arriving."

While two sailors attached the ship to the dock and let down the gangplank, he stood beside an even more excited woman as her eyes roved over those waiting for them.

"Uncle Charles is home! And he brought the wagon to take us to the lighthouse station." She looked up at him. "You will come with us, won't you?"

As he smiled down at her, he nodded.

When they walked in, Norma saw that Auntie had prepared a feast for them good enough for the return of the prodigal son. Norma didn't feel she'd been gone long enough to merit this, but she knew it made Auntie happy. While they ate, they related to her aunt and uncle all that had transpired while they were gone.

After all the dessert was eaten and Alf returned to his quarters, Uncle Charles rested his forearms on the table. "As soon as I arrived home, my wife told me a lot about you, Mr. Logan. I've been fascinated with all the things I found out. I want to thank you for protecting our girl while you were away."

Drake stared at her uncle's face without flinching, even though the words hadn't sounded very friendly.

"I've come to care deeply for Norma, and I'd like your permission to court her. Since my father and I have a thriving business, and we have ships that come this way, I'll be able to stop by to see her often. My desire is to see her achieve all her dreams. If she wants to open a practice, I can help her do that. And there are other ways she can use her medical abilities, if that's the direction she wants to go." His face looked like a stiff mask, and he kept his eyes trained on her uncle.

After this staring match between the two men she loved the most, Uncle's eyes twinkled. "I'm afraid you're asking the wrong person, young man. Do you know whether Norma wants to be courted or not?"

She had to clench her teeth to keep from saying something she might regret.

"No, sir. I'm not sure." Silence hung heavy in the room like a sail when the wind died down.

Finally, Drake sought her gaze and locked his with it. "My dear Norma—"

She felt heat travel up her neck, through her cheeks, to her hairline. *What a time to become flushed like this.*

"May I have the honor of courting you with a goal of marriage?"

That last word was her undoing. *Marriage.* She glanced at her hands. They'd been impulsive when they kissed, but he had never said anything about love and marriage.

Oh, she loved him with all her heart, but she hadn't been sure about his feelings before now. Gazing up at him, she read the uncertainty in his eyes as he awaited her answer.

"Yes. . .yes. Being courted by you would be wonderful." Tears filled her eyes.

He brushed them away with his thumbs. "I love you, precious Norma."

His lips descended to hers, and she met them with glad anticipation. This kiss swept her away from the lighthouse station to a private place where they were alone. After it ended, he leaned his forehead against hers and breathed deeply as their hearts beat as one.

They parted, and when she looked around, no one else was in the room. When had her aunt and uncle left?

It didn't matter. Drake once again took her to that magic place they had just visited.

I hope Uncle Charles doesn't insist on a long courtship.

Dear Readers,

Thank you for buying our collection. I hope you enjoy our stories as much as we enjoyed writing them.

A few things about this story. I try to make everything in my books historically accurate, so I do a lot of research. Almost everything in my story is authentic. Norma and Drake and their story is fiction. I did use the actual names of the lighthouse keeper, the first assistant lighthouse keeper, and the second assistant lighthouse keeper at Whitefish Point Lighthouse station in 1902. I couldn't find the name of Charles Kimbell's wife, so I just called her Auntie in the story.

Shelldrake was a sawmill town. It later became a ghost town, and now even that is gone.

The Whitefish Point Lighthouse was the first lighthouse on Lake Superior, established in 1849.

Packet boats were authentic. So were steamships. The two cities named Sault Ste. Marie (pronounced Soo Saint Marie) are sister cities, one in Michigan, the other in Ontario, Canada. A few years before the time my story is set, a railroad bridge was built to connect the two cities, and there was even a part of the bridge where pedestrians could walk across to the other city.

Lena Nelson Dooley

Multipublished, award-winning author **Lena Nelson Dooley** has had more than 900,000 copies of her 48+ books sold. Her books have appeared on the CBA, *Publisher's Weekly*, and ECPA bestseller lists, as well as Amazon bestseller lists. She is a member of American Christian Fiction Writers and the local chapter, ACFW-DFW. She's a member of Christian Authors' Network and Gateway Church in Southlake, Texas.

In addition to her writing, Lena is a frequent speaker at women's groups, writers' groups, and at both regional and national conferences. She has spoken in six states and internationally. *The Lena Nelson Dooley Show* is on the Along Came a Writer Blogtalk Radio network.

Lena loves James, her children, grandchildren, and great-grandchildren. She loves chocolate, cherries, chocolate-covered cherries, and spending time with friends. Travel is always on her horizon. Helping other authors become published really floats her boat, with over fifty having their first book published after her mentoring. The high point of her day is receiving feedback from her readers, especially people whose lives have been changed by her books.

Visit her website at www.lenanelsondooley.com.

The Wrong Survivor

by Marilyn Turk

Chapter 1

Au Sable Lighthouse
September 1911

Pausing from her daily lens polishing, Lydia Palmer peered through the windows of the lantern room high above the sapphire-blue water of Lake Superior at the boat heading toward the dock below.

She squinted, shielding her eyes against the glare of the bright afternoon sun. It was the lighthouse tender bringing their monthly supplies. Maybe it was bringing some mail too. Anticipation fluttered in her chest. Was there a letter from Nathan? He'd sent one every month since last spring when he left with his brother to work on a freighter.

She'd eagerly waited for each supply boat, hoping there'd be another letter from him, but none had arrived in the last two months. His parents, Assistant Keeper Drake and Mrs. Drake, hadn't received one either. Lydia sighed. How could she bear the next two months without hearing from her fiancé before the shipping season ended and he returned home?

The boat disappeared beyond her line of vision as it neared the boathouse.

Eager to find out if it brought word from Nathan, she hurriedly climbed down the ladder to the room below, then lifted her long skirt to keep from tripping as she rushed down the wrought iron spiral steps of the lighthouse. When she reached the bottom, she ran into her father coming in the lighthouse door.

His hands stretched out to catch her. "Whoa! What's the hurry, Lydia?"

Breathless, she said, "The supply boat is coming in to the dock. Maybe it brought a letter from Nathan this time."

Papa held her by the shoulders. "Calm yourself. Don't be disappointed if there isn't one. Sometimes it's hard to send letters from the ships."

She wouldn't give up hope though. There had to be news from Nathan. "But maybe there is. I have to find out."

"Fine. I'll go with you to the boathouse and get our supplies."

He let her go, and she hurried out. Mama was in the yard, beating a rug that hung on the clothesline.

"Mama! The supply boat's here!"

Mama glanced up.

Lydia didn't wait for her mother's response but rushed around the assistant keeper's house toward the dock. She started down the hill with Papa following behind but stopped when she saw Mr. Drake walking up the hill helping another man who leaned on a crutch. The man's hat hid his face from view, but something was familiar about the tall stranger whose dark hair curled out from the hat and over his collar.

Lydia's breath caught. *Nathan?* Yes, it had to be. She ran down the hill to meet him, but when the man looked up, she froze.

It wasn't Nathan. The man who was a mirror image of her fiancé was his younger brother, Jesse. She looked behind him toward the dock where men were unloading supplies. Surely, Nathan was here too, if Jesse had come home.

"Jesse, where's Nathan? Why isn't he with you?"

Jesse fixed a solemn gaze on her so unlike his normal carefree personality. He glanced at his father then shook his head.

As if she'd been punched in the stomach, Lydia collapsed into herself. "No!" she screamed.

Her legs went limp. Papa caught her before she hit the ground. Bits and pieces of information floated around her ears. A storm. Ship wrecked on a reef. Ship split in half. Sank. Jesse survived. Nathan did not.

As Jesse settled into the chair in his childhood home, his mother stood beside him with her hand on his shoulder, sobbing into her handkerchief. His father stood on the other side of him, speechless. Jesse hung his head but stole glimpses of Lydia lying on the sofa where her father had carried her, wishing he could go to her.

Each sob from Ma twisted Jesse's gut. And now fresh pain knifed through him seeing Lydia's misery. If only he could have spared her the news. If only he'd had someplace else to go. But where else would he go besides home? He'd stayed in Grand Marais for over a month until he was well enough to come home. Even though the shipping company wanted to send a notice to his parents, Jesse insisted he be the one to break the news about Nathan. He still needed to recuperate from his own injuries, including a broken ankle that hadn't healed yet. But more than anything, he had to see Lydia, explain what happened, and console her.

Jesse shuddered as the cries of his shipmates resonated through his mind. When the ship crashed into the reef, throwing him into the water and separating him from his brother, he'd called out Nathan's name until he had no more voice. He never saw his brother again. If only they'd stayed together. If only Nathan hadn't gone with him. If only. . .

But there was nothing he could do. He hadn't been able to save Nathan, and he couldn't bring him back. And no amount of his own pain would make up for the pain he'd caused everyone else.

How could he ever explain to dear, sweet Lydia? His heart pulled him toward her, his arms yearning to hold and comfort her, but that would never be possible. She would never forgive him for taking her future husband away. She wanted Nathan's arms around her, not his.

He shouldn't have convinced Nathan to go with him on a last grand adventure together as brothers. He'd teased him and cajoled him to have a final chance at freedom before settling down and becoming a lighthouse keeper like their father. Like Lydia's father. Jesse was the one who wanted to get away from the boredom of the lighthouse and discover the thrill of a mariner. A thrill that would never return.

And now Lydia was paying the price for his boredom. His grand adventure.

A warm wet muzzle rubbed against his hand.

Jesse tore his gaze away from Lydia to look at his dog, Buddy, sitting at his feet. The coal-black Newfoundland's bushy tail thumped on the floor as his luminous dark eyes studied Jesse's. Only his dog could show such blameless love or maybe even sympathy, if dogs could feel such things. Jesse lifted his leaden hand to stroke Buddy's head, and the dog whimpered. Buddy seemed to know something was wrong.

"Hi Buddy, you old mutt," Jesse whispered, choking back tears as he leaned over to hug the dog's head. Buddy responded by licking him on the face. Those licks were most likely the best welcome home he was going to receive.

"He's been sitting at the door since you and—since you left," Pa said.

Jesse straightened and nodded, trying to smile, but the effort was pointless. Wiping his wet eyes, he glanced back at Lydia, who hadn't moved from where she lay on the sofa. Had she fainted? Was the news too much for her? He fought against the urge to go to her. But he had no right.

As if reading Jesse's mind, Buddy stood and walked over to the sofa. He stuck his nose under Lydia's reddish-gold braid, which had fallen over her face, and began nuzzling her. She reached out to pet the dog's head, signaling her return to life. Brushing her hair out of her eyes, she pushed up to a sitting position and looked around as if to orient herself.

When her gaze landed on him, her eyes registered recognition. Then they darkened and smoldered, filling with tears. The searing accusation in her eyes stung Jesse. There was no doubt about her feelings toward him. And obviously, there was no chance for forgiveness.

Chapter 2

"Lydia, take these clothes and hang them out to dry." Mama shoved a basket full of damp clothes toward her. "The fresh air will do you good."

Sighing, Lydia took the basket and lifted her gaze to her mother. The basket might as well have been full of rocks. "I don't feel very well, Mama."

Mama put her arms around Lydia's shoulders and squeezed. "I know you're hurting. We all are. But we must get on with living."

Pushing the screen door open to the backyard of the keeper's house, Mama held it so Lydia could pass through. Lydia carried the heavy basket down the stone steps and over to the clothesline. The brilliant sun was blinding after she'd been shut up for weeks in her bedroom with the curtains drawn. She dropped the basket on the ground and arched her back to stretch it. A brisk October wind blew off the lake, stinging her face. The water glistened with sunshine diamonds, a sight she used to find enchanting. But the vast lake had lost its charm when it betrayed her and stole Nathan.

Her eyes welled with tears again. When would she ever run out of tears? Sick of crying, she lifted the edge of her apron and dabbed her eyes. A bark from nearby caught her attention as a stick landed by her feet. She glanced down to see Buddy sitting beside her, panting and looking at her with imploring eyes. *Woof!*

Lydia looked over toward the Drakes' house. Her heart leaped when her first glance deceived her into believing she saw Nathan. But it plummeted when she realized it was only Jesse. Sitting on a bench behind his house some fifty feet away, his crutch beside him, he lifted his arm and waved.

"Sorry. He was supposed to bring it back to me," he called, offering a wry smile.

She was in no mood to play, but Buddy barked again, picking up the stick and dropping it on her foot this time to convey what he wanted.

"All right, you pest. I'll throw it this time, but don't bring it back to me." She picked up the stick and tossed it in Jesse's direction. The dog dashed off after it. To her relief, he took it to Jesse this time. She wiped her hands on her apron, took a clothespin out of her apron pocket, and held it between her teeth. Picking up a sheet from the basket, she grabbed the corners and snapped it to get the wrinkles out before tossing it over the line. She secured the sheet with clothespins before the wind could blow it away. Quickly, she hung up another sheet, hoping to place a shield between herself and Jesse, certain he was watching her.

Why did he have to be outside at the same time she was? Seeing him was a fresh reminder of her loss, not that she needed reminding. The emptiness in her heart would not let her forget.

Buddy returned once again with the stick.

"Buddy, I'm busy. I don't have time to play!" She grabbed the stick and threw it as far away from her as she could, restraining herself from throwing it over the cliff toward the water. The big black dog lumbered after his toy, tail wagging. Hopefully, she'd be finished hanging the laundry before he returned.

When she completed her task, she picked up the basket and went back inside where Mama sat at the small kitchen table peeling potatoes.

"Mama, do you need me for anything else?" Lydia asked.

Mama lifted her head, eyeing her. "Not right now. Why?"

"I'd like to go for a walk."

"To the lighthouse?"

"No. Not right now." Lydia hadn't returned to the lighthouse since she'd been told of Nathan's death. She didn't want to risk the chance of running into Jesse or his father. Nathan had hoped to become the second assistant keeper when he returned and they got married. No doubt Mr. and Mrs. Drake were suffering his loss as much as she was, but facing them meant revealing her anger toward their other son. She would spare them that anguish.

She went out the front door and strode away, making sure she was out of Jesse's view. She walked past the redbrick oil house and kept going, not knowing where she was heading. Just away. Away from everyone's inquisitive eyes. Avoiding the assistant keeper's home, she walked past the privy and the barn, across the field, then down the hill toward the fog signal building. She stopped at the brick structure and scanned the area, noting a steamer far out on the lake as it headed toward Marquette. If only she could be on the steamer so it could take her away from here, away from everything familiar, every reminder of Nathan and the future that had been lost with him.

She continued down the hill to the water's edge then plopped down on the seawall marking the entrance to the station boathouse. From here, she could see Grand Sable Dunes to the east, reminding her of happier times, times when she, Nathan, and Jesse had explored the area together. Had it been so long since the three of them were that carefree? When life was untroubled and adventurous?

They had such great fun, especially when Papa let them take the boat out to explore the multicolored shoreline of Pictured Rocks. She'd loved seeing all the caves and unusual rock formations, especially her favorite, the one they called Miner's Castle. A smile eased across her face at the scenes running through her mind, scenes where Nathan and Jesse had shown how brave they could be. Or foolish. The brothers were fearless as they jumped off the rocks into the water, certain they were immune to harm. Exploring the nearby forests, discovering the waterfalls, everything the three of them had shared brought them closer together.

She heaved a sigh as the memories pierced her heart. Life would never be the same again. Never again would the three of them be together like they used to be. Of course, when Jesse left for his first season on the boats, he had changed everything.

It'd been a shock when Jesse announced he was leaving. He'd talked about going on great adventures, but she never expected him to leave. She thought he intended to be a lighthouse keeper like their fathers, but she discovered that unlike Nathan, lighthouse keeping was not his dream. Lydia had missed him terribly, feeling as though she'd been forsaken. But while Jesse was gone, she and Nathan had grown closer. Nathan had revealed his feelings for her, and before long, they were no longer childhood playmates but an engaged couple.

When Jesse returned, the three didn't fit together as they had before. Jesse had almost become an outsider. Lydia was glad to see him again but couldn't allow herself to show it. She was Nathan's fiancée by then. Besides, Jesse hadn't cared enough about her to stay. The tension between the three of them became uncomfortable, as if Lydia and Jesse were vying for Nathan's time. And Jesse had won. Lydia's anger resurfaced as she remembered Nathan giving in to Jesse's persistent urging to experience life working on the lake before the marriage.

Lydia picked up a small rock beside her and flung it as far as she could then watched it splash into the water. She picked up another, repeating the motion and hurling the stone with all her might, as if the stone carried her hurt and rage with it. She stood, searching the ground for more rocks to throw then continued to hurl them into the lake, almost losing her balance with the effort. *God, why did You let this happen?* She threw another rock, then another, as memory after memory renewed her pain. She continued throwing rocks until her arm ached and she was exhausted, her eyes burning with angry tears.

Finally, she stopped and brushed off her hands before wiping them on her apron. She cast one last glance at the lake, then blew out a breath, turned, and stomped uphill toward home. Lifting her eyes to the lighthouse rising between the two keepers' houses, she noticed the glint of the sun reflecting off the glass of the lantern room, a signal beckoning her to return. The lighthouse had not betrayed her, remaining at its post as always. After dinner, she'd visit her old friend and her refuge.

Jesse had gone back inside his house after playing fetch with Buddy. From the upstairs bedroom window, he saw Lydia down at the boathouse. He watched the entire time she pummeled the lake with rocks, her long, golden braid flying with each toss. Small as she was, she'd always had a good throwing arm. More than once he'd been pelted by her when they were kids and he'd raised her ire by teasing. Fortunately, she'd only thrown pinecones at him instead of rocks. No doubt she was angry now.

In a way, he was glad to see her display such wrath. At least she was showing strength, a characteristic he admired in her. Lydia was no weakling. She pulled her weight at the station, never seeming to tire, but rather enjoying the work. Not only did she help with the lighthouse chores; she was brave. Even though she had her limits when it came to some of the stunts he and Nathan did, she seldom backed down from a challenge. He hadn't been around many women, but the girls he'd known in school were such sissies. Lydia was different.

What had she been doing for the last three weeks? She'd disappeared into her house after he returned. Had she fallen ill? Was it possible for someone to be physically sick from grief? Yes, all he had to do was look at himself for the answer. He'd had little appetite since the shipwreck. Ma chided him for losing weight, even though she too wasn't eating much. Jesse missed his brother, and the pain of being responsible for everyone's sadness weighed on him like a boulder pressing down on his shoulders.

But Lydia wasn't the type to stay inside for long, especially when the weather was nice. She loved the outdoors, enjoyed exploring the area as much as he and Nathan had. He was relieved to see her come outside, even just to hang clothes on the line. In the past, he'd have run over to talk with her. But running was out of the question now. At least until his ankle mended. Even if he could have run, the accusing glare in Lydia's eyes alone would've stopped him like a ship dropping anchor. Had she simply been avoiding him?

How he longed to talk with her like they used to. Ever since the accident, he'd wondered what her reaction would be. Would she blame him or sympathize with him? But now he knew. She blamed him. How could he ever apologize enough for her to forgive him? He shook his head. No, he didn't deserve her forgiveness. If only he could explain what happened, how he had tried to reach Nathan. But what difference did it make? He didn't save his brother. His throat constricted as he choked back a tear. Why did he have to talk Nathan into going with him? Why did Nathan agree?

When Jesse returned from his first season on the lakes, he discovered that Nathan and Lydia had become more than friends. She'd been like a sister most of their lives, but there were those times he wanted her for himself alone. But he knew

Nathan did too, so he went away and left her with him. He shouldn't have been surprised to learn that while he was gone they had decided to get married. He had pushed his own feelings for her aside.

Jesse turned away from the window. His gaze fell upon the other twin bed in the room—Nathan's bed. The void in the room was like the gaping hole in his heart that his brother, his best friend, had left.

His stomach knotted, and his eyes threatened tears. He remembered the night before the ship hit the reef. He and Nathan had been on the deck, gazing at the stars, when Nathan turned to him and said, "Jesse, if anything ever happens to me, promise me you'll take care of our girl." Jesse had laughed him off at the time. But did Nathan have a premonition that he wouldn't return? How could he keep that promise when Lydia wouldn't have anything to do with him?

And now Jesse questioned his motives for asking Nathan to leave. Was he trying to keep Nathan away from Lydia? Could he be so selfish? He clenched his fists then grabbed his crutch and hobbled out of the room. He couldn't stay in there with the memories it held. Making his way to the stairs, he gripped the handrail and hopped down to the first floor, then crossed the room to the front door.

"Where are you going, Jesse?" Ma said, wiping her hands on the kitchen towel on her way to help him.

"Back outside. I can't stand to be cooped up in here."

Ma pushed the screen door open and held it while he navigated the stoop.

"I know you can't, but soon you'll be able to get around better. Healing takes time."

Jesse glanced at his mother. Was she referring to his ankle or something more? Ma nodded, affirming her statement, but he could see sorrow lingering in her eyes, the pain she tried so hard to hide from him.

"I'm not sure everything can be healed, Ma."

"Perhaps never completely, Jesse. But the pain gets duller over time, and God will comfort us with good memories of Nathan."

Jesse reached out for his mother, embracing her as he fought back tears. "I'm so sorry."

She patted him on the back. "Quit blaming yourself. The shipwreck wasn't your fault. You hear me? It wasn't your fault!"

He pulled back and sniffed, wiping his eyes with the back of his sleeve. Then he eased his way down the steps, with his mother acting as a railing. Buddy came running from around the house at the sound of the door slamming shut.

Woof!

"Now Buddy, settle down. Don't make Jesse fall!" Ma scolded, commanding the dog to sit with her pointed finger. "Be careful, Jesse. This ground is so uneven."

He couldn't even go for a walk, except to the privy, and even that took great effort. "I think I'll sit right here on the stoop for a while." Jesse withdrew his pocketknife and a small piece of wood from his trousers.

"Well, call me if you need me."

After his mother went inside, Jesse turned the wood over in his hand, studying the grain. What would he whittle out of it? He couldn't tell yet, but he knew the wood hid a secret that would only reveal itself once he began carving.

When Lydia came up the hill, Buddy ran over to greet her. She stopped then bent over to pet him. Jesse's pulse quickened as she came closer. Her face was flushed, adding a rosy glow to her cheeks. Was it possible she'd become more beautiful since he left?

"Did you leave any rocks on shore?" Jesse said, trying to tease a smile out of her.

She glanced at him, surprised. "You were watching me?"

He shrugged. "I couldn't help myself. I remembered what a good arm you had when we used to see who could throw the farthest."

"And did you remember who won?" She was near the steps now.

"Hmm. Me?"

She shrugged. "Maybe once or twice." She glanced at his hands. "What are you making?"

He held up the piece of wood for her to see. "I'm not sure yet. Would you like me to make something in particular?"

She lifted an eyebrow then shook her head. "No." She turned abruptly and continued past the house.

He winced. She obviously didn't want to be around him.

Buddy sat at the bottom of the steps sniffing the air.

"What is it, Buddy? What do you smell?" Jesse gazed around the countryside, his view taking in the forests, the lake, and the dunes in the distance. "Fall's coming, isn't it? I feel it too. There's a cool nip in the air, and the trees are beginning to show some color." What trees still remained near the light station. He glanced toward the dunes and saw the giant log slide leading from the top to the lake below. Normally when winter returned, so did the loggers who cut down the trees that ended up on the slide to be floated down the lake to the sawmills.

But for the past two years, the logging business in the area had slowed after all the trees near town had been cut down. Grand Marais had dwindled to barely a hundred people since the lumber company and the sawmills closed and the loggers moved to other areas to find more trees. Jesse felt for the townspeople who'd based their livelihood on the logging industry, but he was glad he didn't hear trees falling anymore. Lydia felt the same way. She'd been outraged when she, he, and Nathan stumbled across a section of the forest that had been cleared since their previous visit. He and Nathan had to restrain her from going to the lumber camp and giving the loggers a piece of her mind.

He chuckled, shaking his head. She could be pretty feisty. You always knew what she was thinking, either from the look she gave or she'd tell you flat out. Nothing coy or mysterious about Lydia. And that's why he knew how she felt right now. What she hadn't said was spoken loud and clear through her eyes. After all, he deserved it.

Even her angry words would be better than not talking to him at all. When they were good friends, they'd been able to talk about most anything. But when he lost his brother, he lost Lydia's friendship too, and he doubted he'd ever have it back.

Chapter 3

Lydia, please eat something."

"I'm not very hungry."

"You've been pushing those potatoes around your plate long enough," Mama said at dinner. "Would you please put some in your mouth?"

Lydia stabbed a forkful of potatoes and shoved them in then forced herself to swallow.

Papa reached out and placed his hand over hers. "You should talk to Jesse."

She jerked her head to look at her father. "Why? I have nothing to say to him."

"You can show your respect and extend your sympathy. You lost your intended, but Jesse lost his brother."

Emotions warred inside her. Didn't Papa realize it was Jesse's fault?

"Your father's right," Mama said. "Jesse's grieving too."

Lydia's eyes filled with tears. "But he's the reason Nathan was on the ship!"

"Don't be unkind, Lydia," Mama said. "He didn't force his brother to go."

"You need to stop blaming him." Her father's eyes darkened, piercing her conscience. "Don't you think he blames himself enough already?"

Lydia's mouth dropped open. Why didn't her parents understand?

"Excuse me." She scooted her chair back from the table. "I'll get the dishes."

As she reached for the plates, her father caught her arm. "I could use your help cleaning the lantern room, if you're up to it. Mr. Drake and I have been working on the foghorn lately and haven't gotten around to the windows and brass."

Lydia mulled over the request.

"Of course, Papa. I'll take care of it first thing tomorrow." She welcomed the opportunity to help at the lighthouse.

"Thank you." He nodded with a slight smile. "You have a knack for making everything shine and look new."

Papa's praise warmed Lydia because she'd always taken pride in polishing the brass of the lens and keeping the windows spotless. Ever since she was a child and Papa had first given her some responsibility at the lighthouse, she'd tried to do her best, proving she was capable of being a lighthouse keeper herself one day. Of course, women were seldom granted such a position. But it wasn't unusual for wives of keepers to serve as their assistants. That was the dream Lydia and Nathan had talked about, that when he graduated from assistant keeper to principal keeper at his own lighthouse, Lydia would serve as his assistant. Her heart squeezed, knowing that dream would never come true.

The next morning, Lydia walked to the lighthouse and entered the side door. Her heart was heavy as she approached the steps to the tower. Lifting her skirt with one hand and holding the railing on the wall with the other, she trudged up the stairs, a task she'd done many times before, counting each of the ninety-eight steps as she ascended. But today, her feet were like lead and the steps higher than ever before. She stopped at the landing where the cleaning supplies were kept and withdrew what she needed before continuing. When she reached the top of the winding stairs, she hitched her skirt to her waistband to go up the ladder into the lantern room.

As she climbed through the opening and stood beside the huge Fresnel lens, the vast panorama of Lake Superior greeted her through the windows. The sight never ceased to inspire her as it stretched from east to west. Here in the tower high above the world, she felt closer to God and thankful for His magnificent creation. Although she'd never seen an ocean, she couldn't imagine any body of water larger than what lay in front of her. Somewhere on the other side, Canada's shores laid claim to the lake as well. Much as she wanted to stay angry at the lake for taking Nathan, Lydia's spirits lifted at the sight of its sparkling water on this beautiful fall day. And yet the lake could be fickle—beautiful one moment, then ugly and treacherous when storms blew in. How well she knew the way the lake could slam helpless ships onto reefs like the Au Sable reef, which lay just below the water in front of the lighthouse.

Lydia took a rag and some polish and began cleaning each little piece of brass and each small piece of glass that made up the lens, knowing how dust could interfere with the light's visibility. The job was painstaking and slow, but it kept her busy and gave her the satisfaction of doing work that was important. After a while, she transferred her attention to the glass windows, making sure no smoke had stained them. The more she cleaned the inside of the glass, the dirtier the outside looked. She squeezed through the small door leading to the gallery and stepped into the wind. Papa had warned her against going outside when the wind was strong, but today, it blew gently and slightly cool. She wiped and scrubbed the glass, her arm complaining from yesterday's rock-throwing frenzy.

When Buddy barked down below, she peered through the railings to the ground. Buddy was running circles around Jesse while he clumsily maneuvered his crutch across the yard, stumbling a couple of times when he stepped on uneven ground. She didn't want to watch him, but she couldn't take her eyes away. He looked pitiful, so unlike the strong, active man he used to be. *Serves him right.* Where did that thought come from? Had she become so hard-hearted she enjoyed seeing him suffer?

Just then, Buddy bumped into Jesse and he lost his balance and fell to the ground. As he pushed up to a sitting position, the dog rushed over to lick his face as if to say he was sorry. Jesse reached out to pet the animal but didn't attempt to stand. Couldn't he get up by himself? Lydia glanced away briefly, embarrassed to see his humiliation. She fought the urge to go help him, her anger subsiding at the sight of him so helpless. Jesse drew up one knee and laid his forehead against it. Had he hurt himself even more, or was he just resting until he could get up? She became self-conscious as she watched him. Had he seen her up here?

Jesse lifted his head and looked around, but not up, thankfully. She didn't want him to know she'd been watching him. But she couldn't just stand there and do nothing. She had to go help. She turned to go back inside the lantern room, but out of the corner of her eye, she saw Mrs. Drake come around the corner of their house. Spotting Jesse on the ground, she rushed over to help him up. Thank God someone had come to his aid, someone besides her.

Lydia stepped back inside but continued to watch through the window as Jesse's mother helped him to his feet. Once he was standing, Jesse nodded to his mother and waved her away as if to say he didn't need any more help. After she left, Jesse looked down at the ground and shook his head then lifted his face to the sky. Lydia backed away from the window. She'd hate for him to know she'd seen the whole incident. How embarrassed he must be to rely on someone else like that. Knowing Jesse and how much his independence meant to him, Lydia could imagine his frustration.

If they were still friends, she wouldn't have hesitated to help him. She would have rushed down the stairs to his side. But that was before. She turned away, not able to look at him anymore, and tried to ignore the way her stomach tightened. Why couldn't she let herself get through the wall that separated them since the accident?

He would have helped you.

She winced as a shard of guilt pierced her mind.

The lantern room darkened, and Lydia glanced over her shoulder to look outside. She gasped at the sight—a huge bank of gray clouds rolled across the water toward the lighthouse. *Dear Lord, fog.* She better let Papa know so he could light the beacon early and turn on the fog signal. Soon the dreaded noise of the screaming steam-powered foghorn would begin blaring.

She shuddered as the fog crept toward the lighthouse, a phenomenon that always frightened her the way it enveloped the lake and changed everything familiar into a mysterious ghostly world—a world that deceived ships and hid the dangers of the lake even more. Perhaps the fog wasn't as fierce as the storms that roared in with violent winds and shook the buildings, but it was no less treacherous.

She ran down the steps and out the door, heading to the fog signal building. She'd forgotten Jesse was outside until Buddy appeared at her heels.

"Something wrong?" Jesse called out from his spot on the wooden bench.

She jerked her head his direction but didn't stop. "Fog!" She pointed toward the water. "I'm going to tell Papa. He's with your father down at the fog house working on the signal. Hope they've got it fixed."

Jesse shoved himself up from the bench, grabbing the crutch. "I'd ask if there's anything I can do, but I'm sure I can't, at least not today." He glanced down at his foot and crutch then looked up with a sheepish grin. "Can't even race you to the signal building today."

She wanted to snap a quick retort but bit her tongue.

"Next time you can race me," she said over her shoulder as she hurried on.

"And I'll let you win," he shouted after her.

He watched her disappear around the corner of his house. If only he could get around better. He knew all too well the threat fog brought with it. Skeletons of ships still littered the beach near the lighthouse, testifying about the dangers just off shore. The mist drifted steadily onto land, cloaking the buildings in a haze. Moisture soon penetrated his shirt. He'd have to be careful getting back inside as his surroundings disappeared into the blanket of white. Fortunately, he knew the safest direction to head, as long as he didn't get disoriented. If he were to go toward the lake, he might end up falling off the edge of the cliff.

Once when he and Nathan were children, that very thing had happened when they played hide-and-seek outside on a foggy day. He shuddered at the memory of when he slipped over the edge, grabbing hold of a tree branch that broke his fall before he could plummet to the rocks below. Thank God Nathan heard his cry for help and came to his rescue, pulling him back up to safety. Jesse expelled a frustrated breath. He couldn't even return the favor.

Jesse made his way over to the house and felt his way around to the front steps, then hobbled up them and inside. Grabbing the stair rail, he limped upstairs to his bedroom, plopping down in a chair beside the window to stare into the haze. How many ships were out there? How many would find their way back to safe harbor?

At least he wasn't on one of them. Nor would he ever be. He had no intention of ever being on the water again. He shuddered as the memory of sinking below the frigid waves ran through his mind again. As soon as he was able, he'd have to find work somewhere else. Nathan had wanted to be a lighthouse keeper like their father, but Jesse had vowed to do something more exciting, to go places and see new things.

But now he no longer cared about such things and just wanted to stay on solid ground.

He could hire on at one of the logging camps, but it sickened him to see the verdant forests reduced to stumps and rubble. Sure, it was a way to make a living, but could he make himself do something his heart wasn't in? Or maybe he could work in a lumber mill. At least he wouldn't have to participate in harvesting the trees. However, now that the nearest mill was closed, he'd have to go farther away to find work.

Why should he stay around here anyway? Lydia. He'd hoped they could console each other over Nathan's death. But now he knew the impossibility of that wish. She didn't want him here, and renewing their friendship seemed unlikely. Anything more would be impossible. He'd never be able to share his true feelings for her knowing those feelings would never be returned.

A mournful sound moaned into the fog, resonating through him as the fog-horn started up. He too was in a fog, trapped inside and smothered in a cloud like everything else, not only physically, but mentally as well, with no clear idea about his future.

But he wouldn't give in. He couldn't. Just because he was injured didn't mean he had to be a weakling. He didn't blame Lydia for not wanting to be in his company. Why would a woman want a man who was so helpless? He had to regain his strength, if he was ever to regain her respect.

Downstairs, a feminine voice called out. "Hello? Mrs. Drake?"

Lydia. What was she doing here? Where was Ma? He pushed to his feet and hopped across the room to the top of the stairs.

"Lydia, I'm here. Come on in. I'll be right down." He held on to the railing, clenching his jaw as he mustered the strength to slowly ease down the stairs, trying to make the effort look easier than it was.

Lydia stood inside the door holding a pot in both hands. Her forehead puckered as she watched him. "Do you need any help?"

"Nah. I'm getting pretty good at this." Could she tell he was lying? He hopped the last step down to the floor and released a breath then glanced at her and smiled.

"Mama made a batch of soup and wanted me to bring some over." She looked around the living room toward the kitchen. "Where's your mother?"

"I suppose she went to the barn." He waved his hand toward the window. "Hope she can find her way back in this stuff. Soup sounds good. Tell your mother thank you." He looked down at his bandaged foot then back up at her. "Would you mind taking it to the kitchen?"

"Of course, I'd be happy to." She headed to the kitchen, and he did his best to catch up with her.

"Sounds like they got the foghorn working." Maybe he could keep her here awhile longer.

She set the pot down on the stove then faced him. "Yes, thank God. And not a moment too soon."

"Guess we'll have to put up with the noise for a while." He offered a smile.

"Yes." She clasped and unclasped her hands and shifted her eyes as if afraid to look straight at him.

"Would you like to sit a minute? I'm sure Ma would like to thank you for the soup herself." He motioned to the sitting room. "Please. I could use some company."

She gave him a worried glance then looked away. "I suppose I can, for a little while. There's not much else to do right now."

He'd be happy for any time she gave him. They went into the other room, where Lydia sat in the rocking chair by the fireplace. He lowered himself onto the sofa, laying the crutch beside him. Lydia stared at the braided rug between them and started rocking.

"I've never liked the fog," she said, not looking up.

"I know. I remember how it used to scare you. I don't like it either."

She lifted her gaze. "I suppose it's pretty frightening when you're on a ship in it too."

He nodded. "It's eerie. All you can hear is the water slapping the side of the ship as it cuts through the waves. Seems like nobody talks, just listens."

"Everyone is quiet?"

"Yes, it helps to hear the foghorns and know their location."

She nodded, returning her gaze to the rug. "That makes sense."

Jesse looked around then clapped his hands together. "How 'bout I take you on in a game of checkers?"

Lydia glanced up at him, and the glimmer of a smile eased across her face. "Are you sure you remember how to play?"

"Some things you never forget—like beating you in checkers." He grinned, knowing how she hated to pass up a challenge. Maybe it would work.

She stood and put her hands on her hips. "Jesse Drake, how dare you claim to beat me! Where's the checkerboard?"

Jesse pointed toward the dining room. "On the sideboard."

When she headed across the room, he heaved himself up from the sofa and limped after her. She picked up the board and the checkers and spread them out on the table. "I'll take red."

"Your lucky color?" He smiled as a shred of hope bubbled through his gloom. She always chose red, a reminder of their past times together. Was there a glimmer of possibility their lives could return to a semblance of yesterday when they'd enjoyed each other's company?

"Absolutely!" There it was, the sparkle in her eyes he loved seeing. Those eyes that changed color with her mood, it seemed. Nathan said they were hazel, but sometimes they looked green, then magically would change to brown with flecks of gold, like her gilt-spun amber hair. Today, they were the color of the emeralds one of his shipmates carried, claiming the stones came from South America. How he had missed those eyes.

Soon he and Lydia were engaged in a combative game of checkers, testing each other's skill. Lydia twisted a strand of loose hair, pursing her lips while she concentrated on her next move. Long as he could remember, she'd twiddled with her hair when she was deep in thought. Did she even know she was doing it? He doubted it. His pulse increased as he studied her, the silken skin and delicate features. Had she always been so pretty?

He forced himself to refocus on the game. She picked up his checker and moved it.

"You don't have to cheat, you know," he teased.

Her eyes grew wide. "What? How dare you accuse me of cheating!"

He pointed to her mistake, and she blushed.

"Oh dear, I didn't mean to do that," she said, moving the piece back where it had been.

He pulled on his beard. "Are you sure it was there?"

"Of course!" She flipped her braid indignantly over her shoulder with her left hand while slapping the table with her right.

The action startled Buddy, who barked and trotted over to investigate. The big dog stood on his hind legs and put his front paws on the table, sniffing the tabletop.

Jesse laughed and said, "Buddy! Get down!" As he pushed the dog from the table, the animal's claws caught in the lace tablecloth and pulled it down with him, scattering checkers in all directions.

Lydia burst out laughing, and soon they were both laughing while trying to find the checkers and put them back on the table. Lydia knelt on the floor while Jesse leaned over from the chair to reach what he could.

They were still smiling and chuckling as they straightened the tablecloth and rearranged the checkerboard then tried to reposition the checkers where they had been before.

"I believe I was here," Lydia said, placing a red piece on the board.

"No, it was here," said Jesse, his hand closing over hers. Warmth rushed up his arm when his skin came into contact with hers. She glanced up at him, eyes wide with surprise. For a moment, their gazes locked, and he was reluctant to remove his hand.

Ma poked her head into the dining room and said, "Can I get you two some coffee or tea?"

Lydia jumped and retrieved her hand. Jesse turned to face his mother. "Didn't hear you come in, Ma."

"I came in the back door." She looked from Jesse to Lydia. "Hello, Lydia. I heard laughter when I came in and couldn't imagine who was here."

Her face pink, Lydia leaned back in her chair. "I brought you some bean soup Mama made today."

"I saw the pot on the stove. Tell her thank you."

"Buddy upset our checker game, and we were trying to remember where we were," Jesse said, pointing to the board.

Lydia glanced at the checkerboard then the wall clock. "I had no idea I'd stayed so long." She scooted her chair back and stood. "Jesse, I don't think either of us is going to win today. I better get home."

Jesse laid his hands on the table to stand.

"Don't bother getting up. I can find my way out."

He stood anyway. "I need to stretch my legs. I can at least walk you to the door."

She shrugged then watched him maneuver. Moving toward him, she reached out. "Can I help you?"

Jesse shook his head. "Thank you, but I can do it. I'm getting the hang of this thing." He smiled at her and lifted his crutch.

"Knowing you, you'll be rid of it in no time."

"Can't be soon enough." He hobbled toward the front door with her.

Mrs. Drake called out from the kitchen. "Be sure to tell your mother thank you. I know we'll enjoy the soup. Your mother makes the best bean soup I've ever tasted."

"I will," Lydia replied.

Jesse held open the door for her, leaning against it as she stepped out on the stoop. She turned around to face him. "At least you have the winter to heal before you go back to the work on the boats."

The remark caught him off guard. He stared at her, trying to come up with an answer. How could he tell her he wasn't going back to that life? And why he wasn't. Was she so anxious for him to leave again? His future was uncertain now, except for one thing. He was in no hurry to leave her again.

"Maybe I'll heal quickly and do something else."

Lydia's big eyes grew even bigger. "Do something else? What else would you do?"

"Could be a logger. Or even work in the mines."

Her mouth dropped open. Was that a look of surprise or alarm?

"You? But I thought you liked working on the lake."

He shook his head. "Not anymore."

Lydia tilted her head, studying him. But the question in her eyes never made it to her lips, and she shrugged before turning around, descending the steps, and vanishing into the fog.

Chapter 4

How long would they have to endure that dismal sound? The fog had already lasted two weeks, and the foghorn persisted, like a cow with its head stuck in a fence. No sense complaining about it though, since the noisy signal was as necessary as the lighthouse when the fog hid the light. A ship out on the lake would be grateful for the warning.

Lydia stuffed cotton in her ears to shut out the noise. Like a butterfly inside a cocoon, all she could see through the window was haze. Funny that even the lighthouse, so prominent in its position between the two houses, could be hidden behind a blanket of fog, the white of the tower blending into the mist.

She hadn't seen Jesse since the day they played checkers, but she couldn't stop thinking about the time they'd spent together. She mulled over their conversation. What had he meant by his comment to stick around longer? Why wasn't he going back to the boats? He'd been so anxious to get away from the lighthouse before, so why would he want to stay now? Surely he had no intention of being a lighthouse keeper. Had the shipwreck scared him away from the water?

She joined her mother in the warm kitchen. Picking up her apron hanging from a peg on the wall, she said, "Can I help do something?"

Mama rolled out some dough on the counter. With a biscuit cutter in hand, she pressed circles into the dough. She nodded. "You can grease the baking sheet."

Lydia took the can of lard and spread a thin layer on the metal pan, then she picked up the dough circles and placed them on the pan. When she finished filling the sheet, she opened the oven door and slid it in then wiped her hands on her apron.

"Mrs. Drake told me you and Jesse played checkers when you took the soup over," Mama said, putting away the flour.

"We did."

Mama crossed her arms and scrutinized Lydia's face. "I was glad to hear that. Did you have fun?"

"Fun?" Lydia suddenly felt guilty. Was she supposed to have fun?

"Yes, Mrs. Drake said she heard you two laughing."

Lydia's face heated. "Oh, we just laughed at Buddy."

"I see. Well, perhaps you could go back and play another game of checkers today."

Lydia shook her head. "I don't feel very well today. Maybe another day."

Mama quirked her mouth then pointed to the cupboard. "Go ahead and get the dishes out for supper." She picked up a dish towel and brushed flour off the counter then faced Lydia with a hand on her hip. "I've been thinking. Maybe you'd like to go visit your sister in Munising and stay with her awhile."

Lydia started. "Go to Sarah's house? Why, is something wrong with her?"

"Not that I know of, but Lord knows she could use some help with the children. She's got her hands full with three little ones. And a change of scenery might be good for you."

"When would I leave?"

"You could go after the fog lifts. Your father and I think you should spend the winter with her. What do you think?"

"The whole winter? That's a long time." The aroma of hot biscuits drifted through the room.

"Just a few months. Pretty soon, the lighthouse will shut down for the winter anyway. And you know how cut off from town we are when the heavy snows come." Mama opened the oven door, peeked at the browning biscuits, then closed it. "We can talk more about it later. Let's get the table set for supper now. I don't know if Papa will be able to join us or not, since he and Mr. Drake are taking turns stoking the fire for the foghorn."

Lydia took three bowls out of the cupboard then opened a drawer and retrieved three silver soup spoons that had belonged to her grandmother. Someday the spoons would be hers. Someday, when she got married and set up her own house. Her heart squeezed at the sight of the spoons, a reminder she would no longer be moving into her own house anytime soon. She took a deep breath then walked to the dining room.

"I wonder if Papa needs me in the tower," she said, placing the spoons on the embroidered tablecloth of the small dining room table. "I can go up there if Papa wants me to."

"You can ask him when he comes for supper." Mama pulled the steaming biscuits out of the oven and set the pan on the stove next to the pot of stew. "But since we don't know when that will be, let's not wait to eat."

Lydia held the bowls while Mama ladled stew into them. Stew always tasted best on chilly, foggy days like today. As Lydia carried the bowls to the table, Mama brought a pitcher of milk and a plate with the biscuits. She set them down then took her seat. Lydia sat across from her mother, and they bowed their heads.

"Lord, thank You," Mama prayed, "for this bounty which we are about to receive. Please protect those on the lake in this fog. Amen."

Lydia selected a warm biscuit. Taking a bite, she savored the flavor before crumbling half of it into her stew.

"Jesse's ankle should be getting better," Mama said.

Lydia shrugged. "I'm sure he's pretty tired of not being able to get around like he wants to."

"I'm sure he is. He'd probably feel better all-around if he could move normally."

"He never did like sitting still," Lydia said after swallowing a spoonful of stew.

"None of you children did, especially you and Jesse. Always had to be doing something." Mama nibbled her biscuit.

Lydia studied Mama a moment, considering her remark. Why didn't she mention Nathan? Now that Lydia thought about it, she couldn't remember Mama speaking Nathan's name since the day Jesse arrived with news of his brother's death. Was she trying to protect her by not mentioning him?

"I suppose that's why Jesse left to work the boats. He was bored here."

"Guess he'll be returning to them when he heals, and the shipping season starts up again." Mama reached for the butter dish.

"I don't believe he will. He said he'd be looking for another kind of work."

Holding her biscuit aloft, Mama said, "He did? What, pray tell?"

"He said he might stick around."

"Would he be an assistant keeper?"

Lydia heard the unspoken words "like his brother." She shook her head. "Jesse never wanted to be one before." *Before the shipwreck.*

Mama studied her biscuit as she spread it with butter. "Facing death can cause a man to rethink his priorities. Maybe he's changed his mind about following his father's work."

Lydia focused on finishing her meal. Would Jesse ever be content to be a keeper? When he first came back, she'd been eager for him to leave again. But now, she wasn't sure she wanted him to go away. But what if he stayed? How long would it be before he got the urge to run off again?

Lydia stood, extending her hand to her mother's dishes. "I'll take those if you're done."

"Thank you." Mama followed Lydia into the kitchen. "I better make a fresh pot of coffee for your father."

Lydia washed their bowls and silverware. Leaving them in the dish rack to dry, she wiped her hands and made her way into the sitting room. The evening fog permeated the house with its damp chill.

"Should we start a fire in the fireplace?" Lydia called out to her mother.

"Oh yes, please do," Mama said, joining her in the sitting room.

Lydia took three logs from the small stack on the hearth and placed two of them side by side on the iron grate. From the wooden tinderbox, she chose four pieces of kindling and laid them between the logs. Reaching on top of the mantel, she grabbed a long match, then struck it on the brick and lit the kindling at each end. When the flames consumed the kindling, she added the third log on top of the stack. Soon the flames licked the logs, radiating heat into the room.

From her spot next to the hearth, Lydia looked to the window. It'd be dark soon. She quickly went to work lighting the two kerosene lamps. Mama joined her and sat in her chair beside one of the lamps, then leaned over and picked up her embroidery from the basket on the floor by the chair.

"What are you working on now, Mama?" Lydia leaned over to view the design.

"This will be a sampler for baby Helen. I've made one for each of the other two girls, so Helen has to have one too."

With three granddaughters, Mama never tired of making things for them. Lydia didn't care much for embroidery—she always got the thread tangled—so she'd given up trying. Maybe one day Mama would embroider something for Lydia's children. Pain etched her conscience. Would she ever have children?

Lydia walked over to the traveling library box the lighthouse supply ship had brought. She opened the doors of the wooden bookcase and examined the titles of the books lined up on the two shelves inside. Lydia loved to read, and the weather had given her plenty of time to browse the books since the library box had arrived. She'd already finished three of the books. She chose another then took it to the chair opposite her mother.

Mama glanced up from her work and eyed the book. "What's the title of that one?"

Lydia held up the book, displaying the title. "*A Little Princess*, by Frances Hodgson Burnett."

"Hmm. Sounds interesting." Mama returned her attention to her embroidery. "Let me know if you like it. Maybe I'll read it too."

Lydia doubted she would. When Mama wasn't busy working, she embroidered. The book held Lydia's interest a short while before her mind wandered back to the day she'd played checkers with Jesse. They'd had fun, almost like they used to. She chuckled, remembering Buddy's interference in the game.

"Read something funny?" Mama asked.

"Hmm?" She didn't realize she'd laughed out loud. "Yes, I suppose so."

Mama lifted an eyebrow before going back to her embroidery.

Wonder what Jesse was doing now? Was he as bored as she? She was certain of it. Maybe he'd like a book to read. She put down her book and went to search for one he might like.

"The book isn't good?" Mama asked.

"Oh, it's fine. I just thought maybe the Drakes might like to read some of them. I might take some over."

"Now? It's almost dark."

Heavy footsteps scraped the doormat outside before Papa came in, huffing from his walk up the hill from the fog house. He hung his hat and coat on the hat rack then faced the women. "I thought I'd grab some dinner before I go back out. Mr. Drake is keeping the steam boilers going now, but I'll need to relieve him. I checked on the lantern on the way here, but I doubt any ship could see it in this fog."

"I'll get your supper for you." Lydia took a book from the bookcase and stuffed it in her apron pocket before scurrying into the kitchen. She filled a bowl with stew, then took two warm biscuits from the oven, placed them on a saucer, and carried the food to her father seated at the table.

"Is there any hot coffee?" Papa asked.

"There is. Mama just made a fresh pot."

She went back to the kitchen, poured a cup, and took it to him.

"Thank you, Lydia." Papa took a swig of the hot brew and blew out an exhausted breath. "Just what I needed." He looked at her. "No one's in the tower right now, and I could use some help. Would you mind going up and keeping watch until either I or Mr. Drake can relieve you?"

"I'll be glad to, Papa." She grabbed her shawl from the back of her chair, wrapped it around herself, then headed to the door.

"You be careful," Mama said.

"Don't worry, I will." Wet air slapped her face when she stepped outside into the dusky mist. She glanced up, just making out the dim light in the tower. Pulling her shawl up to cover her head, she inched forward. Reaching out with one hand, she patted the side of the lighthouse around to the door, then pulled it open and went inside. She tied the shawl around her shoulders then climbed the damp steps to the landing before ascending the ladder to the lantern room.

The lighthouse appeared to be suspended in the clouds. She could barely make out the roofline of the assistant keeper's house on one side and her house on the other. Picking up the telescope, she peered through it toward the water, squinting to see if anything was visible on the lake. But she might as well have been looking at the steam coming off a boiling pot, for nothing else could be seen.

Except for the rumbling rotation of the lens machinery that muted the foghorn, all was quiet inside the glass room. Like the fog trying to penetrate the walls of the lighthouse, loneliness threatened to overtake her.

Reaching into her pocket for a handkerchief, she felt the book she'd taken from the bookcase for Jesse. She pulled it out and studied the worn leather cover. *The Return of Sherlock Holmes.* Lydia opened the book and perused the table of contents. Jesse would enjoy the book with its collection of mysteries.

When they were younger, Jesse entertained her with stories he made up about the caves they found in the Pictured Rocks cliffs. She smiled as she remembered some of the stories he'd created with his wild imagination, stories of fearful pirates, Indian ghosts, and insane loggers. Lydia chuckled at the vision of Jesse acting out the characters in his stories. He could make her laugh, which was one of the reasons she'd always enjoyed being with him. Like the other day when they played checkers. She craved that kind of company again, but was it fair for her to enjoy being with Jesse? Was it fair to Nathan's memory?

Jesse stoked the fire and watched the embers dance around. He stared at the blaze but didn't see it. All he saw was Lydia's face, smiling when they played checkers. His hope of being friends had been rekindled. It was so good to see her laugh again. He'd always gotten a thrill out of making her laugh, especially when she was angry or pouting. How he loved the way her face lit up and her eyes sparkled when she was happy. He wanted so badly to make her happy again, if she'd only let him. But he wasn't sure how she felt toward him. Her reaction to the news that he might not leave was hard to interpret. Was it disappointment he'd seen or just confusion? Why did he harbor hope she wanted him to stay?

Playing checkers with Lydia had been the best thing that had happened to him since the accident and, for a short while, had lifted the burden he'd been carrying. But was it fair for him to have fun with Nathan's fiancée? What right did he have to happiness when Nathan had none? No, he shouldn't stay. He couldn't take Nathan's place.

Lydia didn't know he had feelings for her. At one time, he and Nathan had even joked about which of them would end up marrying her. What if Nathan had left instead? Would Jesse have been the one she would have chosen? His heart raced at the thought. But he'd given up that hope when he discovered Nathan and Lydia were going to be married. Now it was too late.

Winter was approaching and the boat traffic on the lake would end. But he'd never go back to the boats again. The memory of the shipwreck still haunted him. His heart thumped in his chest as he remembered how he'd almost drowned, helpless under the waves, then the desperate prayer, *"Lord, save me."*

And then he was free, swimming to the surface and breaking through, gasping for air. But Nathan was gone. God had answered Jesse's prayer, but even his prayer had been selfish. Instead of asking God to save "us," he only asked prayer for himself. Jesse hung his head, swallowing the hard lump in his throat. *I'm sorry, Nathan. I'm so sorry.*

Chapter 5

The next day, Lydia hurried through breakfast and her morning chores. Sunlight brightened the fog as it tried to find an opening. Her spirits lifted at the possibility of the fog going away. She'd made up her mind to take the book to Jesse as soon as she could. But before she had a chance, Papa asked her to go to the tower and stand watch until Mr. Drake relieved her.

She made her way to the lighthouse and climbed to the top. Peering through the telescope was difficult with the glare of the sunlit haze in her eyes. Not that it mattered, since she wouldn't be able to see anything before the fog was gone.

When Mr. Drake arrived in the lantern room to relieve her, he shook his head and sighed.

"Sure wish Jesse could help us. I know he does too."

"What has he been doing?"

"Not much, whittling a little. Reading whatever he can find." Mr. Drake picked up the telescope and aimed it toward the lake. "He's also been walking back and forth in the house, testing out his ankle."

"Jesse never has liked to sit around much. Maybe he'll be able to walk without his crutch soon."

"He told me you two played checkers." Mr. Drake lowered the telescope and looked at Lydia. "Thank you for spending some time with him."

Heat rushed to Lydia's face. "I. . .well, we were both bored."

"His mother said it did him good. Maybe you can come back over and play another game of checkers. Or cribbage."

"We've always enjoyed trying to beat each other," Lydia said.

Mr. Drake smiled. "You can go now. I think the fog might lift by this afternoon, thank God."

He turned to face the water, and Lydia backed down the ladder to the stairs.

She reached the bottom of the stairs and paused. Should she take the book to Jesse? Or should she just go home? She started toward his house then stopped. Why was she nervous about seeing him again? She did get the book for him. The least she could do was give it to him. Or she could give it to his father to give to him. She glanced up the stairs. No, she wanted to give it to him herself.

Buddy barked when she knocked on Jesse's door. If Mrs. Drake opened the door, she'd just shove the book into her hand and leave. But the wooden door opened and Jesse stood there behind the screen door, eyebrow hitched.

"Hello, Lydia. Have you come back for a rematch in checkers?" He gave her a teasing smile.

"Wh–what?" she stammered. "No." She held up the book. "I just brought you this."

He pushed open the screen door. "A book? Come on in, and let's see it."

She took a step inside and placed the book in Jesse's outstretched hand. Her fingers brushed his briefly, and the shock of his touch radiated up her arm. She withdrew her hand quickly and clasped it with her other.

Jesse's gaze followed her hand then lifted to her face. Lydia's breath caught at the intensity in his eyes before she forced herself to look down at the book in his hands.

He returned his attention to the book as well, studying the cover. "Sherlock Holmes?" Opening it, he flipped a few pages, then ran his finger down the list of titles. "Look at all these stories." Glancing up at Lydia, he said, "Have you read any?"

She found a loose strand of hair and twisted it around her finger. "No, not yet. The book came in the traveling bookcase, and I thought you might like it."

"I'm sure I will. Thank you." He gestured to the sofa. "Have a seat?"

Lydia eyed the sofa. "I should check to see if Mama needs me. I just left the tower when your father came on duty."

"Come on, Lydia. You can spare a few minutes, can't you?"

"I suppose so, just a few." Buddy followed her as she crossed to the sofa and sat on the edge of the cushion. The dog put his head in her lap and she rubbed his furry ears with both hands.

Jesse limped over to the sitting area where his crutch was propped up next to the fireplace, and dropped into a chair nearby.

"He'll let you do that all day long." Jesse nodded toward the dog.

"Have you quit using the crutch?" A flicker of joy for his recovery tried to surface.

Jesse looked over at the crutch. "I'm trying not to use it in the house, at least." Glancing back up to her, he offered a wry smile with a twinkle in his eye. "If this fog hangs on much longer, I'm going to go to the fog house and help shovel coal. I've been pretty useless."

"Your father said the fog might lift today. The sun is trying to break through, so they might not need your help after all."

"Can't say I'm disappointed. 'Bout had my fill of that noise."

"I agree. It can get on my nerves."

"But soon as I get my 'legs' back, I'll race you to the boathouse."

She fought the smile but couldn't keep it from forming. Scenes from their past footraces played through her mind, spurring fond memories of happy times. "I'd win anyway, even though you do have longer legs."

"We'll see. Actually, I'd be content to just go for a walk right now."

Lydia twisted a piece of her hair, glancing out the window. "Me too. This fog makes me feel like a prisoner."

"I know what you mean."

Lydia's head jerked to face him as his words sank in. He was more a prisoner than she was. "I suppose you do."

Jesse nodded as he glanced at his foot. "When the fog clears, why don't we go for a walk? Maybe you can keep me from falling down." He lifted his gaze to her with hope-filled eyes.

Take a walk with him? Something fluttered in her chest at the prospect. Could she allow herself to do that? She looked back toward the window. "Maybe."

"Lydia, look at me. Please." Jesse's soft voice forced her to face him again. "Could we be friends again? Please? After all, we're not strangers. We've known each other half our lives. There's no reason for us to act so uncomfortable when we're together."

She fought the urge to argue. Wasn't Nathan's death a reason? "I want to be friends again. I really do. I wish we could have fun like we used to. But I'm not sure we can. I mean, what about Nathan? Is it right for us to go on like he never existed?"

Pain etched Jesse's eyes. He turned away before wiping his face with the back of his sleeve. When he spoke again, his voice was barely above a whisper. "I don't know. I miss him too. I'm not pretending he didn't exist. He was my brother, part of who I am. But I don't think Nathan would want us to be strangers. Do you?"

Her eyes filled with tears, and her defenses crumpled as she broke down, sobbing.

"I'm sorry, Jesse. I guess I've only been thinking of myself, my own feelings, and not thinking about yours."

He pushed up from the chair, crossed the short distance between them, then knelt before her. Taking her hands in his, he said, "It's all right. I understand. It's my fault Nathan's not here."

She wiped her eyes to look at him. Was it really his fault? His gaze searched her face, and a tear trickled down his cheek, wrenching her heart. He was hurting as much as she was.

"Jesse, I—I know this is hard for you too."

He nodded then laid his forehead against her skirt. The room closed in around her. She desperately wanted to reach out and comfort him, but for some reason, she couldn't. Not yet.

When he lifted his head, she had no more words. She needed air, needed to think. She stood and gathered her shawl around her shoulders.

"I better go." She moved toward the door, and Jesse made no effort to stand. Buddy lifted his head from his paws and watched her with inquisitive eyes.

When her hand reached the doorknob, Jesse spoke. "Lydia. I'm sorry. Can you ever forgive me?"

She paused a moment, yearning to say yes, but couldn't get the word out because saying yes would feel like she was letting go of Nathan and the future she'd dreamed with him. Instead, she opened the door and walked out.

Jesse held his breath as the door closed behind Lydia, closing the door on any hope of renewing their friendship as well. Although she didn't say it, her actions spoke loudly.

She couldn't forgive him for his brother's death. Why did he think she would? He didn't even forgive himself. If only he had died in the shipwreck instead of his brother. Why did God allow him to survive? So that he could be tortured by guilt the rest of his life?

He lowered his head, lifted his arm to wipe his face, then stood. The book she'd brought him was resting on the table. Why did she bring it to him? If she couldn't be his friend, why would she do something so thoughtful for him? Maybe she felt sorry for him. Yes, that was it.

He reached for the crutch and threw it into the fireplace, watching as a red glow began to eat away at its tips. He didn't want anyone's sympathy, especially Lydia's. And he wouldn't need her help. When had he ever needed it? All he wanted was her forgiveness, but she would never be able to give it to him. Yet a different kind of yearning gnawed at him. Was it only forgiveness he wanted from her? Had he imagined something else existed between them, something he'd longed for but hidden?

It didn't matter. Lydia wanted nothing to do with him. He hadn't been able to tell her what happened. She didn't care if he had tried to save Nathan. He had failed, and that was all that mattered. He had failed to bring Nathan back to her.

Well, he wouldn't stick around and be a sore reminder to her. It was time he moved on as soon as he could. He didn't want to be helpless anymore. Carefully putting pressure on his injured foot, he took a step, then took several more. With sweat beading his brow, he crossed through the living room into the dining room and entered the kitchen where Ma was ironing.

She glanced up as he reached the sink and leaned against it. Setting the iron down, she lifted the shirt she was pressing and rearranged it on the ironing board.

"Did I hear you talking with Lydia?" She resumed her task.

"Yes. She brought me a book." He took a glass from the cabinet, poured some water into it, and took a sip.

"Oh? That was nice of her."

Jesse drained the glass.

"She didn't stay very long, did she?"

"No." He set the glass down, watching his mother work the iron into the creases of the shirt, making them disappear.

She paused and looked up at him. "What is it, Jesse?"

"Lydia made it clear she can't be my friend. Ever."

"Did she? I'm sorry. I thought you two were beginning to get along."

"I thought so too, but it looks like we were both wrong. She's too angry and too hurt."

"Surely she'll come to terms with the situation someday and want to be friends again."

"I doubt it. But even if she does, I won't be here much longer anyway. She doesn't want me anywhere near her, and I don't want to be where I'm so unwanted."

"Your father and I want you here. Are you planning to go back to the boats come spring thaw?"

He shook his head. "No. I don't know where I'll go or what I'll do, but it won't be on the boats again." Jesse blew out a breath. "Guess I'll join a lumber camp somewhere. Or I could work in the mines."

"You've never wanted to do that before."

"It's a living, and I've got to do something."

His mother picked up a water-filled mason jar with holes punched in the lid and sprinkled water on the shirt. When she resumed her ironing, she aimed her next words at the iron in her hand. "If you're trying to get away from Lydia, you might not have to go anywhere else." She looked up. "Mrs. Palmer told me Lydia is going to spend the winter in Munising with her sister. In fact, she might leave pretty soon."

Jesse straightened. "Is that so? Well then, at least I won't be here when she gets back."

Ma put down the iron and held up the shirt, surveying it for more wrinkles. As she did, she looked past the shirt toward the window. "It's clearing up outside, thank God."

Jesse followed his mother's gaze. If only things were more clear in his mind.

Chapter 6

Bright sunlight shone through the lace curtains. Lydia blinked, wondering why it was so bright. Then she realized the fog had lifted and the air was quiet. Thank God, the foghorn had stopped.

She got out of bed and rinsed her face in the water basin. After rebraiding her hair, she put on her shirtwaist and skirt, then went downstairs to breakfast.

"Good morning," Mama said as she entered the kitchen.

Lydia looked past her mother to the window behind her. "It's nice to see the lake again."

"It's already the end of October and a beautiful fall day, clear and cool."

Mama handed Lydia a bowl of hot oatmeal then grabbed a spoon and followed her into the dining room. "I already ate breakfast with your father."

"I suppose it's time to clean the brass of the lantern again."

Mama nodded. "Did Jesse like the book you gave him?"

Lydia flinched at the memory of Jesse's hurt but kept her eyes on her bowl. "He was glad to get it." But probably not glad she had come over.

"I'm pleased to hear you did something nice for him. No doubt he was happy to see you."

Lydia didn't reply because she wasn't convinced her mother's statement was true. She had meant to do something nice for him, but she hadn't made him happy. In fact, quite the opposite was true. She had made him more miserable, if anything.

"Lydia, now that the fog has lifted, you can pack your things to go to Sarah's."

Lydia swallowed her oatmeal. "So soon?"

"Yes, while the weather's nice. We don't want to wait until the first snowfall."

"How will I get there? Are you going with me?" Lydia finished her breakfast and stood.

"The supply boat will be here again in November, so you can take it to Munising. You're old enough to go alone. I'll stay here with Papa."

"I see." Lydia carried her dish into the kitchen and rinsed it. "I'm going to the tower now, if you don't need me for anything else."

"Actually, I haven't collected the eggs yet. Will you please go to the barn and get them?"

"Of course." Lydia took a basket from the top of the cupboard and headed out.

Dew glistened off the grass as it reflected the bright sunlight. The cool air reminded her that soon everything would be covered with snow. She entered the barn and headed toward the area where the hens roosted. As she reached into each nest, she imagined what the next four months would be like away from here at her sister's house. Definitely not quiet, with three young children in the house.

Lydia loved her three nieces and looked forward to seeing them again. Her sister lived in town, which made the winter more bearable, having more people around. Lydia would be able to shop in nearby stores as well as attend regular church services at the little white clapboard church, something she couldn't do at the lighthouse. She should be excited about the prospect of going to Sarah's. The winters here at the lighthouse could be brutal and lonely. If not for the keepers' families, one could feel desolate and abandoned.

Would Jesse stay here all winter? What would he do with himself? She pushed the thought away. It was no concern of hers.

Lydia finished collecting the eggs and turned to leave. Rustling overhead made her step back and glance up.

Meow. A gray tabby poked its head out from the loft and looked down.

"Meow to you too," she said to the cat.

The cat jumped down and rubbed against Lydia's skirt. Lydia set the basket down on the ground then sat on a barrel, and the cat jumped up in her lap. Lydia stroked the cat's fur while the animal purred its gratitude.

"Will you miss me, kitty?" Lydia asked the cat.

Would Jesse miss her if she left? Had he ever missed her? She wished she knew.

Finally, she put the cat down and stood, brushing off her apron. She carried the basket back to the house and gave it to her mother. Mama peered into it.

"Three today? Good. I was thinking about making a cake."

"A cake? Is it someone's birthday?"

"No, no special occasion." Mama's eyes brightened. "I know, it can be a going-away cake for you!"

Lydia smiled, not sure she wanted to celebrate leaving. "If you don't need me anymore, I'll be up in the tower."

"All right. I'll see you later."

Lydia spent the rest of the morning in the tower room. The curtain was drawn on the side of the lantern room that received the morning sun, as the hot sun could damage the lens. The room grew stuffy, and Lydia opened the door to the gallery for some fresh air. The wind whistled as it gusted off the water. A couple of schooners sailed swiftly along with the wind.

When she finished dusting, she closed the gallery door. The lovely day beckoned her outside, so she decided to go for a walk. Being inside for so long was a test of her patience. She popped her head into the house to tell Mama where she was going. "Mama! Mama?"

She didn't get an answer, so she headed away from the lighthouse toward the beach. The beach had always been her favorite place, one of the places where she, Nathan, and Jesse had played when they were young, discovering treasures that had washed ashore and making up stories about their origin. But as she got older, the beach was her place of refuge, especially when both the boys left, and had become her place to pray and talk with God.

Was God angry with her now? She wouldn't blame Him if He was, because she was angry with herself too. *"Be ye kind one to another."* Her parents had taught her the Bible verse since she was a child. But she hadn't been kind to Jesse, and she was ashamed of herself.

A sparkle on the beach caught her attention, so she followed the shine to its source, a smooth stone, wet from the waves. She leaned over and picked it up, turning it over in her hand and admiring the dark blue stone with gold flecks reflecting the sunlight. Such a simple thing, just a rock, as Nathan would say. But Jesse would like it. He used to bring her pretty rocks to add to her collection. Jesse—her friend.

When she was younger, she'd wondered which brother she liked the best. Sometimes it was Nathan, but other times it was Jesse. The brothers had a lot in common, but they were different too. Jesse had been the more adventurous brother and, if she dared admit it, the most fun to be around. He was exciting and funny, eager to explore new things and places. Maybe that was the biggest difference between them. Maybe the reason she chose Nathan was because he was safe. He would always stay with her, but Jesse would leave to see new things. Besides, Nathan was the one who expressed his affection toward her, and Jesse hadn't.

A wave splashed at her feet, and she jumped back, lifting the edge of her skirt. She looked out over the lake and noticed the rollers had gotten larger. The wind had picked up, and she drew her shawl more tightly around her shoulders. The temperature was dropping as the sun lowered in the sky. The days were getting shorter, a sure sign of winter.

She and Nathan were supposed to have been married in the spring. But what did she have to look forward to now? She might as well go to her sister's house. There was nothing left here for her, especially if Jesse left. Deep inside, she didn't want him to leave. The way he'd apologized to her broke her heart. If only she'd been able to reach out to him, comfort him the way he needed to be comforted.

Lydia lifted her gaze toward the sky where the clouds were gathering into menacing clusters and the threat of an approaching storm.

The wind increased, and she tightened her shawl. But there was something else she had to see before she turned back. She leaned forward and pressed on, away from the lighthouse, drawn to what lay ahead. The incoming waves tried to cover it up, but she spotted the wreckage anyway. The ruins were always there, the wooden beams still displaying the spikes that were supposed to hold the freighter *Sitka* together.

The freighter had wrecked on the reef, and waves pounded the ship until it broke into pieces. Only a few years had passed since the accident, and she could still remember the excitement at the lighthouse when it happened. Thanks to the heroic efforts of the Grand Marais lifesavers, the ship's crew had been saved.

To this day, she could see the happy, relieved faces of the men brought to the lighthouse to warm up after the harrowing event. Lydia had helped serve coffee as they profusely thanked her for the hot beverage. All the men had been rescued and were grateful to be alive.

That was the way things were supposed to be. Shipwrecks were always possible with the unpredictability of the lake. But lighthouses were there to watch out for those in trouble. Lighthouse keepers like her father and Jesse's father spent their lives looking out for mariners in distress and providing for their safety.

Jesse had been saved. And she was thankful he was.

"Forgive." Lydia looked up and glanced around. Where had that voice come from? She closed her eyes and prayed. "Father, forgive me for being unforgiving." A peace filled her, and she felt like a weight had been lifted off her chest. She needed to let Jesse know she had been wrong to blame him for Nathan's death.

Her hair slapped her face as the wind forced it loose from the braid. She reached to hold it out of her eyes as a wave hit her, almost knocking her off her feet. As she turned around, the white lighthouse perched atop the bluff was a sharp contrast against the darkened sky. The waves loomed tall as they rolled toward the shore, and she quickened her step to get away from them. As lightning flashed on the horizon, the sails of a schooner could be seen out on the lake.

"Dear Lord, please keep those people safe in this gale," she breathed.

The waves encroached farther and farther onto the shore as she fought to take each step toward the lighthouse. Her dress dragged, wet and heavy, and the wind cut through her like ice. She shouldn't have stayed out so long.

"Have you seen Lydia?" Pa called from the front door. "A storm's about to hit, and her parents haven't seen her for a couple of hours. Mrs. Palmer is worried about her."

Jesse looked up from his book. "No. I haven't seen her today." Nor had he expected to see her again after yesterday.

"Last thing she told her mother was she was going up in the tower. No one knows where she went after that. She needs to get inside quick."

Jesse pushed up from the sofa. "I'll help look for her."

Ma came in from the kitchen wiping her hands on her apron, her brow pinched. "Jesse, are you sure you're ready? What if you fall?"

Anger seethed through his limbs. "I'll take that chance. It's time I did something worthwhile around here."

"Where's your crutch?" Ma's eyes searched the room.

Jesse eyed the fireplace. "I don't need it anymore."

He made his way across the room, testing each step. Thankfully, the pain was finally gone, and he could put his full weight on his foot. As he crossed to the door, his father reached out a hand to help, but Jesse waved him off. "I can do this, Pa." He aimed his gaze at his father's eyes. "I have to do this."

Pa nodded and stepped back so Jesse could walk out. "Where are you going to look for her?"

"The beach. I think I know where she went."

"All right. Be careful, son. I'll go to the fog signal building and look around there and toward the dunes. Mr. Palmer is up in the lighthouse."

Jesse grabbed his slicker hanging by the back door and shrugged into it before stepping outside. Wind blasted him as he made his way down the steps, while Buddy rushed out alongside. Turning away from the lake, Jesse planted his feet firmly on the ground and headed around the house. The closest access to the beach was beyond the lighthouse and past Lydia's house.

The beach was one of her favorite places to go, just as it had been his. Memories of the three of them playing pirates on the beach and finding buried treasure ran through his mind. Most of the scenes had taken place near the ruins of the shipwrecks, the only real element in their stories. Jesse shuddered against the gale-force winds, squinting to find the footpath that led to the beach. A glance at the incoming breakers sparked panic in his heart, and he hurried to find the path. His eyes roamed the shoreline looking for a sign of Lydia while fear gripped his throat.

Buddy ran ahead, barking. "Do you see her, Buddy?"

The dog disappeared down the side of the bluff, directing Jesse to the path. He took a few steps down, scanning the beach for signs of Lydia. His pulse raced as heavy raindrops began to fall. Buddy barked excitedly in the distance, and Jesse followed the sound. Finally, he saw her stumbling along the beach with Buddy running and barking beside her. The waves had invaded the shore and were tugging at her dress, as if they were trying to pull her out into the lake. No. No, they couldn't have her.

Running toward her, he yelled, "Lydia!"

She looked up, and her eyes widened. "Jesse?"

Words were useless with the noise of the storm, so he didn't try to answer but instead threw his arm around her and pulled her away from the water. She shivered from the wet cold, and he held her tightly to warm her. He kept his eyes focused on the lighthouse and away from the water as they headed back. Together, they fought the wind and rain to the foot of the trail.

He pushed her ahead of him as they scrambled up. Once at the top, he hugged her next to him as they plodded through the storm to Lydia's house. The door opened when they approached, and Lydia's mother reached her arms out to her daughter, pulling her inside. Jesse hesitated, unsure if he should follow or not.

"Come on in, Jesse, and warm up," Mrs. Palmer said.

Jesse removed his slicker at the door before he went inside.

Mrs. Palmer threw a quilt over Lydia, who stood shivering by the flaming fireplace. "Here, Lydia. Sit by the fire and get warm. Then you'll have to get out of those wet clothes." Turning to Jesse, she said, "Thank you so much for finding her. I'm so glad to see you can get around again."

Jesse gazed down at his feet then back up at Mrs. Palmer. "I've been working on it every day. Besides, I had to see where Lydia went."

"Well, thank the Lord, you're healed. You two sit there and get the chill off, and I'll get you some hot coffee to warm your insides too."

They sat in silence when Mrs. Palmer walked away. Lydia's shivering slowed, and color returned to her skin. Wet tendrils of hair framed her face like a woman in a Renaissance portrait. She'd looked so frail when he found her, as if she could've been knocked down and washed away by a strong wave. A tremor of fear raced down his spine. He couldn't let that happen to Lydia.

"Thank you." Her voice was so soft, he wasn't certain he'd heard her. She looked away from the fire and studied him. "You don't need a crutch anymore."

Jesse shrugged and grinned. "Nope. It's gone, and good riddance too."

Mrs. Palmer came in with two steaming cups and handed them each one. "This should help." She faced Lydia. "Didn't you notice the storm approaching? How far did you go?"

Lydia shook her head. "I'm not sure. I just kept walking and didn't realize the weather had changed until I headed back."

Her mother glanced from Lydia to Jesse. "Well, thank God Jesse was here. I better go check on dinner." She patted Jesse on the back. "Jesse, you stay as long as you like. No need to get back out in that." She hurried to the kitchen, leaving them alone again.

Chapter 7

He had come looking for her. Even though she'd been unkind to him, he'd come looking for her. And he could walk on his own again.

Lydia stared at the coffee, cradling the steaming cup in her hands and letting the warmth penetrate her arms. She lifted her gaze to Jesse, who sat staring at the fireplace. She'd never realized how handsome he was. His dark hair curled over his collar, and an unruly lock fell onto his forehead. His chiseled features were shadowed by a new-growth beard, making him look older. He had changed since he left to work the boats. And not just in his appearance.

"Why? Why did you come looking for me, Jesse?"

He looked up at her with surprise. "I had to."

She tilted her head and watched his Adam's apple bob up and down. "Did someone tell you to?"

He shook his head, glancing down then back to her. "Lydia, I didn't want anything to happen to you. I couldn't bear the thought that you'd needed help and I had done nothing."

"You could've hurt yourself again."

Jesse frowned. "I was more afraid of you getting hurt."

"I'm surprised you cared, after the way I've been treating you."

"Of course I care about you, Lydia. I always have." He winked at her. "Even though you can be ornery."

Lydia's face warmed, and it wasn't from the coffee. The intensity of his gaze caught her by surprise and conveyed more than his words. What was he telling her? And then the truth hit her.

"You tried to save Nathan, didn't you?"

Jesse's eyes darkened then filled with unspilt tears. He nodded, looking down at the floor. "Yes. I tried, but I failed."

She waited, sensing he wanted to say more.

"The two of us were standing next to each other when the ship slammed into the reef. Both of us were knocked down, and the next thing I knew, the ship was breaking apart. I looked for Nathan, called out his name, but there was so much noise, men crying out for help, the wind blowing, the ship groaning and creaking. I didn't hear him. Then I saw him on the other half of the ship just before another jolt threw me into the water."

Jesse wiped his face with the back of his sleeve and sniffed. "I tried to swim to the top, but my foot was tangled in a rope." He choked back a sob. "I thought I would drown, but I wanted to find Nathan. Somehow, I got my foot out of the rope and made it to the surface. But when my head came out of the water, I didn't see Nathan anywhere. I screamed his name again and again, but the waves kept crashing over my head.

"Then I heard someone call out to me from the lifeboat. I saw it about twenty feet away, so I swam to it and they pulled me in. I asked if they'd seen Nathan, but no one had." Jesse's head drooped. "I couldn't save him."

Lydia's heart wrenched seeing Jesse in so much pain. She set her cup on the small table beside her then stood and went to him, placing her hand on his head. "You would have, if you could have. I know that now."

Jesse leaned his head against her skirt. "I'm sorry. You were right. I shouldn't have asked him to go with me."

"You didn't know what would happen. And it wasn't your fault the ship hit the reef or that Nathan died."

Her own words echoed through her mind. *It wasn't his fault. Jesse didn't kill Nathan.*

Jesse sat back in his chair and looked up at her, searching her face. "Then you forgive me?"

"There's nothing to forgive, Jesse. I wanted to blame you, but that was wrong of me."

His brow creased. "You're not angry with me anymore?"

"No, of course not. How could I be angry with the man who just saved my life?"

Jesse stood, hovering over her. He was so close she thought she could hear his heart beating. Or maybe it was hers. "I did what any man would do for his friend."

Friend? Why did that word sound so odd now, so insufficient? She stepped back, gazing into his eyes. What else did she want him to say?

"Well, thank you for being my friend and looking out for me."

Gripping her arms, he focused on her eyes. "I hope we can be the very best of friends, Lydia." He pulled her close, and she laid her head on his chest.

Best friends. Somehow, those words didn't convey what she felt this close to Jesse. Her heart pounded as she melted into him. She'd never experienced this sensation with Nathan. She wanted to stay next to him and absorb his warmth, but he gently pushed her back and peered into her eyes.

"I better get home and let Ma and Pa know you're safe. You get dry, and I'll see you after you're rested." The door opened as he reached it, and her father stepped inside.

"Lydia, I see you're here. Good." He glanced at Jesse. "You found her?"

435

"Yes, sir. Well, actually, Buddy did. I just brought her back home." Jesse grabbed his slicker and threw it on.

"Then we're thankful you went after her. Now that I know Lydia's safe, I'll get back to the tower. This storm's a mighty one. Wind's even shaking the tower. God help any ships out in this now."

After the men left the house, something Papa said stuck with her. Didn't she see the sails of a schooner out on the lake before the storm hit? She hoped they hadn't caught the worst of it. The wreckage on the shore came to her mind and she shuddered. Would that schooner's fate be the same?

"Let's get you out of those wet things." Mama came into the room holding Lydia's gown. "I think you better go upstairs, put on something dry, and lie down."

Lydia stood while Mama helped her out of her wet dress and chemise, then held her arms up as her mother dropped the gown over her head. Mama towel dried her hair then drew back the quilt on Lydia's iron bed. Lydia collapsed on the bed as fatigue settled over her.

"There. You rest now." Lifting her eyes toward the ceiling, Mama said, "Dear Lord, thank You for taking care of Lydia, and thank You for Jesse's help bringing her home."

Mama turned to go out the door.

"Mama?"

She turned and faced Lydia. "Yes, Lydia?"

"He tried to save Nathan."

Mama nodded. "I know. He loved his brother."

"I'm sorry I've been so spiteful to him."

"Have you apologized to him?"

"Yes, I did, but. . .*achoo!*" Lydia pulled the quilt up around her neck. "I'm cold."

Mama's forehead creased. "I'll get you another quilt and heat up a brick in the oven to put in your bed."

"Thank you," Lydia mumbled. As she closed her eyes, she welcomed the warmth of the quilt, but it couldn't match the warmth that emanated from Jesse's body when she was next to him.

Jesse stood in front of the fireplace at home, trying to dry out and warm up. He couldn't get Lydia out of his mind. His heart still raced when he thought of her being next to him, and it had taken every ounce of his strength to push her away and leave. And when she looked up at him with those searching eyes, his lips begged to kiss hers. But he couldn't allow himself that pleasure. He would be content knowing they were friends again. At least that's what he'd try to convince himself of.

"Women. Good thing you don't have to worry about them, Buddy." The dog lay on the hearth, lifted his head, and wagged his tail. Jesse squatted to scratch the animal's belly. "Maybe I should stick to dogs. I seem to be able to keep you happy." The tail thumped on the floor in agreement.

The next morning, Jesse was sitting by the fireplace reading the Sherlock Holmes book when his father rushed in. "Jesse, there's a boat stuck on the reef! Grab your slicker. We might need your help."

Jesse stood and stared at his father. "My help? What could I do?" Fear began a steady crawl up his spine, threatening to strangle him.

"Anything that's needed. Now that you're mended, we can use your assistance. Just be ready." Pa turned to go, saying over his shoulder, "Meet me in the lantern room."

All right, Jesse, settle down. He took a deep breath and released it. No reason to fret. At least he'd be on solid ground. But those poor men on that ship. . . He was thankful he wasn't one of them. "Lord, help them," he muttered.

Jesse went upstairs and looked out the bedroom window, trying to see the ship, but he could barely make out the lake's turbulent water through the heavy rain splashing against the glass. Shouts for help sent an alarm to his limbs before he realized the sound had come from his own mind as the memory of his shipwreck came to life again. He shook off the shudder that accompanied the memory. Maybe there was something he could do this time.

He hurried back down and put on his slicker before going outside and over to the lighthouse. His legs had forgotten how many steps there were to climb, but he pressed on to the top and climbed the ladder into the lantern room.

The men turned toward him as he joined them, greeting him with grim faces.

"Good to see you, Jesse," said Mr. Palmer with a nod. He lifted the telescope and fixed it on the water. "There's men hanging on the rigging."

"May I see?" Jesse took the offered telescope and peered through it, shocked at the sight of the ship listing to one side where it was trapped on the reef. He counted six men hanging on the ropes while the waves jostled the ship. How long could they hold on?

"I put a call out to the lifesaving station at Grand Marais. The officer in charge said they'd get here as quickly as possible, but they're shorthanded with two of their men at home sick."

"What if they can't get here in time? Will you launch the station boat?" Jesse asked.

"Not yet. We'll let the men who are better equipped get there first. We could capsize ourselves in this storm."

"So we just stand here and watch?" Jesse searched the men's faces.

"For now, that's all we can do," said Pa. "And pray."

Chapter 8

Lydia woke and tried to sit up, but the heavy quilts held her back. What time was it? Had she slept all night? A glance toward the window told her it was barely daylight, but the heavy rain suppressed the light. The wind roared, shaking the windows like it was trying to get in.

She threw back the covers and sat on the edge of her bed. Agitated voices downstairs told her something had happened. Lydia stood and grabbed a dry dress then scrambled into it. She hurriedly pulled on her stockings and laced up her still-damp shoes. As she passed the mirror, she noticed her hair hanging loose, so she pulled it back and tied it with a grosgrain ribbon lying on her dresser. No time to braid it now.

When she stepped into the downstairs area, Mrs. Drake and Mama looked up from their seats by the fireplace.

"Lydia, you're up already? You were very tired," her mother said.

Lydia shook her head. "I've had enough rest. I heard you talking about something, and it sounded important. What is it?"

The two women exchanged glances. Mrs. Drake spoke up, pausing in her sewing. "There's a ship hung up on the reef."

"Oh dear. I wonder if it's the schooner I saw on the lake yesterday before the storm hit."

"It might be the same one then," Mrs. Drake said.

"Are there people still on it?" Lydia's heart trembled at the thought.

Both women nodded. "Yes, I'm afraid so," said Mama.

Lydia's stomach clenched. "Are the lifesavers from Grand Marais coming?"

"Your father called them, and they're on their way, but they told him they were missing some men who are sick, so they're shorthanded."

"We have to do something! We can't just sit here!"

"Lydia, we're as concerned as you are, but we can't do much to help at this time. Once they bring the men in, we can provide warmth and nourishment to them like we've done in the past."

In the past, Lydia wasn't as concerned. In the past, help arrived, and people were saved. In the past, Nathan was alive. But now she was all too aware that things didn't always work out the way they should.

"I have to go see." Lydia headed to the door and found a slicker hanging beside it. She reached for it as Mama spoke again.

"Lydia, I don't know what you can do. You could just be in the way."

"I'll make sure I'm not. I won't be gone long."

Lydia fought a heavy gust of rain-soaked wind as she made her way to the lighthouse. She tugged at the heavy door before it finally released enough to let her step in, slamming behind her as the wind closed it.

She climbed the stairs, listening for voices above. The gale shook the tower with such force, all sound was quieted except the noise of the storm. It wasn't until she reached the room below the lantern room that she heard the men above her. She grabbed the handrails of the metal ladder and climbed up, poking her head through the opening. A third man stood in the small area with her father and Mr. Drake.

"Jesse?"

He turned around and raised his eyebrows. "Lydia? What are you doing out?" He reached down and helped her through the opening to her feet. "I thought you were resting."

She waved him off. "I was, but I'm fine now." She nodded toward the water where the other two men fixed their gazes. "I heard there's a ship out there on the reef."

He nodded and stepped back so she could pass by in the small space, then pointed to the lake. She stepped over to Papa and tapped him on the shoulder. He glanced over his shoulder and appeared startled to see her.

"Lydia. I didn't know you had come up here."

"May I look, Papa?" Lydia motioned to the telescope in his hand.

He handed the instrument to her, and Jesse stepped up to guide it to the right spot.

Lydia's eyes scoured the water until they landed on the stranded sloop. She gasped at the sight of men hanging on for dear life. Lowering the telescope, she handed it back to her father.

"Are the lifesavers coming?"

Papa nodded. "Soon, I hope."

"Oh dear Lord. Please let them save those men." Lydia shivered and crossed her arms, squeezing them for warmth. She glanced at Jesse, whose face was ghostly pale. No doubt he was remembering his own shipwreck.

"Go on back down, Lydia. You can't do anything here but worry and pray, and that you can do back at the house."

"All right, Papa. But if there's anything I can do, please let me know."

"I will. You can help your mother get things ready for the men once we get them on shore."

She went to the opening and began stepping backward down the rungs. Jesse followed her to the service room below.

They stood in awkward silence while Lydia twirled a strand of hair, waiting for him to speak. His mind appeared to be elsewhere.

"I hope the lifesavers get here soon," she said.

He nodded but didn't speak. His eyes were filled with fear.

Lydia placed her hand on his arm, searching his face. "Jesse?"

His gaze fell on her and recognition registered.

"Jesse, what is it? You're remembering your own shipwreck, aren't you?"

He looked away. Her heart ached for him, and she grasped his trembling hand, squeezing it. Then she spoke out loud. "Lord, please send help to those men. Please show us what we can do to help them too."

"They're here!" Papa's voice rang out above them.

"Thank God," Lydia said. "Looks like our prayer has been answered."

Jesse nodded, but the look on his face didn't agree.

"I want to watch the men get rescued," Lydia said, grabbing hold of the ladder again. "Don't you?"

She wasn't sure he wanted to go with her, but he followed her back up to the lantern room.

The four of them passed the telescope around as they watched the lifesaving boat try to cast a line to the marooned sloop. They cheered when the line held fast. But the rocking waves made it difficult for the boats to get too close to each other, preventing sailors from escaping. Lydia gasped when a huge wave descended on the lifeboat, briefly obscuring it from view.

"Thank God," she said, when it reappeared.

The lifesavers tossed out a ring, and a man caught it and put it over his head, holding on as the rescuers pulled him aboard. Four men were rescued from the sloop, but two remaining clung to the rigging and wouldn't attempt to catch the ring.

The officer in charge of the rescue ship waved to the men still on the wrecked boat and pointed to the shore. The rescue boat then headed toward the lighthouse dock.

"Won't they try to get them all?" Lydia's heart sank as the sailors still on the marooned sloop watched the rescue ship leave.

Papa lowered the telescope and turned to her. "I'm sure they'll get them all. Mr. Drake, would you please go meet the rescue boat? Jesse, go with him and help get the men off, then bring them to my house. Lydia, go home and help your mother prepare for the sailors."

The three of them clambered down the stairs and hurried off to their assigned duties—Lydia to her house and Jesse in the other direction toward the dock.

Rain pelted Jesse as he caught the rope the crew member threw him from the rocking boat and tied it to the dock. Balancing close to the edge, he leaned toward the boat reaching for one of the survivors, grabbed his forearm, and jerked him onto the dock. The man stood shivering beside him as the rescuers helped the other three men off the boat. One of the rescuers had a gash on his head and appeared woozy.

"John here took a fall and hit his head on the gunwale when a rough wave hit us. I think he better get inside." The officer in charge put his arm around John and helped him up to the dock, where Jesse steadied him.

"What about the others?" Jesse yelled above the din of the storm.

"We can't get the other two without another man onboard, now that John's hurt. Anybody here that can help?"

Just the idea of being on the rescue ship in the churning water struck fear in Jesse's heart and tightened his gut. "Let's get these men up to the keeper's house," he replied, not giving an answer to the officer. At least Jesse could help the men get comfortable. They all trudged up the hill toward the lighthouse and the keeper's house, trying to keep their footing as the wind fought to push them down.

When they arrived at Lydia's house, Jesse knocked on the door. It was flung open by Mrs. Palmer, his mother standing beside her.

"Come in, come in," Mrs. Palmer said. "Go over there by the fire and warm yourselves."

Jesse and the lifesaving crew followed the men in. Lydia came out of the kitchen carrying a tray with steaming cups of coffee and offered some to each man.

Murmurs of "thank you" ran through the room as the men accepted the hot beverage. Mrs. Drake tended to the cut on John's head.

The officer in charge lifted his cup and nodded to the women. "Thank you, ladies. Take care of these men, please. We hope to return with the others soon."

"There are more out there?" Mrs. Palmer asked. "Oh dear Lord."

"We couldn't get them the first time and wanted to get these men in quickly. Our strongest swimmer is home sick, and now John here, our other swimmer, is hurt." He drained his cup, handed it back to Lydia, and started toward the door, then stopped and faced Jesse.

"Thank you, son, for your help. Can you swim?"

Jesse froze as fear turned his blood to icicles. How could he answer? He used to be a strong swimmer. But since the wreck, he'd vowed to stay out of the water forever. There was no doubt a "yes" meant the officer would ask Jesse to accompany them.

But saying no was a lie. Or was it? Could he still swim? Was he strong enough? Besides, who was he to try to save someone? He'd failed before. He didn't want to fail again.

Lydia stood, tray in hand, waiting for Jesse's answer. Of course he was a strong swimmer. He always had been. Was he hesitating because he wasn't sure about his strength since his injuries? His face had drained of color when the officer asked the question. No, he didn't just doubt his strength. He was terrified. Was he afraid he wouldn't be able to save anyone after what happened to Nathan? Her heart squeezed, feeling his dilemma. She had to do something to help him, because he needed to do something to help others.

She strode toward the men, boldness spurring her on.

"Jesse is one of the strongest swimmers I've ever seen." She steadied her gaze on Jesse, whose eyes widened with surprise.

"That so? Then we need your help to get those last two men. I pray it's not too late. Can I count on you?" The officer's face implored Jesse.

Jesse looked from Lydia to the officer as if searching for an answer. Lydia nodded, encouraging him. Then, drawing himself up, Jesse transformed before her eyes to the man she used to know, the fearless friend she remembered.

"Yes, sir. I'll go with you."

"Good, then let's make haste. Ladies, please say a prayer for us."

"We will," the women chorused as the men went out the door and back into the storm.

Chapter 9

As soon as all the men had been made comfortable, Lydia excused herself and ran back to the lighthouse. She raced to the top and rejoined Papa and Jesse's father in the lantern room.

"Is the ship still afloat? Did the lifesaving boat get back to it yet?" she blurted out while recovering her breath.

"They're both out there," Papa answered. He handed her the telescope.

Lydia focused on the two boats, one dangerously leaning into the water while the other tried to approach. The steady rain made it difficult to see the people on either boat, but she knew one of those forms was Jesse. Her heart raced. Had she been wrong to push him? What if he failed again? What if something happened to him?

She handed the telescope back to her father. "Jesse's out there."

Papa and Mr. Drake turned to face her, a combination of surprise and alarm etching their expressions.

"He is?" Jesse's father asked.

Lydia nodded. "Yes. The officer asked if he could swim. Jesse said he could, and the officer asked him to help, so Jesse agreed."

"Jesse used to be a strong swimmer. I hope he still is." His father turned back to look out the window.

She hoped so too. For the sake of those who needed his help. For Jesse's sake. For hers.

Jesse focused on the two men hanging on to the rigging of the shipwrecked vessel, pushing down the nausea that threatened as waves pummeled the lifesaving boat. The boat was as close to the other as the lifesavers dared to get, lest they too hit the reef.

"We're only about twenty feet away. If they'd let go of the rigging, they could catch the life ring." The officer stood beside Jesse as another crew member held the rope, ready to toss it again.

Indeed, the men appeared to be glued to the rigging. Each toss of the rope resulted in a weak attempt to reach for it.

"Catch the ring!" the lifesaver yelled, encouraging the men to action. "If you don't get off that boat, you'll drown!"

Frustration grew for the lifesavers as their boat tossed in the water while trying to maintain a safe distance from the other ship. Jesse clenched his fists. How could they get the men off?

Thunder boomed overhead as a giant wave jolted the stranded ship, pulling the men so close to the water, the waves covered their feet.

"You must let go!" Jesse yelled.

"Toss it again," commanded the officer in charge.

The ring flew within reach of one of the men, who let go of the ship to catch it. As he did, another wave rocked the sloop and he fell into the water, panicking to find the ring.

"Grab hold!"

The man floundered in the water, unable to reach the ring.

"We need a swimmer to go get him!" The officer faced Jesse, pinning him with his eyes.

"I'll go." Jesse pulled off his shoes and jumped into the chilly water, praying the life jacket he wore would keep him afloat. Water splashed over his head, taunting his dreadful memories to appear. Jesse pushed the memories away. There was no time to dwell on them. He focused on the man in the water, trying to keep him in view despite the turbulent waves and blinding rain.

His arms sliced through the water with strength he didn't know he had as he moved to the panicked man who fought to stay afloat while hollering for help. The ring came within Jesse's reach, and he pushed it ahead of him toward the man.

"Grab hold!" Jesse ordered, extending the ring. He had to keep some distance between himself and the man. Otherwise, the man might grab Jesse and they'd both drown. When the man grasped the life ring, Jesse said, "Put it over your head and arms and hold on! I'll pull you back to our boat."

Thank God, the man did as he was told. Falling in the water had awakened his senses. Jesse swam toward the lifesavers' boat with the man in tow. When they were close enough to the boat, the crew on board tugged the man the rest of the way and pulled him into the boat.

"Help me!" A cry behind Jesse turned his head to the other vessel where the second man was now halfway in the water and hanging on to the side of the boat as it slipped farther under.

"Throw the ring!" Jesse called out as his wet clothes became heavier and heavier.

The crewman tossed the line out again, and Jesse swam toward the ring, grabbed it, and took it to the other man. The man reached out for it and put it over his head and arms, then Jesse started swimming back to the rescue boat. His muscles were screaming as he strained against the waves, now washing over his head repeatedly. Doubt mocked him. Could he make it back to the boat this time? Would his strength hold out?

Lydia twisted her hair, pacing the small area of the lantern room and waiting her turn to look through the telescope. She could see very little of what was happening on the water. But Mr. Drake saw Jesse jump into the water, and no one had seen him come out.

Lord, please protect Jesse. Please bring him back. Jesse had to come back, he just had to. Tears filled her eyes and slid down her face. She didn't want to lose Jesse too.

She hugged herself to quell her anxiety. Where was he?

"I see him! He's pushing another man into the boat. Now they're pulling him in too. He did it!" Mr. Drake's chest swelled with pride. "Lydia, he did it!" He reached out his arms and drew her into a hug.

"Thank God," Lydia said, allowing the tightness in her chest to release.

They watched the lifesaving boat float toward the dock. "Let's go get them," Lydia's father said to Mr. Drake. "We can leave the tower a little while." Facing Lydia, he said, "We'll see you at the house." He smiled at her knowingly.

Lydia hurried back home, flinging the door open as she entered. "They're all safe!"

Smiles appeared on the fatigued men, and audible sighs of relief sounded through the room.

Lydia went over to her mother and Jesse's mother, who rose from their chairs at the dining room table. "Jesse saved the two men."

The women exchanged glances then hugged each other and Lydia too. "Thank You, Lord!" Mama said.

"They're on their way here. Papa and Mr. Drake went to meet them."

"Good. I put another pot of coffee on."

Lydia stood by the front window watching for the men. Her heart leaped when she saw them, and she ran to the door. "They're here!"

Everyone in the room stood to greet the new arrivals and cheered when they entered. Jesse was the last person to enter, and Lydia could hold back no longer, running to him.

She looked up at him. "I'm very proud of you, Jesse. I knew you could do it."

"I wasn't so sure."

She searched his eyes. "I'm so glad you made it back." Tears filled her eyes. "I . . .

I didn't want to lose you."

Jesse studied her face. "Coming back to you was my reason for surviving. It still is."

He pulled her to him, and she fell into his embrace, right where she belonged, with the man who was closer than a friend.

Dear Readers,

In the summer of 2015, my husband, grandson, and I embarked on a mission to visit at least half of Michigan's one hundred lighthouses. Did you know Michigan has more lighthouses than any other state? Our journey took us up the west coast of the lower peninsula, across the Mackinac Bridge to the northern coast of the upper peninsula. We saw lighthouses on and in Lake Huron, Lake Michigan, and Lake Superior.

To reach the 1874 Au Sable lighthouse, we had to hike a mile and a half trail through the woods along Lake Superior's coastline. The walk was pleasant, accompanied by the sound of waves splashing on the shore, but when the woods ended, we stepped into an open clearing and one of the most wonderful lighthouse settings I've ever seen.

Rising above the lake, the white tower stands between two redbrick keepers' houses. From the top of the lighthouse, you can see for miles, starting with the sand dunes to the east that are part of the Pictured Rocks National Lakeshore.

The Au Sable Lighthouse was built at Au Sable Point to warn mariners of the Au Sable reef which lay just below the surface and a mile out from the shore. In addition, the lighthouse was needed to light the midpoint of an eighty-mile stretch of darkened coastline between the Whitefish Point Light and the Granite Island Light.

Although the lighthouse was a major coastal light, the station was as isolated as an island. Besides supply visits from the lighthouse tender, the station's only link to civilization was a winding, narrow foot path twelve miles along the dunes to Grand Marais, Michigan, and this path was impassable during stormy weather when waves washed over the dunes. Life in such isolated conditions took its toll on the keepers, many resigned from lighthouse service after briefly serving at the Au Sable Light.

Keeper Napoleon Beedon and his wife Mary who served as his assistant were severely tested during their first winter at the lighthouse. On December 8, 1876, the day started with a light northerly breeze which by 5 p.m. had churned into a frightful storm that blew down fifty trees around the station. In his station log book, Keeper Beedon recorded that he feared "the lighthouse and tower would be blown down as they shook like a leaf. The wind was NN West, snowing and freezing. It was the worst storm I ever saw on Lake Superior." Three years at the station was all the couple could stand before they resigned.

Today, the site is maintained by park rangers with a volunteer caretaker during the summer who stays on the second floor of the main keeper's house and serves as a tour guide for the museum on the first floor. Maybe you can visit Au Sable, one of my favorite lighthouses, someday too, and see where Lydia and Jesse lived.

Marilyn Turk

Award-winning author **Marilyn Turk** writes historical fiction usually set on the shoreline of the United States. A lighthouse enthusiast, Marilyn is excited to participate in this collection. She and her husband have traveled to over one hundred lighthouses and climbed most of them. In addition, they served as volunteer lighthouse caretakers at Little River Light on an island off the coast of Maine.

Lighthouses always show up in her books, either as part of the setting or in cameo appearances, and on her lighthouse blog at pathwayheart.com. Her book, *Lighthouse Devotions*, features inspiring true stories about lighthouses.

When not climbing or writing about lighthouses, Marilyn enjoys gardening, boating, fishing, and tennis.